THE QUEST FOR ETERNAL LIGHT

B.E. Russell

CONTENTS

1

THE KINGDOM OF STONEHAVEN

The sun rose over the kingdom of Stonehaven in a warm, golden haze—its light dancing across the rolling hills, shining upon tidy farms, and illuminating the spires of the Royal Citadel in the distance. For countless generations, Stonehaven had been a land of harmony, where magic and chivalry wove together to create a society founded on hope and prosperity. Merchants traveled far and wide to bring exotic wares to the bustling markets, and artisans poured their hearts into crafting vibrant tapestries that celebrated the realm's storied past. Knights in polished armor patrolled the roads, ensuring peace and order among villagers who slept soundly under the watchful gaze of the royal family.

Despite its long history of tranquility, an undercurrent of unease had begun to ripple through Stonehaven in recent weeks. Farmers whispered of blighted crops. Shepherds reported missing livestock, their flocks vanishing without a trace. And more troubling still were the rumors of sinister shadows creeping at the edges of the forests—shadows that seemed to have a life of their own. Initially, most dismissed these tales as superstition, or mere illusions cast by the interplay of moonlight and dense foliage. But these stories persisted, multiplying in number and severity until no one could ignore them. Over time, what had started as faint gossip became an unrelenting dread, as though the entire kingdom stood on the brink of a dark revelation.

King Alaric, the monarch who had ruled Stonehaven with wisdom and kindness for nearly three decades, felt the burden of these rumors more keenly than anyone else. Known for his fair judgments and unwavering dedication to his people, he could not sit idly by while his subjects lived in fear. Within the walls of his gleaming white castle, perched atop the Royal Citadel, the king devoted every hour to discerning the cause of these unnerving developments. Advisors and wise scholars from all corners of the kingdom were summoned to the palace to share their knowledge of arcane happenings, to recount ancient prophecies, and to consult dusty tomes about fallen civilizations that had once dabbled in forbidden magic. Despite their efforts, the puzzle remained incomplete—an elusive piece seemed to be missing, an ominous clue lurking just out of sight.

It was High Seer Malachai who first suggested that the unprecedented darkness might be emanating from a corrupted source of magic. Malachai, a venerable magician with hair the color of storm clouds, had served as the Royal Court's chief arcane advisor for many years. Though his vision had grown dim with age, his insights were as sharp as ever. Through weeks of meticulous scrying and the casting of elaborate divination spells, the High Seer concluded that a malignant power, something older and stronger than mere curses, was weaving its tendrils into the fabric of Stonehaven itself. He described it in hushed tones as the *Shadow Nexus,* a place where darkness converged, threatening to spread its vile corruption through the world like a disease.

King Alaric, gravely concerned, convened a secret council of his most trusted aides and generals. They gathered in the War Chamber—a high-ceilinged room lined with tapestries that depicted Stonehaven's triumphs against monsters and tyrants of ages past. A massive circular table dominated the chamber's center, strewn with half-unrolled maps, quills, ink pots, and magical devices that glowed with faint silver light. Candles flickered in iron holders, casting dancing shadows on the walls, eerily reminiscent of the creeping darkness they were all determined to stop.

One by one, knights and counselors revealed troubling reports from every corner of the kingdom. Villagers had encountered monstrous creatures previously unknown to Stonehaven—beings of nightmare with howling voices and burning eyes. Town guards had watched in horror as ghostly apparitions roamed at twilight, draining the life force from weary travelers. Worst of all, ominous black storms had begun to gather unpredictably, thundering across the sky and blotting out the sun, even as farmland below withered in the gloom. No corner of Stonehaven seemed safe anymore, and these alarming developments confirmed that whatever the source of the evil, it was gaining strength rapidly.

"We must act swiftly," declared King Alaric, his usually calm voice trembling with urgency. His steel-gray eyes swept the faces of those gathered. "If this threat is indeed the Shadow Nexus returning, we cannot allow it to take hold in our kingdom. Darkness cannot be permitted to rule Stonehaven, nor spread beyond its borders. Our people look to us for protection—and we shall not fail them."

It was at Malachai's suggestion that King Alaric concluded the kingdom needed more than just a legion of soldiers or the arcane knowledge of his court. They required heroes—individuals who embodied the finest qualities of Stonehaven's highest ideals. These champions would need both formidable martial prowess and a firm moral compass, for the trials that lay ahead would test not only their strength but also their resolve. And so, the king set forth an extraordinary summons to four individuals whose names had reached him through reputation, prophecy, or personal connection—individuals who might together form a powerful bulwark against the tide of darkness.

The first was Sir Cedric, a knight heralded for his unwavering bravery and loyalty. A veteran of countless skirmishes against brigands and raiders on Stonehaven's frontier, Cedric's feats of valor were the stuff of ballads. It was said he had once held a lonely gate against two dozen marauders, emerging victorious with scarcely a wound. Cedric's devotion to chivalric values often set him apart from other knights, who, although gallant, sometimes lacked the humility and compassion he carried in his heart. He had grown up in a modest farming family before displaying a natural talent for swordsmanship in his youth. Given a chance to train in the Citadel's knightly academies, Cedric had risen through the ranks by merit alone. Now, he was one of the realm's most respected defenders.

Next was Lady Elara, a paladin devoted to the Divine Light. She carried a radiance within her that could banish even the darkest nightmares. While many warriors placed their faith in steel, Elara placed hers in the Goddess of Dawn, whose guiding grace she invoked in battle. The pure white insignia of her order adorned her breastplate and shield. People spoke with awe of how she healed the sick with a touch, and how her prayers could repel horrors that would shake the courage of normal soldiers. More than once, Elara had been seen standing vigil at the borders of remote hamlets, ensuring wandering spirits could not harass defenseless peasants. She had dedicated her life to protecting the weak and oppressed, and this vow made her a perfect candidate to stand against the looming darkness.

From the realm's arcane circles came Thalion, an elderly, wise mage of remarkable knowledge and measured demeanor. His connection to Stonehaven's magical currents was both profound and disciplined. Where other spellcasters might harness raw power recklessly, Thalion believed fervently in the principle of balance. He had spent a lifetime studying in the Grand Archives of the Arcanum, delving into scrolls chronicling the world's greatest magical battles and darkest curses. Thalion's mastery of elemental forces, combined with his reputation for humility and patience, made him the intellectual pillar the king's council so desperately needed. With so much uncertain, only someone of Thalion's erudition could hope to decipher the puzzle of the Shadow Nexus.

Lastly, there was Mira, a gifted wizard whose talent for sorcery eclipsed almost every other practitioner in living memory. If Thalion represented the sagacious scholar, Mira embodied the raw might of magic, honed by relentless practice and a mind that thirsted for discovery. Rumor had it that at the tender age of eight, she accidentally froze an entire orchard in the midst of summer. Ever since, she had dedicated her life to learning about the complexities of arcane energy, especially those from primal and interplanar sources. Her skill with illusions and conjurations was legendary, and she had developed her own unique style of staff fighting that paired mesmerizing spellwork with graceful, dance-like movements. Yet, despite her remarkable gifts, Mira was often guarded, as though something weighed heavily on her heart. King Alaric surmised she had her own motivations for responding to his summons, though the exact nature of those motivations remained cloaked in secrecy.

Messenger hawks sped in all directions from the Royal Citadel, each bearing a sealed scroll etched with the royal crest: a majestic phoenix entwined around a golden sun. The message they carried was succinct yet urgent. It spoke of a great and ancient evil stirring in the land, threatening the very essence of Stonehaven, and implored each chosen hero to present themselves before King Alaric with utmost haste. None of the four could refuse such a call. Whether driven by honor, faith, duty, or thirst for knowledge, they knew fate had beckoned them to meet at Stonehaven's heart during this time of crisis.

While the days ticked by awaiting their arrival, the darkness continued its advance. In the northern farmland of Greenwood Vale, villagers whispered of strange silhouettes slithering across the horizon. At dusk, the last embers of daylight seemed devoured by an unnatural blackness that pressed heavily against the lamplight. Men and women, who once toiled contentedly in fields of barley and wheat, found themselves double-bolting their doors and huddling around dwindling hearth fires. Children hid under blankets, comforted only by the lullabies their parents sang—songs passed down for generations to keep fear at bay. Even the birds seemed hesitant to greet the morning sun, as if they too felt the suffocating presence creeping across the land.

Meanwhile, in the southwestern coastal regions, fishermen reported that the once-lively waters had grown eerily silent. Nets came up empty or torn, and eerie shapes could be glimpsed swirling beneath the waves after twilight. Rocky shores, typically full of scurrying crabs and seabirds, looked barren and colorless, as though life itself were retreating before the arrival of something far more ominous than storms. A hush fell over harbors that had thrived on trade, as merchants hesitated to anchor in waters rumored to be haunted by leviathans of shadow.

King Alaric listened intently to every new dispatch that arrived at the Royal Citadel, and with each passing day, his heart grew heavier. Yet he did not yield to despair. He ordered relief caravans to the afflicted towns and fortresses to bolster their defenses. Paladin squadrons were dispatched to oversee the well-being of travelers and pilgrims. Mages lent their powers to fortify city walls with protective wards. All these measures provided a measure of hope—but the unstoppable spread of darkness demanded a more decisive intervention, something beyond the capacity of ordinary warriors.

At long last, the first of the summoned heroes appeared: Sir Cedric. He arrived at midday, astride a proud warhorse draped in a black and gold caparison—Stonehaven's official heraldic colors. Even from a distance, one could sense his composed nobility, his every gesture colored by discipline and humility. As he dismounted in the courtyard, stablehands rushed forward to take his steed. Cedric insisted on helping them unsaddle before he allowed himself even a moment's rest. He walked with firm steps into the grand entry hall, where the guards promptly escorted him to the War Chamber. His posture straight, he placed a hand reverently over his heart when he knelt before King Alaric.

"Sire," he said simply, voice resonating in the chamber's hush, "I stand ready to serve."

Soon after Cedric's arrival, Lady Elara walked through the gilded gates. She bore a silvery longsword at her hip and carried a shield with the sunburst sigil of her order. A gentle aura seemed to emanate from her presence, diffusing the tension in the corridors. Soldiers and servants alike paused to watch as she passed, glimpsing the faint glow at her fingertips—subtle evidence of the divine energies she wielded. Beneath the plate armor, Elara's eyes shone with soft compassion, tempered by steely resolve. When she knelt to the king, the light radiating from her hands cast a comforting brightness that momentarily eased the War Chamber's somber gloom.

Next came Thalion, whose presence in the Citadel was less dramatic but every bit as profound. He arrived in simple but elegant robes embroidered with arcane symbols, a large tome clutched under one arm, and a wooden staff in the other. Though advanced in years, he walked upright, exuding calm confidence. His silver hair flowed past his shoulders, and his kind eyes held a spark of curiosity. He bowed respectfully to King Alaric, the lines on his face creasing into a warm smile. Despite the emergency, it was clear Thalion's scholarly mind was already analyzing the surroundings, the wards in place, and every flicker of magical energy emanating from the Citadel's ancient foundations.

Lastly, in a whirlwind of magical lights, Mira arrived. Courtiers and palace staff near the front gates described her entrance as both astonishing and slightly unsettling—rainbow sparks danced around her figure as she materialized, staff in hand, from what appeared to be a rip in the air itself. Though less rigidly formal than the others, Mira still displayed a measured courtesy when she bowed to King Alaric. A single braid of dark hair fell down one side of her shoulder, framing a youthful face set with serious determination. Where Thalion emanated scholarly patience, Mira brimmed with unbridled potential—a living storm of arcane force contained within a slender frame.

So it was that, within the War Chamber's confines, all four heroes finally stood together for the first time. King Alaric surveyed them with gratitude and relief. Though each was strikingly different—Cedric's knightly stoicism contrasted by Mira's restless energy, Elara's serene devotion counterbalancing Thalion's analytical composure—the king had faith that, united, they could rise to meet Stonehaven's dire threat. All formality aside, the gravity of their charge weighed upon them from the moment they locked eyes.

"Welcome, my friends," King Alaric began, stepping away from the head of the table to face them more directly. "Your reputations precede you, yet I believe even they fall short of the truth of your capacities. The kingdom I love is under siege by a darkness none of us have seen before. If it is indeed what the High Seer believes—the Shadow Nexus— then Stonehaven's future hangs by a thread. I have asked you here, not merely to share our plight, but to entrust you with what may be the most critical mission of our age. I beg you—help us safeguard this realm from a fate of eternal night."

The four heroes listened intently as King Alaric recounted all the harrowing evidence of the darkness's spread. He spoke of the newly formed black storms, of monstrous attacks in once-peaceful villages, and of the slow drain on the kingdom's vitality. Malachai stood by, occasionally interjecting observations about arcane energies or referencing ancient records that told of cataclysmic events in eras long forgotten. The tension in the room was palpable, every flicker of candlelight seeming to highlight the lines of worry etched across the king's face.

As the king finished, Cedric inclined his head. "Your Majesty, you have risked much in calling upon us individually. I offer my sword and my life to protect Stonehaven. But I must know... do we have any idea where this darkness originates? Can the Shadow Nexus be found and destroyed?"

Malachai cleared his throat, the dryness of age and magic crackling in his voice. "There are theories," he said. "A hidden place rumored to exist deep in the western wastes. The only references we've found are in crumbling manuscripts dating back to an era when this land was not yet called Stonehaven. These references speak of a source of negative energy that was sealed away by powerful rites, rites we no longer possess in full. However, the wards that once bound it may be weakening, allowing corruption to seep out. We cannot be certain yet—but if we can gather more information, perhaps we can locate this place precisely."

"Then we must gather this information swiftly," Thalion concluded, stroking his beard in thought. "Time is of the essence. My king, if you'll permit me, I can make copies of relevant tomes and begin cross-referencing them with the Arcanum's archives. However, we'll also need direct evidence from the affected regions. We cannot rely solely on theory."

King Alaric nodded. "Exactly so. Brave explorers and scouts have ventured into these shadow-touched areas, yet many have not returned. Those who did were not the same—often struck with trembling nightmares or cursed injuries that resisted healing. Your fellowship must first travel to these places, discern the nature of this corruption, and then decide how best to counter it. Stonehaven's resources are at your disposal. Use them well."

Elara, who had been silent, finally spoke. Her voice was calm, yet carried an intensity that could quell any lingering doubt. "I feel the stirrings of a great darkness in my prayers," she said. "As though an ancient evil calls out to me from beyond the boundaries of our realm. My goddess grants me strength, and I vow to stand against this threat until my final breath. The people of Stonehaven will be safe again."

Mira nodded in agreement, though her face held a spark of something unresolved—perhaps a personal vendetta or memory that fueled her purpose. "I've studied phenomena like these. Shadow magic often manifests in illusions and corruption, but its root is always more tangible than we might guess. If we find that root, I can help tear it out."

From the gloom of a corner, High Seer Malachai stepped forward, staff tapping against the stone floor.

"Before you depart," he said, "the four of you must be properly equipped. The darkness you face can twist even the bravest heart into despair. We have prepared wards and artifacts to bolster your resolve. Use them wisely, and remember that unity is your greatest shield."

After hours spent pouring over maps and strategizing potential routes, the meeting adjourned. The king personally escorted the heroes through a hidden corridor leading to a small armory. Various magical relics and pieces of gear hung from the walls, each radiating an otherworldly aura. King Alaric presented Cedric with a newly forged longsword, its blade etched with runic inscriptions that glowed faintly when lifted—a token of the royal house bestowed only on the most valiant defenders of the crown. Cedric thanked the king, feeling the weight of this honor resonate in his heart.

Elara received a polished shield overlaid with the symbol of a golden phoenix. According to Malachai, the shield contained a fragment of celestial power that could amplify her divine blessings in times of dire need. She gazed upon it with reverence, quietly offering a prayer of gratitude and a vow to use its power in service of the greater good.

Thalion was entrusted with a staff carved from living heartwood and inlaid with silver filigree. At the top shimmered a crystal that Malachai claimed had come from a meteorite centuries prior. Though the staff was ancient, it hummed with renewed vigor as Thalion ran his fingers along its runes. He smiled, marveling at its craftsmanship and remarking that the synergy between his own magic and this artifact was almost immediate—another sign that destiny had guided them here.

Finally, Mira was offered a small orb, black as the night sky yet flecked with motes of light that seemed to swirl within it like stars. Malachai called it the Eye of Astrum, a focusing gemstone that heightened the user's aptitude for complex spellcasting. When she held it, Mira felt a surge of energy pour into her, igniting a sense of possibility she had only vaguely perceived before. She slipped the orb into a pouch at her waist, feeling its comforting weight, certain that it would help her push the boundaries of her magical repertoire.

Shortly before dusk, King Alaric and the court convened once more in the courtyard to offer a formal blessing for the heroes. Though it was still early in their quest, the entire Citadel felt the significance of this departure—like the beginning of a new, uncertain chapter in Stonehaven's history. Bells tolled solemnly as the four champions, now girded with relics and renewed determination, stepped forward onto the cobblestones. Torches flickered against the advancing twilight, and a hush fell over the assembled guards, nobles, and curious onlookers.

"Sir Cedric, Lady Elara, Thalion, and Mira," King Alaric announced, his voice resonating with the gravity of this moment, "by the authority of the crown and with the blessings of the realm, I send you forth. May your valor never falter, may your hearts remain pure, and may the Light guide you to victory. Return to us in triumph, for Stonehaven stands behind you."

With that, the courtyard erupted in cheers and well-wishes, though the tension beneath the fanfare was unmistakable. The four heroes felt a collective tightening in their chests—a mixture of excitement, resolve, and dread. Each looked to the others, sharing a moment of silent understanding: from this point onward, their fates were entwined, and the land they called home depended on their success.

They rode out under the dimming sky, their path taking them through the torchlit streets of the capital city. Crowds parted reverently, some bowing, others chanting prayers or tossing small flowers in the heroes' wake. Beyond the city gates, the road wound through gentle hills and well-tended farmland. Only a short time ago, these same fields would have appeared serene, a testament to the kingdom's enduring prosperity. But in the creeping twilight, the farmland seemed subdued, with an unsettling hush that replaced the usual nocturnal chorus of crickets and owls.

Within hours, the gloom deepened. Dark clouds obscured the moon, transforming the sky into a starless expanse. Trees in the distance loomed like silent sentinels, their outlines flickering each time distant lightning illuminated the horizon. Even the air felt different—a chill that raised goosebumps on bare skin. Cedric, riding at the vanguard, tried to keep his thoughts focused on the mission. He had faced bandits, mercenaries, and even monstrous creatures in the wild before—but never had the very atmosphere itself felt so oppressive.

Elara spurred her steed close to Cedric's. "Do you feel it, Sir Knight?" she asked softly, her expression grave. "It's as though each breath carries a weight I cannot quite name."

He nodded. "I do. And I suspect we'll feel it more strongly the closer we draw to whatever has taken root in this kingdom."

Behind them, Thalion and Mira rode in silence, though their senses were similarly heightened. Thalion traced subtle patterns in the air, performing small cantrips to detect magical fluctuations. His brow furrowed with concern at the feedback he received: intangible pulses resonated through the environment, as if strings of corrupted energy had been plucked somewhere unseen, sending echoes through the land. Mira gripped her staff more tightly, resisting the urge to siphon that energy for study—dark magic held an allure she found dangerous to indulge, especially without fully understanding its source.

Soon, the party reached an old roadside shrine dedicated to the Goddess of Dawn—a simple stone structure where weary travelers traditionally left offerings of flowers or food as thanks for safe journeys. Now, the shrine was in disrepair. The door was battered off its hinges, and the sculpted figure of the goddess lay crumbled in the dirt. Their horses snorted nervously, stamping the ground as a cold wind whistled through the open spaces. Without exchanging words, Cedric dismounted and approached the ruined shrine. He knelt, gingerly lifting a broken fragment of the goddess's carved hand.

"This is sacrilege," Elara muttered, dismounting to join him. Her voice carried a tremor of anger. "To desecrate a holy place like this... something truly vile is at work."

Cedric gently placed the fragment on a nearby rock, his gaze darkening. "The question is, who or what did this? Was it random, or part of the rising darkness?"

Mira raised her staff, letting the tip glow with soft white light to illuminate the shrine's interior. "I see footprints. They're large—larger than any human's." She traced her finger around the edge of a deep impression in the dirt. "Could be some type of ogre or troll... but the shape is off."

Thalion stepped closer, conjuring a faintly shining symbol in the air. When the symbol touched the ground, it flared with energy, revealing ghostly outlines of what might have transpired here moments or hours before. A swirl of inky shapes flickered across their vision, almost like living shadows lunging at something. Then, with a hiss, the vision dissipated, and Thalion staggered back, pressing a hand to his temple.

"Shadows," he whispered, breath uneven. "Creatures of living shadow. They tore through here... and I suspect they gave no mercy. The aura they left behind is cold, raw."

Elara clenched her fists around her shield strap. "Then we have confirmation of the rumors. These shadow fiends aren't just illusions—they're real. We must press on, warn the local villages, and perhaps rally them to fortify their altars and shrines."

A silent resolve settled over the party. Under normal circumstances, they might have paused to rest for the night, but the spreading darkness left no room for delay. They remounted their horses and pressed forward, guided by flickering torchlight and Thalion's occasional magical orbs. The road felt eerily deserted; not a single traveler, merchant caravan, or messenger was in sight. All of Stonehaven's usual livelihood seemed frozen in anticipation of something dreadful.

Hours later, when they finally spotted the scattered lights of a small town nestled near the base of a gently sloping hill, relief swept through them. The settlement was called Oakenshade—a rustic place once known for its cheerful inns and taverns that served honeyed ale. Yet as the heroes approached, they found the sturdy wooden gates barred, and watchmen peering from the parapets with anxious faces. Torches sputtered in the damp wind. From above, a guard bellowed, "Who goes there?"

Cedric raised his sword in a peaceful salute. "We come by the king's summons. Open your gates. We carry no threat to this town."

The guard hesitated, holding the group at arrow-point for a tense moment. Then, after hurried whispers among themselves, the heavy gates creaked open just wide enough for the four riders. Inside, Oakenshade's once-vibrant main square stood nearly empty. A handful of townsfolk clustered in the glow of lanterns, their eyes brimming with suspicion or desperation. The heroes dismounted slowly, giving the spooked guards no reason to mistrust them further.

A gaunt man in a brown cloak stepped forward, eyes shadowed. "Apologies for the cold welcome," he said, voice shaking slightly. "We've had more than our fair share of trouble these last few nights. My name is Rowan; I help run the town watch."

Lady Elara offered him a warm smile, her posture radiating compassion. "Well met, Rowan. We come in the name of King Alaric. We understand there have been… disturbances."

Rowan barked a mirthless laugh. "Disturbances doesn't begin to describe it. The creatures… they slither in the darkness, they stalk our streets. Good men and women have vanished, taken from their beds or ambushed on the roads. We bar our gates at sundown now. No one enters or leaves at night if we can help it."

Thalion gently placed a hand on Rowan's shoulder. "We understand. Have you or your neighbors witnessed these creatures directly? Are they truly formed of shadow, as we suspect?"

The man nodded slowly. "Shadows, yes. At least they looked like living shadows, shaped into beasts or men—it's hard to say for sure. They slip under doors, through cracks, then vanish. I lost my brother to them a fortnight ago."

Cedric's jaw clenched. "I swear to you, Rowan, we will do what we can to end this threat. Tonight, we will stay here and help protect the town."

Rowan's eyes glimmered with the faintest spark of hope. "We would be grateful for any help you can give. We've tried everything—spreading ashes at doorways, lighting bonfires, calling on traveling priests to bless our homes... But each night, we lose more. Some vanish. Others are found... changed... as if something drained them of their essence."

By now, the entire town guard and a few ragged townsfolk had gathered around, drawn by the presence of these heroes who carried themselves with the kind of confidence only legends possessed. Elara took a moment to speak to the wounded, offering gentle healing to those who needed it. Mira paced the perimeter, quietly weaving spells of detection in the air, trying to sense any immediate threats lurking beyond the flickering lantern light.

As midnight approached, the group decided on a watch rotation. Cedric, donning his new runic longsword, volunteered to patrol the streets with a handful of the more stalwart guards. Elara planned to remain in the central square, healing the injured and standing ready to repel any direct assault with her divine shield. Thalion and Mira took to the rooftops, using their vantage point to scan for magical anomalies and prepare for a swift intervention if something attacked from above or from a hidden angle. The villagers, bolstered by the heroes' presence, set about reinforcing barricades and torch lines with renewed vigor.

The wind picked up, howling through the narrow alleys and rattling shutters on darkened houses. Clouds swallowed the moon entirely, plunging Oakenshade into a near-pitch blackness that only the scattered torches and magical lights could penetrate. Cedric's armor glinted with faint runic light each time the wind parted the shadows, a beacon of hope to the anxious guards. The hours ticked by slowly, each minute stretching taut with expectation, as though the entire town was holding its breath.

Then, a piercing scream echoed from somewhere on the outskirts. Cedric spun on his heel, shouting for the guards to follow. Down a muddy lane leading toward a cluster of small cottages, he saw flickers of movement—shapes that didn't quite conform to any creature of flesh and bone. The shadows seemed to stretch unnaturally, as if peeling themselves off the walls to slither across the ground. Heart pounding, Cedric raised his sword, feeling the runes flare with protective light as he moved toward the threat.

A farmer, pale as death, stumbled onto the lane, his face frozen in terror. Behind him, one of the shapeless black forms lashed out with a tendril-like limb. Cedric lunged, sweeping his sword through the darkness. The blade bit into something intangible, yet the creature recoiled with an unearthly hiss, scattering like ink in water. The farmer collapsed, gasping, barely alive. Cedric scooped him up and called for help, steadying his sword arm in readiness.

Meanwhile, on the rooftops, Mira gasped as she felt an abrupt pulse of malevolent energy. "Thalion, do you sense that?" she whispered, voice trembling with adrenaline. "It's coming from the far edge of town. There might be more of them than we thought."

Thalion nodded grimly. "We must drive them out or destroy them. Focus on limiting their movement. I'll attempt to disrupt whatever magic animates them."

In near-synchronization, Mira and Thalion conjured bright orbs of arcane light, hurling them across the thatched rooftops to illuminate the shadowy shapes. Startled by the sudden glare, several figures lurking near the edges of the light hissed and retreated. Thalion chanted a series of incantations that caused strands of shimmering energy to curl from his fingertips, weaving through the air like silken ribbons. Where these ribbons touched the shadowy entities, they twitched violently, as though in pain. Some dissolved entirely, fading back into the darkness from whence they came.

On the ground, Elara rallied the frightened townsfolk to stand their ground. Her shield, emblazoned with the phoenix crest, emanated a soft glow that repelled the creeping shadows. She guided the able-bodied to form a protective ring around the weaker or injured residents. Each time a shadow creature tested the circle of light, Elara's divine power surged forth, forcing it back with sparks of holy fire. In the midst of this turmoil, she prayed under her breath, calling upon the Goddess of Dawn to guide her hand

and safeguard Oakenshade from the malevolence that had gripped it.

As the fray continued, Cedric engaged multiple shadow fiends in quick succession. His sword's runic inscriptions blazed with every strike. Though his opponents seemed insubstantial, each clean blow caused them to disperse in shrieks that echoed unnaturally. Through the swirling chaos, Cedric's mind remained focused. He remembered all his training, all the times he had pledged his life to defend the innocent. Tonight, that oath was tested in ways he had never imagined: to battle shapes that seemed spawned from pure nightmare. Yet he held firm, relentless in his pursuit of every last abomination.

Bit by bit, the heroes gained the upper hand. The brilliant spells from Thalion and Mira prevented the shadows from converging or ambushing en masse, while Cedric and Elara performed a methodical sweep at ground level. After what felt like an eternity, the last of the creatures hissed and slithered away into the depths of the night. A hush fell over Oakenshade—broken only by the ragged breathing of guards and villagers who had witnessed the confrontation.

In the aftermath, torchlight revealed a grim scene. Several townspeople lay unconscious from the assault, though mercifully none appeared fatally wounded. Cedric helped the farmer he had saved find his family, while Elara offered healing prayers. Mira and Thalion took a moment to recover their composure, leaning on their staffs as the toll of heavy spellcasting coursed through their limbs. The extent of the havoc wrought by the shadow fiends weighed on them like a tangible burden, yet they had succeeded in preventing any further abductions or worse.

Rowan, the town watchman, approached them with eyes brimming with gratitude. "You saved us," he said, voice quavering with both relief and lingering fear. "Thank you… all of you. Without your intervention, who knows how many more we would have lost."

Cedric mustered a small smile, though his eyes reflected the tension still thrumming in his veins. "We did what we came to do, Rowan. But the fight is far from over. These attacks are just the beginning if the Shadow Nexus's power continues to grow. Oakenshade is safe tonight—but we'll need to make sure you have the resources and knowledge to protect yourselves."

Thalion glanced at the horizon, where the faintest hint of dawn lightened the sky. "King Alaric sent us to learn and to push back this looming darkness," he said. "We've accomplished part of that tonight, but the real threat—the source—remains hidden. I suspect it will only get stronger if left unchecked."

Elara nodded firmly. "We must move on as soon as possible, to investigate more of these incidents and piece together the location of the Shadow Nexus. But before we go, we'll reinforce Oakenshade with wards and teach the watch how best to combat these shadow creatures. We cannot be everywhere at once, but we can leave each place a little safer than we found it."

Mira, exhausted yet determined, added, "Tonight showed us what we're up against. If these fiends are just a fraction of the power seeping into Stonehaven, we need to be ready for far worse. Still, it's heartening to see that they can be driven back."

As the first rays of sunlight finally broke over the eastern hills, Oakenshade stirred from the terror of the night. Survivors emerged from locked homes, blinking in the morning's glow, offering hushed thanks to the heroes who had saved them from a fate unknown. Children clung to their parents, and the elders bowed their heads in reverent gratitude. Though the entire village felt the weight of the darkness that still lurked beyond their borders, there was a renewed sense of possibility in the air—proof that the horrors could be challenged, if not yet vanquished.

Gathering their belongings and seeing to their horses, the heroes prepared to depart. Rowan, supported by a handful of watchmen, stood at the gates to bid them farewell. A fragile optimism had replaced his earlier hopelessness; the knowledge that four extraordinary champions were out there fighting for Stonehaven uplifted his spirits. With heartfelt farewells, the companions promised to return if Oakenshade ever found itself in dire need again.

And so, the journey continued. The group pressed onward, determined to uncover more clues about the Shadow Nexus and its rising power. Though still strangers in many ways, they were bound by a growing camaraderie forged in battle. Each had seen the other's strengths, recognized the distinct qualities they brought to the fellowship, and sensed an unspoken bond that would only intensify as they delved deeper into Stonehaven's mounting crisis.

Thus concluded the first leg of their quest—a single night's stand against the creeping darkness in a quiet town that might have otherwise been lost to oblivion. Yet for Sir Cedric, Lady Elara, Thalion, and Mira, it marked the true beginning of a greater destiny. A silent oath, unvoiced yet unmistakable, was sealed: they would stand against this encroaching evil, each contributing their unique gifts, each willing to risk life and soul to safeguard the realm they cherished. Though the shadowy path ahead was fraught with peril, hope still kindled in their hearts. The timeless ideals of courage, unity, and sacrifice lived on, lighting a path through the encroaching blackness. Stonehaven, once peaceful and untroubled, now depended upon these four heroes to usher in a new dawn—and they would not fail.

2

THE CALL TO ADVENTURE

The first rays of dawn spilled over the rooftops of the Royal Citadel, igniting the sky in a wash of pink and gold. Within the high marble walls, a sense of apprehension mingled with quiet excitement, for this day was unlike any other in recent memory. Although Stonehaven's capital city often buzzed with activity—merchants haggling in cobblestone streets, guards marching in polished armor, and nobles crowding the palace halls—today felt different. Whispers of encroaching darkness lingered everywhere, fueling speculation and fear. Yet just as strong was the flutter of hope, for word had spread that four extraordinary individuals were assembling under King Alaric's command to confront the looming menace.

The corridors of the Citadel stretched wide, lined with ancient tapestries depicting Stonehaven's proud history. Serpentine dragons locked in battle with valiant knights. Sorcerers channeling the primal elements of nature to defeat monstrous hordes. And in the center of a grand hallway, the largest tapestry of all showed the legendary Phoenix of Stonehaven—a symbol of rebirth and radiant light—rising from the ashes of a forgotten age. Golden thread woven through the fabric caught the morning light, giving the bird an almost living luminescence.

Down this corridor walked Sir Cedric, his footsteps echoing against the polished tiles. As a knight of great renown, he had traversed these halls before—most recently at the king's initial summons—but never with a mission so daunting. Newly arrived from his overnight vigil in Oakenshade (the small town he and his newfound companions had protected from shadowy fiends), Cedric wore the exhaustion of battle lightly upon his strong features. Sleep had been scarce, but his determination hadn't wavered. He still carried the runic longsword the king had bestowed upon him, its faintly glowing symbols a constant reminder of his promise to defend Stonehaven.

At the end of the corridor stood a pair of ornate doors, fashioned from oak and inlaid with silver filigree. Two Royal Guards stood watch, each bearing a halberd with the Phoenix crest etched into the blade. They inclined their heads in greeting, recognizing Sir Cedric. Without a word, they pushed open the heavy doors, allowing him to enter the War Chamber.

Inside, the atmosphere was hushed yet electric. Tall stained-glass windows bathed the large circular table in kaleidoscopic colors of reds, blues, and greens. Around the table stood the king's closest advisors, along with the Court Mage High Seer Malachai, scribes with quills poised over parchment, and knights resplendent in ceremonial armor. At the chamber's far end, upon a slightly raised dais, stood King Alaric himself—regal in a robe of deep crimson, trimmed with fur, and embroidered with the golden Phoenix crest. His posture remained upright, but the worry etched on his face revealed the weight of the kingdom's troubles.

King Alaric's gaze shifted from a quiet conversation with Malachai to greet Cedric. A smile touched the monarch's features. "Sir Cedric," he said, his voice measured, "I welcome you again to our council. Our kingdom owes you and your companions a debt for your vigilance in Oakenshade."

Cedric bowed, placing a fist over his heart in salute. "Your Majesty, the threat was grave, but we prevailed— thanks in no small part to the allies I fought beside. I trust they will arrive momentarily."

Even as he said it, the doors opened again. Lady Elara entered, the aura of her divine power subtly lighting her path. In the day's bright glow, she looked every bit the paragon of faith: her polished armor gleamed, the insignia of the Goddess of Dawn prominent upon her breastplate, and her white cloak trailed behind her in pristine folds. She paused just inside the chamber, scanning the faces of those assembled with calm conviction.

"Elara," King Alaric greeted, acknowledging her with a respectful nod. "Stonehaven welcomes your devotion and the blessing of the Divine Light you carry."

She returned his nod, stepping forward to stand by Cedric. "My prayers for guidance brought me here swiftly. We have seen the darkness firsthand, Your Majesty. We are ready to learn what we must do to banish it."

Soon after, a quiet hush fell as two more figures stepped in together: Thalion, the elder mage whose robes of deep violet shimmered with intricate arcane symbols, and Mira, the youthful wizard whose staff and belt pouches bristled with magical potential. Thalion exuded an air of scholarly calm, while Mira's eyes shone with barely contained curiosity and determination. They took their places beside Cedric and Elara.

Standing as one, the four formed a striking tableau: the disciplined knight, the radiant paladin, the wise mage, and the prodigiously gifted wizard. Each brought a distinct energy into the room, yet a silent accord passed between them. Their destinies were now bound together, and the kingdom's salvation depended on their unity.

King Alaric cleared his throat, stepping down from the dais to address the gathering more directly. "My loyal advisors, honorable knights, and guardians of Stonehaven," he said. "We stand on the brink of an unprecedented threat. My scouts bring ever-more dire reports from across our lands: farms blighted, lakes blackened, and families forced to flee from horrors that prey upon them in the night. Even so, I have faith. Faith in our resilience, and faith in these four heroes whom fate has delivered in our hour of need."

A rustle of agreement moved through the War Chamber. Though weariness showed on many faces, there was also relief—relief that at last a plan was taking form, a promise that not all hope was lost.

King Alaric glanced at Malachai, prompting the High Seer to step forward. The old magician's robes, a dark shade of blue embroidered with arcane runes, swept across the floor as he joined the circle. His expression carried both intensity and fatigue; indeed, Malachai had scarcely left his tower these past weeks, working tirelessly with the Royal Library's archivists and his own mystical apparatus to pinpoint the origin of the spreading darkness.

"Friends," Malachai began, his voice sonorous and steady, "we have spent sleepless nights tracing the surge of malevolent energy that plagues our kingdom. All signs confirm our worst fears: this evil arises from what our forebears once called the *Shadow Nexus*. In ancient times, it was said to be the convergence point of negative energies—a wellspring of corruption that, if left unchecked, could engulf entire realms in eternal night. We long believed it was sealed or destroyed by our ancestors. But the wards that once held it at bay appear to have weakened. Now, the nexus stirs once more, seeping its darkness into Stonehaven."

An anxious murmur filled the room. Though the name "Shadow Nexus" was new to many ears, its implications were easy to grasp. Cedric felt a cold prickle along his spine; even among the bravest knights, the notion of facing an ancient, near-mythical corruption would test the heart. Elara pressed her lips together, reflecting on the vow she had taken to banish all that was unholy or profane. Thalion's keen eyes flicked from Malachai to the dusty tomes lying open on the table, no doubt containing centuries-old texts referencing the nexus. As for Mira, her grip on her staff tightened, as though her entire being yearned to unravel the mysteries behind such dire magic.

King Alaric gazed from one hero to the other. "And so we call upon you: Sir Cedric, Lady Elara, Master Thalion, and Mira. The kingdom needs you to seek out the Shadow Nexus, to find a way to cleanse or destroy it before its influence spreads beyond our borders. Will you accept this charge?"

It was Cedric who spoke first, voice clear. "Your Majesty, I swore an oath to safeguard Stonehaven from any evil that threatens it. I stand ready to uphold that vow. I accept."

Elara placed a hand over her heart, the faint glow around her intensifying for a moment. "As a paladin of the Divine Light, I cannot turn away from this scourge. I too accept, pledging my faith and my life to this cause."

Thalion inclined his head. "It is a mage's duty to steward arcane knowledge and protect balance. If the nexus truly threatens the natural order, I will do all in my power to help restore equilibrium. I accept."

Mira's eyes shone. "Darkness this potent can't be allowed to exist unopposed. I accept, Your Majesty, and I will bring every ounce of magic I possess to this quest."

A tangible sense of relief spread through the chamber. The king's eyes momentarily closed, as though he offered a silent prayer of thanks. "I am humbled by your courage. Stonehaven is stronger for your unity."

Malachai gestured to the large table strewn with maps and grimoires, inviting the four champions to step closer. Spread out were detailed charts of Stonehaven's diverse terrains—dense forests, mountain ranges, rolling plains, and hidden valleys. Several areas were circled in red ink, including a thick patch of woodland labeled *The Gravenshade Woods* in the southwestern region.

"This is our first concern," Malachai said, tapping the circled woodlands. "Gravenshade Woods has become the epicenter of unusual activity: vanishing travelers, ghostly apparitions, and a creeping darkness that clouds the sky even during daylight hours. I suspect the corruption seeping from the nexus is especially strong in that region. Investigating these woods should be your initial step."

"Precisely," Thalion agreed, leaning over the map. "The forests are known for their centuries-old groves and hidden grottos. If the nexus's energy is concentrated there, it might serve as a clue—perhaps a sign of where the wards have failed or where the magic is bleeding into our realm."

Elara looked up from the map. "High Seer, what do we know of the creatures reported there? We encountered wraith-like shadows in Oakenshade, but rumors from the southwest mention monstrous beasts and unnatural storms."

Malachai sighed. "We have conflicting reports. Some claim to have seen twisted beasts—wolves, boars, and other forest dwellers warped by shadow. Others speak of phantoms materializing between the trees. My scouts also found the remains of bizarre ritual sites. Sadly, details are scarce, as few explorers return unharmed. Your mission will be one of discovery as much as combat."

Cedric nodded solemnly. "Then we will be prepared for any threat, mundane or magical."

King Alaric motioned toward several crates in the corner of the chamber. "Before you depart, accept these gifts. Stonehaven's artisans and smiths have worked tirelessly to craft items imbued with protective magic. We cannot accompany you in your travels, but may these relics ease your path."

From the nearest crate, a steward lifted a polished shield embossed with a golden phoenix. He presented it to Cedric, who already carried a runic longsword. "Sir Cedric," the king said, "while you already bear the blade that was commissioned in your name, this shield has been infused with wards to deflect dark energies. May it protect you and those you defend."

Cedric's breath caught at the craftsmanship. Tiny runic inscriptions glowed around the shield's circumference. He bowed. "Thank you, Your Majesty. I will wield it with honor."

Next, the steward retrieved an amulet with a shimmering opal at its center, attached to a delicate silver chain. Malachai offered it to Elara. "Lady Elara, this amulet resonates with divine magic. It will bolster your healing spells and strengthen the wards you cast against evil. Wear it close to your heart."

Elara cradled the amulet in her palm, sensing a comforting warmth radiating from it. She bowed her head in gratitude. "May it serve the cause of light."

A second steward approached with a rolled parchment tied with a silken cord. He passed it to Thalion. "Master Thalion, these are transcripts of the oldest incantations we could salvage regarding the nexus. Many lines are fragmented, but you may glean new insights by studying them. In addition, we have embedded a minor enchantment that allows these pages to withstand the elements, so you need not fear water or fire. Guard them well."

Thalion accepted the scroll with reverence, his studious gaze already scanning the first lines of text. "This knowledge could prove invaluable. I will safeguard it and employ it wisely."

Finally, an elegant bracer inlaid with faintly glowing crystals was brought forth for Mira. "We call this the Astral Bracer," Malachai explained. "It augments the wearer's arcane focus, making higher-level spells more feasible in moments of crisis. Use it with caution, Mira—too much power too quickly can be perilous."

Mira slipped the bracer onto her left forearm. The crystals pulsed in subtle rhythm with her own magical aura, and she felt a surge of energy ripple beneath her skin. "I understand. Thank you for entrusting me with this artifact. I won't abuse it."

With these gifts bestowed, King Alaric stepped back, surveying the four heroes assembled before him. "Brave champions, our hopes travel with you. The Royal Citadel will provide what support it can—more supplies, horses, and an escort to the outskirts of the Gravenshade Woods. But once you enter those trees, you will likely be on your own. The darkness is cunning. Trust each other, rely on your strengths, and do not underestimate what lurks in the shadows."

A respectful hush fell upon the War Chamber. The four bowed once more to the king. In those final moments, a palpable sense of destiny filled the air. Guards, advisors, and knights shared resolute nods; scribes paused in their note-taking to watch the heroes as they strode from the chamber. Their footsteps echoed down the corridor, accompanied by the faint clinking of armor and the soft hum of magical wards.

Preparations for departure went swiftly. Word of the newly formed band of heroes spread throughout the city, so much so that by the time they reached the Citadel's massive gates, a curious crowd had gathered. Some wore hopeful smiles; others gazed in awe at the quartet who would soon ride forth against the forces of darkness. Children peered around their parents' skirts, whispering excitedly, as though glimpsing living legends from a fairy tale.

True to his word, King Alaric had arranged a royal escort to see the group safely to the borders of the Gravenshade Woods. Two dozen mounted knights, each bearing Stonehaven's phoenix crest on their cloaks, waited in formation along the winding avenue leading out of the city. Sturdy horses for the heroes were provided as well. Cedric took the reins of a noble gray stallion that pawed the ground with impatience, while Elara chose a gentler mare with a creamy coat. Thalion, accustomed to lengthy walks, hesitated but ultimately mounted a mild-tempered bay gelding. Mira, never one to shy from new experiences, swung onto her black mare with agility.

A hush fell as a herald stepped forward, trumpeting a short fanfare that echoed between the stone walls. Then, in a ringing voice, he proclaimed, "Behold, the Heroes of Stonehaven! By royal decree, let none impede their quest nor withhold the aid they require, for upon their success rests the future of our realm!"

The crowd responded with a roar of cheers and applause, though underlying it all was the tension of a people who knew how desperately they needed a miracle. Sir Cedric, leading the procession, raised his sword in a silent salute to the gathering. Elara pressed a hand to her heart, offering a gentle smile. Thalion maintained a measured nod, while Mira waved, a flicker of her usual playfulness shining through her serious demeanor.

At last, the massive city gates, constructed of iron-bound oak, groaned open. With a clatter of hooves on cobblestone, the escort set out, flanking the four heroes in two disciplined lines. Banners emblazoned with the phoenix emblem fluttered in the brisk morning air. It was a grand departure indeed, one reminiscent of the old stories of crusading paladins or triumphant returning armies. Yet despite the pageantry, each hero bore a solemn understanding that their work had only just begun.

They passed through the outer districts of the capital, where the buildings gradually became smaller and more spaced apart. Merchants and peasants craned their necks to see the riders pass. Many made the sign of protection, or offered small tokens—bread loaves, wildflowers, even hastily scrawled notes of gratitude. It was an outpouring of faith unlike anything Cedric had seen in his years of service. He felt humbled and a touch overwhelmed.

Once beyond the city limits, they rode across gently rolling farmland. The smell of tilled earth and blossoming wildflowers filled the air, a reminder of Stonehaven's beauty and fertility. Occasionally, they glimpsed the devastation wrought by the encroaching darkness—withered patches of crops, or blackened tree stumps. Yet for the most part, the day remained bright and clear, a testament to what they fought to preserve.

Eventually, the road diverged from farmland, meandering into dense thickets where the forest canopy grew ever more intertwined. Birds called from within the leafy depths, and a slight hush descended on the company. Trees towered overhead, their branches swaying in a breeze that carried a whisper of something old and mysterious.

By late afternoon, they reached a junction where a thick post stood, arrows pointing in various directions to different Stonehavenn towns. One arrow read, "Gravenshade Woods—5 Miles." The knights drew their horses to a stop, forming a loose circle around Cedric, Elara, Thalion, and Mira.

"Here is where we part ways," announced the knight-captain leading the escort, a tall man with salt-and-pepper hair. "By the king's command, we dare not bring the entire troop into the forest. Stories abound of knights who vanish if they stray too close to that accursed wood. But rest assured, we'll remain stationed here for two days' time. Should you need to retreat, we will hold this post, and you can find us for resupply or medical aid."

Cedric dismounted momentarily, clasping the captain's forearm in a sign of mutual respect. "Thank you for bringing us this far. May the Light protect you and your men."

The knight-captain saluted. "And may it protect you, Sir Cedric—and all of you." He turned to the rest of the knights. "Form ranks, men! We make camp here."

As the soldiers set about establishing a secure perimeter, the four heroes continued onward, following the narrow path that wound deeper into the forest. The further they went, the thicker the canopy, until the sunlight dimmed to a greenish twilight beneath the branches. The calls of forest creatures became sporadic, as though something had driven them away or stifled their voices. An uneasy hush replaced the natural symphony of wind and wildlife.

Elara glanced around, her gloved hand resting on the amulet at her neck. "I feel a heaviness here. Not just the closeness of the trees... something deeper, more malevolent."

Mira nodded. She lifted her staff, letting its tip shine with faint illumination. The beam cast flickering patterns onto moss-covered trunks. "The magic in the air tastes… tainted, if that makes sense. Raw, but twisted. It's like an undercurrent pulling everything toward darkness."

Thalion stroked his beard thoughtfully. "The nexus's influence may be stronger here than we anticipated. Let us remain vigilant. The first sign of trouble often comes in subtle ways—like an odd hush or the absence of natural wildlife."

Cedric slowed his horse, peering down the narrow path that soon turned into a tunnel of interlocking branches overhead. "We should find a place to make camp before nightfall. The stories of these woods at night are grim."

They pressed on, now on high alert. Their earlier conversation and easy camaraderie gave way to silent watchfulness, each scanning the shadows between the gnarled trees. The forest felt ancient—thick vines coiled around trunks as wide as cottages, and the ground was padded with centuries of fallen leaves. Here and there, faint wisps of bluish glow drifted in the still air like ghostly fireflies. Elara carefully touched one with her gauntleted hand; it shimmered and vanished, leaving a faint chill behind.

Eventually, they found a small clearing where a trickling stream provided fresh water, and the overhead canopy gave just enough space to let in a dim circle of light. Cedric dismounted first, patting his weary stallion. "We can rest here," he said, turning to the group. "We have enough daylight to gather firewood and set up a defensive perimeter."

Elara nodded, swinging down from her mare. "Agreed. I can ward the perimeter with a small circle of protection, though it won't hold back every threat if we're attacked in force. It should, however, deter or weaken minor fiends."

Mira flicked her staff in a careful pattern, conjuring a handful of floating motes of light that drifted around the clearing. "And I can set alarm spells near the edges, too. If anything crosses that line, we'll know immediately."

Thalion, already rummaging in his satchel, retrieved some chalks and a small jar of powdered silver. "I have a few protective runes we can inscribe on the trees. Layering multiple wards is wise. The deeper we go, the darker it may become."

They set about these tasks methodically. Cedric and Mira ventured a short distance from the clearing, searching for firewood and kindling. The area was surprisingly barren of dead wood, as though the forest itself was hoarding its resources. Still, they managed to collect enough to build a modest campfire. Meanwhile, Elara traced sigils in the dirt, softly chanting prayers to the Goddess of Dawn. Thin bands of golden energy glowed briefly and then sank into the earth, signifying that her blessings now guarded the perimeter. Thalion sketched runes with chalk on prominent tree trunks, scattering the powdered silver as he chanted. These runes shimmered with a faint purple glow before fading from sight.

As dusk approached, a sense of unease settled upon the clearing. Shadows elongated, forming bizarre shapes that seemed to shift whenever one glanced away. A hush fell upon the entire forest, as if the dense trees held their breath. Once the fire crackled to life, its warm glow provided some comfort, drawing the four companions to sit in a loose circle around it.

For a moment, the subtle interplay of firelight on their faces made them look like old friends around a casual campfire, rather than newly acquainted adventurers thrust into a realm-threatening quest. But the tension in their eyes betrayed the reality: the darkness was no mere rumor, and the forest around them felt saturated with its presence.

Cedric stoked the fire, gazing into the dancing flames. "Malachai said the Gravenshade Woods is our first stop, but we know so little of what we're supposed to find here. The darkness is real enough... but how do we trace it back to its source? Where do we even begin?"

Elara inhaled slowly, folding her hands together as though in prayer. "My vow is to protect the innocent, and that vow brought me here. If the Goddess wills it, we will find signs—like footprints or corrupted shrines—that can guide us. I have faith."

Thalion tugged gently at his beard. "In many texts, references to the nexus speak of anchors or conduits—places of concentrated negative energy that feed the main source. If we find any such place, or even a site of sacrilegious ritual, we may be able to glean the location of the nexus itself."

Mira listened quietly, occasionally glancing into the surrounding darkness, as if expecting it to lunge at them. "Between Elara's divine sense and Thalion's arcane knowledge, we should be able to sniff out anomalies. I can also cast detection spells specifically for necromancy or curses. If something truly malignant is stirring here, we'll sense it."

They continued sharing theories as the flames licked the cool night air. Gradually, however, the conversation stilled. A heaviness in the atmosphere pressed upon them, the hush broken only by the flicker of the fire and the distant rustling of leaves. No owls hooted, no nighttime insects hummed. It was as though the forest itself were locked in an uneasy standstill, waiting to see what intruders might do.

At length, Elara announced she would begin a watch rotation. "We'll take turns standing guard," she said. "I doubt we'll sleep soundly in these woods, but we must conserve our strength. Cedric, you and I can alternate shifts. Thalion, Mira, you two can alternate as well, unless you'd prefer to remain awake together for arcane reasons."

Thalion gave a small smile. "We can manage. My magic doesn't require me to meditate as elves do, but I can manage a light trance that's enough to refresh me somewhat. Mira, you'll need proper rest to keep your casting ability sharp."

Mira nodded, relieved. "I'll catch a few hours of real sleep, then I'll relieve you. Let's hope nothing stirs tonight."

Though the plan offered some reassurance, no one truly expected a peaceful night. Still, they had to try. Setting aside weapons but keeping them within arm's reach, the four heroes settled around the fire. Cedric took the first watch, methodically pacing the edge of the clearing, shield and sword at the ready, occasionally glancing at the runes on the trees. He could feel the subtle hum of protective magic in the air. He was grateful they'd prepared a layered defense; though intangible, it felt like a bulwark against the forest's intangible menace.

As the hours crept by, one shift gave way to the next. Elara replaced Cedric at some point, offering him a gentle smile before he settled onto his bedroll. Her shield glimmered faintly with celestial light as she knelt in silent prayer. Thalion, half-dozing, occasionally roused himself to inscribe a quick note or formula in his journal by the firelight, spurred on by some half-formed dream of arcane equations. Mira lay sleeping fitfully, fingers unconsciously curled around the staff resting beside her.

Then, just before midnight, something stirred. A rustle came from the underbrush. It was soft, but in the oppressive quiet of the forest, it sounded like a branch snapping underfoot. Elara froze, pressing a hand to her ear, every sense alert. The perimeter wards hummed in her mind, a vague awareness that they had not yet been breached—but the movement was definitely close.

She rose, carefully stepping away from the fire so as not to cast her silhouette in stark relief. Her shield, clasped in her left hand, glowed faintly as she readied her right hand for a quick invocation. "Who goes there?" she called softly.

No answer. Only the faint crackle of leaves. She advanced a few paces, peering between the dense tree trunks. Moonlight penetrated the canopy here and there, illuminating patches of moss and gnarled roots. Nothing seemed obviously amiss. Yet the hair on the back of her neck stood on end.

Suddenly, a shape lunged from the shadows. Elara caught the glint of eyes—feral, blazing with unnatural luminescence. Before she could react, the creature collided with the invisible ward that shimmered along the clearing's edge, hurling it backward. It let out an inhuman screech, part snarl, part hiss.

Instantly, Cedric bolted awake, as did Thalion and Mira. "To arms!" Cedric shouted, scrambling upright, sword in hand. Mira flung out her staff, conjuring a bright orb of light that illuminated the undergrowth beyond the ward's perimeter. What they saw caused their hearts to clench with alarm.

A twisted stag, its antlers warped and dripping with some dark ichor, stood hunched just beyond the ward. Its fur was mottled gray and black, patches missing as though eaten away by rot. Where its eyes should have been, twin pits of glowing crimson light stared at them with ravenous intensity. Even as it clattered to its hooves, dripping jaws snapped at the magical barrier, sending sparks flying.

Elara's shield flared as she channeled her divine power. "By the Goddess of Dawn, step back, foul beast!" Her voice rang out, echoing through the clearing. The creature hissed, baring teeth that looked more like jagged shards of bone than the flat molars a deer should possess.

Cedric sprinted to her side, shield raised, sword glinting with runic power. "Stay behind the ward! Let it come to us if it dares." He glanced over his shoulder at the others. "Thalion, can we—"

But Thalion was already weaving a spell, arcane energy swirling around his hands. "If it's truly corrupted by shadow magic, a proper dispelling might weaken its connection." He intoned a string of ancient words, sending a beam of shimmering violet light across the ward line. The moment it touched the undead stag, the creature let out a blood-curdling scream, part animal terror and part demonic rage. It staggered, black fluid oozing from its eyes and mouth, as though Thalion's magic were dissolving whatever dark force animated it.

Seizing the opportunity, Elara hurled a radiant bolt from her free hand. "By the Light!" she cried, striking the creature squarely in the chest. A flash of brilliance flooded the clearing, forcing the others to shield their eyes. When the glow subsided, the stag had collapsed into a heap, its body smoking. For an instant, it convulsed, then lay still—reduced to a lifeless husk of twisted bones and rotting hide.

Silence descended once more. Mira hurried forward, staff at the ready, her heart thudding in her chest. "Is it... truly dead?"

Elara stepped closer, her shield still aglow. "I sense no residual evil within it. It's at peace now—or as close to peace as such a corrupted creature can ever be."

Cedric scanned the gloom, half expecting more abominations to charge from the woods. Nothing stirred. The wards thrummed quietly, unbroken. Thalion lowered his hands, letting his energies dissipate. A wave of weariness washed over him—this short confrontation had demanded powerful spells. But relief followed: they had prevailed.

"Another grim sign of the nexus's corruption," Thalion murmured, resting a hand on his staff. "This forest is teeming with creatures twisted by that foul energy."

Mira knelt beside the stag's body, though she didn't dare touch it. The stench of decay filled her nostrils. "Poor thing... once, it was just an animal, part of the natural balance. Now it's this... monstrosity. We're truly out of time. Every living creature here is at risk of corruption."

Cedric's expression hardened. "Then we must press on at first light, deeper into these woods. Whatever cursed magic lurks here is strong. We can't waste time. If there are more abominations about, we'll need to be cautious."

Elara lingered for a moment, murmuring a soft prayer over the twisted remains. A faint glow trailed from her fingertips, as if granting the creature a final bit of dignity. Then she rose, turning to the others. "Let's secure our defenses and maintain vigilance through the night. Tomorrow, we search for answers."

They intensified their watch, doubling their ward spells. One by one, they caught what rest they could. The oppressive atmosphere never relented, and every stray sound or creaking branch made them tense, but no further attacks came. The night passed in uneasy stillness, leaving them to wonder what deeper horrors might lurk.

Dawn arrived in a pale imitation of its usual brilliance, filtered through the thick canopy of warped branches overhead. Instead of a golden sunrise, the clearing filled with a sickly gray light. The air felt cold and damp, as though the forest resented the warmth of day. Despite the gloom, Cedric, Elara, Thalion, and Mira rose and readied themselves, hearts set on exploring further.

After a brief meal of travel rations, they dismantled their camp. The wards were allowed to dissipate, though Thalion pocketed leftover chalk and silver powder, and Elara retrieved the symbols she had placed—small runed stones, each etched with sacred scripts. Mira scanned the remains of the twisted stag. During the night, it had further decomposed into black sludge, sending an acrid smell into the air. She grimaced but forced herself to approach, staff in hand. A quick detection spell confirmed there was no lingering magic. The creature was truly gone.

They pressed on, guiding their horses deeper into the forest. The path quickly narrowed until it was little more than a winding game trail, choked by gnarled roots and creeping vines. Cedric dismounted to lead his stallion on foot, worried the steep terrain and dense undergrowth might harm the animal's legs. The others followed suit, proceeding in a slow, single file.

The further they ventured, the more signs of corruption they found. Here, a cluster of mushrooms oozing black sap. There, a stream whose water ran an unnatural shade of purple. A few times they passed the skeletal remains of forest creatures, sometimes bearing strange runic carvings. Each discovery heightened their sense of urgency.

After an hour or more of tense progress, the path opened into a low, misty hollow. At its center stood a stone monument covered in moss, partially collapsed. Cracked steps led to a rectangular platform, weathered by centuries of exposure. The mist clung to the monument's base, swirling in sluggish patterns.

"I've never heard of any ruin in these parts," Cedric remarked, carefully tying his horse's reins to a nearby branch. The others followed suit, keen to investigate on foot.

Thalion's eyes widened with scholarly interest. "An ancient shrine, perhaps. Or something older. The architecture suggests a pre-Stonehavenn civilization— notice the runic style on those cracked pillars?"

Mira stepped closer, staff raised to illuminate the worn symbols carved along the stone. "These runes are... they resemble a dialect I've seen in the Grand Archives' section on lost tribes. Give me a moment to decipher."

Elara fanned out, shield at the ready, scanning the tree line. "I'll keep watch. Something about this place feels off."

As Mira knelt to examine the inscriptions, Thalion joined her, running his hands over the stone to sense residual magic. The runes spiraled inward toward a central depression in the platform, forming what might have once been a ritual circle. Faint lines of blackish residue traced their path, as if someone recently used the circle for a dark ceremony.

"I can't make out every word," Mira murmured, trailing her fingertips over the runes. "But phrases like 'Gateway' and 'Beyond the Veil' recur. There's also a reference to something called 'Umbra... Ubrum...' Hard to read."

Thalion pressed his palm to the central depression. "There's definitely an echo of magic here—strong, but old. Could be an anchor to that negative plane we suspect."

Cedric hovered nearby, uneasy. "If a ritual took place, maybe that's how the local wildlife is being corrupted. Some vile sorcerer or cult might be funneling the nexus's power here."

Elara, still keeping watch, spoke without turning. "We should destroy this altar, cleanse it if we can. We can't risk leaving such a conduit intact."

Thalion nodded thoughtfully. "Agreed. But let's first gather whatever knowledge we can. A site like this might hold clues. Perhaps a clue to the path we must follow or a protective measure we can replicate."

Carefully, Mira and Thalion took notes. Mira sketched the runes onto a spare parchment, while Thalion recited incantations to glean the altar's original purpose. Meanwhile, Elara and Cedric moved around the perimeter, searching for tracks or signs of recent visitors. It was Cedric who made a grim discovery: a small clearing near the back of the monument, where a circle of charred earth and the remains of black candles suggested a nefarious ritual had been performed not long ago.

"Over here," he called quietly. Elara joined him, her expression darkening as she surveyed the charred remains. In the center lay a cluster of bones—small, likely an animal's—arranged in a star-like pattern. Remnants of dried blood spattered the ground, forming cryptic sigils.

Elara closed her eyes, whispering a prayer. "This is evil. Sacrificial magic, almost certainly. They might have been testing ways to harness or amplify the nexus's power."

Cedric exhaled slowly. "Then we have to assume there are practitioners within these woods—a cult, warlocks, or something akin. We can't let them continue."

The pair returned to Mira and Thalion with the news. Mira shuddered at the mention of ritual sacrifice. "That confirms it—someone is actively using this place. We can't leave it intact."

Thalion finished his arcane analysis, shaking his head. "This site's energies are deeply woven into the forest. Destroying the altar physically might only be a partial solution. A thorough cleansing ritual is needed."

"I can lead a consecration prayer," Elara suggested. "But to be fully effective, we need holy water and a strong protective circle."

Cedric's brow furrowed. "We have some holy water in our supplies, though not a large quantity. Would it be enough?"

Elara nodded. "I believe so, if Thalion and Mira aid me with arcane wards. Together, we can disrupt the corruption saturating this place."

The plan formed swiftly. They would enact a cleansing rite, combining Elara's divine power, Thalion's knowledge of ritual magic, and Mira's raw arcane force. Cedric would stand guard, ensuring no hidden cultists or twisted beasts ambushed them mid-rite.

Elara retrieved a small vial of holy water from her belt pouch. She walked the perimeter of the platform, sprinkling droplets and murmuring prayers. Each bead of water hissed against the stone, releasing faint wisps of black smoke. Thalion stood at the center, staff planted firmly on the ancient carvings, chanting a litany of dispelling words. Meanwhile, Mira circled in the opposite direction from Elara, tracing glowing runes in midair with her staff, which she occasionally flicked to send pulses of energy through the space.

Cedric watched from the edge, scanning the trees. At first, all seemed quiet. But as the cleansing progressed, the air grew dense, charged with tension. The swirling mist around the altar shifted to a murky black color. An unnatural wind whipped through the clearing, carrying a distant wail that set Cedric's nerves on edge.

"Elara! Thalion! Mira!" he shouted above the gust. "Be prepared—the forest doesn't like what you're doing."

Elara poured the last of the holy water in the center depression. She held her shield high, exuding golden radiance that clashed with the swirling darkness. Thalion's voice soared in pitch, culminating in a resonant phrase that shimmered with arcane potency. Mira's staff glowed brighter, arcs of violet lightning crackling from its tip.

With a collective surge of power, the trio unleashed their energies. Elara's divine light flared, channeling through the holy water. Thalion's staff flamed with purple runes that spiraled into the stone. Mira's lightning crashed down, focusing on the central depression. The altar quaked with a deep rumble as the combined forces of holy, arcane, and elemental energies assailed the corruption.

A shriek reverberated through the clearing—whether from the nexus itself or some lurking entity was unclear. The black mist convulsed, recoiling from the center of the platform as though in agony. For a heartbeat, a swirl of ephemeral figures appeared—ghostly shapes of what might have been the region's former wildlife or the spirits of sacrificed victims, freed from the clutches of vile sorcery. Then, in a final, echoing wail, the darkness imploded, leaving behind only a slight swirl of pale smoke that dissipated into the air.

Silence fell, broken only by the ragged breathing of Elara, Thalion, and Mira, each drained from the effort. The atmosphere in the clearing felt notably lighter, as if a foul stench had finally lifted. The stone platform, once stained with black residue, now looked inert—still ancient and worn, but free of the malignant presence.

Cedric exhaled in relief. "Well done. That was... intense."

Elara leaned on her shield, sweat beading her brow. "The site is cleansed, at least for now. If the cult returns, they won't find easy footing here."

Thalion nodded, though he looked pale. "Let's hope it stays that way. We can't be certain how deeply the corruption runs, but this will disrupt any immediate attempts at channeling the nexus's power."

Mira gazed around the clearing. "That scream... it might have alerted other dark forces that we're here, actively challenging them. We should remain on guard."

Cedric agreed, helping Elara back to her feet. "We'll rest a moment, then move on. The deeper we go, the closer we come to the heart of this darkness. We can't turn back now."

Thus, in the pale morning light, they stood at the cleansed altar, hearts pounding from their first direct encounter with the nexus's hold on the forest. A modest victory, but a significant one. They had proven they could resist the darkness, even strike back. Yet each hero sensed the battles ahead would only grow more dangerous.

They left the ancient monument behind, a silent testament to the unholy rituals once performed there. Despite their fatigue, a new resolve coursed through them. If they could purge one site of corruption, they could do it again—and perhaps, eventually, purge Stonehaven of the nexus entirely. But first, they had to uncover more secrets, follow every lead deeper into the woods, and test the limits of their courage.

As they remounted and continued their journey, the forest seemed to watch them with awakened sentience. Twisted vines uncoiled from branches as they passed, dripping with rotted leaves. Dark hollows in tree trunks appeared as gaping mouths. The hush that fell over the Gravenshade Woods was no longer just eerie—it was vigilant, as though the entire land now recognized the four heroes as intruders bent on unraveling the Shadow Nexus. Indeed, if the nexus and its minions took heed of their presence, the road ahead would be fraught with ambushes and dread.

Yet there was another side to the coin: Freed spirits—those glimpsed in fleeting shapes of silvery light—might aid them, guiding them along hidden paths or revealing crucial clues. The heroes clung to that possibility, forging on beneath the dense canopy where day felt like dusk, buoyed by the knowledge that they had already made a difference.

Soon, the faint sound of a distant waterfall reached their ears, and the trail curved sharply around a mossy knoll. The party exchanged looks. That might be their next destination, or the next place where corruption had taken root. Through adversity, they had grown more confident in each other's abilities. Sir Cedric trusted Thalion's measured counsel; Lady Elara's faith bolstered Mira's spells; and Mira's raw power complemented Cedric's martial prowess. In synergy, they moved as one.

Ahead lay a hundred unknown perils, from grotesque monsters warped by the nexus to the cunning mages responsible for the vile rituals. But for the first time since leaving the Royal Citadel, a spark of optimism flickered among them. They could fight back. They could reclaim the land from darkness. They had answered the call to adventure—now they would see that promise through.

Thus ended the first true day of their mission, forging deeper into the Gravenshade Woods on a path that no map fully charted. With each step, the haunting shadows whispered stories of what was lost, and what might yet be saved. With hearts alight and resolve unbroken, the heroes advanced, determined to ensure that Stonehaven's story would not end in darkness, but in the enduring flame of hope.

3

GRAVENSHADE WOODS

A hush settled over the Gravenshade Woods as the four heroes pressed deeper into its domain. Overhead, a seemingly endless canopy wove thick branches together, filtering sunlight into faint greenish beams. The ground beneath their boots felt spongy, thick with rotting leaves and moss, while the wind carried an unsettling sound—like hushed, distant voices that rose and fell with the sway of the ancient trees. It was no wonder this forest was called the Gravenshade Woods; the very air seemed alive with secret murmurings, as though centuries of unspoken tales clung to every gnarled trunk and tangled root.

Sir Cedric led the party on foot, guiding his gray stallion by the reins. He moved with care, wary of hidden pitfalls and snaking vines. Occasionally, he paused to check for tracks in the damp soil—any sign that travelers or monstrous beasts had passed recently. At his side, Lady Elara kept her shield strapped across her back, a comforting weight that gleamed faintly despite the gloom. Meanwhile, Thalion and Mira followed closely, each scanning the dark corners of the trail for magical anomalies. Though they had braved Oakenshade's haunting shadows and cleansed a corrupted altar on their way here, the heart of the forest promised far greater challenges.

Their progress was slow. The Gravenshade Woods had no well-traveled roads—only meandering trails that faded into clusters of foliage, or wound around towering trees with trunks thick as fortress walls. In the distance, crows croaked, and once in a while, something skittered just out of sight. The group's breath plumed in the chill air, though whether the forest was truly cold or simply leeched warmth away with its eerie presence was hard to say.

"We should rest a moment," Cedric suggested, pausing when the path curved around an ancient oak. Its trunk was riddled with knotholes like hollow, unblinking eyes. He patted his stallion's neck. "The horses need a breather."

Elara nodded. "And so do we." While her divine powers could sustain her stamina in battle, she felt the forest's oppressive aura weighing on her spirit. Pulling a small canteen from her hip, she sipped water and offered it around. "Anyone else thirsty?"

"I'll take some," Mira said softly, stepping closer. Her dark hair was pulled back into a braided coil, though a few tendrils had escaped, plastered to her forehead by sweat. She had been on edge for hours, her posture rigid, as though anticipating an ambush at any moment.

Thalion cleared his throat. "I'm fine for now, Lady Elara. But I suggest we keep our rests short. The longer we linger, the more likely something unsavory comes looking for us." The elderly mage spoke with a calm authority, yet he, too, wore signs of fatigue—shadows under his eyes, a subtle tremor in his hands.

Cedric gave a curt nod of agreement. "We won't tarry. Once the horses have had enough of a break, we continue."

As they huddled near the oak's broad trunk, a gentle rustling drew their attention upward. A tangle of vines draped over a thick branch, and from behind the leaves came the sudden flutter of wings. A startled pigeon—pale, with a patch of missing feathers on its breast—burst out and flew into the deeper woods. The abrupt motion set the entire party on edge. Mira clutched her staff more tightly, and Cedric reflexively stepped in front of Elara, scanning for danger. But nothing else emerged from the vines.

"I hate this place," Mira muttered under her breath. "Feels like the forest itself is watching us."

Elara placed a reassuring hand on the young wizard's shoulder. "Stay strong. We've faced evil before, and we will do so again."

They resumed their journey, forging deeper into the labyrinth of towering trunks and twisting roots. Gloom thickened with each passing hour. The sunlight, already meager beneath the canopy, waned until it was difficult to tell how close they were to dusk. Shadows coiled at the corners of their vision, and the ever-present whispers in the boughs above seemed to intensify. At times, the hushed voices almost sounded like a lament, a sorrowful choir echoing from a time long past.

Eventually, the path opened into a small clearing ringed by ancient trees whose bare, contorted branches reached inward, forming a kind of living enclosure overhead. Thick moss covered every rock and root, so soft underfoot that it felt like stepping on damp cushions. At the far side of the clearing lay a tumble of old stone blocks, half-buried in the earth. Vines had overtaken them, but faint glyphs carved

silent cry. Others reached out with claw-like hands that trailed vapors of cold energy. As the specters drew closer, the forest's temperature seemed to plummet. Cedric could see his own breath turning to white mist before his face.

"Everyone, form up!" Cedric ordered, stepping protectively in front of Thalion and Mira. "Elara, are these the spirits of the dead, or illusions?"

Elara gripped her shield, heart pounding with adrenaline. "They're real enough. Restless souls, bound here by dark magic. I can feel their hunger... they want life force."

Before anyone could respond, the ghostly figures surged forward with eerie speed, arms outstretched to latch onto the living. The clearing erupted in chaos. A flurry of spectral shapes swooped in from all sides, reaching for the warmth and vitality of the heroes.

Cedric swung his runic longsword in a wide arc. The blade flared with a blue-white glow, and where it connected, ghosts reeled back, shrieking voicelessly. Yet even a direct hit didn't banish them entirely; they dissipated momentarily, only to rematerialize a few paces away. Nearby, Elara held her shield aloft, channeling a burst of divine light that pushed several spirits back with a flash of golden radiance.

Thalion planted his staff on the ground, chanting in a deep, rhythmic tone. Wisps of violet light spun around his wrists, coalescing into a sphere that he propelled outward. The orb expanded into a shimmering barrier, buying them a brief respite from the throng of ghosts. Those on the outside clawed at the barrier, their pale hands sliding over the surface as if trying to find a weak point.

"That won't hold them for long," Thalion hissed, sweat beading his temple. "We need a plan."

Mira, staff in hand, surveyed the swirling mass of ghosts. "We might be able to exorcise them if we combine Elara's divine magic with a powerful banishment spell. But we'll have to hold them back long enough to cast it."

Elara nodded. "I can invoke a holy circle. It'll weaken their hold on our realm, at least temporarily. Mira, can you craft a banishment incantation to target multiple entities at once?"

Mira's eyes flashed. "I'll try. But I'll need time to shape it—maybe a minute or two."

Cedric grimaced, glancing at the shimmering barrier. Tiny cracks of glowing cracks were already forming where the ghosts had begun to break through. "You'll have your time. Thalion and I will distract them. Elara, you focus on that holy circle."

Elara closed her eyes, pressing a hand to her amulet. She murmured a prayer to the Goddess of Dawn, voice trembling with urgency. As she prayed, her shield radiated ever-brighter, and motes of golden light drifted around her, forming the outline of a circle on the ground. It slowly expanded, each glowing line inscribed with runes signifying purity and protection.

Meanwhile, Mira knelt, staff across her lap, focusing intently. She traced intricate runic patterns in the air— spirals, lines, and symbols that shimmered with arcane promise. "I'll gather the energy I need. Keep them off me," she muttered.

The barrier faltered. With an otherworldly shriek, the ghosts found the cracks and flooded through. Thalion gritted his teeth, staff blazing with purple arcs. "Cedric, now!"

Cedric charged into the fray, sword shining like a beacon in the gloom. He swung at the first wraithlike figure, slicing it across the torso. The ghost shuddered, momentarily flickering out of existence, only to reappear an instant later at his flank. Another one rushed him from behind, spectral arms outstretched. Cedric managed to raise his shield in time, but a jolt of icy dread coursed through his arm, as if the spirit had siphoned a fraction of his warmth.

"Stay together!" Elara commanded over the din. She strode forward, shield leading. Another group of ghosts soared straight at her, arms swiping with intangible claws. But her shield flared with holy power, blasting them back. Each time they recoiled, fragments of shimmering ectoplasm sizzled in the air. Yet they kept coming, relentless, driven by an insatiable hunger for life energy.

Thalion, his barrier now collapsed, switched tactics. Calling upon the elemental forces he had studied for decades, he slammed his staff into the ground. A web of crackling lightning erupted outward, electrifying the soil. Though the ghosts weren't fully corporeal, the surge of magical electricity disrupted their forms, making them flicker in place. Some drifted upward, keen to escape the sizzling arcs.

But the ghosts were numerous. Even as Cedric, Elara, and Thalion strove to keep them at bay, more emerged from the swirling fog. They ranged widely in form—some with sorrowful expressions, others twisted by rage or despair. One particularly large spirit loomed a head taller than Cedric, brandishing what looked like the phantom shape of a rusted halberd. It swung at Cedric with a soundless snarl. He parried, but the impact still sent a chill racing through his body, as though the halberd existed in both worlds at once.

"Goddess, give me strength," Elara murmured, voice tight with concentration. She poured more power into the circle beneath her feet. Inch by inch, golden runes etched themselves into the moss. The circle's circumference glowed, releasing waves of warmth that pushed back the cold. Ghosts that ventured too close to Elara's position recoiled, hissing in silent agony.

While the paladin stabilized the circle, Mira's staff glowed with intensifying brightness. Her lips moved in silent incantation, weaving a complex tapestry of arcane forces. Sparks of white and silver crackled around her, forming a swirling vortex at the staff's tip. She could feel the presence of the ghosts straining at the edges of her awareness, their despair and anger almost overwhelming. Holding her focus demanded every ounce of willpower.

Suddenly, a particularly swift ghost darted around Cedric's guard and lunged at Thalion. The elder mage only partially evaded. Ethereal fingers grazed his shoulder, draining a sliver of his life force. Thalion gasped, stumbling as weakness coursed through him. His vision blurred for an instant, and a cold sweat broke out on his brow.

Cedric dispatched another nearby ghost with a powerful slash, then pivoted to interpose himself between Thalion and the attacking spirit. "Are you all right?" Cedric asked, breath ragged.

Thalion nodded weakly, regaining some composure. "Yes, but I'll need a moment." He lifted his staff again, forcing himself to focus. "They can drain our energy. Everyone, be mindful—prolonged contact could be fatal."

Elara caught fragments of Thalion's warning. Grim resolve set in her expression. "I'm nearly done," she called to Mira, who knelt within the luminous lines. "Once the circle is complete, its aura will weaken them significantly. Hurry, Mira!"

Mira, eyes closed in fierce concentration, clasped the staff between her hands. The swirling vortex at the tip crackled with arcs of luminous energy. She could sense the ghosts all around—frigid presences pressing in from every side. She reached deeper into her reserves of magic, drawing upon the bracer Malachai had given her, focusing her mind on a singular purpose: *Banishment.*

With a final surge, Elara pressed her gauntleted hand to the ground, completing the last symbol of her holy circle. Rays of golden light spiraled outward, bathing the clearing in radiant brilliance. The chill in the air momentarily receded, and the ghosts twitched, as though pinned down by a sudden force. Some tried to flee but found themselves partially anchored by the circle's glow, their ephemeral forms shimmering with conflict.

"Now!" Elara shouted, meeting Mira's gaze.

Mira stood, staff raised high. The vortex of magic at its tip had grown into a swirling orb the size of a melon, pulsing with a mesmerizing interplay of silver and white. "All of you, back away!" she called to her companions.

Thalion and Cedric heeded her command, scrambling to the relative safety of Elara's circle. Cedric pressed close to Elara, shield locked with hers, while Thalion mustered what strength he had left to erect a smaller ward around them.

The ghosts, though battered by divine light, circled restlessly, as if preparing another wave of assault.

Mira's voice rose in a chant that echoed across the clearing. It was a primordial incantation, older than modern Stonehavenn tongue, each syllable tinged with arcane potency. The swirling orb of banishment magic expanded to a blazing sphere, and Mira thrust her staff forward, releasing a torrent of power.

Silver-white light lashed across the clearing, striking ghost after ghost. A cacophony of unearthly shrieks rent the air—though the sound was more felt than heard, reverberating in the mind like a chorus of anguished voices. Ghosts were hurled backward, evaporating into wisps of pale mist where the banishment magic touched them. Some dissolved instantly, while others resisted for a second or two before disintegrating with echoes of sorrowful cries.

In mere heartbeats, the swirling phantoms were gone, their once-overpowering presence fading like a bad dream chased off by dawn. Silence descended. The clearing felt abruptly warmer, the color returning to a world previously ensnared by ghostly gloom. A few motes of spectral energy lingered in the air, drifting upward like lost fireflies until they, too, vanished.

A stunned hush fell over the group. Their breathing was ragged, each grappling with the adrenaline crash. Cedric lowered his sword, scanning for any sign of residual threats. Finding none, he cautiously stepped out of Elara's circle. "It's over... for now," he said, voice laced with lingering tension.

Elara rose to her feet, letting her shield rest at her side. The divine lines she had etched in the ground were already fading. She murmured a soft prayer of thanks, relief evident in her posture. "Well fought, everyone. Those souls... they were truly lost."

Thalion wiped sweat from his brow, leaning on his staff for support. He felt drained, as though he'd aged another decade in those few minutes of combat. "If we encountered that many restless spirits in one location, it suggests a deep wound in the spiritual fabric of these woods—likely connected to the Shadow Nexus."

Mira nodded, though her eyes seemed distant. She could still feel the echo of the ghosts' despair reverberating in her thoughts. "They... they were so full of sorrow. It was like they had no choice but to lash out, hunting for life they no longer possessed."

Cedric rested a hand on her shoulder, offering a comforting squeeze. "We did what we had to. Think of it as setting them free from torment."

"Yes," Thalion agreed gently. "Their souls can hopefully find rest now, instead of being bound here by corruption."

They took a few moments to tend to each other. Thalion checked everyone for signs of life-force drain. Elara, channeling soft healing energies, restored minor vitality to the group, helping them recover from the ghosts' chilling touches. Though the party was still fatigued, they felt physically sound enough to continue.

Yet the fight had not been without gain. As the clearing returned to relative calm, Cedric walked among the mossy stones, noticing that in the wake of the ghosts' banishment, some of the ancient carvings had become clearer. A faint shimmer lingered across certain glyphs, as if the confrontation had peeled back a layer of obscurity.

"Thalion," he called, kneeling by a newly revealed symbol. "Look here."

The mage approached, eyes narrowing. The glyph resembled a spiral swirling inward, surrounded by stylized shapes reminiscent of doorways or portals. Thin lines branched outward from the spiral's edges, each ending in a small rune. "Fascinating," Thalion murmured. "This might be a depiction of a boundary between realms."

Elara joined them, scanning the glyph. "Could it relate to the nexus as a bridge to some dark plane?"

Mira, curiosity piqued despite her fatigue, knelt as well. She traced a cautious finger near the spiral. "I see something else. This smaller inscription—these characters look like references to cardinal directions or... vantage points?"

Thalion nodded slowly. "If I interpret this correctly, it might be a stylized map. One that points to a place where the boundary between our world and a darker realm is thinnest. Possibly an entry to the Shadow Nexus itself—or a route leading closer to it."

Cedric exchanged looks with the others. "That sounds like a lead we can't ignore."

Elara exhaled. "Agreed. We came here looking for clues, and now we have them. But deciphering an ancient map inscribed on half-buried stones is no easy feat."

Still, the four set about carefully copying the newly revealed glyphs. Mira used a piece of charcoal and paper, sketching every line and symbol in painstaking detail. Thalion scribbled notes regarding potential translations, cross-referencing them with bits of knowledge gleaned from the cleansing site they had visited earlier. Elara and

Cedric stood watch, though the forest seemed calmer after the ghosts' defeat—at least in this clearing.

Once they finished, Thalion tapped the final lines of his notes. "We'll need more context to fully understand this. Possibly comparing it with the transcripts King Alaric's scribes gave me. But we do know one thing: the glyphs confirm the presence of potent rifts in these woods."

Mira rolled up the charcoal sketch. "Let's keep moving. If the ghosts have found no rest until now, it's because something keeps them chained. That something must be undone."

Leaving the clearing behind, they pressed deeper. The forest's gloom felt fractionally less oppressive, though it was impossible to say if that was due to the banishment of the ghosts or simply a shift in atmosphere. Birds remained scarce, but the party heard the occasional rustle of small woodland creatures—perhaps the local fauna sensed that the immediate threat had lessened.

Nevertheless, the party proceeded with caution. Each step was deliberate, every sense on high alert. The hours slipped by without further incident. The faint sound of running water guided them to a narrow stream, which glinted silver under the feeble sunbeams piercing the canopy. The water here seemed cleaner than the earlier streams they'd encountered—no trace of the purple tint or foul odor associated with corruption.

"Finally, something that isn't threatening," Mira said, a note of relief in her voice. She bent to fill a canteen, tasting the water first. "Seems safe enough."

Elara joined her, filling her own container. "We should probably rest here for a short while. Our magic reserves aren't infinite. The fight with the ghosts took a toll on each of us."

Cedric agreed but insisted on setting a watch perimeter. "We can't assume peace just because the stream runs clear," he warned, scanning the thick undergrowth.

"Agreed," Thalion said, gingerly settling onto a fallen log. He unrolled one of the scrolls from King Alaric's court, carefully comparing its archaic symbols with the notes they'd just made. "I'll take this chance to see if we can glean anything more about that spiral map."

They spent the next hour in quiet activity. Mira and Elara took the horses a short distance upstream, letting them drink and graze. Cedric circled the perimeter, sword at his hip, alert for trouble. Thalion immersed himself in cross-referencing runes. Only the gentle burble of the stream and the whisper of the canopy accompanied them. For a moment, it was almost tranquil—an interlude in a land that seemed otherwise dominated by dread.

As the party regrouped, Thalion's brow furrowed in sudden focus. He traced a finger along a line of runes on the parchment. "Strange," he murmured.

"What is it?" Cedric asked, stepping closer.

"These transcripts from the royal library—here, they mention an entity called 'The Keeper of Keys,' said to guard thresholds between realms. And our stone glyph references a gate of some sort. It can't be coincidence."

Elara lowered her canteen, her expression turning serious. "So we might be dealing with an actual guardian? Is it friend or foe?"

Thalion shook his head. "Unknown. The texts are fragmentary. 'The Keeper of Keys' might be a literal gatekeeper—someone or something entrusted with sealing or opening passages to the Shadow Nexus."

Mira approached, still drying her hands after leading the horses back. "If we can find this Keeper, maybe they'll know how to seal the nexus completely."

"Or they might be guarding it on behalf of darker forces," Cedric countered. "We can't be sure."

Elara adjusted her shield strap, taking in the forest around them. "Regardless, it's the best lead we have. Where do we go from here?"

Thalion tapped the spiral design. "The geometry suggests an inward route, likely further west if I interpret these partial directions correctly. That lines up with older legends claiming the Shadow Nexus lay in the west, beyond the great mountains. If we continue in that direction, we may find more runic markers guiding us."

Cedric took a deep breath. "Then we do it. We press on westward, cautious but determined."

Despite the seriousness of the discussion, a sense of purpose rallied them. Their brush with the ghosts had been terrifying, but it had also hardened their resolve. They had survived—and even liberated some restless spirits—proving that the darkness, while potent, was not invincible.

Eventually, day slid into dusk, though in the Gravenshade Woods the difference was nearly imperceptible. The forest ceiling darkened, and the temperature dropped further. Keen to avoid another night battle like they'd faced in Oakenshade, they decided to find a defensible place to camp.

They stumbled upon a large boulder ringed by stunted, twisted trees whose trunks formed a natural barrier on three sides. Setting their tents against the rock, they left only one angle of approach, which they could guard easily with wards and a watch rotation. Cedric and Elara collected what sparse firewood they could scrounge from fallen branches, while Mira and Thalion set alarm spells around the perimeter. The gloom thickened fast, but they managed to start a small fire—its crackling flames a fragile sphere of light in a realm of encroaching shadows.

Dinner was a modest affair: travel rations of salted meats, dried fruit, and hard bread softened by a bit of water or warmed by the fire. The flicker of the flames cast dancing silhouettes on the boulder behind them, turning each hero's face into a shifting mask of light and darkness.

Elara led a quiet prayer before they ate, thanking her goddess for their survival and asking for continued guidance. Cedric, not usually a man of devout faith, nevertheless lowered his head respectfully, sensing the comfort the brief prayer brought to his companions. Thalion simply closed his eyes, perhaps lost in contemplation of arcane secrets. Mira stared into the flames, mind flickering between images of the ghosts they had faced and the uncharted path ahead.

After the meal, Thalion produced the transcripts again, reading them by the light of the fire. Elara checked over her gear, ensuring no dents or cracks compromised her shield or armor. Mira scribbled thoughts in a small notebook, planning potential incantations for future dangers. Cedric sharpened his sword, methodically dragging a whetstone along the runic blade. The cyclical *shhkk, shhkk* of steel on stone was oddly soothing amid the quiet forest.

Conversation was sparse, each weighed down by the day's events and the threat of tomorrow's unknowns. Yet a subtle camaraderie had taken hold. The four had battled together, relied on one another in mortal peril, and come out stronger. That bond—tempered by shared fears and hard-won victories—offered a bulwark against the forest's oppressive aura.

As night deepened, they established their rotation. Elara took first watch while the others tried to rest. She stood at the edge of the firelight, shield resting against the trunk of a dead tree, its emblem faintly glowing in the dim. The moaning breezes of the Gravenshade Woods caressed her hair, carrying those ever-present murmurs. She tried to ignore them, focusing on the steady breathing of her sleeping companions and the soft crackle of the flames.

An hour passed with no incident. Then two. At length, she gently woke Cedric to take over. The knight rose, shrugging off his bedroll. The two exchanged a few whispered words:

"Nothing stirred," Elara reported quietly. "Even the whispers seemed calmer than usual."

Cedric nodded, eyes still adjusting. "Get some rest. You've earned it."

Elara smiled, exhaustion evident in the slump of her shoulders. She unbuckled her gauntlets and curled up near the fire, trusting Cedric to keep them safe. The knight moved to the perimeter, boots crunching lightly on dead leaves. He let his gaze roam the darkness, keenly aware that malevolent eyes could be peering back from behind every trunk and vine.

The hours crawled by. The fire dulled to embers, but Cedric fed it enough kindling to maintain a soft glow. Occasionally, the whistle of wind through branches mimicked faint cries, making him tighten his grip on his sword. But no threat emerged.

He roused Mira for the third watch. The wizard, though young, had proven her steel in the ghostly battle. She yawned, rubbing her eyes, and Cedric returned to his bedroll. Mira paced near the fire, staff in hand, scanning the twisted silhouettes of the forest. She imagined she could still see ghostly faces in the gloom, but each time she stepped closer, it was just a trick of the light against the bark.

At last, the final shift fell to Thalion, who relieved Mira so she could catch a brief rest before dawn. The elder mage set his staff upright in the earth, leaning on it while he watched the horizon lighten by barely perceptible increments. A swirl of arcane runes occasionally flickered around his fingers, perhaps a subtle warding or a comforting habit. Long years of study had taught him patience—patience to wait, observe, and glean knowledge even in the stillness of night.

True dawn never came in brilliant hues here in the Gravenshade Woods, but eventually, the canopy took on a softer gray tint. The forest stirred with whatever life it still possessed. Thalion gently woke the others.

They broke camp quickly, quelling their small fire with dirt and making sure no trace was left. Their horses, spooked but unharmed, were bridled and calmed. Soon, they resumed their westward journey. Fog clung to the undergrowth like a ghostly shroud, swirling around their ankles.

Mira took the lead this time, guided by the partial translations of the spiral map. She claimed she sensed a pull of arcane energy that grew stronger in a specific direction. As they walked, Thalion occasionally paused to test the air with small detection spells, verifying that they were indeed following a faint thread of magical resonance.

Elara and Cedric talked in low voices, strategizing about how to handle future encounters. If the forest was teeming with ghosts and other horrors, they couldn't rely on the same banishment ritual every time. Overuse would drain Mira's reserves. Elara considered ways to intensify her protective auras, while Cedric brainstormed tactics to keep potential foes at bay. They agreed that Thalion's mastery of elemental spells and illusions might offer new angles—perhaps illusions to misdirect or trap spectral foes before they closed in.

Though the morning was still, a sense of anticipation crackled in the air. If they were heading toward a hidden rift or gate, what would they find guarding it? More restless spirits? Twisted beasts? Or possibly, living cultists who sought to harness the nexus's power?

A rhythmic sound soon emerged from deeper in the forest—*drip, drip, drip*—like water trickling from a rocky outcrop. The party followed it, cresting a small ridge over which the fog thinned. On the other side, they found a shallow ravine cut into the forest floor. At the ravine's heart, water seeped from the rocks, forming a pool whose surface reflected the dim canopy like a mirror. The clearing around the pool was circled by standing stones, each carved with runes reminiscent of the ones they had seen at the ghost-haunted clearing.

Mira's eyes widened. "This must be a confluence—a place where magical ley lines meet. I can feel the energy swirling."

Thalion closed his eyes, inhaling deeply. "Indeed. It's potent, like stepping onto a crossroads of arcane currents. But it's... tainted. There's a resonance of darkness here as well."

Elara peered at the standing stones. Some were partially toppled, others laced with thick vines. "This looks similar to the altar we cleansed, but more expansive. Could it be an older site, or a direct node feeding the nexus?"

Cedric dismounted, leading his stallion toward the ravine's edge. The ground was soft, muddy in places. "We should be careful. The illusions or guardians here might be stronger than anything we've faced yet."

The party approached the pool. A sense of hush enveloped the area, as if the forest were holding its breath. Sunlight, diffused through the canopy, lit the water's surface with a pale glow. Closer inspection revealed faint patterns swirling just beneath the water—tendrils of shimmering black, reminiscent of ink dissolving in water.

Mira took out a small glass vial. She crouched at the bank, carefully filling it with the tainted water for later study. "Look at it up close," she said, holding it up. Dark wisps danced within the clear liquid as though alive. "Corruption from the nexus, no doubt."

Elara moved to examine one of the standing stones, running her hand over the chipped runes. Unlike the earlier ruins, these carvings were far more elaborate—spirals intersecting with jagged lines, small symbols that looked vaguely like eyes or gates. "Could be a ritual site for crossing realms," she speculated. "Perhaps the cult that performed sacrifices at the altar also used this place."

Thalion kept his staff at the ready. "I sense residual energies that might attract or spawn lesser spirits. This place is essentially a magnet for arcane phenomena."

Cedric was about to suggest a plan for investigating each stone when a sudden disturbance shattered the stillness. The water in the pool rippled violently, as though struck by a heavy force. Dark plumes erupted, swirling upward in a pillar of inky mist. The ground trembled, knocking Mira off balance. A low moaning echoed throughout the ravine.

"Not more ghosts," Cedric growled, gripping his sword.

From the swirling mist, vague shapes manifested, each trailing streams of black vapor. They looked like wraiths akin to the ghosts they had banished, but these forms were darker, more concentrated. Their eyes glowed with a violet radiance that burned with malevolent intent. Unlike the previous ghosts, whose forms wavered in pity and torment, these exuded a malevolent purpose.

Elara gasped. "They're not just restless souls. They're... siphons of darkness. I can feel them tugging at my aura."

Indeed, the entire party felt a pull, as though invisible threads tried to yank at their spirits. Thalion recognized this phenomenon from old texts describing "Void Wraiths"— amalgamations of negative energy, rumored to drain not just life force, but hope and sanity as well.

The largest wraith, nearly twice the size of a man, rushed Mira first—perhaps sensing her potent magical energy. She barely raised a ward in time, the ephemeral creature smashing against her barrier with a soundless impact. The shockwave jarred her arms, sending sparks of magic scattering. Another wraith zoomed toward Elara, purple eyes boring into her. The paladin planted her shield, meeting it head-on. Where her holy emblem clashed with the wraith's misty substance, a swirl of gold and black hissed like acid meeting a base.

Cedric and Thalion sprang into action. The knight tried a forward slash at one of the smaller wraiths, but it darted aside with impossible agility, passing near enough to brush him. A jolt of cold anguish stabbed Cedric's heart, causing him to stumble. Memories of past failures and regrets flared unbidden, as though the wraith had tapped into his psyche.

"Cedric!" Elara shouted, noticing his distress. She slammed her shield into the wraith attacking her, then pivoted to throw a burst of radiant light at the wraith harassing Cedric. The golden flare scorched across the wraith's side, eliciting a seething hiss. The creature recoiled, releasing Cedric's mind from its influence.

Meanwhile, Thalion channeled a chain-lightning spell. Purple forks of electricity arced from his staff, striking first one wraith, then leaping to the next with crackling vigor. Though the wraiths convulsed under the assault, the effect wasn't as decisive as hoped; their forms disintegrated partially, but they re-coalesced moments later. "They're resilient!" Thalion warned.

Mira recovered her footing. Her eyes narrowed with determination. "Then we hit them with everything we have. Elara, I need your divine synergy again!"

Elara nodded, too occupied to respond verbally. She thrust her shield at the nearest wraith, unleashing a pulse of radiance. The entity screeched, swirling in agitation. With the wraith momentarily disoriented, Cedric dashed in, landing a punishing slash that cut straight through its center. The creature exploded in a shower of black vapor, flickering out of existence. A hint of relief flashed in Cedric's eyes—one down, at least.

Thalion and Mira moved in tandem next. Thalion conjured a vortex of wind that corralled two wraiths together. Their smoky bodies thrashed against the gale, but it kept them from scattering. Mira then channeled a raw bolt of arcane energy straight into the swirling mass, the staff's bracer glowing bright. The resulting impact unleashed a shockwave that tore both wraiths apart, their shrieks fading into the breeze.

That left the largest wraith—the one that had attacked Mira at the outset. Elara engaged it in a furious melee, shield radiating lines of holy power. The wraith fought back with an aggression that belied its intangible form, swirling around Elara like a writhing serpent. Every time she scored a hit with her sword, the wraith seemed to splinter, only to snap back moments later. "It's too strong," she gritted out. "I need help!"

Cedric sprinted forward, ignoring the pounding in his chest. Together with Elara, he tried to trap the wraith between shield and blade, forcing it into a narrower shape. The entity shrieked, looking for an escape route. As it slipped around the side, Thalion struck with a well-timed burst of flame. Fire didn't usually harm specters, but laced with arcane potency, it singed the wraith's essence. Meanwhile, Mira raised her staff overhead, channeling a final, piercing lance of astral light.

"Get clear!" she yelled. Elara and Cedric obeyed, diving aside. Mira hurled the lance of light straight through the wraith. The creature convulsed, its form warping violently before collapsing into a swirl of black mist that evaporated into nothingness.

In seconds, the clearing returned to a tense stillness. The water in the pool stabilized, no longer boiling with dark energy. The party, panting and trembling, regrouped on the bank.

"That was... intense," Mira said, chest heaving. She could still feel the residue of that draining presence, a lingering ache in her spirit.

Thalion checked his own condition, patting his robes for any sign of physical injury. "Void Wraiths," he confirmed grimly. "I've read about them, but never expected to see them. They feed not just on life, but on the essence of one's mind and emotions."

Cedric frowned, recalling the sudden surge of negative memories. "No wonder I felt so... lost for a moment." He steadied himself, turning to Elara. "Thank you for intervening."

She offered a reassuring nod. "That's why we stand together. Had I been alone, that big one might've overwhelmed me."

Despite the danger, their victory had yielded more valuable experience. The group felt a renewed sense of camaraderie, each member relying on the other's strengths in the heat of battle. Moreover, these Void Wraiths, stronger manifestations of corruption, seemed to confirm that they were nearing a major junction in the Shadow Nexus's spread.

"You notice how the wraiths emerged right after we approached the confluence pool?" Thalion observed. "They were likely drawn by our presence—our living energy—and the heightened magic of this area."

Elara slowly circled the pool, her boots squishing in the mud. "Places like this might be fueling the nexus's power. Or the nexus is fueling them. Either way, these confluences are critical."

Mira studied the swirling black tendrils beneath the water's surface. "I wonder if cleansing it, like we did at the altar, is possible. But that might require a different ritual—this pool is part of a vast network of ley lines. We'd need more preparation."

Cedric, too, considered the water. A faint reflection of his own face gazed back, tinted by shadow. "Let's not attempt it without a solid plan. We can't risk awakening an even larger threat."

As they caught their breath, Thalion noticed a faint glimmer in the mud near the pool's edge. He bent down, carefully wiping away the muck. "There's something here," he murmured. "A... medallion?"

He lifted a small, round object inscribed with unfamiliar runes. Its surface glowed faintly with subdued red light. Though caked with sediment, the craftsmanship was exquisite—clearly magical. "This medallion might be a key of some sort," Thalion guessed.

Elara joined him, eyeing the runes. "Or a relic from one of the cultists. Maybe it dropped during a ritual. But it doesn't look like any holy symbol I know."

Mira frowned in concentration, passing her staff over the medallion. "I sense raw negative energy bound within. A container, maybe, or a conduit?"

Cedric gripped the hilt of his sword, still uneasy. "Great. Another puzzle piece that might attract trouble. But it could also be what we need to reach the Keeper of Keys, if that legend is more than rumor."

Thalion pocketed the medallion carefully. "We'll examine it later with the proper wards in place. For now, let's move away from this confluence. We have what we came for—a clue and more proof of how far the corruption has spread."

They left the ravine, making their way back up the ridge. Although battered by two fierce battles in a single day—first the ghosts, now the Void Wraiths—they felt emboldened by their growing synergy. Each confrontation honed their teamwork, and each discovery added another piece to the nexus puzzle.

By late afternoon, they located a slightly more welcoming stretch of forest where sunlight managed to pierce the canopy in flickering patches. A scattering of flowers grew around the base of a large, healthy tree, a rare sign of thriving natural life. The group decided to rest briefly, letting their horses graze and refreshing themselves.

As they settled into a wary calm, Elara led a short ceremony. She touched each of her companions lightly on the shoulder, channeling a soft restorative warmth through them. "Let us not forget the cost of this journey. Each clash with dark forces saps our strength and tries to break our spirits. Yet we endure because we fight for Stonehaven, and for each other."

Cedric inclined his head, gratitude shining in his eyes. "We've come a long way in a short time. There's no one else I'd rather face these threats with."

Mira offered a small smile. "I used to study magic for the sake of knowledge. But ever since the king's summons, I've realized there's a higher calling—to use what I've learned to protect lives."

Thalion's gaze traveled across the forest. "We do this not just for ourselves or even for Stonehaven alone, but for all who might suffer if this corruption spreads. The nexus threatens the very balance we hold dear."

Nightfall wasn't far off, and they would soon have to decide whether to push on or make camp. The Gravenshade Woods showed no sign of relenting. Still, they had survived two major encounters, gleaned vital clues, and even discovered a peculiar medallion that might prove crucial in the trials to come. The ephemeral ghosts and the potent Void Wraiths had tested them, forced them to use every ounce of skill and faith. And they had emerged not unscathed, but triumphant in small yet significant ways.

They gathered at the center of the clearing, forming a loose circle around a low-burning fire. Cedric unrolled the map they carried, placing Mira's charcoal sketches and Thalion's notes beside it. By comparing the runes they had found on the confluence stones with the references in King Alaric's transcripts, they began piecing together a probable route westward, toward what might be the Shadow Nexus's outer boundaries—or at least a major stronghold of its corrupt influence.

Elara traced a line on the makeshift chart. "If these runic directions are accurate, we'll pass through a region the old texts call the Sorrow Glen. It's said to be haunted by echoes of a battle from centuries ago."

Thalion nodded. "Given what we've faced so far, we should assume the worst. The spirits we saw today might be a mere taste of what's to come."

Cedric's voice was firm. "Then we prepare. We've gained experience fighting these spectral foes. Next time, we'll be ready."

Mira, though tired, wore a look of determined optimism. "And we'll refine our rituals, maybe adapt the cleansing technique if we face another confluence or shrine. The more we thwart the nexus's corrupt sites, the weaker its hold on Stonehaven becomes."

Each nodded in agreement, a new layer of resolve settling upon them. The day had been long, and the night likely held further trials, but they were no longer novices stumbling blindly. They were becoming a true fellowship—knight, paladin, mage, and wizard—united by purpose and tempered by adversity.

As the last vestiges of daylight faded, they chose to camp under that one relatively healthy tree, hoping the patch of vibrant flora indicated less corruption in that spot. While Thalion and Mira set the usual wards, Cedric busied himself gathering enough fallen branches to maintain a modest fire through the night. Elara double-checked her armor straps, mindful that even a hairline crack could prove disastrous in the next spectral assault.

The hush of the forest descended once more. The wind sighed overhead, rustling leaves in a pattern that almost resembled speech. Flickers of movement at the edge of vision kept them alert, though no direct threat emerged. Each hero retired to a short shift of rest, trusting that whoever stood watch would rouse them at the first sign of danger.

In the flickering glow, Thalion spent a final hour studying the newly acquired medallion. He noted the runic phrases that glinted faintly on its surface, cross-referencing them with half-forgotten texts. A partial translation suggested themes of "opening," "sacrifice," and "key." The word "Umbra" also appeared. Though the details remained elusive, it was enough to confirm the medallion's significance.

Thus ended their third day in the Gravenshade Woods—a domain aptly named, for it thrummed with secrets and threatened to overwhelm any intruders with unrelenting gloom. But the party persevered, forging ahead despite the weight of dread that pressed in from all sides. They had faced spectral ghosts hungry for life force and wraiths of darker origin, each confrontation an unspoken reminder of what awaited if they faltered. In the aftermath, they gleaned new insights, uncovered hidden artifacts, and strengthened their bond.

As the party drifted to a half-slumber, Elara found herself gazing at the stars, dimly visible through a break in the canopy. She recited a silent prayer, asking the Goddess of Dawn to guide them to further victories, to grant peace to the restless spirits they had encountered, and to illuminate the path to the Shadow Nexus. For if this was but the beginning, what might they face when they finally stood at the nexus's heart?

Night settled fully, and the forest's whispered lamentations continued, a chorus of wind through leaves and unseen voices carried from ages past. Yet amid that haunting melody, four courageous souls kept their vigil. Tomorrow would bring new tests of their teamwork and faith; tomorrow they would resume the quest to dispel the darkness threatening Stonehaven's future. Still, for this fleeting moment, they allowed themselves a quiet sense of accomplishment—small embers of hope glowing in the vast expanse of night.

Their final thoughts before sleep claimed them were of unity and purpose. They had survived the Gravenshade Woods' first horrors together. They had wrested knowledge from ancient ruins, banished malevolent specters, and uncovered relics hinting at deeper mysteries. Though the darkness loomed, they knew they were not alone. And in that knowledge, their resolve grew ever stronger, a spark of light in a forest of shadow, carrying them onward into the challenges yet to come.

4

THE WYVERN'S LAIR

The morning light filtered weakly through the Gravenshade Woods, staining the leaf-laden forest floor in patches of gold and shadow. Sir Cedric, Lady Elara, Thalion, and Mira roused themselves from their modest campsite, each bracing for another day of perilous exploration. The air felt heavier here than it had in the outskirts of the woods—cooler, quieter, the birdsong all but silenced by a pervasive, uneasy hush. They had grown accustomed to the eerie atmosphere, yet no amount of experience could fully shield them from the slight chill that danced up their spines whenever the forest's distant whispers rose in pitch.

The four heroes gathered around a small cooking fire, its coals still aglow from the previous night. Elara ladled out portions of a simple oatmeal they'd prepared with dried fruits, offering a few scraps of bread to the horses. Though rest had been fleeting, they were grateful for what little sleep they had managed before the forest's nighttime noises frayed their nerves once more.

"Anyone else sense a change in the air?" Cedric asked quietly, glancing at the gnarled trunks around them. The knight had spent his watch listening for the faintest hint of threat. He was used to the tension of dark places by now—

creeping illusions, spectral shapes—but something about this new day felt off. "It's like the forest is... disturbed."

Elara looked up from the fire, a light of concern in her gaze. "I feel it too. We've encountered so much corruption already, but there's a different kind of menace in these parts. Almost... raw power."

Thalion nodded, stirring his tea. "Given the intensity of the negative energies we've observed, I suspect we're nearing another focal point of the Nexus's influence. That, or a massive creature that thrives on the darkness."

Mira, holding her staff across her knees, let out a contemplative sigh. "It's possible. We heard rumors from traveling merchants that a winged beast was terrorizing the forest's edges. We assumed it might be some lesser drake or an oversized bird corrupted by the Shadow Nexus, but maybe it's something more formidable."

The group exchanged uneasy glances. The last thing they wanted was another pitched battle. Nevertheless, they had pledged to vanquish evil and protect the innocent; if a monstrous creature threatened nearby villages, they could not ignore it. With that unspoken resolve, they finished their scant breakfast, doused the fire, and readied themselves for the day's journey.

They set out along a narrow path twisting westward, guided only by the half-deciphered glyphs from Thalion's notes and Mira's own sense of arcane currents. The progress was slow. Fallen logs and thick underbrush forced them to lead the horses on foot, weaving carefully between jagged roots that snaked across the forest floor. Ominous shapes flickered at the edges of their vision, vanishing whenever they turned to look. Now and again, a rush of black-winged ravens spiraled through the canopy, cawing as if to warn them of dangers ahead.

About mid-morning, they broke out of the densest part of the woods and emerged onto a rocky ledge overlooking a valley. Sunlight washed across the scene, revealing a patchwork of farmland beyond the forest's border. A winding dirt road cut across the fields, leading to a small hamlet. Even from a distance, it was clear the settlement bore scars. Several rooftops were partially collapsed, plumes of dark smoke curling upward. Fields lay trampled, with fences broken. Tiny figures were scurrying about, likely villagers attempting to salvage what they could.

"This must be one of the villages we heard about," Cedric said, exhaling. "It looks like it's been ravaged recently."

Elara turned to the others. "We should help them. If a creature is truly terrorizing these people, stopping it is part of our mission. The corruption of the Shadow Nexus might be emboldening or warping whatever is attacking."

No one disagreed. Though they'd been focused on hunting for the Nexus, the vow they had made—to defend Stonehaven from any darkness—took precedence. They led the horses down a scraggly path winding out of the woods, stepping carefully to avoid loose stones that might tumble dangerously downslope.

Once they reached level ground, the route grew smoother, albeit muddy in places from a recent rainfall. Their approach did not go unnoticed. Before the group reached the hamlet's outskirts, a handful of weary-looking men armed with pitchforks and crude spears stepped onto the road.

"Halt!" one of them called, though his voice trembled. He looked no older than twenty, and his knuckles were white around the pitchfork's handle. "Identify yourselves!"

Cedric raised his empty hands, stepping forward in a display of peace. His sword remained sheathed at his side. "We mean you no harm. I am Sir Cedric, knight of Stonehaven. My companions and I heard there was trouble here."

The young man glanced at Cedric's well-made armor and then eyed Elara's shield with its glowing emblem, Thalion's staff, and Mira's wizardly attire. Although frightened, the villager seemed to draw a small measure of hope from their presence. "Apologies, travelers. These are dangerous times. We can't afford to trust easily."

Elara moved to Cedric's side, her expression gentle. "We understand. We've come to see if we can help with your... troubles."

A slight commotion behind the makeshift guards parted them, revealing an older woman with gray streaks in her hair. She carried herself with the bearing of someone who had seen too many hardships. "I'm Rosemary, the head of this village," she said. "If you're here to help, then by the grace of the Light, we welcome you. But be warned: We've been beset by a terrible wyvern for weeks."

"A wyvern?" Thalion repeated, stroking his beard. "That's more fearsome than a mere drake. They can be cunning as well as strong."

Rosemary nodded gravely. "It has attacked our fields, devoured livestock, and even destroyed parts of our homes. We tried to erect defenses, but our weapons are no match for its claws and fire-breath."

Elara's brow furrowed. "Fire-breath? Wyverns typically rely on poison or noxious fumes. Are you sure it's a wyvern, not a dragon?"

"It's definitely a wyvern," the older woman insisted. "We've seen it up close. It has a barbed tail and two hind legs, not four. But it spews some sort of molten acid that sets everything ablaze."

Cedric rested a hand on his sword's hilt. "Such a creature could easily hide in the forests or the nearby hills. Has anyone tracked it?"

Rosemary shook her head. "We've lost men who attempted to chase it. Rumor says its lair is in a cave beyond the forest ridge, near the old quarry. But no one has returned to confirm."

"Then we'll look into it," Mira said quietly, though her voice carried determination. "We've fought creatures of the Shadow Nexus before. We can handle a wyvern."

At that, murmurs rippled among the villagers. Many of them bore tear-stained faces, while children clung to their mothers. It was clear how desperate they were. Rosemary bowed her head. "We have little to offer in return, but we will feed you, stable your horses, anything you require. Just please, end this nightmare."

The heroes spent a brief hour in the village, verifying the location of the rumored lair and assessing the scale of destruction. Thalion spoke to some survivors who described how the wyvern roared through the sky like a thunderstorm, leaving trails of smoldering wreckage. Cedric examined footprints in the muddied fields—a set of colossal, reptilian tracks, spaced about the width of a barn. The deep gouges in the ground confirmed that whatever they faced had immense weight and power.

Once they'd gathered enough information, Cedric took the lead, reassuring Rosemary that they would do all in their power to slay the wyvern. The villagers prepared a modest meal, offering dried meats, bread, and a hot stew. Though the party felt uneasy taking provisions from those who had so little, they accepted in the spirit of unity, promising to return victorious.

Guided by local rumors, the companions set out to find the old quarry where the wyvern supposedly nested. They left their horses in the village's care, not wanting to risk the animals spooking in the face of a massive predator. The trek from the farmland back into denser woodland was short but tense, the canopy swallowing them once again in shifting green shadows. Soon, the farmland behind them was out of sight, replaced by silent pines and tall spruces that creaked in the breeze.

An hour passed. Then two. The ground grew rocky, sloping upward toward the region's higher terrain. Large boulders dotted the path, some carved with ancient runes that Thalion recognized from earlier nights of study—warnings or boundaries once set by the forest's ancient inhabitants. Winds gusted, carrying the faint smell of sulfur.

At last, they spotted a crooked sign staked into the earth, its lettering nearly faded: *Quarry Road.* A steep trail ascended beyond it, a switchback climbing a cliff face half-smothered in vines and lichen. This had to be the route. Cedric drew his sword, Thalion prepared a detection spell, and Elara gripped her shield. Mira hovered behind them, staff in hand, scanning for any trace of movement overhead.

The climb was arduous. Loose stones skittered beneath their boots, and the wind whipped around hair and cloaks with unexpected force. But after nearly another hour of exertion, they reached a ledge that overlooked a wide bowl-shaped valley of dark, jagged rock. Centuries ago, workers had mined valuable ores from this place, but the site was abandoned long ago. Now, the quarry had partially flooded, forming a small, murky lake in the center. The air stank of rot and acrid fumes. Enormous bones—possibly from livestock or even giant forest creatures—littered the far bank. With dawning horror, the party realized this was undoubtedly the wyvern's feeding ground.

"There," Elara whispered, pointing. On a cliff side to the north, a gaping cave mouth yawned like an open wound in the rock. Charring around the entrance indicated repeated blasts of heat or acid. The ground leading inside was scorched black, scattered with broken stone. Tracks of monstrous claws marred the ground.

Mira wrinkled her nose. "We can try to sneak in, but a creature that large will sense us quickly."

Thalion nodded. "Wyverns are known to be territorial. If it detects us, it'll come out to fight or flush us from the quarry."

Cedric's jaw tightened. "We should draw it out. Fighting it in those tight corridors would be a death sentence."

Elara studied the terrain. "There's a plateau just above the cave. If we can get up there quietly and set a trap or vantage point, we might stand a chance at ambushing it. Then we're not stuck on the ground if it decides to take flight."

They deliberated the plan for a few minutes. Eventually, they decided to climb a ridge overlooking the cave, hoping to secure high ground. From there, they would attempt to lure the wyvern out. The risk was immense—an airborne wyvern was lethal, but being trapped in a cave was worse. With the approach settled, they carefully circled to the northern rim of the quarry, keeping low and moving with as much stealth as their gear allowed.

The route to the upper ledge was perilous: a narrow game trail skirting the cliff's edge, gravel sliding with each footstep. Twice, Cedric had to catch Mira's arm to keep her from tumbling onto jagged rocks below. Elara, used to traveling in her heavy armor, found the climb taxing, but she soldiered on with stoic determination. Thalion quietly chanted a feather-light cantrip to lessen the burden of each footfall. At last, they reached a rocky outcrop that jutted above the cave's mouth, partially hidden by a row of stunted pines. From that vantage, they could see into the cave's entrance, a dark tunnel leading further into the bowels of the earth.

They arranged themselves in a semi-circle, taking cover behind boulders and low shrubs. Elara readied her shield, whispering a soft prayer for protection. Mira prepared a concentrated bolt of arcane energy, staff tip glowing a faint blue. Thalion's free hand crackled with the potential for elemental magic. And Cedric knelt near the cliff's edge, breath steady, sword in one hand and a small dagger in the other. He scanned the gaping maw below. All was still.

Minutes dragged on. The wind gusted, swirling dust into their eyes, but the cave remained silent. Cedric squinted, trying to discern movement in the darkness. "Maybe it's out hunting," he muttered under his breath.

No sooner had he spoken than a deep rumble echoed from within the cavern. It was a guttural, scraping sound, like claws raking stone. A moment later, a pair of glowing yellow eyes appeared, glinting in the darkness. The party tensed. Slowly, the wyvern stalked into view, each step making the ground tremble. Its scales were a mottled green-black, ridged with bony spines. Two enormous leathery wings folded against its flanks, and a serpentine tail swung behind it, crowned with a vicious barbed stinger. The creature's head was draconic, jaws drooling a noxious green fluid that hissed where it dripped onto the rock.

For a heart-stopping instant, the wyvern sniffed the air, muscles coiling beneath its scales. Then it reared back on its hind legs, releasing a roar that reverberated through the quarry, shaking loose small stones from the ledge above.

Cedric exhaled. "Now."

Mira raised her staff. A brilliant streak of light tore through the air, aimed directly at the wyvern's massive chest. The beast flinched, letting out a shriek of surprise. Thalion followed up with a crackling lance of lightning, arcs dancing from his fingertips. Elara stood, brandishing her shield high, channeling holy energy that cascaded in a radiant beam, searing the wyvern's flank.

Caught off guard, the wyvern staggered back, its wings flaring. Blackish blood oozed where the spells impacted, sizzling on the rocky ground. However, the creature recovered with alarming speed, letting out another ear-splitting roar. It stretched its wings wide, launching itself into the air with a single powerful leap. Gusts of wind buffeted the heroes, forcing them to brace against the rocky ledge.

Suddenly, the wyvern pivoted mid-flight, swinging its tail. A glistening droplet of acid launched from the stinger's tip, spraying the ridge with a pressurized jet. Elara raised her shield just in time, the metal hissing under the corrosive onslaught. Thalion conjured a protective ward, but small droplets scorched his cloak, leaving charred holes. Mira dived behind a boulder, narrowly avoiding the scalding spray.

Cedric, shielded by Elara's stance, scrambled to his feet. "We need to get it back on the ground!" he shouted.

Thalion grunted, raising his staff. "I can ground it, but I'll need a moment." The mage began weaving an incantation, drawing power from the swirling air. Meanwhile, Cedric sprinted to the side, finding a vantage near a tall pine, determined to flank the creature if it landed. Mira popped out from behind her cover, hurling a volley of luminous orbs that slammed into the wyvern's wing membranes. Though the blasts tore small holes in the leathery skin, the beast remained aloft, screeching in rage.

Elara advanced, sword in one hand, shield in the other. She locked eyes with the wyvern, calling upon her paladin vow to shield the innocent and banish the monstrous. A golden glow enveloped her blade, amplifying its destructive potential. "Try me, beast," she murmured, setting her jaw.

With a thunderous flap, the wyvern swooped low, aiming its fang-filled maw at Elara. She raised her shield, bracing for impact. The collision sent her skidding backward, boots scouring deep furrows into the loose gravel. Sparks flew as the wyvern's jaws clamped around the shield's rim. For an instant, it seemed Elara might be torn apart, but she let loose a surge of divine light. The wyvern recoiled, hissing, a smoking wound on its snout.

Capitalizing on the distraction, Mira hurled a concentrated bolt of arcane power at the creature's flank. At the same moment, Thalion completed his grounding incantation. A sharp gust of wind slammed down from above, forcing the wyvern's wings to fold. The beast tumbled to the rocky floor below in a crash that sent dust and pebbles spiraling skyward.

Cedric seized the opportunity. He dashed along the rocky outcrop, leaping down a small slope with controlled grace. As the wyvern tried to regain its footing, rearing its spined tail in fury, Cedric lunged, sword angled for a decisive strike. But the wyvern twisted at the last second, swiping its clawed forelimb. The blow caught Cedric's side, metal squealing as claws raked across his breastplate. Though the armor held, he was knocked sprawling, pain rippling through his ribs.

"Cedric!" Elara cried, racing to his side. She took a defensive stance above him, parrying the wyvern's next strike. The tail whipped in, stinger poised to deliver a deadly injection of acid. But Thalion and Mira were already reacting. Another burst of lightning scorched the tail, while Mira conjured an ice-lance that impaled the barb, temporarily freezing the acidic sacs.

Enraged, the wyvern whipped its head around to blast them with molten fluid from its maw. The entire area fumed with toxic vapors. Mira coughed, eyes watering, while Thalion threw up a quickly improvised shield of swirling wind to push the fumes away. Elara, heart pounding, helped

Cedric stand, checking that his armor hadn't been corroded. He nodded, grimacing but not yielding.

"We need to cripple its wings or tail," Cedric hissed. "If we keep fighting it on all fronts, we'll wear ourselves down."

Elara agreed. She summoned a fleeting aura of healing, easing the sharp ache in Cedric's ribs. "I'll hold its attention from the front. You two circle behind, aim for the tail. Thalion, Mira—provide cover!"

Even as they spoke, the wyvern lunged again, jaws snapping dangerously close. Elara charged, shield high, sword slicing across the beast's muzzle. Every strike left searing trails of golden light, eliciting shrieks of fury. Yet it wasn't enough to kill something this massive. The wyvern battered her with a forelimb, nearly toppling her, but she held firm, unrelenting in her duty.

Circling wide, Cedric grit his teeth against the pain in his side. With the creature focused on Elara, he closed in behind it, sword at the ready. The tail swung violently, forcing Cedric to duck. He retaliated with a powerful slash across the scaly hide. Sparks flew, and a deep gash opened in the wyvern's flank. Reddish-black blood spilled onto the stone. The monster roared, trying to pivot, but Cedric rolled away, narrowly avoiding another deadly swipe.

Meanwhile, Thalion recited a new incantation, harnessing the elemental energy swirling around them. Electricity crackled in the air, coalescing into a dancing sphere above his staff. At his signal, Mira joined her power to his, sending arcs of purple-tinted lightning into the sphere. Their combined magic erupted in a blinding fork that streaked into the wyvern's side, burning a charred line along its scales. The stench of scorched flesh filled the quarry.

Roaring in agony, the beast unleashed a torrential stream of acid from its jaws. Thalion and Mira dove apart to avoid it, the sizzling liquid melting the stone in seconds. For a moment, the smoke and fumes obscured the battlefield. Elara coughed, eyes stinging, maintaining her shield to guard against further sprays. Cedric used the confusion to scramble around the flank, determined to end the fight before the wyvern regained the upper hand.

Emerging from the haze, the wyvern locked eyes with Cedric. Its lips pulled back, revealing rows of jagged fangs dripping with venomous froth. Both adversaries paused, as though acknowledging the finality of this clash. The knight steeled himself, drawing on every ounce of training and courage. His vow to protect Stonehaven rang in his mind, fueling his resolve.

He sprinted forward, sword raised. The wyvern snapped its tail around, but Cedric ducked low, muscles aflame as he forced himself into a desperate roll. He came up under the beast's belly, slashing upward. Scales parted, blood splattered. The wyvern howled, thrashing so violently that stones rained from the cliff walls. Cedric's sword arm trembled with the impact, but he refused to let go.

Elara seized the advantage: she charged with a defiant roar, plunging her blade into the wyvern's flank. Divine sparks danced along the metal, intensifying the wound. Mira fired off a volley of arcane missiles, each cracking into the wyvern's side, further weakening its gargantuan form. Thalion conjured a final bolt of searing lightning that struck the creature's chest, scorching scale and sinew.

The wyvern teetered, eyes rolling in pain. Its tail whipped out one last time, forcing Elara to block with her shield. The stinger snapped off in the collision, sending acid splattering across the ground. With a final, anguished roar, the beast staggered to its knees.

"Now, Cedric!" Elara shouted.

Cedric gathered his strength and leapt. His sword, glowing faintly with residual arcane energy from the storm of spells, came down in a decisive arc. The blade pierced the wyvern's thick neck, slicing through muscle and bone. Time seemed to slow as the beast issued a final rasping growl, then collapsed under its own weight. Dust billowed, pebbles skittered, and the quarry grew eerily silent.

For a long moment, no one moved. Then Thalion exhaled shakily, leaning on his staff. Mira lowered her hands, arcs of leftover magic dissipating around her. Elara fell to her knees, clutching her shield, sweat pouring down her face. Cedric stood panting, sword embedded in the wyvern's throat, overwhelmed by the enormity of the victory.

They had slain a creature that could have ravaged entire armies. With the threat ended, relief washed over them like a breaking dawn. But the cost weighed heavily: each was bruised, some lightly burned by acid, and all were exhausted.

After binding minor wounds and catching their breath, the group moved to examine the dead wyvern. Up close, its size was staggering: it spanned at least thirty feet from snout to tail, with a wingspan that could blot out the sun. Great spines jutted along its back, each as thick as a man's arm. The stench of acrid blood and rancid breath forced them to cover their noses. Still, their mission was clear: retrieve any sign or clue that might help identify whether the creature was tied to the Shadow Nexus.

It was Mira who first noticed something unusual in the beast's scales. Near its shoulders, multiple plates had grown in bizarre patterns, discolored with blackish veins that pulsed faintly. She ran her hand gingerly across the corruption, feeling a strange hum of residual magic. "This is definitely not normal," she whispered. "It's like the creature was partially tainted by external sorcery."

Elara nodded, her gaze somber. "Could the nexus have infected the wyvern as it did the ghosts and wraiths we encountered? That might explain the acid breath and abnormal aggression."

Thalion leaned in, using a small illumination spell to inspect the blackish streaks. "I suspect so. These lines remind me of the same arcane scars we've seen on corrupted beasts. The question is whether the wyvern was forcibly twisted, or if it willingly consumed some source of dark power."

Cedric, still breathing heavily, placed a hand on his sword's hilt. "In any case, it was a threat to innocent villagers. We did what needed to be done." His eyes flicked to the jagged lines marring the wyvern's hide. "But if there's any insight we can glean from this creature—like the cause or location of the corruption—it might help us find the nexus."

Mira nodded. "Let's see if there's something like a mage's brand or a runic marking on its underbelly or near the head. Sometimes cultists brand beasts they subjugate."

They spread out, carefully examining the wyvern. The rest of its body appeared typical for its kind—thick scales, a barbed tail, a draconic head. But near its chest, half-hidden beneath a scale the size of a small shield, they found a curious marking: a swirling rune etched directly into the creature's flesh. The lines glowed faintly with a deep purple luminescence.

Thalion's eyes narrowed. "That's not a brand I recognize from Stonehaven's usual circle of warlocks. This... might be older, more primal."

Elara placed a hand above the rune. She could sense a faint malevolence radiating from it, reminiscent of the altar sites they'd purified. "Whatever this symbol is, it bound the wyvern to some dark purpose. We should remove it."

Cedric slid his blade under the large scale, prying it up with a grunt of effort. Beneath, the flesh was blackened, the rune carved directly into muscle. Steeling himself, Cedric cut away the marked tissue with grim efficiency. The moment the tainted flesh separated from the body, the faint luminescence sputtered out, leaving only a dull husk of black. A vile stench rose, and he flung the piece aside, wincing.

Mira conjured a small flame in her hand and burned the corrupted fragment to ash. The group watched the dark smoke curl into the quarry's sky, relieved to see the sinister brand destroyed. Yet in the process, something else tumbled free from beneath the scale: a single plate that glimmered with an otherworldly sheen, different from the rest of the wyvern's hide. It was about the size of a human hand, etched with faint lines reminiscent of the runes they'd seen near the old confluence sites.

"That's odd," Elara remarked, picking the scale up gingerly. Despite its size, it felt surprisingly light. "I've never seen a wyvern scale with this kind of pattern."

Thalion examined it, eyes alight with curiosity. "These lines appear to form a partial glyph, possibly an indicator of location. Wyverns sometimes accumulate magical residue, but this is beyond that—it almost looks like a map in miniature."

Mira cast a minor detection spell, watching as wisps of azure light traced the edges of the scale. "It's definitely infused with energy. But not the same foul corruption we saw in the flesh. This is... older. Could it be connected to the nexus's preexisting magical network?"

Cedric sheathed his sword, stepping closer. The scale glinted with greenish iridescence under the midday sun, overlaid with a labyrinth of swirling lines. "Maybe that's how the cult or whoever's behind this was steering the wyvern, or maybe the wyvern found something in the nexus region and it imprinted on its scales."

Elara pursed her lips. "Regardless, it might be the key to unraveling another piece of the puzzle. Thalion, think you can glean any more from it later?"

"I'll certainly try," replied the mage. "If it's a clue to the nexus's location, we can't afford to overlook it."

With that, the group secured the mystical scale in a leather satchel, wrapping it in cloth to prevent any inadvertent magical surges. They did one final sweep, ensuring no other arcane elements clung to the wyvern's remains. The rest of the body, massive and motionless, would remain a grim testament to the forest's lethal transformations.

Weary from battle, the heroes made their way back down the quarry trail, heading toward the village to deliver news of their victory. A hush had settled over them, partly from fatigue but also from the weight of what they'd discovered. This single monstrous wyvern was but one threat among many, twisted by ancient magic, perhaps orchestrated by a hidden force. What deeper horrors awaited them as they pressed on?

By the time they reached the hamlet, late afternoon light slanted across the fields. The villagers, on edge all day, rushed to greet them, eyes wide with hope. When Cedric raised his gauntleted hand to signify success, an audible gasp spread through the crowd. Children cheered, and adults wept with relief. Rosemary, tears in her eyes, approached the party with trembling hands.

"It's... gone?" she whispered, voice hoarse.

Elara nodded. "We have slain the wyvern that plagued your lands."

A collective cheer rose, though it was laced with exhaustion. Villagers crowded around, some offering small tokens of gratitude, others simply falling to their knees in prayerful thanks. Many gazed at the heroes with reverence, as though they had just witnessed a miracle. Cedric felt a stab of humility, for he knew well how close they'd come to losing. But the sight of these people's relief renewed his resolve.

They accepted meager gifts—a pouch of freshly ground wheat, a small wooden charm to ward off evil, a handful of herbal poultices. Rosemary insisted they take lodging in the communal hall for the night. Though the group initially planned to press on, the day's battle had taken its toll. They realized resting among grateful villagers might be the reprieve they needed.

Under the communal hall's sloping roof of thatch and timber, the townsfolk prepared a simple feast. While half the building's windows were boarded up, and debris still littered the floors, the atmosphere was celebratory. A handful of farmers played a lively tune on handmade flutes, and children danced, their fears momentarily forgotten. The smell of roast vegetables and salted pork wafted through the air, offering a welcome contrast to the acrid stench of the quarry.

Seated on rough wooden benches, the heroes found themselves at the center of attention. Everyone wanted to hear how they defeated the wyvern, from the roars of battle to the final blow. Cedric recounted the fight in modest terms, emphasizing that each of his companions played a crucial role. Elara, ever pious, attributed their victory partly to her goddess's favor. Thalion and Mira gave only brief explanations of their spells, conscious not to overwhelm the villagers with arcane details.

After the meal, Rosemary approached with a small, carved oak box. Inside lay a necklace set with a cloudy quartz stone. "We once used this charm to bless our crops," she explained. "It's not much, but it brings fortune. We'd like you to have it—perhaps it will bring you success on your quest."

Elara accepted it with gratitude, slipping it around her neck. Though the stone held no obvious arcane signature, it felt warm against her skin, a reminder of the village's heartfelt thanks.

Night fell, and the group found themselves drifting into an uneasy sleep on straw pallets. Outside, a gentle rain began to patter against the roof. Cedric, half-dozing, let his mind wander to the mystic scale they'd retrieved. Could it truly point them to the Shadow Nexus? Or would it lead them astray? At least they had rid Stonehaven of one monstrous threat and saved this village from ruin.

Shortly before midnight, a thunderclap startled them awake. Flashes of lightning illuminated the hall through gaps in the shutters. For a moment, Cedric felt his heart race, thinking of the wyvern's thunderous presence. But as the afterimage faded, he remembered it was dead. All that remained was the echoes of fear and the permanent scars left on the people here.

The next morning, they rose with dawn to the soft drumming of rain on thatch. Though the villagers would have liked the heroes to stay longer, both to celebrate and to bolster morale, the four knew they had to continue their quest. Easing the immediate threat was one step; discovering the root cause of all these horrors was another. With heartfelt farewells, they packed their gear, gathered their horses, and prepared to ride on. Rosemary insisted on sending them off with baskets of bread, dried fruit, and fresh water. "May the Light protect you," she said, voice quavering with emotion.

Before departing, Thalion discreetly asked if any of the villagers had glimpsed strange lights or heard rumors of cultists in the area. One old man recalled seeing dark-robed figures traveling north under cover of night, carrying torches that glowed with an unnatural purple hue. It happened many weeks ago, before the wyvern attacks. No one dared to follow them, fearing black magic. It was meager intel, but it hinted that dark practitioners might be roaming these lands, possibly orchestrating the infiltration of shadow energies.

"At least we have another lead," Thalion said as they mounted their horses, turning to the others. "Dark-robed figures heading north. It could tie in with the scale's markings."

Mira nodded, tucking her staff across her saddle. "Let's examine the scale once we make camp tonight. Maybe I can replicate a scrying spell keyed to its aura, see if it resonates with anything in the region."

Cedric adjusted his reins, the fresh bruises on his torso protesting with each breath. "We'll follow the road, then turn back into the forest. The Gravenshade Woods extends northward in patches. We might pass near other outlying settlements that also need help."

Elara drew up beside him, shield strapped to her horse's flank. "We should remain vigilant. The wyvern was formidable, but if the Nexus truly warps beasts, we might face even more dangerous creatures ahead."

They rode in a somber formation, the gentle rainfall softening the dusty road into a slick path. Though the villagers had been saved, the larger threat remained. Yet the party sensed a renewed unity—battle had forged them closer, each relying on the other's strengths when survival hung by a thread.

For much of the day, they traversed rolling hills and sparse woodlands. Shafts of pale sunlight broke through the clouds, illuminating the mist that hovered over fields. Rarely, they passed a farmer's cottage or a small cluster of huts, but these were mostly abandoned. Fear had driven people to gather in larger villages for protection. The roads were eerily quiet, reminiscent of a land preparing for war.

By late afternoon, the terrain shifted again. Dense conifers loomed ahead, forming another curtain of forest—one that local maps indicated was part of a northern stretch of the Gravenshade Woods. Cedric signaled for a halt, guiding the horses to a shallow stream for water. The group dismounted, each stretching sore muscles from the previous day's ordeal.

"Let's camp here," Cedric suggested. "We have enough daylight left to gather firewood, and the stream offers fresh water. It'll give us time to study the scale more thoroughly."

No one objected. They set about their tasks with an unspoken efficiency that came from fighting side by side. Elara knelt in prayer, blessing the area to deter any lurking spirits. Mira cast a minor ward around the perimeter to alert them of encroaching threats. Thalion rummaged through his pack, producing the mystical wyvern scale. He placed it on a flat rock by the stream's bank, eager to examine it more deeply.

As twilight descended, Mira sat cross-legged before the scale, staff laid across her lap. Thalion stood behind her, quietly offering suggestions for detection spells. The rest of the camp glowed with the warmth of a small fire, where Cedric and Elara kept watch. Between bites of salted jerky and sips of herbal tea, the two would occasionally glance at the scale's faint gleam in the dusk light.

Mira started her incantation, weaving threads of arcane force that manifested as faint lines around the scale. "If I can sense an echo or resonance, it might show us how it's tied to the nexus," she explained, eyes half-lidded in concentration.

Thalion added a layer of his own magic, using the knowledge gleaned from ancient runic texts. Slowly, a swirling pattern of ghostly shapes emerged above the scale, forming a hovering outline of something reminiscent of a topographical map. In the ephemeral light, the shapes looked like contoured ridges and valleys.

Elara edged closer, entranced. "Is that... the landscape around us?"

Mira nodded. "In part. But it also shows what looks like a deeper layer, maybe subterranean passages or a network of magical lines."

Thalion pointed to a particular swirl that pulsed faintly. "This might indicate a place of concentrated shadow energy. See how it aligns with the patterns of corruption we've encountered in the southwestern portion of the forest?"

Cedric studied the image, recognizing the approximate shape of the region near the quarry and the old shrines. "Then that must mean this pulsating point is further north, probably beyond what we can see on normal maps."

Mira let out a slow breath, releasing the incantation. The floating image faded like morning mist under the sun. "So it's basically telling us to continue north. Possibly toward higher mountains or a hidden valley. The scale is more than a clue—it's practically a compass to the nexus's location."

A hush fell. Each of them felt a pang of foreboding. If the nexus truly dwelled in the desolate north, they would face longer journeys, more monstrous creatures, and unknown cultists fueling the darkness. Yet a flicker of determination lit their hearts; the quest felt more urgent than ever.

"We press on," Elara said softly. "Just as we promised King Alaric, and all those who suffer under the shadow. The wyvern was a step, but the true evil lies ahead."

Cedric nodded, gaze fixed on the dying embers of their campfire. "We've come too far to turn back now. We have a lead—let's see it through."

The night passed without incident, the wards and Elara's blessing seemingly enough to keep malevolent forces at bay. Come dawn, they doused the fire, packed up their gear, and resumed their journey. Spirits were mixed: relief at having saved a village from a monstrous wyvern, tempered by anxiety over what terrors the Shadow Nexus still harbored.

Yet something had changed between them. The near-fatal fight against a formidable foe, culminating in a trophy scale that now guided them, had crystallized their unity. Each member of the party felt a deeper trust in the others' strengths. Cedric's bravery, Elara's faith, Thalion's wisdom, and Mira's arcane prowess combined into a seamless front. They were no longer just four summoned heroes; they were a cohesive team, forging a legend that might one day echo through the halls of Stonehaven.

With the morning sun cresting low in a cloudy sky, they rode northward, the mystical scale tucked safely in Thalion's satchel. In the distance, the trees of the Gravenshade Woods rose like silent sentinels, beckoning them into deeper shadows. The whispering wind seemed to carry a portent of challenges yet to come—and perhaps, the promise of answers. One crisis in Stonehaven was resolved, but the next lay just beyond the horizon, waiting to test their resolve once more.

Though the road ahead would undoubtedly bring more peril, the heroes felt a renewed sense of purpose. If they could slay a corrupted wyvern, then they could stand against whatever else the Shadow Nexus birthed. Their unity, tested in fire and acid, shone brighter than ever. Thus, with hearts both wary and resolute, Sir Cedric, Lady Elara, Thalion, and Mira continued their quest, pressing onward into the unknown. Each step carried them closer to the looming darkness that threatened Stonehaven—yet each step also carried them further along a path of heroism, forging a bond that no shadow could easily break.

5

ALLIES AND ENEMIES

A sliver of pale dawn light peeked over the tops of the twisted pines, marking the heroes' departure from the rugged forests that had tested them so harshly. Sir Cedric, Lady Elara, Thalion, and Mira rode at a measured pace, bones still weary from their relentless battles: first the spectral ghosts, then the deadly wyvern. Though the realm ahead promised new dangers, the promise of seeing civilization again—an actual town with warm beds—stirred a note of optimism in their hearts. With the dark outlines of the Gravenshade Woods receding behind them, the four companions turned their sights on Brighthaven, a bustling settlement rumored to be a haven of trade, learning, and open-mindedness.

For days, they navigated well-worn roads that snaked across rolling hills. Wild poppies dotted the verges of the dirt path, and the scent of blooming clover sweetened the breeze. Compared to the oppressive gloom of the forest, the open skies and bright farmland felt almost jarringly cheerful. Local farmers waved politely from their fields; at first, these strangers riding with weapons and arcane staves caused some raised eyebrows, but an unspoken courtesy prevailed. After all, the heroes carried themselves with the quiet confidence of seasoned adventurers, and the villagers seemed relieved just to see anyone who might stand against the growing rumors of darkness spreading through Stonehaven.

They made camp under star-studded skies and pressed on at first light. Each day's travel made them more aware of the changes they observed in the land: In some places, crops flourished, while in others, entire fields lay blighted, as if a silent gloom had devoured their vitality. The four debated whether this creeping corruption was an offshoot of the Shadow Nexus or some other ill omen. Either way, it reminded them of the grave nature of their quest.

At last, on a brisk morning graced by scattered clouds, the party climbed a gentle rise to behold Brighthaven in the distance. The town lived up to its name: Sunlight glinted off rows of white-walled homes, and its tiled roofs were painted in warm earth tones. A tall clock tower dominated the skyline, and at the highest point sat a proud temple spire dedicated to the Goddess of Dawn. Unlike the capital city's imposing walls, Brighthaven's defenses were simpler—a reinforced wooden palisade and a single iron gate that admitted travelers by day.

A sense of relief settled on Sir Cedric as he guided his horse forward. Despite the many trials they had faced, this place exuded an air of welcome, like a sanctuary for the weary. Lady Elara, who had glimpsed the temple spire, felt a flicker of comfort that somewhere within Brighthaven's walls, her faith's presence remained strong. Thalion, for his part, eagerly anticipated restocking rare spell components and visiting local scholars who might shed light on the arcane mysteries behind the Shadow Nexus. And Mira, quietly watchful, hoped to find some measure of normalcy after the terrors of the Gravenshade Woods.

They approached the gates at midday. Guards wearing simple plate-and-leather armor eyed them cautiously but without overt hostility. One guard, a lanky fellow with a scar across his cheek, raised a hand.

"Halt there," he said, though not unkindly. "What business brings you to Brighthaven?"

Cedric dismounted, offering a courteous nod. "Travelers in need of rest—and perhaps new supplies. We've been tasked with investigating the spread of darkness in these parts on behalf of King Alaric. My companions and I have come a long way."

The guard exchanged a look with his fellow, then nodded. "We've heard rumors of monstrous creatures in the west. Well, Brighthaven welcomes peaceful travelers—especially those who aim to keep these roads safe. Mind your manners, and you'll find fair trade within. If it's lodging you seek, the Gilded Lantern on Main Street offers a decent night's sleep."

With that, the gates opened to admit them. The party guided their horses through, thankful to be greeted without suspicion or alarm for once. On the other side lay a busy thoroughfare lined with bustling shops, taverns, and market stalls that overflowed with local produce. Children scampered between wagons, laughter brightening the midday air. Street vendors hawked fresh pastries and trinkets from far-off regions. A group of traveling minstrels strummed lively tunes, serenading passersby.

"It's hard to believe that the same darkness we saw in the forest might threaten a place like this," Mira mused, scanning the bright faces of people busily going about their errands. "They don't look worried at all."

Thalion sighed. "Give them time. Darkness can be subtle. Sometimes it strikes so fast that a community has no chance to prepare."

Elara's gaze wandered to the distant temple spire. "True. Still, I sense pockets of fear among these people. They might not show it openly, but there's a tension in the air."

Cedric agreed, noticing how a few of the townsfolk glanced at the group's weapons with a hint of apprehension. "Let's find that inn, stable our horses, and see what news can be found. Maybe the local guard or mayor can provide leads."

It didn't take long to locate the Gilded Lantern—a cozy, two-story establishment marked by a swinging wooden sign painted with a golden lamp. The inn's stable boy, a freckle-faced teenager, offered to groom the horses for a modest fee. The party gratefully handed over the reins, then entered through the wide double doors.

Inside, the Gilded Lantern's common room bustled with midday patrons. Merchants conferred over ledgers, a traveling bard plucked a gentle tune, and a few locals sipped ale while chatting about the latest gossip. The aroma of spiced stew and fresh bread wafted through the air. A sturdy woman with a warm smile—presumably the innkeeper—beckoned them to an empty table.

"Welcome, travelers!" she called in a cheerful tone. "I'm Odalys, mistress of the Gilded Lantern. Fancy some hot stew and a place to rest those weary bones?"

Cedric nodded, removing his gauntlets. "That would be wonderful, Odalys. We've been on the road for quite some time."

She handed them menus, her practiced eye sweeping over their armor and magical staves. "I can see that. You all look like you've seen plenty of excitement. Soldiers or adventurers, are you?"

Elara exchanged a glance with the others. "Adventurers, I suppose. We're investigating the spread of a dark influence in Stonehaven—and we've fought more than our share of horrors along the way."

Odalys' warm expression tempered with concern. She gave a quick nod. "Aye, well, you may find that not all is bright in Brighthaven. We're better off than some places, mind you, but troubles of the night have crept in here and there. Missing livestock, strange sightings by moonlight. You'll want to speak with the town guard or even the mayor if you're digging deeper. I'll fetch your stew—and some bread from the morning's bake."

She bustled away. The four heroes settled at the table, scanning the room. They spoke in low voices, mindful not to alarm the other patrons with talk of necromantic beasts and monstrous corruption. Yet they noticed a handful of folks staring, curiosity evident. Word traveled quickly in small towns, and well-armed newcomers rarely went unnoticed.

After a hearty meal, they inquired about rooms. Odalys offered them two adjoining chambers on the second floor. Grateful for the prospect of real beds, they accepted. Thalion paid in advance, leaving a little extra. Then they parted ways in the main hall—Mira and Elara to gather supplies, Cedric and Thalion to find the local authorities. They agreed to reconvene at the inn by dusk.

Stepping out into the afternoon sun, Elara and Mira made their way through Brighthaven's winding lanes toward the central market. Wooden stalls formed rows under a canopy of colorful tarps. Vendors of all sorts displayed bright cloth, fresh produce, carved trinkets, and potions in glass bottles. Shouts of "Fresh fish!" and "Best fruits in Stonehaven!" filled the air, mingling with the joyful chatter of townsfolk haggling over prices.

Mira couldn't help but smile. After so many nights on the road, seeing normal life continue was oddly comforting. She stopped at a stall selling alchemical ingredients—dried herbs, ground minerals, rare oils. Carefully examining the wares, she picked out a few items to replenish her magical components, chatting briefly with the vendor about local rumors. The merchant, a stout woman named Carina, mentioned that caravans from the north had reported strange nocturnal travelers. Some wore cloaks even in warm weather, and more than once, unmarked wagons traveled under heavy guard. Mira stored those tidbits in her memory, suspecting it might connect to the broader darkness creeping through Stonehaven.

Meanwhile, Elara ventured to a blacksmith's booth. She needed to mend a dent in her breastplate from the wyvern battle. Though she could channel healing miracles, metalwork required a craftsman's skill. The blacksmith, a middle-aged man with burn scars on his forearms, hammered out the dent with precision. Conversation drifted to local troubles: apparently, livestock had been found drained of blood in nearby farms, a grim sign that made Elara's skin prickle. Vampires? Or some lesser thrall?

Elara regrouped with Mira near a stall that sold sweet pastries. Over delicious honey-tarts, they exchanged the unsettling rumors they'd gathered. Although neither used the word "vampire" outright, the suggestion hovered in the air. Drained livestock, nighttime visitors in cloaks—these were the hallmarks of vampiric activity. The two women resolved to share this with Cedric and Thalion later. If vampires were indeed operating here, the party had to be prepared for cunning foes, not just mindless beasts.

While Elara and Mira scoured the markets, Cedric and Thalion walked toward the town hall, hoping to meet with the mayor or at least one of her councilors. The building proved easy to find, a sturdy brick structure near the center square. A small crowd waited outside—farmers petitioning for lower taxes, messengers bearing letters, and local citizens with official complaints.

A town guard, noticing Cedric's armor and the tall staff in Thalion's hand, approached. "Looking for someone, sirs?"

Cedric flashed a polite smile. "We'd like to speak with whoever's in charge. It concerns unusual events: attacks, sightings of dark creatures, that sort of thing."

The guard nodded. "You'll want Mayor Adalene. She's inside hearing petitions. Though, as you can see, it might be some time before she can address you."

Thalion stepped forward, brandishing a small medallion with King Alaric's crest. "We're on royal business. If it's not too much trouble, can you let her know we're here? We appreciate your assistance."

The guard's eyes widened at the crest. "I... certainly. Wait here a moment." He hurried inside, leaving Cedric and Thalion under the curious gazes of the townsfolk. A few recognized the royal symbol and muttered among themselves. It wasn't every day that the crown took interest in local matters so directly.

Soon enough, a well-dressed attendant emerged from the town hall, beckoning them in. They navigated cramped hallways lined with wooden benches until they reached the mayor's office. Inside, behind a modest desk piled with scrolls, sat Mayor Adalene. She was a composed woman in her late forties, with a streak of silver in her dark hair and an air of brisk efficiency. A pair of reading spectacles perched on her nose, and she set them aside as Cedric and Thalion entered.

"Greetings, travelers," she said, her tone welcoming but tinged with curiosity. "My guard says you carry the king's crest. How may Brighthaven assist you?"

Cedric bowed respectfully. "Madam Mayor, I am Sir Cedric, and this is Master Thalion. We've journeyed to Brighthaven seeking any information about a corrupt influence spreading across Stonehaven—an ancient evil known as the Shadow Nexus. In the course of our travels, we've encountered horrors in the Gravenshade Woods and glimpsed signs of dark forces lurking near your region. If you've experienced unusual attacks or suspicious visitors, that knowledge may be crucial."

Adalene's expression grew grave. "I see. This might explain the troubling reports I've heard—farmers finding animals mysteriously drained of blood, travelers who vanish at night. I've tried dispatching a militia to investigate, but they found no trace of the perpetrators. We fear it may be some roving band of cultists... or worse."

Thalion nodded. "We've reason to suspect vampiric activity, among other threats. While we don't wish to incite panic, we can't ignore the signs. If vampires are establishing a foothold in Brighthaven, they likely have a hidden nest—or allies among the populace."

The mayor's fingers drummed on the desk, anxiety etched into her features. "That's a dire accusation, Master Thalion. We pride ourselves on being a bastion of peace and scholarship, but we're not blind. I've already asked the local guard to enforce curfews, though it's done little good. If you can help expose and eliminate this threat, you'll have my support. Is there anything you need from me?"

Cedric considered. "We'd appreciate introductions to the town guard's captain, any witnesses to these incidents, and, if possible, private lodging secure enough to plan our next steps. Though we've taken rooms at the Gilded Lantern, we suspect prying eyes abound."

Mayor Adalene nodded. "Captain Farim is a good man. I'll arrange a meeting. As for witnesses, I have a list of farmers who reported drained livestock. Let me gather those records. You can remain here or return tomorrow."

Thalion inclined his head in thanks. "We'll gather our companions first, then come back tomorrow morning for those reports. In the meantime, please maintain vigilance. Vampires can appear deceptively normal, or ensnare others to do their bidding."

Adalene sighed. "The last thing we need is betrayal from within. Very well. I shall do what I can."

They exchanged farewells. Outside, Cedric and Thalion confided in one another that the mayor seemed genuine, but the hints of infiltration disturbed them. For a vampire nest to operate effectively in a place like Brighthaven, it would likely have bribed or manipulated locals. Their steps quickened, eager to rendezvous with Elara and Mira at the Gilded Lantern and share all they had learned.

The four reunited in a private corner of the Gilded Lantern's common room. By then, the sun dipped low in the sky, painting the streets in warm oranges and purples. Over a modest meal, they quietly shared the rumors of drained livestock, clandestine shipments, and missing travelers. Hushed conversations turned to the likelihood that a vampiric nest had taken root. The possibility set them on edge; vampires, while not unbeatable, presented unique challenges. Their powers of charm, transformation, and regeneration made them formidable foes. Worse, if they had embedded themselves among the populace, distinguishing ally from enemy would be no simple matter.

"Captain Farim might be a good place to start," Cedric concluded. "If we can coordinate with the guard, we'll have more eyes and ears on the ground. The mayor's willingness to help is a boon."

Mira nodded, sipping her tea. "We also have to keep watch for sabotage. If vampires suspect we're onto them, they could strike first—or incite others to turn on us."

Elara gazed around, mindful of the other patrons. Though no one seemed to be eavesdropping, the sense of hidden tension never left her. "I'll speak with the local temple tomorrow, see if they've recorded any unnatural visits at night. A place of worship for the Goddess of Dawn might repel or at least unnerve these creatures, which could force them into more desperate actions."

Thalion tapped his fingers on the table. "We should also look into arcane wards. If we can identify the vampires, isolating them would be easier. But let's not jump to conclusions. Let's gather hard evidence, or we risk accusing innocent people."

They agreed on a plan: In the morning, split tasks between gathering intel from Captain Farim, speaking to farmers and possible witnesses, and seeking out any magical or divine means of detecting vampire activity. If all went well, they might flush out the nest quietly. If not, a confrontation was inevitable.

Before retiring to their rooms, they asked Odalys if she'd heard anything about strangers lurking around the inn. She merely shrugged, explaining that travelers come and go, and she rarely saw suspicious behavior. Still, she offered to keep an eye out for them. The group thanked her, parted ways, and slipped upstairs.

Night fell over Brighthaven in a hush occasionally broken by distant laughter or the bark of a stray dog. In the small hours, a drizzle began to patter on the inn's rooftop, lulling the weary adventurers into a restless sleep. Unknown to them, a pair of red-tinged eyes watched from an alley across the street, quietly measuring the heroes' silhouettes in the second-floor windows.

Dawn broke under a sky of molten pink and gold, a fitting tribute for a place named Brighthaven. The heroes rose, groggy but resolute, sharing a quick breakfast in the inn's common room. They made their way to the guard barracks, a sturdy structure near the eastern wall. The sign above its archway bore Brighthaven's sunburst crest, an emblem promising vigilance and order.

Inside, they found Captain Farim, a tall, broad-shouldered man with keen dark eyes and a short, well-kept beard. His uniform was practical: chain mail over a quilted gambeson, a short sword at his hip. He greeted them politely but with the guarded caution of a man who'd seen too many well-armed strangers pass through. Nevertheless, the mention of King Alaric's crest softened his demeanor.

They convened in a small office. Farim offered them seats at a long wooden table. Papers and ink pots cluttered the space; obviously, the man had been tracking multiple issues simultaneously. He wasted no time.

"So you're the ones Mayor Adalene mentioned," Farim said, voice grave. "Vampires, is it? My men have heard rumors of pale figures prowling farmland by night, leaving livestock drained. The farmers think it's a pack of wolves, but the condition of the bodies says otherwise."

Cedric folded his arms. "Yes. We're concerned it's not just random. Vampires often appear in small covens or operate under a master with a broader agenda."

The captain let out a weary sigh. "We're stretched thin dealing with bandits along the trade routes. If there's a vampire threat, we need proof—and guidance. Don't get me wrong; I'll help however I can. But accusations of vampirism can sow panic. I can't arrest people without evidence."

Thalion nodded. "We wouldn't ask you to arrest innocent citizens. But we suspect infiltration, possibly among traveling merchants or wealthy patrons. Vampires sometimes pose as aristocrats, using charm to manipulate towns."

Farim frowned. "We do have a few new merchants in town. Some left quickly after a few nights. Others remain, but I can't say any have raised alarms... except rumors about one well-dressed man who arrives after dusk to hold private dealings. He calls himself Calisto, claims he's from the east, dealing in exotic silks."

Mira exchanged a glance with Elara. A merchant who only appears after dusk? That was a red flag. "Where can we find this Calisto?"

"Usually at the Gold Leaf Emporium, a warehouse near the docks. He rents a small office there for nighttime transactions."

Elara rubbed her chin. "Nighttime dealings. Very suspicious indeed. We'd like to see him for ourselves."

The captain hesitated. "I don't have direct evidence that he's a vampire, but I can't deny it's odd. The warehouse is heavily guarded, and no one sees him by day. It's your call if you want to investigate. Just don't start a panic."

Cedric nodded firmly. "We'll proceed with caution. Thank you, Captain Farim."

In parting, the guard captain promised to send one of his men—Lieutenant Rowan—to discreetly assist if needed. He also provided the names of farmers who had seen prowlers on their land: the Forester family in the north fields, the Kroger estate by the river. Armed with these leads, the party left the barracks, determined to catch the elusive Calisto in the act.

Splitting up, the companions spent the remainder of the day pursuing their investigations. Thalion and Mira visited the farmers, confirming accounts of tall, pale figures who moved too quickly to be mortal. The creatures vanished into the night, leaving behind dead animals drained of blood. Meanwhile, Cedric and Elara headed to the local temple, where the resident clerics confirmed that an unusual number of townspeople had approached them about nightmares and unexplained bite marks. Though these folks had since vanished, likely fleeing their shame or fear, it solidified the suspicion that a vampire presence lurked in Brighthaven.

By late afternoon, the group reunited in a secluded alley behind the Gilded Lantern. The tension was palpable. If Calisto was indeed a vampire or connected to them, confronting him directly could be dangerous—especially since he employed armed guards. They decided on a stealthy approach: wait near the Gold Leaf Emporium until nightfall, watch who entered or left, then confront him if the evidence supported it.

As dusk draped the town in purple shadows, they slipped into position: the Emporium was a large brick building by the river's edge, a loading dock out front stacked with crates. The windows were shuttered, allowing only thin lines of golden light to escape. A pair of armed men in black cloaks patrolled the perimeter, talking in hushed tones. Several wagons stood parked by the dock, bearing no obvious markings. The entire operation exuded secrecy.

The heroes waited behind a stack of barrels, the night air chilled by a light breeze off the water. Cedric quietly tested the edge of his sword. Elara clutched her shield, channeling a subtle prayer of protection. Mira readied a detection spell to sense undead, while Thalion prepared illusions to cloak them if needed. Tension coiled in their muscles, each alert for the slightest sound.

At last, the doors opened with a grating squeal. A tall man emerged, clad in a finely tailored coat, his skin unnaturally pale under the moonlight. His hair was slicked back, and a faint smirk curved his thin lips. Behind him followed two more figures, similarly pale, though their eyes gleamed red in the darkness. Guards parted to allow them passage, bowing obsequiously. The party recognized that gesture: it was the deference of minions to a superior.

Elara's senses prickled. "Vampires," she mouthed silently.

Cedric gestured for quiet. They waited, hoping the trio would move out into the open. But the group lingered by the warehouse entrance, conversing in hushed tones. Mira tried to inch closer. The floorboards of the loading dock creaked beneath her subtle footsteps. She cast a minor cantrip to sharpen her hearing.

"—shipments to the northern keep," the tall man was saying. "We mustn't fail. Our patron's patience grows thin."

One of the pale followers hissed, "More adventurers have arrived in town. There are rumors they destroyed a wyvern. They might cause trouble."

Calisto—the tall man—narrowed his eyes. "We'll handle them. If they search for us, we'll strike first. The Shadow Nexus demands obedience, and we are sworn to see its influence spread. Stonehaven must kneel."

Mira's heart pounded. The mention of the Nexus confirmed it: these were not just opportunistic vampires but active agents of the darkness. She eased back to rejoin her companions, trembling with adrenaline.

Cedric nodded grimly when she relayed the conversation. "No more doubt—we confront them now. If they slip away, we lose our best chance to unravel this nest."

Before they could spring into action, a faint clank behind them made them freeze. Another group of black-cloaked figures had appeared from the shadows. The heroes found themselves surrounded—a classic pincer maneuver. Feral red eyes shone in the alley, accompanied by low hisses. They had walked into an ambush.

A tense heartbeat passed, then the vampires attacked. The ambushers lunged with preternatural speed, hissing and baring fangs. Cedric and Elara met them head-on, steel flashing under the moonlight. Cedric's blade connected with one attacker's chest in a powerful thrust. To his alarm, it barely penetrated the vampire's unnatural flesh. Only repeated strikes to vital spots or the use of enchanted weaponry would truly harm them.

Elara raised her shield, channeling a burst of divine light from the goddess. The closest vampire reeled back, snarling in pain as the radiant energy seared undead flesh. "They fear the Light!" Elara shouted, pressing the advantage. Another pale attacker circled behind her, only to recoil when she turned, shield blazing. Where her shield's emblem glowed brightest, the vampires hissed and retreated.

Meanwhile, Thalion unleashed a wave of arcane force. Purple flames crackled from his staff, wrapping around the ankles of two attackers. Though the flames wouldn't kill them outright, it slowed their movement significantly. "Mira!" Thalion called, "They're pinned—hit them now!"

Mira, staff in hand, traced an intricate sigil in the air. A swirling orb of light formed at the tip, intensifying until it burned with brilliant energy. She hurled it at the entangled vampires, the impact releasing a shockwave of luminous force. Both creatures shrieked, staggering, smoke rising from their scorched garments. One collapsed, dissolving into ash, while the other scrambled away, heavily injured but still alive.

Despite these successes, more vampires emerged from the warehouse and the alley. Calisto himself stood on the loading dock, arms crossed, a sardonic grin playing on his lips as he watched the fight unfold. "So these are the vaunted heroes," he murmured. "Perhaps a worthy test of my new minions."

Cedric parried a vicious swipe from one vampire, a gaunt figure with elongated claws. Sparks flew where steel met razor-like nails. The creature's eyes glowed with a cunning malevolence. With a fierce grunt, Cedric pivoted, driving the pommel of his sword into the vampire's temple. It stumbled, giving Cedric an opening to slash across its neck. Yet the vampire did not fall easily; it hissed, still clawing at him. Only when Elara advanced, sword alight with divine fury, did the undead fiend recoil and dart away.

"They're playing with us," Elara spat, breathing hard. "We need to break through or risk getting overwhelmed."

On the other side of the skirmish, Thalion found himself grappling with a lithe female vampire, her speed astonishing. She evaded his blasts, darting in close to rake him with her claws. Blood blossomed on Thalion's sleeve, though he refused to cry out. Summoning a surge of wind, he threw her back against the warehouse wall. Even pinned, she hissed, baring elongated fangs that dripped with venom.

Mira sent arcs of lightning crackling toward the group of minions. The spell caught three at once, locking them in convulsions of pain. Yet another vampire popped out of the shadows behind her, mouth parted in an inhuman snarl.

With no time to turn, Mira braced for impact—but a crossbow bolt whistled through the air, striking the vampire squarely in the chest. It collapsed, writhing, as a second bolt found its heart. The creature disintegrated into ash.

Surprised, Mira whirled to see Lieutenant Rowan and a handful of Brighthaven guards rushing in to aid them. "Reinforcements!" she cried in relief.

Rowan nodded, reloading his crossbow with a speed born of desperation. "Captain Farim sent us. Seems we arrived just in time!"

With the guards adding crossbow fire, the vampire thralls found themselves outmatched. One by one, they fell or fled, screeching into the night. The heroes pressed their advantage, cornering the remaining enemies against the warehouse wall. Elara held her shield high, the radiant symbol flaring with righteous power that forced the vampires backward. Cedric's sword and Thalion's spells cut off their escape.

Calisto watched the rout with cold detachment. "Pathetic," he drawled, stepping forward at last. "Fine. I'll handle this myself." In a burst of inhuman speed, he lunged at Elara, claws slashing. She blocked the blow, but the impact reverberated through her shield arm. The tall vampire's strength was monstrous.

Cedric surged in to flank. Calisto danced aside, moving like a blur. He lashed out with one pale hand, seizing Cedric by the throat in a crushing grip. The knight choked, sword dropping from his hand. Elara gasped, slashing at Calisto's arm, but the vampire twisted away, dragging Cedric backward.

"We can't kill them all, but at least I'll have a hostage," Calisto snarled, fangs bared. "Perhaps I'll drain you, knight, so your friends know the price of meddling in my affairs."

Mira and Thalion converged, desperation fueling their spells. Thalion conjured a blinding flash of light, aiming to disrupt Calisto's senses. The vampire hissed, momentarily disoriented, loosening his grip on Cedric's throat. Mira seized her chance, launching a streak of brilliant arcane energy that slammed into Calisto's chest. He staggered, releasing Cedric entirely. The knight collapsed to the ground, coughing.

Enraged, Calisto glared, his eyes burning red. He made as if to lunge again, but realized the tide had turned. Guards now formed a ring with crossbows trained on him, Elara's shield glowed like a blazing sun, and Thalion's staff crackled with lethal magic. Even a vampire lord had limits.

"This isn't over," Calisto hissed. With a supernatural leap, he vaulted over a crate, disappearing into the darkness beyond. Lieutenant Rowan cursed, firing a bolt that missed wide. The final stragglers among Calisto's minions also scattered into the alleyways, leaving behind only ashes, blood spatters, and the acrid stench of burned undead flesh.

In the sudden stillness, the heroes stood panting, adrenaline still coursing through their veins. Lieutenant Rowan and the guards approached, crossbows lowered but still at the ready. Overhead, the moon slipped behind a cloud, plunging the scene into half-light. A few stray crates smoked where spells had singed them.

Cedric rubbed his bruised throat, voice hoarse. "Thank you for the timely rescue," he managed, nodding to Rowan.

The guard's eyes flicked to the piles of ash swirling in the breeze. "We should be thanking you. Without your stand, these fiends might've gained even more ground in Brighthaven. Captain Farim suspected something was brewing tonight... We came as soon as we could."

Elara approached Rowan, offering a tired but grateful smile. "We owe Captain Farim our gratitude. It's clear you saved us from being overrun."

Thalion glanced toward the direction Calisto fled. "He escaped, but we've wounded him. That should buy us some time. We need to discover where he's holed up... and who else might be part of his coven."

Mira nodded, retrieving her staff from where it had clattered. "At least we confirmed the threat is real. Vampires are here, allied with the Shadow Nexus, no less. Brighthaven is in danger."

Rowan motioned for the guards to spread out, searching the perimeter for any sign of returning vampires. None remained, though the ground bore evidence of the brief but furious clash: scorch marks, blood spatter, scattered weapons. "I'll report this to the captain and Mayor Adalene immediately," Rowan said. "You all should come with me. If the townspeople see you standing with the guard, they'll know you're allies."

So they walked together through the dimly lit streets, the hush broken by the occasional bark of a watch dog or the flicker of a lantern in a window. Word of the battle must have spread with unnerving speed; though it was late, heads appeared in doorways, and murmured questions followed them: "Is it safe?" "What happened?" "Are those the heroes from the inn?" Lieutenant Rowan answered in brief, urging people to remain indoors for their safety.

By the time they reached the guard barracks, a small crowd had gathered. Captain Farim stood near the entrance, arms folded, a stern expression etched on his face. But when he saw Cedric clutching his throat, Elara's shield glowing with divine residue, and Thalion's robes singed, he understood a grave confrontation had just occurred.

After Rowan's succinct report, Farim spoke: "So Calisto is confirmed a vampire, leading a group of undead. This is worse than I feared—but you've exposed them, which is more than we managed in months. The people must know they have champions willing to protect them."

Mayor Adalene arrived soon after, hair disheveled, having been roused from her bed. She listened to the tale with eyes wide, occasionally pressing a hand to her mouth in shock. "All this... in our very streets. By the Light, we owe you a debt." She bowed her head to the heroes. "Now, the entire town will see you for what you are: saviors in this dark time. Anything you need, you shall have it."

Cedric raised a hand. "We don't do this for reward, Mayor. Only to ensure Stonehaven's safety. Still, we might ask for your cooperation in searching the city for Calisto's lair. He won't hide forever."

Elara seconded this. "Also, we should warn your people about the signs of vampiric presence: those who only appear at night, fear holy symbols, have pale complexions, or maintain suspicious business dealings. That might flush out conspirators."

Adalene nodded fervently. "At first light, we'll alert the public. But carefully—no panic. Captain Farim will coordinate a plan to identify and isolate suspected individuals. We'll also ask the local temple to provide wards of protection for the households that want them."

Lieutenant Rowan chimed in: "And we'll double the night patrols. Our men may not be as experienced in fighting vampires as you, but we're quick learners. We'll station archers with silver-tipped arrows, too."

The crowd listening in the courtyard murmured approval. Fear still lingered in their eyes, but hope shone alongside it. A few townspeople stepped forward, uttering words of gratitude and vowing to aid however they could—spreading warnings, offering safe houses, or volunteering in the guard. It was a tangible testament to how the heroes' stand had kindled a spark of resistance in a town that only hours earlier felt helpless.

With the immediate threat quelled, the mayor insisted the heroes rest. But before they could retire, an elderly man pushed through the crowd, leaning on a cane. His face was lined with age, but his eyes were bright with urgency.

"Begging your pardon, good sirs and ladies," he said in a wavering voice. "I'm Harriman, a scholar here in Brighthaven. I've studied local history, especially the legends of vampiric lineages. I must speak with you—privately, if possible."

Intrigued, the group glanced at each other, then at Captain Farim. He shrugged. "Harriman is well-known, though somewhat reclusive. He might have knowledge worth hearing."

So they ushered Harriman into a smaller side room adjacent to the courtyard. By lantern light, the old scholar explained that he had been researching old manuscripts from the city's founding era. One volume described a clandestine sect that once built catacombs under Brighthaven. This sect was rumored to practice blood rites, presumably worshipping vampiric lords. Though the sect was believed purged centuries ago, Harriman speculated that remnants might still exist, hidden in underground passages.

Mira exchanged a startled look with Thalion. "That could be where Calisto is hiding... a subterranean labyrinth beneath the city."

Harriman nodded. "Yes, child. In an old portion of my notes, there's mention of an entrance in a ruined crypt near the temple courtyard, sealed long ago by wards. But I fear those wards might be weakened by the corruption you speak of."

Elara felt a chill. A secret crypt beneath the temple's courtyard? If that was compromised, the entire city could be threatened from below. "This is vital information," she said softly. "Thank you, Harriman."

The scholar looked relieved, as if unburdened of a terrifying secret. "If you truly seek the source of Brighthaven's vampiric infiltration, that crypt is where I'd look. But be warned: the old texts mention traps and guardians placed by the sect. It will be no simple matter to venture there."

Cedric closed his eyes briefly, steeling himself. "We've traversed haunted woods and faced a wyvern's claws. We'll manage. The bigger question is: do we have time to rest, or must we strike tonight?"

Harriman shook his head. "The wards, if not fully broken, might hold a little longer. A day or two, perhaps. But the sooner you act, the less chance the vampires have to reinforce their lair."

With that dire note, the group thanked Harriman and emerged into the courtyard once more. The mayor, catching wind of the crypt, insisted they plan carefully. Captain Farim offered to station guards near the temple courtyard in case the vampires tried to flee or ambush. The heroes agreed. That left one final question: rest or strike?

Elara, eyes heavy with fatigue, said, "We can't fight effectively if we're exhausted. A few hours of sleep might save us from mistakes. Let's reconvene at dawn, prepare wards and silvered weapons, then descend into the crypt."

The others concurred. And so, with a final round of thanks from the gathered townsfolk, they trudged back to the Gilded Lantern, limbs aching, minds buzzing with the revelations of the night. Word had spread that they drove off a vampire ambush, and as they walked, small crowds parted for them like waves, whispering admiration.

Inside the inn, Odalys fussed over their cuts and bruises, providing hot tea and warm towels. She seemed on the verge of tears, repeating how grateful she was for their defense of Brighthaven. The heroes offered humble reassurance, then ascended to their rooms. For the second night in a row, they slept fitfully, haunted by images of red eyes, fanged smiles, and subterranean crypts brimming with untold horrors. Yet the knowledge that the townsfolk now trusted them—and that they'd formed a plan to root out the danger—was a balm to their weary spirits.

Morning arrived with a crisp clarity, as though the stormy tension of the previous night had been swept away by fresh breezes. At dawn's first light, the heroes gathered in the Gilded Lantern's common room, checking gear and bandaging lingering scrapes. Cedric's throat still bore faint bruises, but he could speak normally. Elara's shield glimmered with renewed blessings, while Mira's staff hummed with energy from her restorative meditations. Thalion's robes had been patched and cleaned, but the determined set of his jaw hinted at no illusions about the trials ahead.

They stepped out into Brighthaven's main square. Captain Farim waited, along with a contingent of guards armed with crossbows and short swords. Mayor Adalene was there as well, flanked by Harriman, the scholar, who clutched a satchel of scrolls. A handful of curious citizens milled about, though the mayor urged them to maintain a respectful distance. After the horrors of last night, everyone understood the stakes.

"The crypt entrance is in a neglected corner of the temple grounds," Harriman explained, his voice quivering with excitement and fear. "I'll show you the way."

Farim stepped in. "My men will secure the perimeter. If you manage to flush out vampires from below, we'll be ready."

Cedric thanked him. "We're grateful, Captain. The more we can coordinate, the better the chance we sever this coven at its root."

The heroes marched through Brighthaven's winding streets, watched by silent onlookers who seemed torn between awe and dread. In half an hour, they reached the temple courtyard—a tranquil space of flagstones and hedges, overshadowed by the temple's tall spire. Normally, worshipers and clergy bustled here, offering prayers to the

Goddess of Dawn. But that morning, the courtyard was deserted, the atmosphere heavy with a sense of foreboding.

Harriman led them to an overgrown corner behind a marble colonnade, where vines choked a small grate set into the ground. Ancient runes circled its rim. Though many were faded, Elara sensed a weak divine presence; indeed, old wards to keep something sealed below. She knelt, murmuring a prayer, but felt only a flicker of the protective magic that might have once been formidable.

"We'll break this seal carefully," Thalion said. "No telling what traps might remain."

Mira stepped forward, staff in hand. "Let me try to unravel it gently. If it's warded, I can disarm it without setting off a backlash—assuming I read these runes correctly." She began chanting a quiet incantation, tracing patterns in the air. Tiny sparks danced over the grate's metal. At first, the vines shriveled, releasing the rusted edges. Then the old runes flared once with a golden glow before flickering out entirely, like a candle guttering in a draft.

A dull *clunk* sounded, and the grate lifted. Stale air wafted up, smelling of mold and something older, more malevolent. Cedric peered into the darkness, hand on his sword hilt. "This must be it—our entry into the catacombs. Let's go."

Elara touched her amulet. "May the Light guide us."

With a final nod to Captain Farim and Harriman, the four heroes descended a narrow spiral of stone steps. The temperature dropped immediately, and the walls dripped with moisture.

Darkness engulfed them as the grate sealed above, footsteps echoing on the narrow stone steps. A chill breeze stirred the stale air, thick with a damp musk that clung to the catacomb walls. At first, only the soft glow of Thalion's illusions and the warm halo of Elara's shield lit their way, revealing decades—perhaps centuries—of dust coating old carvings. Mira's staff hummed faintly, its tip aglow with an arcane orb that cast dancing shadows along the tight corridor.

Sir Cedric led the descent, sword in hand. **Clink. Clink.** Each footfall resonated with caution. The spiral staircase eventually widened into a low-ceilinged passage, the walls carved with faded reliefs—sun motifs, winding vines, and fragments of runic text. Once, this might have been a sanctified undercroft. Now, it lay neglected and all too silent.

Elara brushed her fingers over a carved sun symbol. A weak pulse of holy resonance stirred under her touch, as if the old wards recognized her faith. "These wards... They still carry traces of light magic. But they're almost extinguished."

"They'll offer little protection if vampires have truly made this place their lair," Thalion said quietly. He turned in a slow circle, illusions flickering across the walls. "We should be wary of illusions or traps they might have set in defense. Vampires love cunning deceptions."

Mira, trailing her staff along the floor, peered into branching side passages. Broken sarcophagi, collapsed archways—signs of a place once revered, now defiled. "No telling how far these corridors run. If Harriman's books are right, an entire labyrinth might lie beneath Brighthaven. We could get lost if we rush."

Cedric nodded, jaw set with quiet resolve. "One step at a time. Let's search methodically. Keep your guard high. If we can locate the main crypt or nest, we'll cut off the head of this vampiric threat."

With unanimous agreement, they advanced deeper. Cobwebs draped corners, and rivulets of water trickled along cracks in the floor. Now and then, a faint scratching noise or subtle scuffle made them pause. Yet each time they investigated an alcove, they found only ancient bones, half-collapsed tombs, or rats scurrying out of reach. The tension grew taut, like a string wound too tightly. They knew something lurked here.

Their vigilance paid off upon reaching a wide chamber supported by twin rows of columns. Sparse moonlight filtered through a grate overhead, illuminating dust motes in the stale air. The columns bore chipped reliefs of robed figures, their faces scratched away—defilement by some long-ago intruder. At the chamber's center stood a massive stone sarcophagus, its lid askew.

Elara approached carefully, shield raised. Mira moved alongside her, staff tip flaring to reveal a yawning gap where the coffin's lid had been pried open. The interior was empty, save for tattered wrappings and a moldering cloak. A stale, fetid odor hung around it.

Cedric knelt, examining the marks on the sarcophagus' edge. "Claw marks. Something forced its way out... or in," he observed grimly.

Before they could speculate further, a rustling hiss emanated from behind one of the columns. Eyes turned, muscles tensed. Thalion conjured a quick illusion—a luminous figure stepping forth to bait any hidden foe. Immediately, a pair of gaunt, pale arms lunged from the shadows, raking at the illusion. Unsuccessful, they snapped back in frustration.

"Show yourself," Cedric commanded, edging toward the column with sword poised.

From the gloom emerged two vampire thralls, gaunt and feral. Their eyes glowed faintly red, lips curled in silent snarls. One wore a shredded vest, revealing patches of dead flesh. The other clutched a rusted dagger. They hissed, crouching low, ready to pounce.

Elara wasted no time. She stepped forward, shield blazing with a surge of holy light. The thralls shrieked, recoiling, arms raised to block the glare. One stumbled backward, nearly toppling over broken debris.

In that instant, Cedric lunged, delivering a precise strike at the nearest thrall's neck. While not an instant kill, it staggered the vampire, blackish blood seeping from the wound. Thalion followed with a wave of illusions shaped into ghostly chains that latched onto its limbs. The thrall howled, immobilized.

Meanwhile, the second thrall lashed at Mira, dagger glinting. She sidestepped, staff arcing overhead. A spray of crackling frost hammered the vampire, encasing its arms in ice. It roared in pain and tried to break free, thrashing violently. Mira grimaced, holding the spell as best she could.

Elara sprinted across the crypt, sword raised, sending a burst of radiant energy into the thrall's frozen chest. A muffled shriek echoed, followed by the stink of burning flesh. In seconds, the creature slumped, dissolving into ash. The first thrall, still chained by illusions, hissed in mounting panic. Its red eyes darted between the heroes, searching for an escape route.

"Talk," Cedric growled, leveling his sword at the creature's throat. "Where's your master? Is Calisto down here?"

The thrall sneered, revealing rotted fangs. "Fools," it spat. "Calisto is but a pawn. Our mistress weaves the true threads. You can't stop her return."

Mira exchanged a concerned look with Thalion. Mistress? Another vampiric power behind Calisto? The thrall let out a low cackle. Then its face contorted in agony—some internal command, perhaps from a vampire overlord. It convulsed, smoke rising from its body. Moments later, it collapsed into ash, leaving only a hiss that died in the still air.

"That was no normal death," Elara whispered, gaze on the ash pile. "It seems someone enforced silence upon it, likely by a blood pact. Whoever's controlling them must be powerful."

"Or ancient," Thalion added gravely. "We'd best be careful."

Regrouping, they realized the presence of a greater vampire mistress or master orchestrating these thralls. The notion that Calisto served someone else—a more formidable undead—sent a shiver through them. The crypt stretched deeper, hallways branching in multiple directions. The confrontation just now confirmed they were on the right track.

Pressing onward, they found an arched passage leading down another flight of steps. The air grew colder, laced with an unmistakable scent of decay. At intervals, torches flickered in wall sconces, their flames unnaturally still, as if not truly fed by normal oil. Each step echoed, intensifying the hush.

Mira's detection spell thrummed softly, picking up faint undead signatures ahead. "They're not far," she murmured, sweat beading on her brow. "If they sense us, we might face more thralls."

"Then we strike swiftly," Cedric said, tightening his grip on his sword. "Let's keep illusions at the forefront, lure them out while we maintain an advantage."

Thalion shaped an illusion of a lone guard wandering the corridor, appearing as a hapless mortal. They advanced behind this illusory scout, mindful of traps. Sure enough, a half-hidden door to the left slid open, revealing two vampires armed with short swords. They lunged at the illusion, only to pass right through it. Confused, they turned—but too late. Cedric and Mira unleashed a coordinated assault: his sword cleaved one vampire's arm, and her arcane blast seared the other, forcing it to reel back. Meanwhile, Elara brandished her shield, the faint hum of divine energy repelling the undead.

The ambush ended quickly, the vampires dispatched with minimal fuss. Their ashes scattered, leaving no chance to glean further information. But the momentary confrontation confirmed more minions lurked here, presumably defending a central lair.

Eventually, the group emerged into a large crypt chamber. Rows of ornate stone coffins lined the walls, each bearing chiseled names worn by time. But it was what lay in the center that set their hearts pounding: a recently constructed dais of black marble, inscribed with fresh runes that pulsed faintly with negative magic. An altar, smeared with dark stains, stood on top. Candles flickered in a circle, their flames a sickly violet hue.

"This is no relic of the old temple," Elara said in a tight voice, stepping closer with her shield raised. "They must have built this altar to siphon or store energy. Possibly for performing vampiric rituals."

A side nook revealed a small library of sorts—half a dozen books and scrolls, plus vials of unsettling contents. Thalion scanned the titles, shock twisting his features. "These references to the Shadow Nexus... summoning rites... attempts to amplify vampiric power through an ancient wellspring of darkness."

Cedric exhaled, tension thick in his chest. "So that's the bigger plan. Calisto was a pawn in something far older. Their so-called mistress is likely trying to resurrect or harness the Nexus's vestiges here in Brighthaven. If they succeed, the entire town—maybe all of Stonehaven—could be swarmed again by horrors."

Elara's face hardened. "We must destroy this altar and any relics they use to connect with the Nexus. Quick, before more thralls or the mistress herself arrives."

They moved swiftly, Thalion weaving illusions that dampened the runes' aura, while Elara splashed holy water across the altar, reciting a cleansing prayer. Mira created a shockwave of pure arcane force, cracking the black marble dais. Cedric hammered at the structure with his sword, aiding the arcane blasts. The dais fractured, splintering under combined might. The runes flickered and died, their negative hum silenced.

A chorus of screeches erupted from behind a far archway—clearly, the destruction of this unholy site triggered alarm among the undead. The four braced themselves for a fresh wave of foes. But the sound receded, suggesting a retreat. Perhaps the vampires realized they were outmatched. Or they lured them deeper into a final confrontation.

Satisfied they had neutralized this makeshift shrine, the heroes pressed on. Another corridor led deeper, but the presence of vampiric energies felt weaker now. Thalion suspected the nest might be spread out or in flux. One possibility: if the mistress sensed the altar's destruction, she might flee rather than risk a direct fight. Nonetheless, the party advanced, hoping to root out the vampiric threat entirely.

They found only deserted passages, a few broken coffins, and signs that undead had once occupied these halls—bloodstains, tattered robes, a half-open chest of worthless trinkets. The uneasy hush suggested the vampires had withdrawn. Could it be a trap? Cedric remained on edge, expecting an ambush around every corner. Yet no further attacks came.

Eventually, they circled back to the staircase. The crypt was eerily silent. They had found no grand antechamber or a final boss—just that unholy altar. Elara's intuition whispered that a greater enemy lingered beyond their reach, but for now, the crypt seemed purged of immediate danger. The four ascended, hearts heavy with the knowledge they had won only a partial victory. Calisto and the unseen mistress still roamed free.

Emerging into the daylight, the heroes blinked under the sudden brightness. Captain Farim and Lieutenant Rowan, along with a squad of guards, hurried to meet them.

Tense expressions softened into relief at seeing the party intact.

Elara recounted their findings: the new dais, the vampiric paraphernalia, the subtle references to the Shadow Nexus. Rowans face paled, while the mayor—who had also arrived—listened grimly. "So they prepared a ritual site under our very feet," Adalene murmured, voice trembling with anger. "I'll see that the temple priests reconsecrate every inch down there. We'll post guards too."

Farim nodded, determination in his eyes. "We'll scour every corridor, though we lack your skill in illusions or holy might."

Mira offered a reassuring smile. "We'll coordinate with you. If the vampires retreated, they might be planning to strike elsewhere, or attempt a deeper infiltration. Let's ensure Brighthaven's watch stays vigilant."

The mayor bowed deeply, sincerity shining in her gaze. "You've saved us from unimaginable horrors. Please—let me provide a secure place for you to plan. If you need to remain in Brighthaven, we'll see that you have resources."

Cedric looked to his companions. "We should rest, restock, and maintain a watchful presence. Our journey continues, but for now, ensuring this town's safety is paramount."

Elara and Thalion both agreed. They recognized that this cat-and-mouse with the vampires could be ongoing, but the discovery of the altar was a significant blow to the undead's plans. By forging an alliance with Brighthaven's authorities, they'd stand a better chance at cornering Calisto and exposing the mistress behind him.

As the sun arced overhead, the party returned to the Gilded Lantern for a much-needed break. Citizens along the way paused to express thanks, offering small tokens or heartfelt blessings. Though the day was far from over, a sense of solidarity had blossomed. The heroes realized they had found not only foes to challenge them but also allies eager to stand against darkness. That unwavering support kindled their spirits, reminding them that the deeper they ventured into Stonehaven's perils, the more unity they forged with the very people they sought to protect.

Somewhere in Brighthaven's shadows, Calisto nursed his wounds, his pride stung by the heroes' defiance, waiting for orders from a more sinister power. But in the hearts of the four companions, a renewed resolve burned bright. Allies and enemies alike had been revealed. The stage was set for the next phase of their quest—one that would take them deeper into Stonehaven's secrets. For Brighthaven stood as both a testament to the realm's resilience and a warning that darkness, though pushed back, would not vanish without a final reckoning.

Thus, Chapter 5 drew to a close on the threshold of new discoveries and looming dangers. The heroes had tested their bonds in the chaos of an ambush, gaining fresh allies and deeper insight into the shadow spreading across the land. And in the hush of the Gilded Lantern's upper rooms, they prepared for whatever awaited them in the nights to come, forging plans with Brighthaven's defenders for the battles yet to be fought.

6

THE MINOTAUR MAZE

Sir Cedric, Lady Elara, Thalion, and Mira departed Brighthaven amid heartfelt farewells and renewed vows of alliance. Although their sojourn in the bustling town had been intense—with vampire ambushes, clandestine dealings, and the revelation of an underground crypt—it had also fortified the bond between the companions and the grateful townsfolk. Word of their heroics spread quickly, granting them fresh respect and resources for the continuing quest. Mayor Adalene, the scholar Harriman, and Captain Farim all helped gather information on the next steps toward the Shadow Nexus. Clues pointed northward, to a foreboding mountain range known for labyrinthine passages and legendary, horned denizens: the Minotaurs.

Brighthaven's gates closed behind the heroes as dawn's first light gilded the horizon. Their horses trotted across well-worn roads that soon turned into rougher trails. Every mile put more distance between them and the relative safety of the town, drawing them nearer to the Labyrinthine Mountains—so named for the winding caverns, sudden cliff faces, and twisting valleys that snaked through the peaks. Ancient stories claimed a tribe of Minotaurs lived there, masters of cunning and brute strength, fiercely territorial and rarely welcoming to outsiders.

Cedric guided his gray stallion at the forefront, watchful for signs of trouble. The events in Brighthaven still weighed on his mind: Calisto the vampire had escaped, and while the heroes had disrupted his plans, Cedric couldn't shake the feeling that they would cross paths again. Nevertheless, they had little choice but to proceed. The Shadow Nexus stirred with every passing day, and time was a luxury they did not possess.

Behind him, Elara's posture remained upright, though her expression bore weariness from previous battles. She rested a hand over her heart, feeling the gentle resonance of her goddess's protection. She silently prayed for strength, mindful that the deeper they ventured into uncharted territory, the more difficult it would become to keep the party safe. Nearby, Thalion rode in thoughtful silence, occasionally conjuring small illusions of the mountainous terrain in the air to confirm their route, while Mira alternated between studying a map and gazing at the shifting clouds, her magical senses attuned to any arcane disruptions that might signal danger.

They traveled for several days. The farmland and rolling hills gave way to rockier soil, sparse forests, and increasingly steep inclines. The temperature dipped as the elevation rose. Nights became cold, forcing them to huddle around campfires, exchanging half-spoken concerns about the trials ahead. Rumors abounded: travelers told of monstrous creatures lurking in the ravines, swirling mists that could lead explorers astray, and cryptic stone formations bearing strange carvings.

But of all the stories, the accounts of Minotaurs proved most concerning. Passersby spoke in hushed tones about horns as wide as an axe blade, hooves that stamped the ground like thunder, and a rigid warrior society that forced outsiders to prove their worth—or perish trying. Some caravans even claimed the Minotaurs had built a monumental maze high in the mountains, a living fortress that no ordinary traveler could penetrate.

This knowledge both intrigued and alarmed the heroes. Elara pointed out that a fierce tribe might also harbor a strict code of honor; it was possible the Minotaurs could be reasoned with. Cedric, however, remained skeptical, recalling war stories in which Minotaurs had razed entire garrisons. Thalion believed diplomacy and knowledge of ancient customs might be the key, while Mira took heart in the possibility that cunning illusions and strategy could outwit raw strength.

Late on a blustery afternoon, the group found themselves at the base of a massive cliff that loomed like a fortress wall. Thick clouds gathered overhead, obscuring the higher peaks. A winding path cut into the rock, leading upward in sharp switchbacks. Just as they decided to ascend, thunder rumbled in the distance.

"We can press on or camp here," Cedric suggested, eyeing the darkening sky. "If we continue, we risk getting caught in a storm on the ledge."

Elara tested the air, her senses flaring with caution. "A storm in these heights could be dangerous. A single misstep could send us tumbling."

Yet Thalion stroked his beard thoughtfully. "We're close to the outskirts of Minotaur territory. If we camp here, we might be spotted by their scouts. They patrol the foothills, I've heard, to watch for trespassers."

Mira nodded in agreement. "Better to find some measure of higher ground. Maybe we'll spot a cave or outcropping to shelter us from the weather."

Thus, they continued upward, leading the horses with care. The wind picked up, lashing them with stinging droplets of rain. After an arduous climb, they discovered a shallow cave partially hidden by boulders. With relief, they guided the horses inside, then set about making camp. The interior smelled faintly of old moss and stale air, but it was mercifully dry. They built a small fire, using gathered brush and leftover kindling.

Outside, the storm raged, lightning illuminating the cliffs in eerie flashes. Thunder boomed, echoing against the crags, and for a time, conversation was impossible. Each hero sat lost in thought, the swirl of wind and rain outside mirroring the chaos in their minds. When the storm finally waned, Mira broke the silence with a quiet comment about the land's wild beauty. Elara concurred, adding that such grandeur often sheltered both wonders and terrors.

Night wore on, and one by one, they slipped into restless sleep, each haunted by the knowledge that they stood at the threshold of a realm belonging to powerful, unpredictable foes.

Come morning, the storm clouds had retreated, replaced by a clear blue sky. The newly washed rocks glistened, and rivulets of water trickled down crevices. Mounting their refreshed horses, the party resumed the ascent. The switchback trail was slick from the rain, forcing them to proceed slowly. As they climbed, they noticed the environment changing: the vegetation grew sparse, replaced by hardy shrubs clinging to patches of soil. Strange, jagged rock formations jutted from the mountainside, some adorned with carved symbols that resembled horns or spiraling mazes.

Mira halted her horse at one such carving. "Look at this," she said softly. "It's a labyrinth symbol. And here—horn-like glyphs. Definitely Minotaur script. Must be marking their territory."

Thalion dismounted to inspect it. His keen scholarly eye took in the chiseled lines, the style reminiscent of ancient runic shapes. "They seem to be warnings, or perhaps challenges. If I'm not mistaken, this section reads: 'Prove your strength or turn back.' Another part references a labyrinth—a test of worth."

Cedric exchanged looks with Elara. "So it begins. We may be forced into this test if we want safe passage or answers."

Elara nodded, glancing across the rugged landscape. "Let's remain open-minded. If the Minotaurs hold valuable knowledge about the Nexus's location, we have to approach them carefully. We can't afford a full-scale battle with an entire tribe."

Pressed for time but committed to caution, they proceeded further. The path wound around a craggy peak, and as they cleared the bend, an imposing sight greeted them. A natural plateau stretched ahead, dotted with stone pillars and arranged in a pattern that resembled a giant circle. Farther beyond, the towering entrance of a carved tunnel glowed in the morning light. Standing at the mouth, like statues come to life, were two Minotaurs—each easily seven feet tall, muscular torsos rising above powerful legs, thick horns curving menacingly.

The Minotaur sentinels noticed the heroes at once. They hefted enormous axes and took a few steps forward, hooves striking the stone with a resonant thump. Although menacing in appearance, their posture seemed more guarded than overtly hostile. Cedric raised his empty hand in a universal sign of peaceful intention, though he kept the other hand close to his sword.

One of the Minotaurs spoke in a deep, rumbling voice. "Strangers. Why do you enter the lands of Clan Mazehorn? Speak quickly."

Thalion moved forward, staff angled downward to show he intended no threat. "We are travelers on a quest to stop a great darkness called the Shadow Nexus. Our path leads us through these mountains. We seek safe passage and perhaps counsel, if your clan allows it."

The second Minotaur snorted, exhaling a gust of steam in the chilly air. "The labyrinth is no place for the weak. Turn away, or face the trials."

Elara took a step closer, shield lowered. "We mean no disrespect. We come as allies, not conquerors. If your labyrinth is a trial we must pass, then we shall. But only if you permit us to attempt it."

A tense silence followed. The first Minotaur sized them up, scanning Mira's staff, Thalion's scholarly composure, Cedric's knightly bearing, and Elara's paladin aura. Finally, he gave a curt nod. "You speak with respect. Our clan's ways dictate that outsiders must prove their worth by surviving our maze. Only then may you earn an audience with the Clan Elder. If you fail, your bones remain in the labyrinth forever."

Cedric's jaw tightened. "We accept."

With a low grunt, the sentinel turned and gestured for them to follow. The other Minotaur remained behind, presumably to guard the entrance from additional intruders. Leading the companions past the stone pillars, the Minotaur guided them toward the massive tunnel opening. The air within was cool and dank, the walls adorned with carved symbols akin to those they'd seen on the path.

"Enter. The labyrinth will test your mind, body, and spirit," the Minotaur said. "Return here, unbroken, and we shall see if you are worthy to speak with the Elder."

Lanterns lined the entry passage, flickering with a pale glow. The floor sloped downward, gradually revealing a network of tunnels branching in multiple directions. Each corridor looked identical—rough-hewn stone walls, an arched ceiling, and sporadic runic markings that offered no obvious guidance. A damp, earthen smell permeated everything, mingling with the faint odor of old fires.

Once the sentinel left them, the companions stood at a central junction, uncertainty pricking their nerves. The labyrinth's reputation preceded it: rumor spoke of hidden traps, illusions, and illusions designed to break one's will. If these rumors held any truth, they needed to tread carefully indeed.

Thalion raised a hand, conjuring an orb of pale light that hovered above them. "My illusions might help if the corridor is rigged to confuse us. But we should also watch for physical dangers—pitfalls, hidden blades, anything."

Mira glanced at the runes on the walls, trying to decipher their meaning. "Minotaurs often see mazes as sacred. This might be as much a spiritual journey as a physical puzzle. Let's proceed slowly."

Elara advanced first, trusting her divine senses to alert her to unnatural traps. Cedric followed, sword halfway drawn for quick defense. Step by step, they delved deeper, each corridor they chose seeming to twist back on itself. More than once, they ended up at the same junction, though from an unexpected angle. Frustration mounted, but they kept calm, systematically marking intersections with chalk so they wouldn't repeat mistakes.

An hour passed, maybe more. The labyrinth's winding passages tested their patience. Eventually, they emerged into a large chamber lit by torches. Rows of towering stone columns supported the high ceiling, and at the far end, a massive gate blocked their path. In front of the gate stood two hulking Minotaurs, each gripping a huge club.

As soon as the heroes set foot inside, the Minotaurs rumbled in unison, "To go beyond, prove your strength."

The two guardians charged, clubs whistling through the air. Cedric and Elara rushed to intercept them. The chamber erupted in the clamor of steel on stone. One Minotaur slammed its club down with crushing force, causing cracks in the floor. Elara blocked with her shield, knees buckling under the weight of the blow. Cedric darted to the flank, sword slicing, but the Minotaur's hide was tough as leather, and it shrugged off the shallow wound.

Meanwhile, the second Minotaur roared and barreled at Thalion and Mira. Thalion conjured a barrier of swirling wind, slowing the brute's approach. Mira unleashed a volley of arcane missiles, each bursting against the creature's fur. While this caused it to stagger, the Minotaur's momentum remained formidable. It forced its way closer, swinging its club in a deadly arc. Mira ducked, heart pounding, narrowly avoiding a direct hit.

Elara counterattacked her adversary with a burst of divine light, channeling her paladin's gift into her blade. The Minotaur recoiled, stunned by the radiant energy searing its flesh. Cedric seized the opening, thrusting his sword into a gap between the beast's ribs. With a pained bellow, the Minotaur collapsed to its knees, then fell.

Across the chamber, Thalion's wind barrier faltered under the second Minotaur's onslaught. Sensing the ward's imminent collapse, Mira conjured a dazzling flash of light to blind the creature. The Minotaur roared, stumbling, as Thalion summoned a spear of crackling lightning. With expert precision, he hurled it through the beast's torso. The smell of singed fur filled the air as the monstrous guardian toppled, head lolling to the side.

Panting, the heroes regrouped, each nursing bruises and shallow cuts. "That was direct," Cedric managed, catching his breath. "No puzzle, just raw strength."

Elara wiped sweat from her brow. "We passed the test, but at a cost. Let's see if there are more challenges ahead."

Beyond the massive gate lay a spiral staircase leading downward. Blue torches provided an eerie light, reflecting off damp stone. The stairs ended in a long corridor carved with lines that formed intricate geometric patterns. The floor itself was a mosaic of tiles, each boasting a different symbol. At the far end, an iron door barred the way.

When the group approached, a stone plaque on the wall flared to life, revealing a spectral Minotaur visage. In a resonant voice, it intoned: "Strength you have displayed. But the labyrinth also demands wit. Choose your path with care, or let your bones rattle in the depths."

A faint grinding noise followed. Suddenly, the floor tiles shifted. Sections rose or fell an inch, forming a puzzle-like surface. Patterns of runes glowed across certain tiles: some blazed with a warm hue, others flickered with a ominous red tinge. It appeared the corridor might be riddled with pressure plates or arcane triggers.

"Clever," Thalion murmured. "We can't just walk across. One wrong step might trigger traps. Possibly illusions or lethal devices."

Mira nodded, kneeling to examine the nearest tile. "The runes correspond to Minotaur numerals, or maybe letters. I see repetition that might indicate safe tiles."

Elara and Cedric stood back, letting the two arcane minds puzzle it out. Meanwhile, they kept watch for any movement in the corridor's shadows. A subtle hiss or click could mean spikes, flames, or worse.

Carefully, Thalion recited possible sequences that aligned with the labyrinth's script. He stepped onto a tile marked with a swirl pattern. Nothing happened. Encouraged, he tried another. A slight rumble built beneath their feet, and the swirl of an overhead glyph brightened, but no trap was triggered.

Mira added her own reasoning. "The Minotaurs likely made a path spelled out by the correct arrangement of glyphs. They incorporate their sense of honor—perhaps the word for 'courage' or 'truth.' Let's see." She advanced, stepping systematically on tiles that matched a specific pattern of runes referencing labyrinth mythology.

Occasionally, the corridor trembled if she erred, so she quickly readjusted.

At length, they reached the far side, panting from the mental strain. The door slid open, revealing the next corridor. A sense of triumph brightened their spirits, though they knew the labyrinth likely had more surprises in store.

The labyrinth continued in a serpentine fashion, presenting loops, dead-ends, and hidden passages. After hours of trial and error, they began recognizing subtle architectural hints: a stone relief here, a repeated symbol there. With perseverance, they navigated winding tunnels, avoiding pitfalls by spotting telltale cracks or discolored tiles. Despite their caution, they sustained minor scrapes—once, a dart trap grazed Cedric's shoulder, and another time Mira nearly stepped on a floorplate that would have released a spiked gate. Lady Elara's healing gift mended their wounds as they pushed onward.

Their vigilance paid off. They gradually made headway into the labyrinth's deeper chambers, each more elaborate than the last. The Minotaurs had engineered an impressive network, presumably honed over generations to challenge even the bravest warriors. Yet the heroes also sensed that each obstacle tested different virtues: raw power, cunning intellect, calm in adversity. It struck them that the labyrinth was more than a fortress—it was a spiritual crucible, shaped by the tribe's core values.

Eventually, exhaustion gnawed at them. They found a relatively safe nook—a small alcove with a trickling fountain of water—and decided to rest. It was impossible to know how long they'd been underground; the labyrinth allowed no natural light. Thalion surmised it had been at least half a day since they entered.

Their conversation drifted to speculation about the Minotaurs. "Why build such a formidable place?" Mira wondered. "Surely they don't expect visitors often."

Cedric shrugged. "It's part of their identity, I suppose. A labyrinth that shapes them from youth to adulthood, teaching them the clan's ideals. Outsiders are either worthy or not."

Elara nodded. "It also helps them keep secrets. If the Shadow Nexus lies near these mountains, the Minotaurs might guard knowledge or artifacts that reveal its location."

Thalion sipped water from the fountain, nodding thoughtfully. "We can only hope that if we survive, they'll grant us the map or clue we need. We're close to our goal—somewhere in these mountains is the next step to confronting the Nexus."

After a brief meal of dried rations, they resumed, hearts steeled. Yet fatigue weighed heavily, and the labyrinth's claustrophobic corridors pressed in on them, draining morale. They reminded themselves of the oath they had taken: to protect Stonehaven from looming darkness. That vow ignited a spark of resolve, carrying them forward into the depths.

A few turns later, they emerged into a cavernous hall lined with tapestries—surprisingly refined for a Minotaur stronghold. The vibrant colors depicted historical battles, ceremonies, and scenes of daily life in a long-forgotten age. In the center stood a large stone dais bearing an ornate brazier. Soft, magical fire glowed at its heart, casting dancing shadows on the walls.

Approaching cautiously, Elara sensed no immediate threat. Thalion examined the brazier's flame. "It's fueled by arcane energy, likely a symbol of the clan's heritage."

"Look," Mira said, pointing to the largest tapestry. It showed a towering Minotaur chieftain forging an alliance with a group of robed figures—possibly human mages. Beneath them, a stylized labyrinth design overshadowed a shape reminiscent of a swirling vortex. "This might be a depiction of how the tribe learned arcane secrets, or maybe it references the Shadow Nexus."

Cedric followed the tapestry's narrative from left to right. "Here, the labyrinth is revered. Then, warriors are tested. And at the end, they stand guard before that vortex shape. It suggests they're keepers of something."

Elara frowned. "Or keepers of a gateway. The Shadow Nexus might be connected to a gateway between realms. Perhaps the Minotaurs took on the responsibility to guard it ages ago."

The significance was clear: the labyrinth wasn't just for ceremony—it could be safeguarding or overshadowing a path to the Nexus. Their determination redoubled, the heroes pressed on, following the hall's exit deeper into the catacombs.

As they advanced, the floor's stonework gave way to a polished surface that reflected torchlight like a mirror. Columns twisted up into the gloom, and a faint haze drifted near the ceiling. With every step, the corridor seemed to shift, contorting in subtle ways. Suddenly, Cedric found himself separated from the group, standing alone in a corridor that looked different. In alarm, he called out, but the echo was distant, as though the others were nowhere near.

Simultaneously, Elara, Mira, and Thalion experienced similar illusions. Each found themselves isolated, the corridor warping into a personal labyrinth. For Mira, the walls exuded swirling patterns reminiscent of illusions she once studied. For Elara, phantom foes lurked at the edges of her vision. Thalion sensed a distortion of arcane energies, a puzzle crafted to confuse even the most disciplined mind.

Cedric, heart pounding, forced calm. "This is an illusion. I must focus." He recalled training that taught knights to center themselves, trusting in willpower to pierce mental deception. Step by step, he navigated imaginary walls, ignoring illusions of monstrous shapes. Eventually, his determination cracked the façade, and he found himself back in a small antechamber.

Elara invoked her goddess's name. A faint glow surrounded her, repelling the illusions. The corridor's haze receded like a bad dream. With renewed clarity, she spotted a faint gold thread along the floor's edge, likely a guiding line left by the Minotaurs for those who overcame the illusions. Following it, she soon rejoined Cedric in the antechamber.

Mira and Thalion used arcane logic, analyzing the illusions' patterns. Mira identified key distortions, dispelling them systematically. Thalion employed an antimagic field that peeled away false corridors. Though they were tested, both found their way to the same antechamber, relieved to see Cedric and Elara waiting.

Their reunion was heartfelt. After illusions of isolation, the sight of each companion was a gift. With cautious gratitude, they realized they had passed yet another test—this one of mental fortitude and trust in themselves.

Beyond the illusion corridor, the labyrinth descended into a wide, open space where natural rock formations merged with carved stone. A subterranean stream bubbled from the wall, creating a small pool that shone like polished onyx. Carved steps led up to a dais overshadowed by a massive statue of a horned Minotaur champion, arms folded in silent vigil.

Approaching carefully, the heroes found the statue's pedestal inscribed with lines of ancient script. Thalion deciphered them: "He who stands triumphant in mind, body, and soul may approach. Those unworthy shall face the Guardian's wrath."

As if on cue, the statue rumbled to life. Stone limbs creaked, red light glowed in its eye sockets, and it stepped off the dais, brandishing a massive stone axe. The Guardian was no ordinary Minotaur but a golem animated by centuries-old magic.

Elara raised her shield, bracing for impact. The Guardian swung its axe with terrifying force, leaving a gouge in the stone floor. Cedric circled to its flank, sword sparking against the statue's rocky hide. The Guardian hardly flinched.

Mira and Thalion combined their spells, targeting the golem's joints with blasts of intense elemental magic. Chunks of stone cracked, but the Guardian pressed on, bringing its axe down in a thunderous crash. The shockwave knocked Cedric off his feet and rattled Elara's shield arm.

In desperation, Elara invoked a potent divine aura, imbuing her sword with radiant might. Each strike chipped away more stone, but the Guardian's form regenerated swiftly, as though feeding on the labyrinth's arcane wards. Thalion realized that an external power must be fueling it. He quickly scanned the dais, noticing runic channels leading into the statue's base.

"Mira, disrupt the runes on the platform!" he shouted. "Cut off its energy source!"

Mira sprinted for the dais, weaving around the Guardian's stomping hooves. She traced a runic cancellation pattern on each etched channel, her staff glowing with concentrated energy. At first, the lines flickered defiantly, but she persisted, chanting a powerful dispel. With a final surge, the runes on the dais guttered, severing the Guardian's link to the labyrinth's reservoir.

Robbed of its sustaining magic, the Guardian weakened. Elara's radiant sword blow cleaved its shoulder, and Cedric followed up with a decisive thrust that shattered the torso. The golem staggered, stone limbs collapsing in a heap of rubble. The red glow in its eyes died, leaving only fragments of ancient craftsmanship behind.

A tense silence followed, broken by the heroes' ragged breaths. Another trial overcome, but the labyrinth was merciless in its demands.

A stone door slid open at the back of the chamber, revealing a tall Minotaur clad in ornate leather and metal. Unlike the silent guardian, this one was very much alive. Muscles rippled beneath the leather straps crossing his broad chest. On his head, two impressive horns were capped with shining steel rings. He carried a war hammer slung across his back and wore a heavy necklace of carved bone and polished stones. Behind him stood two more

Minotaurs, similarly armed but holding themselves with deference to their leader.

They eyed the scattered rubble of the Guardian, then turned to the group. Their leader spoke in a low rumble: "You have survived the labyrinth. Few do."

Cedric sheathed his sword, though he remained cautious. "We seek an audience with your Elder. We've come in peace, hoping to earn your tribe's help."

The Minotaur inclined his head. "I am Serak, War-Captain of the Mazehorn clan. Your prowess in the trials proves you are not trespassers of idle ambition. Follow me, if your limbs still stand."

Exchanging looks that conveyed both relief and guarded curiosity, the heroes trailed behind Serak. The two Minotaur guards flanked them, watchful but not overtly hostile. The labyrinth corridor ahead slanted upward, leading to daylight that spilled in from an arched exit high in the mountain. They climbed into the brightness, blinking as their eyes adjusted.

They emerged onto a wide ledge overlooking a hidden valley nestled in the mountains. Clustered huts made of stone and timber dotted the valley floor, interspersed with pens for livestock and small fields of hardy grain. Smoke rose from chimneys, and the call of distant horns echoed across the peaks. Dozens of Minotaurs roamed the village below—some carrying water, others tending to forging fires. The entire settlement bristled with a communal energy that was more organized than the heroes might have expected.

Serak motioned for them to descend a winding path that led into the heart of the village. As they walked, curious Minotaurs paused their tasks to stare, whisper, or grunt in low tones. Some displayed open suspicion, while others, especially younger ones, stared wide-eyed at the strangers who had allegedly bested the labyrinth's trials.

Elara caught glimpses of what seemed like a rudimentary but well-structured society. She spotted a communal cooking area, an arena for combat training, and even a small shrine where a stone labyrinth icon stood entwined with carved horns. Mira marveled at the intricate blacksmith operations, forging iron with an efficiency that rivaled human forges.

At last, Serak led them to a large, circular lodge built of immense logs and reinforced with bones from colossal beasts. Two carved pillars flanked the entrance, each shaped like a twisting horn. Inside, a central fire crackled in a pit, filling the hall with dancing shadows and the pungent scent of burning.

Seated at the far side of the lodge on a raised dais was the Elder of the Mazehorn clan. Her horns were aged and worn, yet they still curved magnificently. White fur around her muzzle suggested a venerable lifespan. Adorned in ceremonial garb woven with intricate labyrinth patterns, she held a staff topped with a carved horn. Surrounding her were advisors and chieftains, each bearing the stoic pride of the Minotaur race.

Serak bowed before her. "Elder Korath, these outsiders have conquered the labyrinth. They seek your counsel regarding a greater darkness."

Korath's eyes, clouded with age but still sharp with wisdom, fell upon the heroes. She considered them in silence, her gaze lingering on Elara's shield, the runic sword at Cedric's side, and Thalion's staff. Finally, she spoke in a deep, measured voice, "You have done what few can. Why risk such a gauntlet? Speak, and we shall judge your purpose."

Cedric cleared his throat, stepping forward with measured respect. "Elder Korath, we are on a mission to stop the spread of the Shadow Nexus—a great wellspring of corruption that threatens Stonehaven. Our journey led us here, guided by hints that your tribe may hold knowledge of the Nexus's true location. We humbly request your aid."

Elara nodded in support. "We do not seek to violate your lands. The labyrinth has proven both your might and your traditions. We hope to form a bond of mutual respect, so that together we might prevent a catastrophe that could harm all."

A heavy silence filled the lodge. Minotaurs exchanged glances. Some advisors looked uneasy, while others scowled, as if recalling memories of conflicts with humans or other realms. The fire crackled. At length, Elder Korath exhaled a weary sigh. "The Shadow Nexus. That name has not been spoken openly among us for generations. Our ancestors swore to guard certain secrets. Indeed, we hold a map—no, a living tapestry—showing the paths to places of ancient power. The Nexus is among them. Yet we do not give such knowledge freely."

Korath tapped her staff on the dais. "Long ago, our tribe accepted a duty from the Skyhorn Sages. A vow was made that we would protect the labyrinth's secrets from those who would misuse them. Many have come seeking forbidden routes, trying to harness the Nexus for conquest. We have repelled them all. But you... you seek to destroy the darkness. That is a different aim."

One of the advisors, a grizzled Minotaur with a chipped horn, interrupted. "We cannot trust them simply because they speak with honeyed tongues. The labyrinth proved only their skill, not their honor."

Another nodded in agreement. "Our laws demand an oath, sealed with the old rites. If these outlanders break the vow, the labyrinth's curse will find them. Are they prepared for that?"

Cedric glanced at his companions, then back to Elder Korath. "We understand. If an oath is required to ensure we use this knowledge only to protect, we will swear it."

Elder Korath paused, peering at each hero in turn. "Speak your vow, and we shall see if the labyrinth's spirit finds your words true."

A hush settled. The flickering fire cast enormous shadows of horns across the walls. Elara stepped forward, pressing a hand to her heart. "I, Lady Elara of the Dawn, pledge on my faith and my life to use the knowledge granted by the Mazehorn clan only for the purpose of ending the corruption of the Shadow Nexus. I shall not twist it for personal gain, nor bring harm to your tribe by betrayal."

Cedric, Thalion, and Mira each took turns echoing similar vows, invoking the memory of their struggles and the earnestness of their mission. The tension in the lodge was palpable, the Minotaurs' skepticism cut by a growing sense that these adventurers might indeed stand for something bigger than themselves.

When all had spoken, Korath lifted her staff. A dim glow emanated from the labyrinth patterns woven into her garment. It spread across the dais and into the lodge floor, tracing ancient runes that formed a circle around the heroes. For a moment, they felt the labyrinth's presence—an echo of the trials, the illusions, the guardians. A faint pressure gripped their chests, testing the sincerity of their vow. Then, like a sigh of relief, the glow faded.

Elder Korath nodded, satisfied. "Your vow is accepted. May the labyrinth guide you faithfully. Serak, bring the Tapestry of Paths."

Serak vanished into a side chamber, returning moments later with an elongated roll of embroidered cloth. The entire lodge seemed to hold its breath as he carefully unrolled it. Vivid threads depicted mountain ranges, forests, rivers, and arcane symbols superimposed onto each region. Toward the top left, swirls of inky black threads wreathed an ominous emblem—the mark of the Shadow Nexus.

Mira's eyes lit up. "This... this is remarkable. It's more than a map. It shows the ley lines, places where magical energies intersect, and how they converge near the Nexus's location."

Thalion nodded in awe. "Yes, see how the threads form knots at certain points. Those are focal sites—strongholds of power or wards against evil. The Nexus's swirl stands out. It appears deep in the northern wastes, near the boundary of realms."

Elara scanned the tapestry, recognizing some landmarks they had passed, though stylized in labyrinthine fashion. "This confirms our route. Once we leave these mountains, we must head north by northeast to a region that looks... desolate. Possibly a glacial area or a cursed land."

Elder Korath pointed a clawed finger at the swirl. "This is only the approximate site. The Nexus shifts, feeding on energies around it. You will find it hidden behind illusions or corrupt storms. Our tapestry shows the best guess, gleaned from centuries of watchers. Take care: many have tried to breach that domain. None returned."

Cedric took a steadying breath, determination flashing in his eyes. "We shall face whatever it takes."

Korath rolled up the tapestry with an air of finality. "We will not relinquish the original. We will make a copy for you, woven with runic dyes that approximate the magical lines. Use it wisely. If you succeed in cleansing the Nexus, the labyrinth's spirit shall remember your names as guardians of the land."

Over the next day, the Mazehorn clan extended cautious hospitality. The heroes were allowed to rest in a communal lodge where hay bedding and warm furs offered respite from the mountain chill. Hearty stews of root vegetables and goat-meat restored their energy. While the clan's warriors remained stoic and somewhat distant, the younger Minotaurs displayed open curiosity, shyly asking about human towns, mages' spells, and the realm beyond the mountains. Elara answered them gently, mindful not to sow any illusions about the dangers they might face.

Serak took them to the clan's forge, showing off the craftsmanship that produced the labyrinth's weapons. Cedric admired the forging techniques, noting their reliance on meteorite steel. Thalion discussed with a Minotaur blacksmith the secrets of embedding runic enchantments. Mira tried a massive warhammer sized for Minotaur hands, nearly toppling from its weight. Laughter broke the tension, fostering an odd camaraderie between the visitors and their once-suspicious hosts.

By the second evening, the tapestry copy was finished. It glowed faintly with arcane thread. Under Elder Korath's watchful eye, the heroes studied it meticulously, memorizing landmarks and runic notations. They were also given instructions on safe passage out of the mountains—a route that avoided the labyrinth's more dangerous coils.

Dawn came swiftly, the crisp mountain air carrying the smell of resin and wild herbs. The heroes prepared to depart, each silently reflecting on the unexpected alliance forged with the Mazehorn Minotaurs. Before leaving, they gathered in the lodge courtyard one last time. Serak, War-Captain, offered them a single metal horn token inscribed with the clan's seal. "Show this to any Minotaur sentinel you meet in the mountains. They will not hinder you."

Cedric, deeply moved, bowed. "We'll treasure this token—and your clan's trust. Thank you."

Elder Korath stood at the edge of the courtyard, staff in hand, flanked by her advisors. "We shall watch your path, outsiders. Return with the Nexus cleansed, and you shall forever be welcome among the Mazehorn. Fail, and darkness swallows us all."

With those solemn words echoing in their ears, the heroes mounted their horses—retrieved from the labyrinth's entrance—and set off, guided by the directions and the newly woven map. A small honor guard of Minotaurs accompanied them to the mountain pass, ensuring a safe egress from the tribe's territory. The switchbacks and cliffs once again tested their resolve, but now they moved with renewed purpose, the tapestry safely tucked in Mira's satchel.

Once they descended to the lower foothills, the Minotaur honor guard bid them farewell, returning to their hidden valley. The heroes pressed onward, cresting a ridge that revealed a panoramic view of the northern horizon. Jagged peaks gave way to rolling plains that eventually vanished into a distant haze. Somewhere out there, the labyrinth of the mountains gave way to a labyrinth of ice, rock, and twisted magic, where the Shadow Nexus festered.

At camp that evening, they unrolled the tapestry by the fire, tracing the route with a mixture of excitement and dread. Thalion pointed out a series of runic lines crossing near a feature labeled "The Bleak Expanse." That region, it seemed, was a hotbed of negative energy. Mira grimaced, recalling nights of study that warned of cursed storms in those latitudes. Cedric steeled himself, vowing to protect the group whatever came. Elara murmured a prayer for guidance, the glow of her goddess briefly illuminating the runic threads in the tapestry's weave.

While they shared a modest supper of dried meat and foraged herbs, the conversation took a more reflective turn. Mira observed how each trial in the labyrinth seemed to test a different facet of their teamwork—strength, cleverness, unity under illusions. Thalion commented that facing the Guardian golem reminded him how powerful synergy could be: had they fought that construct separately, they would likely have perished. Elara spoke of the labyrinth's spiritual dimension, praising the Minotaurs' blend of martial prowess and ancestral reverence. Cedric quietly admitted that he had misjudged them as mere beasts, but the labyrinth proved the clan was as noble and complex as any human nation.

These insights fueled a deeper sense of camaraderie. Though they were exhausted, the intangible weight of their duty felt slightly lighter, shared among four companions whose destinies had been intertwined. Another day's travel lay ahead—another step toward the unknown threat of the Shadow Nexus. But for once, they felt prepared, at least in spirit.

Late that night, while on watch, Cedric stood at the edge of their firelight, gazing at the mountain silhouette etched against a sky glittering with stars. He could almost imagine he heard the faint echo of Minotaur horns resonating through the passes, a testament to the labyrinth that once tested them. Part of him yearned to see the day when the Shadow Nexus posed no more threat, allowing them to return and share news of victory with Elder Korath and Serak. Would that be possible?

He turned to see Elara approach, also drawn by the night's hush. Her eyes reflected the fire's glow. "We've come far," she said softly. "From the horrors in the Gravenshade Woods to the vampire threat in Brighthaven, and now this. It's humbling."

Cedric nodded, letting out a breath he hadn't realized he was holding. "Every challenge reveals a deeper layer of darkness—but also, we uncover new allies. If we ever needed proof that Stonehaven isn't alone, the Minotaurs gave it to us."

Elara smiled, a faint curve of her lips. "Let's hope we can keep forging these alliances. The road ahead might require every ounce of unity we can muster."

They stood together for a moment, the wind rustling the grasses at their feet, the night sky an endless tapestry above. Perhaps they found a measure of comfort in the shared silence before returning to the circle of firelight, taking solace in the presence of friends.

Dawn arrived in a blaze of color—rosy light spilled over the eastern horizon, painting the foothills in gold. The horses, well-rested and fed on the mountain grasses, snorted as Cedric, Elara, Thalion, and Mira packed up camp. They shared a final look at the mountainous skyline behind them, recalling the labyrinth's echoes and the proud Minotaurs who called it home.

Steeling themselves for the next leg of the journey, they consulted the tapestry's runic lines, verifying the correct heading. North by northeast, across harsh plains, swamps of unknown peril, and eventually into bleak territories that no ordinary traveler braved. Each land, they knew, might harbor its own guardians or curses.

Yet with the copy of the Tapestry of Paths tucked safely away, the vow from the Mazehorn Elder blazing in their thoughts, they felt a renewed surge of determination. They had passed the labyrinth's deadly trials. They had been deemed worthy by the Minotaur clan, forging an alliance that might tip the scales in the war against the Shadow Nexus. Now it was time to face whatever lay beyond the horizon—new terrors, new revelations, and perhaps the final route that would carry them to the very heart of darkness.

Thus, they set forth, hooves clattering on rocky ground, hearts beating in anticipation. The journey had been perilous and would only grow more so, but their unity shone like a beacon in the gathering gloom. Resolute, they traveled on, the labyrinth behind them and destiny ahead, carrying the hopes of Stonehaven—and the silent blessing of Clan Mazehorn—to confront the ultimate evil.

173

the hopes of Stonehaven—and the silent blessing of Clan Mazehorn—to confront the ultimate evil.

174

7

ILLUSIONS OF THE PAST

Wind whispered across a bleak, desolate plain, stirring trails of dust that danced in faint curls around Sir Cedric, Lady Elara, Thalion, and Mira. They had traveled north by northeast, faithfully following the directions given on the tapestry they had received from the Minotaurs of Clan Mazehorn. Though the newly woven map held accurate landmarks and arcane notations, little could have prepared them for this barren expanse: a landscape stripped of warmth and color, where the sky hung heavy and gray. Even in daylight, an oppressive weight settled upon the air, hinting at the closeness of the Shadow Nexus's influence.

Days had passed since their departure from the Labyrinthine Mountains. Their route had taken them across rocky foothills, winding through pockets of twisted woods and dried riverbeds. Every so often, the tapestry's glowing threads indicated new anomalies—spots where the earth bled negative energy, withered flora, or unnatural mists. At each sign of corruption, Elara raised silent prayers for protection, while Thalion studied the phenomenon with a scholar's curiosity, ensuring they remained on track.

Yet as the group advanced deeper into the northern reaches, a subtle shift began to settle upon their collective mood. It was more than just fatigue; a gnawing tension had taken root, as though the land itself exhaled constant dread. Stray thoughts—memories from childhood, regrets, unspoken fears—drifted to the surface of each hero's mind, unbidden and distracting. They found themselves uncharacteristically short-tempered or withdrawn. Even the horses grew restless, snorting and tossing their heads at the slightest disturbance.

One afternoon, the companions rounded a low ridge to discover a wide, flat valley blanketed by a hazy, shimmering mist. Beyond it stretched a craggy plateau ringed by black rock. According to the map, this valley was the only clear route to a pass leading further north. But the tapestry's arcane runes glowed with a disquieting crimson hue whenever pointed at the valley, suggesting intense magical interference.

Elara reined in her mare, peering across the valley. "I sense something... wrong here. As if the very air is saturated with sorrow."

Mira, scanning the terrain, felt the subtle pull of negative energy. "It's more than sorrow. I feel illusions or illusions' potential. Like a dream that could become a nightmare if we step too close."

Thalion stroked his beard, gaze narrowing. "The tapestry indicates a strong confluence of Nexus magic in this region. It might be a dimensional bleed—some realm of distorted reality. Possibly a trap set by the Shadow Nexus itself."

Cedric frowned. "Then we have no choice but to pass through. Let's prepare ourselves. If illusions or visions come, we must remember who we are."

They exchanged resolute nods. Though each felt a chill of apprehension, they were united by a single purpose: to push closer to the Nexus, no matter the cost. Leading their horses at a measured pace, they descended into the valley. The swirling haze thickened around them, obscuring details of the ground. It felt as if they were passing into another dimension.

At first, the group remained tightly clustered. Elara carried a small orb of divine light at her fingertips, while Thalion conjured a protective ward around them. It lasted only a few minutes before flickering out, as though devoured by a greater force. Cedric muttered a warning for everyone to keep eyes on each other. Yet in a sudden shift—perhaps triggered by crossing some invisible boundary—the members of the party found themselves inexplicably alone.

Mira blinked, scanning in confusion. Only a moment earlier, her companions had been walking beside her, the horses' reins in hand. Now, she stood in a mist-shrouded courtyard under a twilight sky. Her staff felt heavier, resonating with a strange tension. All around her, the architecture resembled her hometown's familiar shapes—cobbled lanes, gabled roofs—but they were twisted, half-decayed, as though a reflection of memory.

She called out, voice echoing in stillness. "Elara? Cedric? Thalion?"

No response.

A flicker of movement caught her eye. On the far side of the courtyard, a figure in a dark cloak peered at her. Unnerved, Mira recognized something about the figure's stance—it reminded her of her younger self, hunched under the weight of uncertainty. Then, the figure melted away into the gloom, leaving only a swirl of dust in its wake. Against her better judgment, Mira found herself compelled to follow.

Elsewhere in the same domain, Elara stood in what looked like a dilapidated chapel of the Dawn. The pews were overturned, the stained-glass windows cracked, letting in beams of wan, purple-tinted light. A hush lay over the place, so oppressive that her own breath reverberated in her ears. Nervous, she lifted her shield, calling softly for her friends. A shuffle answered from behind a fallen altar. Elara stepped closer, heart pounding, uncertain what she might find.

To her shock, she saw the form of a kneeling woman in battered armor, golden hair streaked with blood. The woman's posture was bent in despair, a sword resting limply across her lap. Elara approached, a surge of empathy welling in her chest. She reached out a trembling hand. "Are you... wounded? Let me help you."

The woman lifted her face, eyes dull with hopelessness. In the flickering light, Elara felt a jolt of recognition: the woman was a reflection of herself—only older, broken. A ghost of who she might become should she fail in her mission. Elara nearly dropped her shield in alarm as the figure's lips parted in a silent, anguished plea.

Thalion, for his part, found himself in a chamber lined with infinite bookshelves, spines worn and pages scattered across the marble floor. The air smelled of old parchment and decay. Each step he took echoed unnaturally loud. He bent to pick up a fallen tome, only to find its pages filled with swirling scribbles that defied comprehension.

A dreadful sense of familiarity overcame him. He recognized this library as a perversion of the Grand Archives in which he had spent decades of study. Even the architecture matched the corridors where he had once roamed in scholarly curiosity. But now, the place was deserted, silent as a tomb. A whisper fluttered from behind the shelves, calling his name in a voice that shifted between mocking and frightened.

Suddenly, something crashed from above—a shelf toppled, spilling books in an avalanche of knowledge. Thalion dodged aside, heart pounding. When the dust cleared, he glimpsed a figure wearing robes identical to his own, face obscured by a hood. The figure turned, eyes gleaming with arcane light, then vanished into a corridor of impossible angles. Thalion felt compelled to pursue, haunted by the possibility that this was a reflection of his worst failures or unspoken regrets.

Cedric, too, was alone in the hush. He stood on a battlefield, the ground littered with broken spears and shields. A stale wind reeked of smoke and iron, carrying faint echoes of anguished cries. The sun overhead was a bloated red disc, casting everything in a lurid hue. Searching the horizon, Cedric recognized the silhouettes of farmland in the distance—his home region, from before he was ever knighted. Memories flooded him: the call to arms, the first skirmish, the sense of duty that had shaped his life.

As he ventured forward, stepping over a half-buried helm, Cedric froze. Ahead lay a small figure, curled on the ground. A farm boy? The boy's hair was the same tawny shade Cedric himself had in youth, and he wore tattered garments reminiscent of Cedric's old village. As Cedric approached, the boy gazed up with wide, tearful eyes. "Why didn't you save me?" he asked in a broken whisper.

An ache shot through Cedric's chest. He recognized the boy as an echo of those he had failed to protect over the years, the casualties that haunted him. Before Cedric could speak, the boy's form dissolved, morphing into a gaunt soldier's shape—a friend from a distant campaign who had perished under Cedric's command. Then it shifted again, becoming an old mentor who had died in Cedric's arms. Each figure pleaded silently, a haunting tableau of regrets Cedric had buried deep in his heart.

In these separate corners of the Nexus's illusory realm, each hero wrestled with manifestations of their past traumas. The illusions felt uncannily real, stirring raw emotions they had tried to bury. Yet for all the fear and despair these visions induced, a faint glimmer of purpose shone in each hero. They recalled the bonds forged during battles against specters, vampires, and guardians. These illusions, dreadful as they were, offered a chance to confront what still weighed them down—if they could find the courage to do so.

On a winding street reminiscent of her hometown, Mira chased the dark-cloaked figure through half-collapsed archways. Each corner she rounded revealed new shards of her past: a ruined orchard where she had first unleashed her magic by accident, freezing blossoms in the height of summer. Guilt churned in her gut, remembering how her parents had looked on in equal parts awe and wariness. She had always feared being an outcast for her power.

Her staff glowed fitfully, reacting to the swirling negative magic. At last, she cornered the figure in a courtyard overshadowed by a broken fountain. The figure turned, revealing a face that was half Mira's own—pale, tear-streaked, and etched with loneliness.

"You were always afraid," the doppelgänger murmured. "Afraid of being too powerful, of harming those you love. You shut yourself away in books, in illusions, so no one would see your true nature."

Mira felt tears burn her eyes. "I... I just wanted to protect people. I couldn't control it at first."

Her darker self smirked. "And in that fear, you withdrew. Every moment you wanted acceptance, but you also believed you could never belong. Even now, you wonder if Cedric, Elara, and Thalion truly accept you—or if they only tolerate your powers out of necessity."

A pang of doubt tightened in her chest. Yet images of her companions' trust emerged: the times they had shielded her from threats, the laughter shared around a campfire, the unwavering respect they showed for her spellcraft. Gathering her courage, Mira squared her shoulders. "That was my fear, yes. But I've learned that real acceptance comes when you trust others enough to let them see who you are. My magic can do so much good. It's not a curse."

The doppelgänger hissed, illusions swirling around it. "They'll leave you. One day, your power will outstrip your control, and you'll destroy them."

Mira's grip on her staff tightened, a wave of warm energy rising within her. "No. I won't let that happen. I'm growing, learning every day. My friends stand with me, and I with them. I won't cower from my gift anymore."

As her conviction solidified, the illusions around the doppelgänger shattered like glass. The figure's face flickered, twisting in silent agony. A final shriek reverberated in the courtyard before dissolving into motes of black mist. Mira gasped, tears on her cheeks, but her heart felt lighter, as if she had cast off a heavy weight. The illusions parted, and she found herself standing on a bare stretch of ground, the swirling haze receding. A path stretched onward, beckoning her to move forward.

Within the shattered chapel of the Dawn, Elara knelt beside her broken reflection. The other Elara lifted her head, tears brimming. "I failed them all," she whispered, voice raw. "So many have died in my care. I couldn't heal them. I prayed and prayed, but the Light did not answer."

Elara recognized the moment: the memory of a battlefield where she could not save everyone. The sense of inadequacy had haunted her prayers for months, fueling a hidden fear that she lacked the devotion required of a true paladin. She felt a pang of sorrow as she recalled the last time she had visited a war-torn village, where too many had perished despite her healing spells.

"It wasn't that the Light abandoned you," Elara said softly, tears stinging her own eyes. "We simply face limits as mortals. Even a paladin cannot always avert tragedy."

Her reflection cried out, voice thick with pain. "Then what is the point? Why devote ourselves if we can't prevent suffering? Why believe in a goddess who won't stop evil from taking root?"

Elara's throat tightened. "Because there's more to it than guaranteed victory. Faith is a beacon, a guide. The world has free will, and darkness arises from that same freedom. We stand against it, not because we always succeed, but because the Light calls us to save whom we can, to never give up."

The reflection flickered, uncertainty crossing its face. "But the guilt... it crushes me."

Elara placed a trembling hand over her counterpart's. "We carry that guilt, yes, but we also carry hope. Each life we save matters. Each kindness, each victory—no matter how small—pushes back the darkness. That's why I continue. I've come to accept that I can't fix every wound, but I can still be a shield for those in need."

The broken reflection closed her eyes. A faint glow emerged from Elara's touch, growing into a gentle radiance. With a sigh, the reflection dissolved, leaving behind the battered armor on the chapel floor. The walls reassembled, the stained glass shining more brightly. Elara rose, new resolve firm in her chest. She felt the presence of her goddess reaffirmed, as though the Dawn itself had found purchase in her doubts. With renewed composure, she strode through the chapel doors, the illusions melting away.

In the twisted library, Thalion stalked through endless aisles of cryptic tomes. The darkness pressed in, and intangible whispers gnawed at the edges of his mind, suggesting he was unworthy of arcane mastery. At last, he spotted the robed figure again, drifting among scattered scrolls.

"Who are you?" Thalion demanded, voice echoing. "Why do you torment me with illusions of my past?"

The figure half-turned, revealing Thalion's own face, but lined with bitterness and regret. In a resonant voice, it spoke: "I represent your vanity and your fears, old man. All your life, you've pursued knowledge, championed balance. Yet how many times did you sacrifice humility for the sake of discovering forbidden truths? How often did you remain in your tower, while others shed blood to protect the realm? You speak of defending Stonehaven, but you only emerged from your books when it was too late for many."

Thalion clenched his staff, heart pounding. Images flashed across his mind: scholars lost to madness from delving into cursed tomes, entire villages destroyed while he toiled in isolation, convinced that knowledge alone could save them if only he found the right spells. The reflection advanced, eyes blazing with arcane brilliance. "You hide behind caution, but you hoard secrets, letting your wisdom stagnate behind dusty pages."

A swirl of pages erupted in a cyclone around them. Thalion forced himself to steady his breathing. "I did retreat into scholarship, yes. I believed knowledge was the key to preventing catastrophes. But I learned that knowledge must be wielded. We cannot remain idle, waiting for the world to break us. I joined this quest because I realized that knowledge unshared or unused is worthless. My companions remind me daily that action and empathy matter as much as insight."

The reflection's eyes narrowed. "But you fear what you might unleash if you harness the full extent of your magic. The Shadow Nexus itself is born of corrupted knowledge. What if you become an agent of darkness by peering too deeply?"

Thalion mustered a calm, resolute stare. "The risk is real. Yet I choose the path of balance. The deeper I look, the stronger my duty to protect others becomes. My heart is anchored by the bonds of friendship. That is how I avoid corruption."

An aura of calm emanated from Thalion's words, dispelling the swirling storm of pages. The reflection let out a final, furious hiss, then crumbled to dust. The library illusions flickered, revealing a simple corridor ahead. Thalion exhaled, feeling both weary and exalted. He stepped forward, staff tapping gently on the now-solid floor, guided by a new certainty in the synergy between wisdom and compassion.

Cedric stood amid the shifting forms of his past: fallen comrades, terrified villagers, and the child he once was. Each ghostlike figure accused him with silent stares, condemning him for every life lost under his watch. The illusions weighed heavily on his chest, stoking the ancient guilt he kept hidden behind a knight's stoic facade.

He recalled the day he earned his spurs, standing proudly before the knights' council, vowing to protect Stonehaven. But in every war, every mission, some innocents were lost despite his best efforts. Those memories haunted him with the question: *Am I truly worthy to be a knight if I cannot save them all?*

Suddenly, the illusions coalesced into a single towering form—a monstrous visage bearing the faces of those Cedric felt he had failed, eyes glaring with condemnation. It loomed over him, a twisted embodiment of guilt and regret. The wind howled, pressing him to his knees.

Cedric inhaled slowly. He thought of Elara's unwavering faith, Thalion's quiet wisdom, Mira's unstoppable curiosity. They had accepted him—flaws, burdens, and all. He thought also of the times he had protected villages from brigands, turned the tide against monsters, and shielded his companions in battles with specters and vampires. Those were not illusions; they were truths.

With trembling hands, Cedric gripped his sword. "I cannot undo every tragedy. But I have sworn to fight for the living, to honor those lost by preventing further harm. My oath does not require perfection—only the resolve never to abandon the cause."

The monstrous figure roared, launching a wave of oppressive force. Cedric staggered, but he held his ground, sword angled forward. Summoning every ounce of courage, he roared back, a primal shout of defiance that reverberated through the illusion. Light sparked along his blade, surging from the depth of his conviction. The monstrous figure trembled, cracks forming across its many faces. With a thunderous crash, it shattered into fragments of shadow that evaporated into the sky.

Cedric collapsed, breath shuddering, tears in his eyes. Yet relief and clarity coursed through him. He stood again, feeling a renewed sense of purpose. The battlefield illusions fell away like mist, revealing a path leading onward through the haze.

One by one, each hero emerged from their personal trial, stepping onto a broad plain of blackened grass. The swirling haze was still thick, but they could see each other's silhouettes in the distance. Even the horses reappeared, though subdued and tense. The four companions staggered toward one another, relief flooding them as they confirmed that all had survived the illusions.

Immediately, Elara noticed that each person carried themselves differently. Mira's eyes shone with quiet confidence; Thalion's posture exuded resolute calm; Cedric, though still stoic, seemed more open, less weighed down; and Elara felt a warmth in her own heart, her faith burning brighter.

They exchanged embraces, pressing foreheads together in mutual gratitude. Tears glistened here and there, but no one teased or questioned it. In that moment, they understood that the illusions they had faced were not simply nightmares but something the Shadow Nexus forced them to confront—past fears, regrets, and unhealed wounds. And rather than be defeated, they had grown stronger, forging deeper trust among themselves.

After brief rest and whispered thanks, the group continued across the desolate plain. The haze persisted, yet they sensed the worst illusions had passed. Indeed, a faint path revealed itself underfoot, illuminated by stray motes of ghostly light. The tapestry's runes flared in Mira's satchel, indicating they were nearing a crucial juncture. Perhaps the Shadow Nexus itself—or a major gateway to it—lay just ahead.

Though exhaustion tugged at them, the companions pressed on. The sun's dim outline slid behind dark clouds, painting the world in a gray twilight. The plains rolled into a shallow depression where a circle of ancient standing stones rose, each etched with jagged glyphs. Black vines coiled around their bases, pulsating like veins. A dreadful hum emanated from the stones, vibrating through the air.

Cedric set a hand on the pommel of his sword. "Feels like a threshold. Are we sure we're ready?"

Elara nodded, her earlier doubts replaced by a renewed, serene determination. "Whatever lies beyond, we face it together."

Thalion glanced at the tapestry. "We must pass through these stones. It might be a warded boundary. Let's see if we can identify the pattern."

Mira stepped forward, staff glowing. "Wait, I sense a distortion. The illusions might be gone, but a new barrier is here—something physical or magical. Possibly a lesser realm bridging us to the deeper layers of the Nexus."

Sure enough, as they approached, arcs of crackling dark energy leapt between the stones, forming a half-sphere of swirling shadow. The hum intensified, and the wind picked up, whipping the heroes' cloaks. The phenomenon was reminiscent of a portal, but twisted by malevolent power.

"Stand back," Thalion warned, motioning for them to circle the perimeter. Each stone bore a different glyph, and though he recognized some from the Minotaurs' tapestry, others seemed older, possibly pre-Stonehavenn. He concluded they formed a puzzle lock—eight runes that needed activation in a certain sequence.

They spread out, each hero poised at two stones. Under Thalion's direction, they pressed or traced runes in a synchronized manner. Sparks of midnight-blue energy surged along the stone surfaces. When they completed the sequence, the arcs of dark lightning trembled, then parted like a curtain, revealing an opening.

Heartbeats thundered in their ears. Cedric took a measured breath, stepping first through the black swirl. The intangible barrier seemed to cling to him, icy and jolting, but he forced himself forward. Elara followed, praying silently. Mira and Thalion joined as well, leading the frightened horses behind them.

Instantly, the world shifted to a realm of perpetual twilight. The ground was no longer dusty but smooth, glass-like, reflecting inverted images of the sky above. Columns of swirling shadow rose in the distance, bending at impossible angles. Faint, disembodied whispers floated through the air, almost like a lullaby of despair. This was, undoubtedly, a domain under the direct sway of the Shadow Nexus's magic, a place that twisted natural law.

Yet the illusions that had tormented them were absent. Instead, a stifling quiet reigned. The tapestry glowed fiercely in Mira's bag, threads unraveling as if reacting to the proximity of the Nexus's power. Each hero felt tension coil in their muscles, but also an unexpected wellspring of inner strength—born from conquering their personal shadows.

Elara's voice broke the hush. "Those illusions... they might've been the Nexus testing us, trying to break our spirits."

Cedric nodded, gazing at the bleak horizon. "We've each faced our past, our regrets. Now, I believe we're more prepared for whatever is next."

Mira gently patted her staff. "And I no longer doubt that my power is meant for this fight. I'm not the frightened girl in the orchard anymore."

Thalion's eyes gleamed with a mix of somber acceptance and fierce resolve. "We stand on the threshold of the final approach to the Nexus. The real battles lie ahead, but we'll confront them together."

A warm sense of unity enveloped them. In silent agreement, they pressed onward into this strange twilight realm. With every step, the hush seemed to deepen, as though the land itself waited for a final showdown. But the heroes carried a new intangible armor—confidence earned through introspection, solidarity forged in the crucible of heartbreak and healing.

Since time was distorted here, night and day had little meaning. Eventually, they decided to set up a makeshift camp in a relatively sheltered area where jagged pillars rose in a semicircle, providing cover from the howling wind. The ground was eerily smooth, reflecting their faint outlines in dull, ghostly shapes.

Despite the oddness of the realm, they built a small fire using conjured heat from Thalion's spells and bits of driftwood-like debris that drifted in from who knew where. As they gathered around the flickering flames, a hush spread among them, different from the oppressive silence outside—this hush was one of reflection and mutual comfort.

Mira, stirring the pot of stew they managed to piece together, broke the silence. "I never properly thanked you all... for accepting me as I am. I've carried doubts for so long—fearing I'd lose control of my magic." She took a breath, glancing at each companion's face. "But the illusions showed me that you've always seen me for who I am, not just a tool. Thank you."

Cedric gave a gentle nod. "We all fear something about ourselves. But we rely on each other, not just for battle, but for support. I think that's what real fellowship means."

Elara placed a reassuring hand on Mira's shoulder. "Your magic has saved us more times than I can count. The fact that you worry about its misuse just proves how deeply you care."

Thalion, stirring the fire with a piece of broken stone, added, "And we will continue to rely on each other's strengths. We might be the only ones who can do this—to stand against the Nexus. That's no small burden."

Mira passed out small bowls of steaming stew. They ate quietly, each lost in reflection of the illusions that they had vanquished—echoes of old guilt, sorrow, or fear. By confronting their darkest corners, they had shed invisible shackles that might have hindered them in the final battles to come.

Elara found herself gazing at Cedric with new empathy. She had glimpsed hints of his regrets before, but never had she understood their depth. She sensed a similar bond with Thalion, who always kept his secrets behind scholarly detachment, and with Mira, whose bright curiosity had masked insecurities. Now, she felt closer to them all.

At length, Thalion finished his meal and cleared his throat. "In many stories, such trials serve as preludes to a hero's ascendance in skill. Have any of you felt... changes?"

Mira flexed her fingers. "My spells do feel more fluid. Earlier, I tested a small conjuration, and it required half the usual effort."

Elara touched the emblem on her shield, sensing a brighter, more potent glow. "Yes. The Light within me feels more attuned. I can almost hear a chord of divine energy that wasn't accessible before."

Cedric nodded thoughtfully, curling a hand around the hilt of his sword. "For me, it's like I trust my blade—and my oath—more than ever. I sense a unity of purpose in every swing, a clarity of mind that helps me anticipate attacks."

Thalion offered a slight smile. "It seems our triumph over personal demons has, in a way, unlocked deeper potential. The Shadow Nexus's illusions inadvertently became a catalyst for our growth. We must not squander that gift."

In this twisted realm, dawn was a relative concept; the sky merely lightened from pitch black to murky indigo. The group rose, feeling unexpectedly refreshed despite the unnerving environment. A new day beckoned them further into the domain. They extinguished their fire, gathered their belongings, and resumed the journey.

A short distance from their campsite, they came upon a bizarre phenomenon: a vast mirror-like lake, its surface perfectly still. The air shimmered above it, warping reflections of the twisted spires in the distance. According to the tapestry's partial guidance, crossing this water might shorten the route to the next major landmark. But the realm was uncharted; who knew what lurked beneath that placid surface?

"Let's test the depth," Cedric proposed, picking up a piece of debris. He tossed it in. Instead of splashing, the object vanished soundlessly, as though consumed by an illusion.

Mira frowned. "It might be safe, or it might be another trap. Illusory water, or a gateway to some sub-realm."

Elara touched the water with her fingertips, wincing at a jolt of cold energy. "It's real enough, but I sense necrotic undercurrents. Could it be the place where souls drift?"

Thalion, after a moment of contemplation, conjured a floating disk of magical force, setting it to hover a few feet above the water's surface. He guided it gently forward. After traveling a short distance, the disk shuddered and blinked out of existence, dissolving in a swirl of shadow. "It appears the lake disrupts direct arcane constructs. We'll have to approach differently."

Before they could devise a new strategy, a ripple formed on the lake's surface. A ghostly figure rose from the water: a robed shape with indefinite features, likely a sentinel conjured by the Nexus's influence. Its voice echoed in the heroes' minds: "You who have cast aside your fears, do you believe you are free of shadows? The lake reveals all truths."

As it spoke, the surface churned, showing fleeting images—past battles, tears, laughter, heartbreak, triumph. The watchers recognized their own histories playing out in rapid sequence, as if the lake was a cosmic mirror. The robed sentinel's voice resounded, "Will you step forward, or will you drown in what remains unspoken?"

Without hesitation, Cedric stepped to the water's edge. "We've faced our past," he declared, voice steady. "We are not bound by it anymore."

Mira nodded, staff raised in defiance. "Whatever illusions remain, we stand as one."

Elara invoked a soft aura of light. "In faith, we move forward. Fear shall not chain us."

Thalion summoned a glowing rune that hovered overhead, an emblem of resilience. "We accept the trials to come."

The robed sentinel inclined its head, then vanished into the lake. A path of shimmering motes materialized across the water's surface, forming stepping stones. The heroes exchanged resolute glances and proceeded single file. Each step caused the water to ripple, revealing glimpses of old memories beneath their feet—painful moments now tempered by acceptance.

Halfway across, the motes flickered, and for a heartbeat, it seemed they might vanish, plunging the party into the cold depths. But the heroes focused on the unity they had built, anchoring themselves in mutual trust. The stepping stones held. Reaching the far shore, they found the watery illusions fade, replaced by solid ground. They had proven to the sentinel—and to themselves—that they had not regressed into old fears.

Emerging from the half-formed illusions and the swirling energies of the Shadow Nexus's domain, the party stepped onto a rocky expanse of genuine, unwarped terrain. The gloom overhead still churned with ominous clouds, but the immediate haze was gone, as though the realm itself acknowledged the group's steadfastness. They were closer now to the Nexus—close enough that each hero felt a low thrumming in the earth, a reminder that the greatest challenge was yet to come.

A hush of awe descended as they beheld a distant horizon where lightning flickered across the sky. The tapestry glowed faintly in Mira's bag, directing them eastward around a towering formation of black basalt. Thalion surmised that beyond that basalt ridge, the land would drop into a valley rumored to be the Nexus's seat of power. For centuries, none who ventured there returned.

In that moment, Cedric pressed a fist to his heart. "We do this not just for ourselves, but for every life the darkness threatens. Let's not forget all the people we've vowed to protect—Oakenshade, Brighthaven, the Minotaurs' clan, and more."

Elara placed her hand over his, eyes shining with conviction. "And for the memory of those we couldn't save, ensuring that their sacrifices won't be in vain."

Mira lifted her staff, letting arcs of light dance along its crystal tip. "We fight for the future we believe in—one where the Shadow Nexus can no longer claim innocent souls."

Thalion placed a steadying hand on Mira's shoulder. "We have overcome illusions of the past. Now, let us shape the reality of tomorrow."

Thus united, they took the next steps forward, hearts fortified by the knowledge that while the journey had forced them to confront their darkest memories, it had also gifted them with unbreakable resolve. Whatever the Nexus still had in store—be it monstrous legions, cursed storms, or unimaginable illusions—the four stood ready, free of the burdens that once held them back. Their bond, tempered by shared hardships, now glowed like a flame in the deepening twilight, guiding them toward their ultimate destiny.

Nightfall (or the realm's closest equivalent) found them in a small, sheltered depression on the outskirts of the basalt ridge. The thunderheads still raged, flickering with violent electricity in the distance, a macabre prelude to the final confrontation. Camp was set with minimal fuss; no one spoke much, though a gentle undercurrent of warmth hung among them. They needed few words, for their hearts were aligned.

As Cedric took first watch, he gazed out over the desolate landscape, recalling the illusions of the battlefield and the ghosts of those he had failed. Instead of guilt, he felt resolution—and a quiet vow to remain steadfast so that future tragedies might be averted.

Elara quietly prayed beside the embers of the fire, reflecting on the chapel vision. She felt the Dawn's blessing surge through her veins, more vibrant than ever. She would use that power to shield her companions when the worst of the Nexus's fury descended.

Thalion scribbled notes in a journal, detailing the illusions they had witnessed, the new spells he felt stirring in his mind, and the swirl of cosmic forces that governed this realm. He realized that knowledge of one's self was as vital as knowledge of magic in the battles ahead.

Mira sat nearby, staff across her lap. She closed her eyes, inhaling the crisp air. Through trial, she had at last accepted that her powers were not a burden but a gift that bound her to her companions, bridging the gulf between her solitary studies and the larger world. She would no longer shy away from her magic's potential.

A faint hush draped the campsite, broken only by distant thunder. The four heroes leaned on each other in silent camaraderie. The illusions of their past no longer held them hostage, their old wounds now healing. Empowered by unity, they looked to the horizon where the swirling vortex of the Shadow Nexus beckoned them onward.

Together, they had walked through illusions of regret, sorrow, and self-doubt—and emerged stronger. No matter what horrors lay ahead, they now knew that their greatest obstacles were not outside in the gloom, but within their own hearts. Having faced those shadows and dispelled them, they stood poised to confront the darkest evils with unwavering courage, ready to strike a decisive blow against the corruption threatening Stonehaven.

When dawn (or something like it) rose again, they would embark anew—four hearts bound by trust, four souls freed from old shackles, each harnessing deeper powers discovered in the crucible of introspection. Now, at the twilight boundary of the Nexus's domain, their journey would intensify, but their bond and resolve were unbreakable. The Shadow Nexus could no longer exploit their fears; it would find, instead, four heroes illuminated from within, forging onward to reclaim the light for Stonehaven, no matter the cost.

8

THE BEHEMOTH'S ROAR

A frigid wind cut across the stony foothills as Sir Cedric, Lady Elara, Thalion, and Mira emerged from the final stretch of rocky trails. The Labyrinthine Mountains rose behind them like silent sentinels, still partially wreathed in clouds, while the land ahead spread out in a patchwork of rolling fields and sparse forests. This change in terrain marked a new phase of their journey—one that, according to their map and the glowing runes on the tapestry obtained from the Minotaurs, should lead them closer to the location of the Shadow Nexus.

Yet the hush that lay over the countryside felt unnatural. Where one might expect the twitter of birds or the distant lowing of cattle, there was only an eerie stillness. Cedric guided his horse to a halt at the crest of a small rise, scanning the valley below. Beyond a few scattered farmhouses, he saw strangely churned earth and torn patches of land, as though a titanic force had ripped through the fields.

Elara rode up beside him, her shield strapped across her back, eyes narrowed. "The land looks... wounded," she murmured. "Could be bandits or a rampaging warband, but this destruction seems too large-scale."

Thalion stopped behind them, staff in hand. He tapped the ground gently, sensing traces of residual magic. "I can feel a disturbance in the leylines—like shockwaves from something enormous moving across these fields."

Mira, last to arrive, studied the patterns of churned dirt with an analytical stare. "You think it's another manifestation of the Nexus's corruption? We've encountered monstrous creatures before, but these tracks seem even bigger than the Wyvern or the Behemoth we read about in ancient texts."

Cedric nodded grimly. "We can't assume it's anything less than catastrophic. Let's move carefully."

And so they urged their horses down the slope. A steady wind howled across the open land, flattening tall grass and stirring loose dirt into the air. No birds wheeled overhead. Even the sun, climbing high in a bleached sky, felt distant.

As they descended into the valley, the party came upon fields devastated as though struck by a hurricane: fences snapped, barns collapsed, and tilled soil churned into massive furrows. Here and there, fragments of wagons or livestock pens lay strewn about like children's toys cast aside. The closer they drew, the stronger they felt a faint vibration beneath the earth, as if the land itself trembled with dread.

A half-ruined barn stood near a battered farmhouse. Elara dismounted and approached cautiously, calling out, "Is anyone here? We mean no harm!"

Her voice echoed in the emptiness. At first, there was only the whisper of the wind through broken boards. Then a shaky voice replied, "Who—who goes there?" from somewhere behind a leaning stack of debris.

Elara raised a hand, urging the others to hang back. "We're travelers, on a quest to stop the darkness spreading in Stonehaven. We saw the destruction here and came to help."

A figure emerged—a bearded farmer, clothes torn and face smeared with soot. Two younger farmhands flanked him, clutching pitchforks and looking pale with terror. They studied the newcomers, noting the shining armor and arcane staffs, then sank with obvious relief. "Thank the Light someone's come," the farmer said, his voice raw.

Cedric swung off his horse, approaching with palms up to show peaceful intent. "What happened here? Bandits?"

"Worse," the farmer rasped. "A monster, bigger than anything we've seen. It tore through these fields just two nights ago. The ground shook, barns caved in. We barely escaped with our lives." He cast a fearful glance toward the east, where the plains gave way to a distant ridge. "It went that way, roaring. Some say it's a Behemoth."

Thalion and Mira exchanged alarmed looks. Legends of colossal Behemoths—massive, primeval beasts that slumbered in the world's hidden cradles—were known to most scholars, but rarely did they appear in living memory. And if a Behemoth was on the rampage, it might be drawn by the Shadow Nexus's corruption.

Elara reached out to gently clasp the farmer's shoulder. "We're sorry for your losses. Do you know how many were hurt? Is anyone still missing?"

The farmer nodded grimly. "Several folk ran, but some are unaccounted for. We managed to gather survivors at the old mill down the road. We're all too afraid to go after that beast. The last we saw, it vanished over the next ridge, bellowing so loud it shook the windows."

Cedric set his jaw. "We'll track it. If it's truly a Behemoth, we'll do whatever we can to stop it before it ravages more land."

A woman stepped forward from the wreckage, eyes rimmed with tears. "Please—my sister's farm was that way. We haven't heard from her. If you find her..." Her voice cracked. Elara offered a sympathetic nod.

"We'll look," she promised. "Gather your people, keep them safe. We'll return once we learn more."

With that, the companions made a quick check of the area, finding no immediate threats, then resumed their trek eastward, hearts heavy with the knowledge that an unimaginable terror lurked somewhere ahead.

The group pressed onward for half a day, following a trail of devastation: uprooted trees, massive footprints in the mud, and occasional bursts of scorched earth. The destruction carved a path that cut through farmland and into rolling meadows.

Eventually, they heard a deep, resonant rumble echo across the sky—like thunder, yet the sky was only partially clouded. The horses snorted and balked, ears pinned. Another rumble followed, this time vibrating the ground underfoot. Thalion squinted into the distance, adjusting a scrying crystal. "It's near," he said quietly.

Mira's skin prickled with the sensation of powerful magic saturating the atmosphere. "I can taste the corruption in the air. It's like a storm of negative energy swirling around wherever that creature goes."

They pressed on until they crested a broad ridge. Below them lay a shallow vale, and at its center, they finally glimpsed the monster: a massive Behemoth, easily three times the height of a castle's main gate, its limbs like tree trunks. Its hide appeared to be a layer of bony plating interlaced with glowing seams, reminiscent of molten lava. With each step, the ground quivered. The beast paused to roar, and the sound reverberated across the valley, sending flocks of birds scattering.

A row of cottages sat in the Behemoth's path, and the creature was moving inevitably toward them—likely to be destroyed in moments. Cedric set his jaw. "We have to stop it now."

Elara nodded, breathing out. "We do this together. No second-guessing."

Thalion's voice was tight. "A direct assault on a Behemoth is risky. But if we let it reach those cottages, we'll have even more innocent lives lost."

Mira tightened her grip on her staff. "Let's move. We have the advantage of surprise—maybe we can lure it away from the homes."

They galloped down the slope, hooves pounding. As they closed in, the Behemoth swung its colossal head, noticing the riders. It let out a resonant roar that sent tremors through the air. Immediately, the ground beneath the heroes splintered in minor quakes, forcing them to pull the horses up short.

"Dismount!" Cedric yelled, leaping from his stallion before it could throw him. The others did the same, letting the terrified animals retreat.

The Behemoth turned, trampling a grove of trees as it lumbered toward them. Its molten cracks flared, suggesting a buildup of internal heat. Elara, shield readied, shouted for Cedric to circle left while Thalion and Mira hung back.

Cedric sprinted in a wide arc, brandishing his sword. "Hey! Over here!" he bellowed, banging the flat of his blade against his shield to get the creature's attention. The Behemoth's fiery eyes fixated on him, and it charged.

Elara rushed forward, shield glowing with divine light, intercepting the monster's swinging forelimb. The impact thundered, nearly bowling her over, but she braced with a burst of holy power. "Now!" she shouted through gritted teeth.

Thalion lifted his staff. Chanting in low, measured tones, he unleashed a volley of arcane bolts that slammed into the Behemoth's flank. Though each bolt exploded in sparks against the beast's thick hide, it succeeded in drawing its attention away from Elara. Meanwhile, Mira conjured swirling shards of ice that pelted the creature's leg, seeking to cripple its mobility.

Enraged, the Behemoth reared back, letting loose a spew of molten breath that scorched the grass in a wide arc. Cedric dove aside, narrowly escaping incineration. The ground smoked, sending clouds of ash rolling across the battlefield.

Undaunted, Cedric rebounded and lunged, slashing at the thick plates on the Behemoth's foreleg. Sparks flew as steel bit into hardened bone-like armor. He only managed to scratch it, but it was enough to draw a roar of pain from the beast.

"That plating's tough!" Cedric called. "We need a soft spot!"

Elara advanced, driving her blade into the gap near the creature's shoulder. Holy light flared on impact, causing the Behemoth to jerk its massive body sideways. It roared in fury, swinging a boulder-like fist at Elara, who raised her shield and prayed for strength. The blow sent her skidding across the churned earth, her shield sparking with golden embers.

Seeing Elara knocked back, the Behemoth turned its attention to Thalion and Mira, who stood a short distance away, weaving spells. The creature inhaled, chest expanding ominously, and unleashed another blast of scorching breath. A wave of molten energy fanned out across the field, setting brush ablaze.

Mira reacted swiftly, erecting a curved shield of frost. Steam erupted where flame met ice. Thalion reinforced it with a gust of enchanted wind, pushing the inferno away enough to spare them from being roasted alive.

Yet the Behemoth did not relent. With a monstrous snort, it charged again, tearing at the land with unstoppable momentum. Thalion threw up a swirling ward, but the creature's sheer mass shattered it on impact. The mage tumbled backward, struggling to maintain composure as Mira dove to avoid being crushed.

Nearby, Cedric managed to help Elara back to her feet. She coughed, chest heaving. Her armor glowed faintly where the divine power had absorbed much of the impact. "We can't keep trading hits like this," she gasped. "We have to wear it down—find a critical point."

Cedric nodded, grim determination etched on his face. "We'll force it into a vulnerable position. Thalion, Mira— aim for its joints or anywhere the plating looks thinner. Elara and I will try to draw its attacks."

Using a combination of feints and precise strikes, the heroes attempted to herd the Behemoth away from the cottages. Cedric bravely dashed in to slash at the monster's flank, while Elara pounded her shield to hold its attention. Thalion and Mira circled to the rear, looking for gaps in the thick armor along the spine or hindquarters.

As the Behemoth pivoted, it stumbled on uneven ground scarred by its own rampage. Mira seized the moment, conjuring a cluster of jagged ice spears that materialized around the beast's rear leg. She hurled them forward, each spear streaking across the battlefield like a falling star. Several shattered on impact, but one managed to punch through a chink in the plating. A muffled bellow of pain echoed from the creature's massive throat.

Roaring, it swung its tail—a bristling club of spikes— toward Mira. Thalion swiftly intervened, conjuring a barrier of crackling arcane force. The tail slammed against it with an ear-splitting crack, sending arcs of energy dancing through the air. Mira rolled away, breathing hard, staff clenched tight.

Meanwhile, Elara prayed to the Goddess of Dawn, channeling radiant might into her sword. She sprinted forward, meeting the Behemoth head-on as it whipped around. Their collision was deafening: her glowing blade clashed with the beast's molten-surfaced horns, sparks and embers flying in all directions. For a moment, Elara held her ground, face set in fierce resolve.

Cedric leapt in from the side, driving his blade into the beast's shoulder seam. The Behemoth howled, staggering a step. The combined might of Elara's radiance and Cedric's swordsmanship was making a difference, forcing the creature to shift from offense to defense.

Yet in its pain, the Behemoth's molten lines glowed even brighter, and a wave of superheated steam burst from cracks in its hide, knocking both Elara and Cedric back with a scalding blast. They landed hard, gasping as the scorching wave singed cloth and leather.

The fight began taking a toll on both sides. The Behemoth's movements grew more erratic, its breathing labored, smoke billowing from its wounds. The adventurers were likewise battered: armor dented, robes singed, and their magical reserves heavily taxed. The land around them smoldered with scattered fires, and the cottage residents, watching from a safe distance, feared each quake might be their last.

Gritting his teeth, Thalion mustered a fresh surge of arcane power. He could sense the thinning threads of the creature's life force interwoven with the corruption of the Shadow Nexus. If they could strike at just the right spot—some vital junction of bone and molten energy—they might bring the beast down.

He yelled to Mira, "Focus your frost spells on the same wound Cedric just opened! We'll freeze and shatter that plating if we time this perfectly!"

Mira, sweat glistening on her brow, nodded. She began to chant a complex incantation. The air around her crackled with gathering cold, forming a swirling vortex of ice shards and frigid wind. Meanwhile, Elara and Cedric regrouped to keep the Behemoth's attention on them.

"Hey, ugly!" Cedric shouted, bashing his shield to produce a metallic clang. Elara joined in, unleashing a flare of holy light across the beast's face. Dazed and furious, the Behemoth fixated on them, stomping forward.

Thalion seized the moment: with a deft motion of his staff, he conjured an arcane chain that snaked around the Behemoth's near forelimb, tethering it—albeit briefly—to the charred ground. The monster strained, roaring in frustration. That minor restraint was all Mira needed. She unleashed her swirling vortex, aiming it directly at the gaping wound near the Behemoth's shoulder.

A torrent of frost smashed into the wound, forming a lattice of ice that crackled with intense cold. Steam hissed as molten fluid clashed with subzero temperatures. The Behemoth howled, staggering sideways. Cracks formed around the edges of its bony plating.

In that split second, Elara summoned a final reserve of divine might, rushing forward with sword blazing. Cedric flanked her, sword raised high. They struck simultaneously, smashing through the half-frozen plating. A sickening crunch sounded as bone and lava-like flesh split under the combined force of steel, frost, and holy energy.

The Behemoth let out a heart-rending bellow that rattled the sky. The molten glow in its seams flickered erratically. With a shudder, the colossus collapsed to one knee, trembling under its own weight.

Now panting, Cedric and Elara pulled free, stumbling away. The creature teetered, then fell heavily onto its side, the impact sending a shockwave through the ground. Dust and ash plumed high. The monstrous form lay there, sides heaving in failing breaths.

Silence closed in as the Behemoth's labored breaths slowed. A dim glow continued to emanate from the cracks in its hide. Then, with one last weak roar, the beast shuddered and went still. Ripples of negative energy burst out, swirling over the battered battlefield and dissipating into the air like an exhaled curse.

The heroes stood in place, hearts hammering, each one battered and scorched yet alive. For a moment, none dared speak, caught between relief and awe at the magnitude of what they had just accomplished.

Elara fell to her knees, pressing a hand over her ribcage where bruises ached. Cedric dropped beside her, gently steadying her. Thalion sank onto a piece of rubble, leaning on his staff, while Mira rested her hands on her thighs, chest heaving, tears of exhausted relief prickling her eyes.

Some distance away, the cottagers, who had been watching in terror, now erupted in a mixture of cheers and incredulous gasps. A few ventured forward timidly, as though not quite believing the Behemoth was truly dead.

"It's over," Elara whispered, closing her eyes for a moment. "Light be praised."

Cedric squeezed her shoulder gently. "We did it together. No single one of us could've taken it down."

Thalion lifted his head, scanning the monstrous corpse. "I sense a lingering trace of powerful magic... Something inside that creature."

Mira nodded, her voice subdued. "Right. Stories speak of Behemoths absorbing arcane objects or relics. We should investigate."

Approaching the colossal corpse was no simple matter. The heat radiating from its core made the air shimmer, and smoke still drifted from cracks in its plating. The group advanced cautiously, ignoring the stench of scorched flesh and the overwhelming sense of finality that hung around the fallen giant.

Eventually, they located a large, ragged hole near the beast's shoulder—the very wound they had exploited. Thalion and Mira conjured small orbs of light to guide their inspection. Within the seared flesh, they caught the faint gleam of something metallic, half-embedded in thick tissue.

Working quickly, Cedric and Elara carefully pried open the plating. Thalion used a minor telekinetic cantrip to shift charred matter aside, while Mira cast a cooling spell to reduce the intense heat. Bit by bit, the artifact came into view: a broad disc of intricately carved metal, etched with runes that pulsed with a soft, purple-white glow. The disc was about the size of a large shield, though it felt far lighter in Cedric's hands than it looked.

Elara leaned in, surprise evident in her eyes. "This definitely isn't ordinary metalwork. The runes—look, they're similar to some of the symbols we found on the tapestry from the Minotaurs."

Thalion scrutinized the carvings. "I can see references to gateways, thresholds... This might be a key or seal. Given the energies swirling around it, I suspect it's crucial for accessing deeper wards near the Shadow Nexus."

Mira gently placed a hand on the disc's surface, feeling the thrumming current within. "Yes, it resonates with the same magical frequency we've been tracking. The Behemoth must have absorbed or attached itself to this relic, either awakening it or being awakened by it. Perhaps the Nexus's corruption spurred it to rampage."

A hush settled as they realized the importance of this artifact. Cedric exhaled. "So this was not just a random monster. The Nexus's influence likely stirs up ancient horrors, and they carry pieces of the puzzle we need to confront it."

Elara cradled the relic, feeling its power hum against her gauntlets. "We have our second key, then. The tapestry indicated we'd need these relics to breach the final barrier around the Nexus. With the scale from the Wyvern's lair, and now this disc... we're gathering the necessary tools."

The sight of the Behemoth's lifeless body drew a slow trickle of stunned onlookers from the nearby cottages. Some arrived with bandages for the wounded heroes, others brought canteens of water. A few simply stared at the fallen giant in mute disbelief, as though expecting it to stir back to life at any moment.

Elara, leaning on Cedric's shoulder, managed a weary smile at the villagers. "You're safe now," she said gently. "The threat is gone."

Sobbing with relief, a middle-aged woman pressed a small wooden amulet into Mira's hands, calling it a token of thanks. Another villager insisted Thalion take a pouch of medicinal herbs. They had little to offer, but the gratitude pouring from them was immense.

Cedric took a moment to speak to an older man with trembling hands who wanted to be sure the monster was dead. "Gone for good," Cedric assured him. "It won't rise again."

The man nodded, tears glistening. "You saved us... When I saw that beast, I thought no mortal force could stand against it."

Thalion overheard this and gave a small, humble nod. "We're not extraordinary alone, but together we've learned to fight as one. That's all it took."

As dusk approached, the adventurers assisted villagers in clearing some of the debris, ensuring that no immediate threats remained. They found a central barn still partially standing, which provided a place to rest. Though battered and exhausted, they took comfort in the sense of community that emerged among the survivors.

Night fell, stars glimmering faintly behind drifting clouds. Inside the barn, they laid out bedrolls atop scattered hay bales, sharing a simple meal of bread and dried vegetables donated by the villagers. A lantern cast long shadows on the wooden walls.

Mira gingerly rotated her shoulder, wincing at bruises. "If we keep facing creatures of this magnitude, I fear for our survival. We got lucky today."

Cedric, massaging a sore forearm, nodded in agreement. "We'll need new strategies. If the Nexus can awaken more beasts... we have to be ready."

Elara's face showed fatigue, but her voice was resolute. "We have the relic from this Behemoth. Every victory brings us one step closer to sealing the Nexus. And with each battle, we're growing—both in skill and in unity."

Thalion, flipping through his notes on the artifact, added, "I'll study these runes. Perhaps they'll reveal the location of the next key or confirm how to use them all together once we reach the Nexus. For now, though, let's rest."

A hush of mutual understanding passed between them. They had pushed themselves near the breaking point, yet the quest demanded even greater resolve in the days ahead. Eventually, they drifted into uneasy sleep, listening to the distant echo of wind through ravaged fields, haunted by the memory of the Behemoth's final roar.

At sunrise, the party emerged from the barn to find that the villagers had begun the painful process of repairing their homes. Wagons were being righted, roofs patched, and rubble cleared. Though progress was modest, there was a grim sense of hope shining in the farmers' eyes.

Elara offered blessings where she could, healing minor injuries and comforting frightened children. Thalion showed local elders how to set simple wards that might deter lesser horrors. Cedric and Mira helped with heavier tasks, from hauling beams to clearing broken cartwheels, ensuring the immediate area was stable before moving on.

By midmorning, the group gathered near the outskirts of the settlement, horses saddled and supplies restocked as best as the villagers could afford. The relic disc, carefully wrapped in cloth, sat secured to Cedric's saddlebag. The ephemeral hum of its enchantment still tingled in the air around them.

The village elder, a silver-haired woman leaning on a carved staff, approached the heroes. "We owe you a debt," she said softly. "If not for your intervention, that Behemoth would have razed our homes entirely. Though we have little, know that you'll always have refuge here."

Cedric bowed his head. "We're grateful. But truly, your perseverance is what stands out. This land endures hardship after hardship."

The elder smiled through weary lines on her face. "We do our best. Light guide you on your journey."

Exchanging final farewells, the four turned eastward once more. Their injuries—physical and otherwise—had not fully healed, but an iron determination burned beneath the fatigue. They had struck down a colossal Behemoth, preventing widespread carnage. And in return, they gained an artifact essential to breaching the Shadow Nexus's final barrier.

The road ahead wound through gently rolling hills, but the presence of the Nexus hung over them like a gathering storm. Clouds massed in the distant sky, and the tapestry from the Minotaurs still displayed glowing lines that pulsed in sync with the newly discovered relic. Thalion surmised that, once they collected all necessary keys, those lines would guide them directly to the Nexus's hidden stronghold.

In hushed conversation, they revisited the battle's harrowing moments—Elara's near-miss with the Behemoth's fists, Mira's ice vortex, Thalion's arcane wards, Cedric's sword strikes. Each recounted the synergy that had turned near-defeat into triumph, forging a deeper layer of trust. Though they had faced illusions, vampires, labyrinths, and monstrous creatures before, this had been their largest foe yet, both in size and sheer might.

They paused at a small stream to water their horses. The land here was quieter, less scarred, though the emptiness of the roads suggested travelers still feared to move freely. Cedric gazed at his reflection in the stream, recalling the expression of awe—and perhaps fear—he'd seen in the cottagers' eyes when they realized he'd stabbed a Behemoth the size of a fortress.

"We're delving into legendary territory," he said, half to himself. "I never pictured I'd be battling creatures out of old sagas when I first took my knightly vows."

Elara rested a comforting hand on his shoulder. "Destiny shapes us in ways we can't always predict. But we have each other—and we have a cause worth every risk."

Thalion closed his eyes, listening to the rush of water. "We must not become complacent. The closer we draw to the Nexus, the more powerful its defenses. We should use this calm to refine our strategies."

Mira nodded, adjusting the strap of her staff. "Our synergy saved us, but our resources are finite. Let's keep practicing combined spells, like the frost-lightning synergy or the way we shielded each other in the heat of battle. We'll need those tactics."

Resuming their journey, they traveled for another day without encountering major threats, though ominous signs of corruption—blackened patches of soil, twisted plants— became more frequent. Late on the second afternoon, they reached a broad plateau that offered a sweeping view of the plains. The sun dipped toward the horizon, painting the sky in oranges and reds.

They decided to camp there, feeling the land's hush. Thalion spent the evening analyzing the relic disc. He traced the runes with careful incantations, noting how they shimmered in response to certain magical frequencies. Mira assisted, cross-referencing the disc's symbols with the partial lexicon gleaned from the tapestry's labyrinth script.

Elara and Cedric patrolled the perimeter, ensuring no prowling beasts lurked. After dinner, they all gathered around the fire, mulling over the significance of the relic. Thalion shared his preliminary findings:

"These runes correlate to gates or seals. I believe that once combined with the scale from the Wyvern—along with potentially other items—we'll be able to unlock or bypass a barrier that the Nexus established ages ago."

Elara held the disc in her lap, feeling its faint vibration. "That means the Nexus is behind all these monstrous resurgences. If so, we're on the right track, collecting what we need to confront it. But the question remains—how many more relics are out there?"

Mira, weary but determined, shrugged. "There might be more, or just a few. The tapestry suggested multiple keys. But even if we have to fight more Behemoths, we'll do it. We can't turn back now."

Cedric leaned forward, face lit by the campfire's glow. "We've come this far. No matter what abominations stand between us and the Nexus, we'll stand together. That Behemoth was the largest foe we've faced, but each victory fuels the next."

A comfortable silence followed, each companion reflecting on how far they had traveled—both physically and spiritually—since they first united in Stonehaven's Royal Citadel. The trials tested their bonds and forced them to grow, culminating in the slaying of a beast that once would have been unthinkable to challenge.

Eventually, the weariness of the day took over. They set their watch rotations, then settled down to rest under a sky streaked by distant storm clouds. A hush of hope lingered: as horrifying as the Behemoth's rampage was, it had given them the relic they needed. Step by step, the path to the Shadow Nexus revealed itself, and with each step, they grew more certain that they were indeed the ones fated to seal away the ancient darkness before it devoured Stonehaven.

At dawn's first light, a gentle breeze swept across the plateau. Cedric rose to greet the sun, marveling at how the land before them seemed both peaceful and fraught with unseen perils. Elara joined him, eyes closed in a meditative prayer. The relic disc hummed softly in her pack, as if sensing the day's potential.

Thalion finished repacking his notes and spells, offering a quick check of the wards they placed overnight. Mira sipped a small cup of herbal tea, gazing out at the horizon where the sky hinted at storms.

They broke camp, saddled the horses, and once again faced east. The Shadow Nexus awaited. Fresh scars from their battle with the Behemoth reminded them that each confrontation demanded everything they had. But the faith that blossomed among them—born of trust, tested by illusions, tempered in the forge of monstrous battles—was unwavering.

As they rode out, the memory of the Behemoth's final roar lingered in their minds. It was a roar of ancient rage, awakened by the creeping corruption, now silenced by the unity of four heroes who refused to break under its onslaught. That same unity would guide them forward, no matter the monsters yet to come.

In the days ahead, they would face new horrors, unravel deeper mysteries, and push ever closer to the malevolent heart of the Shadow Nexus. But for now, they carried with them the relic so vital to unlocking the final path—and, more importantly, the unspoken pledge to fight for each other and for all the innocent lives threatened by darkness.

With renewed purpose, they left the scene of their victory behind. The countryside stretched endlessly, a stage for the culminating battles that loomed on the horizon. No matter what monstrous roars awaited, these four companions would answer with courage, forging hope out of the deepest shadows until Stonehaven knew light once more.

9

THE ANCIENT LIBRARY

A hush settled over the rolling foothills as Sir Cedric, Lady Elara, Thalion, and Mira continued their trek eastward. The journey had grown ever more ominous since their recent battle with the colossal Behemoth. Though the threat of that monstrous titan was laid to rest—and its relic safely secured—they couldn't help noticing how the land bore fresh scars of corruption and strange disturbances. Trees stood half-withered, streams ran dark, and an unsettling quiet replaced the usual chirping of wildlife. It was as if the Shadow Nexus's influence seeped into every root and rivulet, stifling the pulse of life.

Despite these grim signs, a new determination fueled their steps. Each hero felt a deeper resolve forged by prior trials: illusions that tested their darkest memories, the labyrinth of the Minotaurs, the towering rampage of the Behemoth. They had emerged not just intact but stronger, each discovering a well of inner power—and each trusting in the unity that bound them as a fellowship. Now, spurred by rumors and runic clues from the tapestry they carried, they ventured in search of an ancient library rumored to hold secrets about the Shadow Nexus itself.

The party's current lead was a scrap of old text referencing an "Arcadium of Forsaken Knowledge," a place once devoted to gathering the mightiest spells and records in Stonehaven's earlier ages. Thalion had turned the partial name over in his mind, connecting it with a footnote in the Minotaurs' Tapestry of Paths. In those swirling threads, a faint swirl of symbols indicated a hidden repository of knowledge—concealed behind illusions, wards, or worse.

"Arcadium," Mira had mused, late one night by the campfire. "If that's a corruption of an older word, it might be the same as the Arcadium Librarium from the lost city-states. Or a portion of Stonehaven's magical archives that was never recorded officially."

Elara, intently polishing the damage from her shield, had paused to listen. "If so, that library might hold texts about the earliest conflicts with the Nexus. Perhaps how it was sealed or contained in ages past."

Thalion rubbed his chin, gaze flickering. "Indeed. If we learn the precise purification method, we can do more than just seal it. We might cleanse or destroy the Nexus altogether."

So they had followed the tapestry's faint guidance, traveling days across lonely fields and over a low mountain range until a single rumor from a shepherd guided them to a peculiar ravine. The shepherd, wizened and somewhat reluctant, admitted hearing of "buried halls of old," hidden behind illusions that kept most folk at bay. With each new clue, the sense of approaching something monumental grew.

Eventually, the group arrived at an expanse where the hills curved inward, forming a natural amphitheater of stone. At the center, a jagged crack opened in the earth, plunging down into darkness. Vines and creepers draped the edges, swaying in the breeze. From above, the ravine looked like an innocuous cleft—yet Mira felt strong enchantments humming beneath the surface.

"That must be it," she whispered, heart fluttering. "The wards are subtle, but definitely there. Something down in that fissure isn't normal rock."

Cedric tested the ground at the ravine's lip. "It's stable enough. Let's see if we can find a safe descent."

Moving cautiously, the companions tied ropes around a sturdy outcrop and rappelled down the fissure's shadowy walls. The air grew stale, laced with a faint mustiness reminiscent of damp parchment. Loose stones rattled underfoot. After descending nearly fifty feet, they reached a ledge that wound deeper into the darkness.

Elara held up a small orb of radiance, courtesy of her divine magic, to light their way. "No sign of guardians yet," she noted. "Only stifled air and old spiderwebs."

Thalion cast a simpler glow charm, giving them a second source of illumination. "We must be near an entrance. The tapestry implied a concealed door or arch."

Following the ledge, they spotted an ornate archway half-buried in rubble. Its stone was etched with swirling runes: stylized wings, horned faces, and cryptic glyphs that time had worn thin. A broken keystone overhead bore a single word in archaic script—one that Thalion recognized after a moment's study. "Arcanum," he read. "Or Arcadium, in the older tongue. We're in the right place."

Intrigued, Mira stepped forward, staff at the ready. She gently brushed away moss clinging to the runes. "There's a faint barrier here—like a locked door made of illusions. Let me try to unravel it."

Pressing her palm to the runes, she murmured a soft incantation. Threads of blue-white light shimmered across the arch. With a hiss, the illusions parted, revealing a dusty corridor leading into the cliffside. The air that rushed out smelled of centuries-old tomes and stale magic. A faint sense of foreboding draped the threshold.

Cedric drew his sword, glancing at the others. "Stay on guard. We have no idea what wards remain."

Without another word, they stepped through. Darkness fell behind them like a curtain as the corridor swallowed their lights. Each footstep echoed off walls that once might have been grand, now eroded by time. Ancient sconces dotted the stone, their metal frames rusted, some still holding the remnants of enchanted torches long spent. The corridor sloped downward, gradually widening until it opened onto an imposing set of double doors made of blackened oak.

Elara raised her shield. "This must be the main entrance to the library. Let's see if it's locked."

Cedric tried the handle, expecting resistance. Instead, the doors groaned inward with a push, revealing a sweeping hall beyond. Their lantern-like spells cast overlapping circles of light onto shelves upon shelves of books and scrolls, arranged in labyrinthine rows. Dust motes swirled in the sudden disturbance. A hush clung to the place, as if centuries of silence weighed heavily upon every surface.

Mira's eyes widened. "Incredible," she breathed. "This might be older than any library in Stonehaven's capital. Who knows what knowledge lies here?"

They ventured in, pulses racing. The hall soared overhead, supported by carved pillars depicting robed figures and bestial shapes—a veritable forest of stone statues gazing down from the shadows. At intervals, narrow corridors branched off, lined with more shelves and reading alcoves. Old tables sat strewn with skeletal remains of parchment, lamps, and quills. The floor was layered with dust so thick it muffled their boots.

Elara ran a gauntleted hand across a shelf, wiping away a half-inch of grime. "No footprints," she noted, voice hushed. "No sign of other visitors. It's as though no one's set foot here in decades, maybe centuries."

Thalion nodded thoughtfully, eyes scanning the towering shelves. "If this is indeed the Arcadium or a lost annex of Stonehaven's archives, it's no wonder. The illusions up top might have kept all but the most determined explorers away."

Cedric peered down one of the side aisles, noticing entire racks of scroll cases, many collapsed from rot. "The question is, how do we find anything about the Shadow Nexus in this labyrinth? We could wander for days."

Mira lifted her staff, letting the tip glow more brightly. "Perhaps there's an index or a central reading chamber. Ancient libraries often had a system to organize knowledge by subject."

Elara gave an encouraging nod. "Let's split up, but not too far. We'll each check a few rows, then regroup. Thalion, can you sense any strong magical imprint that might guide us?"

The mage closed his eyes, extending his senses. After a moment, he pointed toward a dim corridor branching off the main hall. "That way. I feel a subtle hum of wards, like a protective net around a cluster of texts."

And so they advanced, weaving carefully between looming shelves. The hush of the library pressed in, as though a thousand phantom scholars still studied in silence. Cobwebs clung to corners, occasionally stirring as the party passed. Through it all, Mira's excitement grew, tempered by caution. It felt as if the knowledge they needed was close at hand—and yet something about the stony gloom set her nerves on edge.

They emerged into a circular reading chamber with a domed ceiling. A mosaic in the center depicted a stylized sun-and-moon motif ringed by runes. Benches and desks lay scattered, decayed from centuries of neglect. Against the far wall, a series of locked cabinets lined up, their doors intricately carved with arcane symbols. This area seemed more organized, as though the librarians had placed especially valuable or forbidden tomes here.

Mira approached one of the cabinets, staff held high for light. "I sense wards, older than anything I've felt. They might be keyed to an archival system... or a trap."

Thalion joined her, carefully extending a palm to the swirling runes on the cabinet door. He murmured a counter-ward incantation, causing the symbols to flicker. After a moment, the lock clicked open with a soft *thunk*.

Inside, rows of scrolls and slender tomes stacked neatly, each labeled in archaic script. Mira's heart fluttered as she gently lifted one. The cover bore the image of a swirling vortex ringed by runic circles—eerily similar to what they had seen in the tapestry referencing the Nexus. "We're on the right track," she breathed.

Elara and Cedric stood guard near the entry, alert for any hidden guardians. But aside from the scraping of the party's boots on stone, the library remained eerily silent. For minutes, Thalion and Mira rummaged through the cabinet's contents, quietly exclaiming at references to "a wellspring of negative energies" and "the ancient rites of purification." Each mention made their pulses quicken—here might lie the method to cleanse the Shadow Nexus entirely.

As the pair gathered the most crucial scrolls, Thalion's brow furrowed. "These references speak of overlapping planes, of an origin predating even Stonehaven's earliest kingdoms. The Nexus may have been a tear in the world's fabric, or a confluence of malignant energies. To purify it, certain artifacts or rituals were used, yet the text is incomplete."

Mira opened another tome, scanning the yellowed pages. "This one mentions a grand incantation known as the 'Song of Severance'—capable of severing the Nexus from our plane. But it references needing certain anchors or relics to stabilize the ritual. Possibly the relics we're gathering."

Elara stepped closer, her curiosity piqued. "So if we combine the keys—the Wyvern's scale, the Behemoth's disc, and whatever else we find—and enact this Song of Severance, we might seal the Nexus for good?"

"More than seal it," Thalion clarified. "If done correctly, we could banish or neutralize it permanently. The texts hint at a final cleansing that once saved Stonehaven in a bygone era. But the details are scattered."

Cedric exhaled, adrenaline surging. "Then we'll gather what we can and fill in the gaps. Let's collect all relevant volumes. We'll copy what we need if we can."

Mira nodded, eyes shining despite the dust. "Yes, we should. But we must be quick. I have a strange feeling we're not alone here."

Her premonition proved correct. As they sorted through the texts, a distant scraping echoed in the library's depths. At first faint, it grew louder: grinding noises of stone on stone, accompanied by the flutter of wings. The party froze, hearts pounding. Then from a high balcony, two monstrous shapes peeled away from the architecture. With heavy flaps of leathery wings, Gargoyles descended into the circular chamber.

Each Gargoyle bore a horned visage and a body of living stone, etched with runic lines that glowed a dull red. Their eyes burned with an inner light. With a raspy shriek, they swooped overhead, smashing into shelves and scattering books. Dust and shards of wood flew.

"Gargoyles!" Cedric shouted, raising his shield. "Looks like they're guardians."

Elara gripped her sword, stepping forward. "They must defend the knowledge here. The wards we broke might have awakened them."

Thalion and Mira quickly set aside the scrolls they'd gathered. The Gargoyles circled once, then dove, claws extended. The party scattered as talons raked the air.

One Gargoyle latched onto a pillar, glaring down with a hiss, while the other soared across the room, swiping at Thalion. The mage erected a barrier that cracked under the stone beast's assault. Sparks flew, forcing him to roll behind a toppled desk.

Mira conjured a blast of arcane light, searing the Gargoyle's flank, but the stone hide resisted most of the magic. "They're tough," she gasped, staff humming with effort. "We need physical force or something that disrupts stone."

Cedric lunged at the nearest Gargoyle, slashing with a runic longsword. The blade screeched against the creature's rocky hide, carving a shallow groove. The beast let out a guttural snarl, swinging a wing that knocked Cedric sideways. Elara rushed to intercept, shield shining with holy energy. She bashed the Gargoyle's chest, and cracks blossomed under the radiant impact. Stone chips rained down, fueling a fierce hiss from the monster.

Yet the second Gargoyle swooped in from behind, nearly catching Elara off guard. Thalion hurled a small thunderbolt, staggering it, while Mira launched a volley of shimmering darts that pelted its wings. The stone beast roared, pivoting in midair.

The library turned into a swirling melee of dust, debris, and flapping wings. Gargoyles battered the shelves, toppling ancient tomes. The heroes dashed in and out of row after row, using pillars for cover. Each strike shook the musty air, echoing up into the vaulted dome.

Cedric circled wide, eyes locked on the Gargoyle that soared near the ceiling. He spotted a stone chandelier overhead, supported by a thick chain. Timing his movement, he hefted a throwing knife at the chain's weak link. The blade clanged, severing it. The chandelier plummeted, slamming into the Gargoyle's back. The creature shrieked, pinned under the broken mass of metal. Wasting no time, Cedric rushed forward, driving his sword between the Gargoyle's shoulder blades. The monster shattered in a shower of rubble, releasing a final, anguished screech.

Meanwhile, the second Gargoyle engaged Elara and Thalion among scattered desks. Its stony talons raked the floor, leaving gouges in the flagstones. Elara deflected a blow with her shield, though the impact jarred her arm. Thalion conjured a lash of arcane energy that coiled around the Gargoyle's ankle, yanking it off balance. Sensing the opening, Mira fired a concentrated burst of frost at the creature's wings, freezing them. The Gargoyle staggered, roared, and tore free with raw strength, fragments of ice scattering.

Elara seized the moment. She channeled divine light into her sword, thrusting it into a crack in the Gargoyle's chest. A blinding flare of energy erupted, and the stone beast crumbled, screeching as it disintegrated into dusty rubble. The echoes of its final roar faded, leaving the library in hushed disarray.

The fight ended as abruptly as it began. Gargoyle fragments lay scattered, and the once-pristine library was even more disheveled—broken shelves, upturned furniture, drifting clouds of dust. The companions caught their breath, hearts racing with the sudden adrenaline crash.

Mira bent over a shattered Gargoyle head, tapping it with her staff. "Incredible," she murmured. "They had layered runes that bind a soul fragment or elemental spirit to animate them. Old magic, indeed."

Elara supported herself against a leaning shelf, wincing at bruises. "They were formidable. At least we know the wards here were top-tier."

Cedric dusted off his pauldrons, scanning the corridor for signs of more guardians. "Seems these two might have been the primary sentinels. We need to be sure there aren't more. But first, we should secure the tomes that mention the Shadow Nexus."

Thalion stepped carefully around the rubble, picking up a few scattered scrolls. "At least we saved these from the chaos. Let's gather as much knowledge as possible—quietly, if we can. Then we'll plan our exit."

They worked methodically, searching nearby shelves and cabinets for anything referencing the Nexus. Through it all, the library's imposing stillness resumed, as though the Gargoyles' presence had been the only spark of life in centuries. Distant corridors beckoned, but mindful of traps, they limited their exploration to the circular reading chamber and adjacent alcoves.

Within an hour, they amassed a small stack of critical texts: half-decayed scrolls detailing early attempts to contain the Shadow Nexus, fragments of incantations for the "Song of Severance," notes on relic usage, and partial maps of rumored strongholds. Mira pored over them, her eyes blazing with intellectual fervor. Despite the dust and exhaustion, she smiled whenever she stumbled on a new piece of the puzzle.

Once they felt certain no further guardians lurked in the immediate vicinity, the group settled in a relatively intact reading alcove. Elara and Cedric kept watch near the door, weapons ready should anything else stir. Thalion spread out the newly found texts on a sturdy table, while Mira perched on the edge, leaning in eagerly.

The old parchments were written in archaic dialects of Stonehavenn. Some lines were smudged beyond recognition, others intact but riddled with symbolic references that demanded a scholar's eye. Thalion guided Mira in translating, each step revealing another facet of the Nexus's history.

"So it's as we suspected," Thalion explained after a while. "Long ago, the Nexus formed as a convergence of negative energies, possibly from another plane. The ancients discovered it could warp reality and birth abominations if not contained."

Mira squinted at a curling corner of text. "Here it explains that initial wards were placed by a coalition of mages and priests. They used artifacts to anchor the wards—artifacts that harness elemental or divine power. Over time, those wards weakened, leading to sporadic reawakenings."

Elara, looking over their shoulders, chimed in. "Then the Song of Severance might be the final measure to not just seal but purge the Nexus from our plane."

Thalion nodded, brow knit in concentration. "Yes. According to this, the Song is a grand ritual, orchestrated with relics that each represent a fundamental aspect of Stonehaven's life force—earth, air, fire, water, and so forth. We already have at least two: the scale from the Wyvern might represent the primal energy of fire, and the disc from the Behemoth might embody earth. But the texts hint at more."

"Water, air, possibly something divine or celestial," Mira added. "We might have to locate them all to fully power the ritual. And each relic must be placed in a precise formation while the Song is chanted."

Cedric, arms folded, frowned thoughtfully. "That means we'll need to keep searching. If the library references them, there may be hints about where the other relics rest—and how to complete the Song."

Rummaging further, they uncovered references to "The Pearl of Tides," rumored to lie in a sunken temple near Stonehaven's southern coasts. Another text spoke of an "Amulet of Dvine Light" hidden in a sky-borne spire. Yet the details were vague or lost. Many pages disintegrated at Thalion's touch, forcing them to piece together half-phrases and cryptic clues.

Elara exhaled, wiping sweat from her forehead. "We'll cross that bridge later. For now, we confirm that we can indeed purge the Nexus if we gather all these relics and enact the ritual. That's more hope than we had before."

Mira's eyes shone. "We also know it's dangerous—any misstep in the Song of Severance might unleash catastrophic backlash. But at least we have a path forward."

Cedric nodded. "We'll track down each relic, then approach the Nexus with the knowledge and the power to end this once and for all."

Thalion rolled up the most vital scrolls, planning to copy them later. "I'll keep these safe. The rest, we can summarize or photographically memorize with illusions, if we have time."

He conjured a minor illusion to imprint key diagrams from the crumbling pages, capturing the arrangement of runes for the Song's culminating verse. Mira replicated the symbols, storing them in her own portable parchment. The synergy of their combined scholarship warmed the gloom of the library, a bright spark amid centuries of dust.

They planned to depart soon, not wishing to linger in a place that might hold more gargoyles or worse. But as they began packing the precious documents, a scraping sound in a side corridor made them all tense. Cedric and Elara readied weapons, Thalion dimmed his glow orb, and Mira froze, staff in hand.

From the shadows stepped three smaller gargoyle-like creatures. Not as large or imposing as the two guardians before, these resembled stone imps—wingless, hunched figures with jagged teeth. They hissed, their eyes glowing with a lesser arcane spark. A savage intelligence gleamed in them, suggesting they were subordinate watchers or sentries.

Cedric moved forward to engage, but Thalion gently touched his shoulder. "They're not charging us. Maybe they're uncertain whether to attack." Indeed, the stone imps seemed to watch warily, as though waiting for a signal or command.

Mira raised her staff. "They might sense we've taken something. Or they could be scouting. Gargoyles often serve as watchers for larger guardians."

Elara approached carefully, shield raised. "We mean no desecration, only to preserve this knowledge. If you can understand, we are not your enemies unless you force us to be."

At her voice, one imp clacked its claws, then advanced. The group braced, but the creature only stopped a short distance away, tilting its stony head as though assessing them. Sparks flickered in its eyes. Then, with a collective hiss, the trio slunk back into the corridor, disappearing into the gloom.

Thalion exhaled. "Strange. Perhaps they're bound to protect the library from those who'd destroy or defile it, rather than from those who—like us—seek knowledge. The bigger gargoyles must've been the first line if we forcibly broke wards."

Mira frowned. "Still, we can't be sure. Let's hurry. No need to provoke them further."

They finished gathering the most critical texts, then double-checked the library's main hall. Satisfied that they had gleaned all possible details about the Song of Severance and the relics, the party prepared to depart.

Retracing their steps past collapsed shelves and columns, they returned to the corridor leading to the ravine. No further guardians emerged. The hush remained unbroken except for the crunch of rubble beneath their boots. At the archway, Mira paused to run a hand over the old script. Despite the dust, she felt a pang of sorrow leaving such a monumental trove of knowledge behind.

Cedric gently touched her shoulder. "We can't save every scroll. But we carry the essential parts with us. That will be enough to save Stonehaven."

She nodded, offering a grateful smile. "I know. Part of me just dreams of restoring these halls, making them a beacon of learning again. Maybe after the Nexus is cleansed, we can see about that."

Elara, overhearing, smiled softly. "One challenge at a time. Let's survive the next leg of our journey first."

Careful not to disturb the illusions outside more than necessary, they exited the massive library gates. The corridor, dimly lit by Elara's orb, led them back to the broken arch near the ravine. Once they stepped beyond the threshold, the portal shimmered shut behind them, as though it never existed. If not for the battered gargoyle rubble scattered inside, one might think the library was just another rumor.

At the ravine's edge, they retrieved their ropes and climbed up, hauling themselves back into the open air. The sun, already dipping westward, cast warm rays across the grass. A swirl of relief accompanied them: although the library had been foreboding, its revelations granted a renewed sense of direction.

They opted to make camp near the ravine, finding a flat patch of ground a safe distance from the fissure. Tired from the gargoyle battle and the mental strain of deciphering ancient texts, the four settled around a small fire. Cedric produced dried meat and fruits for supper while Elara performed a short healing prayer for bruises.

Mira spread out the scrolls they'd salvaged, eager to piece together more details. Thalion joined her, both leaning close to the flickering firelight. Though exhausted, their excitement was palpable—like scholars unearthing a hidden library's greatest treasures. They spoke in low tones, referencing the Song of Severance, the relic alignments, and theories on the purifying ritual's cosmic significance.

Cedric and Elara, meanwhile, discussed the possibility of gargoyles or other guardians reemerging at night. They set up watch rotations, each determined not to be caught off guard. But the evening proved calm, disturbed only by a gentle breeze rustling the grass.

At length, Thalion sat back, rubbing his eyes. "We've definitely confirmed we need at least four or five relics, each symbolizing an elemental or celestial force. That fits with the relics we have: the Wyvern scale likely stands for flame, the Behemoth disc for earth. The texts reference a 'Pearl of Tides' for water, and possibly a 'Amulet of Light' for the air divine aspects. Summoning the Song requires all, plus a final incantation."

Mira stifled a yawn, nodding. "It means more journeys to gather them. But we have a blueprint now."

Cedric, hearing them, joined the conversation. "And once we have all the pieces, we head for the Nexus's lair, enact the Song, and purge it. Simple on paper, but the execution will be... intense."

Elara's expression shone with cautious hope. "We'll face it together. Each step we take has led us here. Let's rest, gather strength, and keep forging on."

When the stars emerged, an almost cheerful hush fell over the camp. Mira found herself unable to sleep, mind abuzz with the revelations from the library. The shadowy illusions that once haunted her dreams seemed distant now—she was enthralled by the possibility of saving Stonehaven from the Nexus's creeping doom.

She wandered a short distance from the tents, gazing at the ravine's outline under moonlight. Memories of the gargoyle fight flickered in her thoughts—the stone shards, the screech of wingbeats. A quiet determination settled in her heart. Yes, they had risked their lives, but the knowledge gleaned was worth it. If the Song of Severance truly existed, and the relics indeed formed its key, they had a real shot at ending this cataclysm once and for all.

From behind, footsteps rustled. She turned to see Thalion approaching with a kindly expression. "Couldn't sleep?" he asked softly.

Mira shook her head, half-smiling. "Too many things swirling in my mind. We're so close, but it feels like the hardest parts are yet to come."

The mage nodded, gazing out at the starlit horizon. "True. But we're closer than we were yesterday. And we're not alone."

They shared a quiet moment, the night breeze ruffling their cloaks. One by one, they'd all faced their personal demons, risked life in monstrous battles, and gleaned secrets from dusty tomes. Now, the path forward was clearer if still fraught with peril.

"Thank you," Mira murmured. "For guiding me in the translations. For standing with me. With all of us."

Thalion placed a hand lightly on her shoulder. "We stand together, or we don't stand at all."

Sunrise found the party rejuvenated. Elara's healing spells and a good rest soothed their bruises, though the memory of the gargoyle fight lingered in stiff muscles. They packed their gear, carefully protecting the retrieved texts in watertight bags. The plan was to head north again, intersecting with a known trade route where they might glean further intelligence about the next relic sites.

Cedric led the way from the ravine, ensuring no hidden illusions reactivated behind them. The library's entrance, concealed once more, appeared as mere stone. If not for the scuff marks of their ropes, one might never guess a wealth of forbidden knowledge lay beneath.

Thalion took a final look back. "If we're successful in cleansing the Nexus, maybe one day we can return to restore and share this library's treasures for Stonehaven."

Elara smiled, adjusting her shield. "That's a worthy dream. But first, we must gather the relics, form the Song, and confront the darkness itself."

They mounted up, urging their horses across the dew-laden grass. The sky glowed with early warmth, a hopeful sign. Each hero carried a portion of the library's lore in their pack or memory. The promise of a final solution to the Nexus's blight kindled excitement despite looming uncertainty.

By midday, they reached a winding dirt road that cut through hilly farmland. The difference from days prior was striking: farmland looked less ravaged, though subtle signs of corruption—stunted crops, jittery livestock—persisted. Villagers they passed seemed wary but not entirely despairing. Word of the Behemoth's defeat had traveled, inspiring a fragile optimism.

Now more than ever, the group realized they must not fail. The land's flicker of hope hinged on eradicating the Nexus's threat. As they rode, they occasionally paused to reassure frightened peasants or exchange news. None, however, knew about the library or the Song of Severance. The general populace remained ignorant of the deeper forces at work.

In the late afternoon, a traveling peddler hailed them from a rickety cart. "Heard tell of strange watchers in the ruins east o' here," he said, tipping his hat. "Some travelers claim winged stone creatures attacked 'em. But you look well-armed. Might not be an issue, eh?"

Cedric nodded with a polite smile. "We encountered something like that. It's been... resolved. But caution is wise."

The peddler shrugged, rattling away with his wares, grateful for the advice. Mira watched him go, feeling a faint sense of guardianship. They had battled the guardians so no further reckless wanderers would meet a grim fate. A small, quiet victory.

That evening, they made camp by a shallow stream. The air held a pleasant chill, and crickets ventured tentative songs from the nearby grasses. Over a modest dinner, the group revisited the library's revelations, clarifying steps:

1. **Gather all elemental relics.** They already had two (Wyvern scale for fire, Behemoth disc for earth) and needed to find the others—especially ones representing water, air, and possibly a divine essence.

2. **Reconstruct or memorize the Song of Severance.** They had partial verses from the library, enough to confirm its existence and general structure, but they required more details. The scrolls held some lines, and illusions copied from the crumbling pages offered hints. Thalion and Mira might piece it together in time.

3. **Confront the Nexus** at its core. Once they possessed all relics and the full incantation, they would venture into the heart of the corruption, likely beyond Stonehaven's northern or eastern frontiers. The tapestry indicated a swirl of darkness that might be miles wide—a place where negative energies poured into the land.

As they mapped out next moves, Elara knelt in silent prayer, asking for guidance. Cedric re-checked their supplies. Thalion jotted notes while Mira quietly hummed a snippet of the half-remembered Song, her melodic voice carrying a subtle magic. An undercurrent of awe passed among them, imagining how that melody, fully realized, might banish an ancient evil forever.

Before rest, they gathered around the fire. A solemn mood fell as each considered how close they teetered to cataclysmic events, yet how real the chance of victory seemed. Mira lifted one of the salvaged texts—its old binding cracking—and read aloud a short passage describing how the ancients once purified lesser rifts with a fragment of the Song. Her voice trembled slightly:

"In unity of flame and stone, of wave and wind, The chords of Dawn's promise we weave to mend— Lattice of life, from darkness unbind, So wholeness and hope forever ascend."

As the words faded, the crackle of the fire resumed. A hush followed, each hero feeling the text's resonance. Then Cedric spoke softly, a hand curled around his sword hilt. "We vow to see this through. If these verses can drive out the Nexus, we'll give all we can to realize them."

Elara placed her palm over his, eyes bright. "And once done, we'll share this knowledge with Stonehaven—so no future generation must relive this threat."

Thalion laid a scroll aside. "Agreed. Knowledge should not be locked away to gather dust or guarded by monstrous sentinels, but shared for the realm's preservation."

Mira smiled, tears glinting in her eyes. "Then let us be the stewards of this library's secrets. We'll carry them forward, enact the cleansing, and restore hope to Stonehaven."

They joined hands in a circle, forging a silent pact to use the library's lore for the greater good, promising that these secrets—once twisted by fear or lost to time—would guide them to banish the darkest threat in living memory.

Morning dawned on a gentle breeze, the land seeming a fraction less grim. Their next destination lay further east, toward rumored coastal regions or lofty highlands. Whispers of the "Pearl of Tides" or "The Amulet of Light" might beckon them in days to come, but for now, they rode on with renewed hearts.

They left the region of the Arcadium behind, ensuring the illusions re-sealed the library's entrance so that reckless wanderers wouldn't accidentally awaken more guardians. From the vantage of a distant slope, the ravine looked like any other rocky cleft—a place of little significance. Yet the companions knew otherwise. There, behind illusions and stone, a treasury of knowledge now lived within them.

As they traveled, they continued refining the partial Song, humming bits of melody or reciting lines to test the flow. Each hero contributed in a distinct way: Elara's sense of divine cadence, Thalion's arcane scholarship, Mira's knack for puzzle-solving, and Cedric's ear for timing and synergy. Though incomplete, the Song of Severance took a rough shape in their minds.

The day progressed without major incident, giving them time to nurse aches from the gargoyle fight and to mentally organize the library's lore. By late afternoon, they forded a shallow river under a crimson sky, searching for a safe campsite. The road ahead promised new perils—monsters, cultists, or lingering corruption—but with the library's secrets in hand, they felt a spark of confidence that no challenge would be insurmountable.

Setting camp near an old oak, they gazed at the horizon's fading light. The memory of towering shelves and the hush of ancient pages still glimmered in their thoughts. Elara reflected that if the library's guardians had left them alive, perhaps some arcane spirit recognized their pure intentions. The library might well remain hidden, waiting until they completed their quest—or until another worthy seeker approached centuries hence.

Cedric polished nicks from his sword, recalling the thrill of besting the gargoyles. "They were fierce," he mused. "But I'm glad we overcame them. Without that, we'd never have gleaned these crucial secrets."

Thalion gave a wry smile. "Indeed. And who knows? Maybe if the library stands once the Nexus is gone, we can revisit it for further truths about Stonehaven's lost eras."

"Every place we go, we realize how vast this realm's history is," Mira said, fiddling with an old scroll. "It humbles me. There's so much we don't know. But at least we have this piece of the puzzle now."

Elara's shield caught a glint of firelight. "And the knowledge might save countless lives. With it, we aim to do more than seal the darkness; we'll exorcise it from Stonehaven's heart."

Their conversation segued into lighter banter—about the dusty smell of old tomes, the improbable idea of Thalion or Mira opening a traveling library, or Cedric's comedic attempts at reading ancient script. Despite the daunting future, they laughed, forging a camaraderie that promised to see them through any horror.

And so ended their chapter in the Arcadium's hidden depths. Though battered by Gargoyles and overwhelmed by the magnitude of half-forgotten lore, they emerged with the truth that the Shadow Nexus could indeed be purified—provided they gathered the right relics and harnessed the ancient Song of Severance. Their presence in the library had awakened fierce guardians, but also awakened the dormant knowledge that might save their world.

Under the star-strewn sky, with a gentle wind rustling the grass, each hero found solace in how far they had come. The illusions that once plagued them felt distant. The beasts and tyrants they had battled seemed stepping stones toward a grander destiny. As they lay down to sleep, the grim hush of the land no longer smothered them; rather, it underscored the importance of their quest.

In the days to come, they would face new trials, from watery depths to lofty spires, from cultist treachery to monstrous abominations. But the library's quiet halls echoed in their memories—a reminder that knowledge, once discovered and shared, held the power to reshape fate. The roars of gargoyles, the hush of ancient tomes, and the radiant bonds of friendship melded into a single chord of purpose.

10

GARGOYLE GUARDIANS

When dawn broke, the group found themselves reflecting on whether they had overlooked something in the Ancient Library. Their hurried retreat—forced by the confrontation with the Gargoyle guardians—had ended their search prematurely. Now they wondered if crucial information had been left behind in those hidden corridors. Perhaps the small stone imps they'd encountered were guarding more vital secrets deeper within.

Resolved to find out, the heroes decided to return. Many sections of the library still lay unexplored, and if there were more guardians patrolling deeper halls, there might be more knowledge waiting to be discovered.

Retracing their path from the previous day, they arrived once again at the ragged slope rising above the Arcadium. Thalion glanced around and remarked, "The illusions near the entrance might be reactivated by now. We should be vigilant—there could be other hidden wards or gargoyles that didn't appear on our first visit."

Elara nodded, adjusting the strap on her battered shield. "Yesterday, we managed to collect some crucial texts. But we only scratched the surface of what the Arcadium's archives might offer. There could be entire wings with more detailed records on the Song of Severance or other relics. If the gargoyles are actively guarding those halls, we should expect a larger, more coordinated fight."

Mira checked the runic inscriptions on her staff, verifying that her spells were prepared. Despite a twinge of nervousness at facing more animate stone beasts, her eyes gleamed with curiosity. "It's risky, yes. But if those old references to the Song of Severance are incomplete, we need everything we can find. The library's secrets could be the key to truly eradicating the Nexus."

Cedric scanned the horizon. The farmland behind them bore quiet scars of corruption, twisted trees, and withered patches of grass. It reminded him how urgent their mission was. "Agreed. We can't rely on partial fragments. We'll venture deeper, handle whatever guardians remain, and secure the knowledge once and for all."

In unspoken accord, they descended into the fissure once again, following the rope they had left anchored to the stony outcrop. The morning wind stirred dust motes around them as they climbed down. Each hero moved with renewed caution—armor freshly patched, spells recharged, hearts resolved to finish what they had started.

Once at the base of the ravine, Mira stepped forward to unravel the illusory barrier that concealed the library's grand entrance. She placed a palm on the carved arch, whispering arcane syllables to dissolve the illusions. The runes shimmered, then parted like a receding veil, exposing the same dusty corridor they had explored before. But the air inside felt different—darker, heavier, as though stirred by an unseen presence.

Cedric ventured in first, sword drawn. "Stay close," he murmured over his shoulder. "We don't know how many gargoyles might have reactivated overnight."

Their boots crunched on chipped stone. The corridor extended into gloom, torches long extinguished. Old sconces clung to the walls, rusted with age. Thalion conjured a small orb of light that bobbed overhead, bathing them in a warm, ghostly glow. The corridor opened onto a familiar foyer—a wide, circular space lined with half-collapsed shelves and rubble.

Elara ran a hand over her shield, calling on a minor protective prayer. "Yesterday, the gargoyles attacked us near the main reading hall. If there are more guardians, they might be deeper in the archives or posted around valuable sections."

Mira nodded, eyes flicking across the shadows. "We should also watch for traps. Some libraries of old used living wards—like gargoyles—to protect critical books, but they might have other defenses, too."

Thalion pointed down a hall to their right. "We didn't explore that wing yesterday. Let's start there. It might lead us to new shelves or antechambers we missed. If the gargoyles are guarding anything vital, that's where they'd likely be posted."

They proceeded into the unknown wing, navigating corridors stacked with mildewed tomes and dusty scrolls. The architecture hinted at a grand design once, with elegant columns and vaulting overhead. Now everything was shrouded in centuries of neglect. Cobwebs fluttered as the party passed, and the faint echo of dripping water resounded in the distance.

Occasionally, they paused to examine titles on the shelves. Thalion recognized references to ancient magic theory, but few direct mentions of the Nexus. Mira noticed a volume describing obscure relics used in ritual banishments, but its pages were eaten away by mold. Still, the deeper they ventured, the more the lingering wards pricked at their magical senses, as if warning them that valuable secrets lay within.

After about twenty minutes of careful progress, they reached a vaulted chamber with multiple branching passages. At the center stood a crumbling statue of a robed figure holding a staff—perhaps a librarian or a scholar immortalized in stone. The statue's gaze seemed to follow them, a testament to the illusions or enchantments woven into the library's design.

Cedric examined the floor, noticing fresh scratches in the dust. "Look here. Something heavy moved through recently—a broad drag mark, plus chipped stone. Could be a gargoyle's talons."

Elara crouched beside him, fingertips grazing the marks. "Yes... and it's heading that way." She nodded toward a dark corridor. The scratch marks vanished into the shadows.

Mira swallowed, feeling a flicker of nerves. "I'd guess multiple guardians might be patrolling. Let's be ready for a coordinated attack."

Thalion signaled for them to continue but remain silent. The tension heightened. Each footfall felt too loud, echoing around the high ceilings. It was as though the library held its breath, poised to unleash its stony protectors at any moment.

Sure enough, as they rounded a corner into a large reading hall, a low rumble echoed overhead. Four gargoyles perched on the crossbeams near the ceiling. Their stone skins bore intricate runes that glowed faintly red. Guttural snarls echoed as they stretched their wings, eyes flaring with an inner light that seemed to register the intruders.

Cedric instantly raised his shield, calling, "We've got gargoyles—four of them!"

The creatures launched themselves from the rafters with stony screeches, swooping down in arcs that kicked up clouds of dust. The library's hush exploded into the clamor of battle. The group spread out, each hero taking a defensive stance.

One gargoyle dove at Elara, talons aiming to rip her shield away. She braced, slamming her shield upward. Metal and stone collided with a deafening crash. Sparks rained, and the gargoyle hissed, launching backward to wheel in the air. Another soared toward Cedric, who swung his sword in a controlled arc, managing to nick the beast's rocky hide and deflect a raking claw.

Mira swiftly muttered an incantation. Frost-laced arcs formed at her fingertips. With a thrust of her staff, she sent a barrage of icy shards at the gargoyles overhead. Two of them roared, battered by the cold projectiles, but their thick stone hides shed shards of ice with minimal damage.

Meanwhile, Thalion conjured a swirling shield of arcane wind, deflecting one gargoyle's attempt to flank him from behind. The stone creature tumbled mid-air, regaining its balance with a flap of heavy wings.

"Focus fire!" Cedric barked, raising his blade. "Try not to split up too far!"

Realizing brute force alone might not suffice, the heroes shifted to a more strategic approach. Elara channeled divine energy into her shield, forging a bright aura that cast the gargoyles in shimmering light. The beasts recoiled, hissing at the holy glow. While they were momentarily blinded, Cedric dashed forward, dealing quick strikes. The sword edges chipped at one gargoyle's stony chest, creating hairline cracks. It screeched, swiping back with a wing that Cedric barely sidestepped.

Mira and Thalion set about corralling another pair of gargoyles. Thalion recited a chant, summoning a swirl of illusions around one beast's head, confusing its senses. Snarling in disorientation, the gargoyle flapped wildly, crashing into a shelf. Mira seized the opening, launching a precise beam of arcane force that shattered a small portion of its wing. With a roar, the creature careened to the ground in a tumble of rubble.

A third gargoyle attempted to rush Elara from above, talons extended. She pivoted, using her shield in a forceful upward bash. Divine sparks exploded on contact, and the gargoyle reeled. Cedric capitalized by sweeping his sword across the creature's midsection, deepening the cracks. Stone chips clattered to the floor.

The fourth gargoyle soared overhead, keen eyes scanning for an opening. Spotting Thalion alone near a pillar, it dove with terrifying speed, jaws snapping. Thalion erected a barrier of crackling energy, but the gargoyle's momentum carried it through the shield, albeit slowed. It crashed into Thalion with a jarring impact, sending him sprawling. Gasping, he scrambled away, staff clutched tight. Before the gargoyle could follow up, Mira hammered it with a cone of force, pushing it sideways into a toppled bookshelf.

Despite their progress, the heroes found themselves beset on all sides. The reading hall's cramped confines and the gargoyles' aerial agility made the fight chaotic. Dust and scraps of paper swirled in the library's gloom, and the stone beasts' roars echoed alarmingly.

One gargoyle, battered but still furious, leapt back onto a high beam. It spread its wings and let out a hideous shriek. In response, footsteps and scraping echoed from an adjoining corridor. More gargoyles?

Cedric's eyes flicked to the corridor. "Reinforcements? We have to finish these four fast!"

Elara pressed forward, channeling a protective aura for her allies. The faint golden glow bolstered Cedric's stamina, Thalion's focus, and Mira's resilience. Encouraged, Cedric lunged once more at the gargoyle he had partially cracked. This time, his sword sank deeper. The beast let out a final rasping howl before shattering into rubble. Cedric stepped away, panting.

Simultaneously, Thalion lashed an arc of lightning at the gargoyle pinned under the collapsed shelf. Stone flesh glowed under the electric assault, spider-web fractures spreading. The gargoyle convulsed, then burst into chunks, leaving only dust behind.

Mira, staff crackling with energy, turned to the creature that had hammered Thalion's shield. She wove a quick incantation of binding: shimmering bands of force looped around its torso, constricting its limbs. The gargoyle hissed, flailing to no avail. Elara rushed in, sword raised high, slamming it down on the monster's neck. Stone cracked, and the gargoyle's head rolled free. The captive body crumbled, scattering across the marble floor.

That left the last of the original four, perched overhead with an angry glare. Rather than dive again, it hopped along the beam, shrieking. The scraping from the corridor drew closer—likely more gargoyles responding to the sentinel's call.

As the heroes braced, two new gargoyles emerged from the corridor. These newcomers stood taller, their stone frames etched with more intricate runes. Their eyes glowed a fiercer red. One brandished a stone spear fused with its forearm, while the other sported a spiked tail. They wasted no time, charging into the hall with thunderous steps that shook the flagged floor.

The perched gargoyle joined them, dropping down in a swirl of dust. Now three formidable guardians faced the heroes—two elite variants and one battered but defiant sentinel.

Cedric's jaw set. "They just keep coming. Let's hold them at the corridor entrance."

Elara dashed forward to block the corridor, shield up. "Form a line!" She signaled Mira and Thalion to remain behind her, while Cedric flanked to the side. This formation would keep the gargoyles from attacking them from multiple angles at once.

The elite gargoyle with a spear hissed, brandishing its stony weapon. Sparks of arcane energy crackled around the spear's tip. In a flash, it lunged at Elara, forcing her to brace behind her shield. The impact rang out like a bell, the force reverberating up her arm. She grimaced, holding firm under the divine aura that reinforced her stance.

Meanwhile, the spiked-tail gargoyle bounded around them, trying to flank. Cedric intercepted, sword clashing with the stone tail in a cascade of sparks. Each collision battered Cedric's arms, but he refused to yield ground, forcing the creature into a stalemate.

Mira, scanning for an opportunity, conjured a swirl of frost at her fingertips. She launched a volley of icicle shards toward the battered sentinel gargoyle, who advanced menacingly. The shards slammed into its cracked torso, chipping off more stone. Staggered, the sentinel still advanced, arms raised to strike. Thalion intervened with a lash of arcane flames that seared the gargoyle's flank. Stone glowed red-hot, fracturing. The creature let out a twisted roar before collapsing into rubble at last.

Now only the two elite gargoyles remained, fighting ferociously. The spear-wielding one hammered Elara's shield again and again, forcing her back step by step. Each strike chipped the stone floor, sending shards ricocheting. Elara's arms shook from the onslaught, but her faith-infused shield glowed brighter with every blow, staving off the gargoyle's lethal power.

"Thalion—help!" she called out.

The mage responded, weaving a chain of wind around the gargoyle's legs. The stone warrior growled, partially immobilized. Elara took the chance to slam her shield into its chest. Holy sparks erupted, pushing the gargoyle off balance. Seizing the moment, she swung her sword in a powerful downward slash. Stone chipped, and the gargoyle lurched, howling in pain. But it wasn't finished yet.

Meanwhile, Cedric squared off with the spiked-tail gargoyle, exchanging blow after blow. The creature's tail whipped around, aiming to skewer him. He ducked, blade angled low, slicing at the gargoyle's abdomen. Chunks of stone fell away, but the monster retaliated with a savage claw swipe, carving deep grooves into Cedric's shield. Gasping, Cedric bashed the gargoyle's face with the shield boss, opening room for a second slash. Stone cracked, and the gargoyle roared.

Mira launched a supportive spell—binding threads of luminous force that latched onto the gargoyle's tail, restricting its movement. Cedric pressed the advantage, shattering more of its stony hide. The gargoyle stumbled, wheezing a guttural growl. Its tail, pinned by Mira's magic, smashed in frustration against the floor. With a final, determined thrust, Cedric drove his sword through the creature's chest, splitting it apart. The gargoyle disintegrated in a spray of debris.

Seeing its ally destroyed, the spear-wielding gargoyle shrieked with renewed fury. It tore free from Thalion's wind chain, lunging once again at Elara. She braced, but the beast caught her shield at an angle, twisting it aside. Its stone spear thrust forward, aimed at her torso. At the last second, Thalion flung a lightning bolt that scorched the gargoyle's arm, deflecting the blow. Elara ducked, returning an upward slash that sliced through the gargoyle's side.

It snarled in agony, stumbling. Elara's shield came around in a brutal bash, and the gargoyle's chest plating shattered. As it dropped to its knees, Mira delivered a finishing ray of arcane frost that snuffed out the faint red glow in its eyes. The gargoyle broke apart, tumbling into a pile of lifeless rubble.

The room fell silent except for the heroes' ragged breathing. Stone shards littered the floor, mingled with tattered books and collapsed shelves. Sweat dripped down Cedric's brow, Elara's arms trembled from exertion, Thalion clutched at a bruised side, and Mira panted from magical fatigue. Yet they had triumphed again, the library's fiercest gargoyle guardians lying in ruins around them.

Elara managed a wan smile. "That... was more organized. They fought as if they recognized us as a threat to something they protect."

Thalion, leaning on his staff, nodded. "No doubt the library wards awakened them with a singular directive: keep intruders away from forbidden knowledge. We're definitely nearing a location with crucial records."

Cedric exhaled, shaking tension from his sword arm. "They almost had us pinned. Our coordinated spells and strategy made the difference."

Mira slid down to sit on a chunk of rubble, staff across her lap. "Agreed. If we'd come unprepared, they could've overrun us easily. Let's not forget this could happen again if there are more wings or hidden vaults."

Thalion surveyed the hall. "We should check the adjoining corridors, see if they lead to a restricted archive. The gargoyles might've been posted near the most valuable texts."

Exhausted but resolute, they took a few minutes to catch their breath, patch minor wounds, and re-secure their gear. Another wave of guardians might lurk deeper in the Arcadium. But the possibility of lost secrets fueling their quest pushed them on.

Skirting the rubble, they followed the corridor from which the elite gargoyles had emerged. It ran deeper into the library, the architecture growing more ornate—ceilings higher, pillars carved with swirling motifs, and doors reinforced with engraved metal. The sense of layered wards hung thick in the air, tingling on Mira's and Thalion's magical senses.

Eventually, the corridor ended at a grand door carved from polished dark wood, bound with a lattice of runic iron. It radiated a faint magical aura, as though locked by more than just a physical mechanism.

Cedric glanced at Thalion and Mira. "Likely the final safeguard. Ready to unravel it?"

Mira stepped forward, carefully resting a hand on the inlaid runes. "Yes... It's a complex locking spell. But the gargoyles that triggered it are gone, so we might bypass it with the right incantation."

Thalion assisted, identifying the symmetrical patterns that formed a puzzle lock. They painstakingly chanted a soft, dual incantation, the runes reacting with sparks. A gentle hum rose, building in pitch until the lock gave a soft click. The door's iron braces retracted, releasing ancient dust into the air.

With a firm push, Cedric opened the door, revealing a short flight of steps descending into a vaulted chamber lit by a faint magical glow. Rows of ornate, locked shelves lined the walls, each sealed with metal gates. A central dais held a large lectern, upon which rested a single, imposing tome chained with iron links.

Elara studied the dais. "A prime vault, no doubt. The librarians must have placed the most dangerous or vital knowledge here, locked behind wards and guarded by gargoyles."

Mira's eyes sparkled despite her fatigue. "If anything in this library references the Shadow Nexus purification, it's likely here."

As they crossed the threshold, a swirl of eerie lights coalesced at the dais. From them emerged a lone gargoyle—larger than any encountered yet, towering with majestic horns and runes that glowed white-hot. Its eyes glimmered with raw arcane energy, and black wings spread wide, the membrane etched with silver lines. This was clearly the apex guardian of the Arcadium.

The gargoyle stepped forward, each footfall shaking the stone underfoot. It raised a massive claw, pointing in challenge. No roar, just a resonant hum vibrating through the hall. The message was clear: turn back or perish.

Cedric squared his shoulders, lifting his sword. "We're not leaving without that knowledge. Let's do this."

Elara formed up on his flank, shield braced. Thalion and Mira stood behind, spells at the ready. In unison, they advanced. The gargoyle narrowed its glowing eyes, wings fanning. For a heartbeat, everything hung still. Then the gargoyle charged with startling speed.

Elara met it head-on, shield blazing with divine radiance. The gargoyle's claw crashed into the metal with a deep gong, nearly bowling her over. Cedric lunged, sword angled for the beast's flank, but it twisted with impossible agility, deflecting his blade with a stony forearm. Sparks cascaded.

Thalion invoked a chain of lightning that snaked across the gargoyle's torso, arcing from rune to rune. The creature hissed, runes flaring brighter as if absorbing some portion of the magic. Sensing that raw arcs of energy might not suffice, Thalion swiftly switched to illusions, conjuring duplicates of himself and Elara to confuse the gargoyle's targeting.

Mira circled behind, chanting a potent frost-laden incantation. She aimed at the gargoyle's legs, hoping to freeze it in place. But the guardian, keenly aware, whipped its tail, sending a shockwave that disrupted her spell mid-cast. A swirl of snow fizzled in the air. Mira stumbled, staff buzzing with backlash.

Elara slashed at the gargoyle's side with a holy-empowered blade, scoring a shallow groove in the stone. The guardian retaliated with a savage backhand that crashed against her shield, sending her sliding across the polished floor. Cedric pressed in from another angle, hacking relentlessly, but the gargoyle's thick plating shrugged off most strikes.

Seeing their initial assault falter, Mira quickly reorganized. She locked eyes with Thalion. "Combine illusions and frost? Distract it so Elara and Cedric can strike vulnerable points?"

Thalion nodded, breathing heavily. "Yes—on three."

As Elara and Cedric held the gargoyle's attention, Thalion conjured a swirl of mirror images around the guardian—copies of the heroes darting in and out, each mimicking movement. Snarling, the gargoyle slashed at illusions, warping its sense of distance.

Simultaneously, Mira conjured a ring of frost-laden runes beneath the creature's feet. The stone floor iced over, creeping up the gargoyle's legs. Weighted down and confused, the guardian roared, thrashing to break free. Stone chipped as it heaved, but for a moment, it stood partially immobilized.

"Now!" Cedric yelled. He and Elara dashed in from opposite sides. Cedric hammered at the gargoyle's left flank, while Elara unleashed a searing flash of holy light from her sword at the right. The combined force fractured the plating around the gargoyle's ribs. A gaping crack formed, glowing with the guardian's internal magic.

The beast howled, wings flaring in a last, desperate surge. Stone shards flew as it broke free from the frost. With a violent spin, it backhanded Cedric across the chest, sending him crashing into a locked shelf. He groaned, stunned. The gargoyle wheeled on Elara, fists raised to pummel her. But Elara, unwavering, raised her shield and prayed for divine intervention. A radiant field shimmered into being, partially absorbing the blow. Still, she was slammed to one knee.

Thalion hurled a bolt of pure arcane disruption at the monster's cracked torso, further widening the break. Meanwhile, Mira directed a narrow beam of intense frost into the same wound. The gargoyle convulsed, an unearthly wail echoing off the high ceiling. Stone flesh began to crumble from within, runes flickering dangerously.

Summoning the last of her strength, Elara drove her sword into the opening. Holy flames surged along the blade, colliding with the gargoyle's core. With a final, shuddering roar, the guardian exploded outward in a shockwave of debris and arcane sparks. Elara flew backward, shield held tight, as fragments rained across the dais.

When the dust cleared, the gargoyle was gone—reduced to rubble and drifting arcane residue. Elara coughed, rising shakily. Cedric, bruised but alive, limped from the collapsed shelf. Thalion and Mira approached, breathing hard. A hush followed, the faint hum of wards fading from the air. It seemed they had vanquished the final guardian.

They stood in a ring of destruction: scattered stone fragments, overturned shelves, and swirling dust. At the dais, the huge tome chained in iron still rested, untouched by the chaos. Its cover bore a strange sigil—two overlapping circles, one black, one white, ringed by cryptic letters. A faint aura pulsed around it, as though the library recognized the heroes' victory and relinquished its treasure.

Cedric carefully stepped onto the dais. "This must be the knowledge the gargoyles were protecting. Let's see if we can open it without triggering more wards."

Elara joined him, pressing a hand to the iron chains. She closed her eyes, whispering a prayer. Light shimmered along the chains, testing them. They loosened with a soft clang, undone by the library's acceptance of the champions who bested its guardians. The massive tome's cover creaked open.

Inside, dense script scrawled across thick parchment, occasionally accompanied by swirling diagrams. Thalion approached with reverence, reading a few lines out loud: "Herein lies the Final Aria of Purification... a compendium of the Great Rifts... the forging of relics, the alignment of star and plane..." He trailed off, eyes widening. "This might be the single most comprehensive guide to the Shadow Nexus we've seen."

Mira glanced at the text, heart racing. "Look—these runes reference the exact mechanism of the Song of Severance, including how multiple relics must be placed in a specific geometry. This is the final puzzle piece we were missing!"

Elara felt tears prick at her eyes. "Then all we risked... all these fights... it's worth it. We have what we came for."

Cedric nodded solemnly, setting a hand on the open pages. "Yes. Now we can fully prepare the ritual to cleanse the Nexus. No half-measures or guesswork. We'll know exactly what must be done."

They spent the next hour carefully skimming the tome, transcribing vital passages onto more portable scrolls. Thalion and Mira took turns reading, deciphering archaic phrases, and charting the instructions for forging synergy among the four elemental relics. The text was dense but methodical, describing how to channel each relic's essence into the Song's final crescendo.

Outside the dais, Elara and Cedric scouted the newly revealed vault. Shelves upon shelves bristled with lesser tomes, though none glowed with the same significance as the chained volume. They concluded that the gargoyles must have guarded this single masterpiece above all else.

The library's deeper secrets might exist, but time pressed. The heroes could not linger indefinitely in these halls, not with the Shadow Nexus intensifying beyond the horizon. Once Thalion and Mira finished copying the key chapters, the group agreed they had secured the knowledge needed.

With the tome's mysteries gleaned, they turned to leave the vault. No further gargoyles emerged, as if the library itself had recognized their worthiness. Or perhaps they had simply slain every last sentinel. Either way, the ancient Arcadium lay quiet, its labyrinth of halls stirring no more illusions of threat.

As they retraced their path, glimpses of the earlier fights—rubble-strewn floors, chipped pillars, gargoyle fragments—reminded them how desperately the library had resisted their intrusion. Yet now, in the hush, there was an almost reverent energy, as though the Arcadium silently acknowledged their rightful cause.

Elara ran a hand along a battered shelf. "I wish we had time to restore these halls. But we can't. The Nexus draws near."

Mira murmured her agreement, eyes lingering on the half-collapsed rows of books. "At least we saved the crucial knowledge from fading to dust. That's what matters."

Cedric and Thalion led the way back to the main entrance. Each corridor felt less menacing, the wards subdued by the defeat of the guardians. Finally, they stood at the threshold near the ravine, illusions parting once more as they stepped into daylight. The sense of returning to the living world was palpable.

Outside, they inhaled fresh air, squinting against the sun. Sweat glistened on their brows, and a light breeze dried the grime of battle. Relief mingled with accomplishment. The gargoyle guardians—fierce, unyielding—had tested every ounce of skill and synergy. Yet together, the heroes had prevailed.

"We owe our survival to teamwork," Thalion observed quietly. "One mistake, and those gargoyles would have overrun us."

Cedric tapped his battered sword hilt. "Agreed. And they were not mindless. They fought with cunning, responding to each other's calls."

Elara gazed into the distance, a determined set to her jaw. "They guarded invaluable knowledge. Now that knowledge is in our hands. We must use it wisely."

Mira settled on a fallen rock, brushing hair from her face. "We will. The details in that tome... It's everything we needed to confirm how to arrange the relics for the Song of Severance. Without it, we'd be stumbling in the dark."

Looking back at the fissure, they beheld the illusions swirl, concealing the library once again. Cedric and Elara exchanged a nod. The Arcadium could rest peacefully now—its guardians silenced, its secrets carried onward for a noble cause.

They decided to set up a modest camp a short distance away, in a hidden hollow where they could rest and tend to wounds. The day had worn on, and each needed time to recover physically and mentally. Cedric pitched a simple lean-to, while Elara fetched water from a nearby stream. Mira and Thalion carefully cataloged the new texts, cross-referencing them with the partial references from before. Their excitement was tangible as they filled in crucial blanks about the Song's synergy.

That evening, they lit a small fire, the crackle providing a comforting counterpoint to the day's tension. Over a meal of dried rations and boiled roots, they recounted the gargoyle battles, marveling at how close they came to disaster. Yet a thread of pride wove through their conversation: they had faced the Arcadium's best defenders and secured the final piece of the library's knowledge.

After dinner, Elara performed a gentle healing ritual, easing bruises and burns from gargoyle claws. Thalion massaged an ache in his shoulder, grateful for the soothing aura. Cedric, by the fire's glow, cleaned and sharpened his sword, reflecting on how their synergy in combat had evolved. Mira carefully reorganized the transcribed notes, ensuring no line of the newly found ritual instructions was smudged.

Late that night, with the campfire reduced to embers, Elara stood on watch, scanning the surrounding darkness. Her thoughts circled around the fierce battles with the stone beasts. She couldn't help but admire the gargoyles' loyalty, in a way—created to protect knowledge from misuse, they had only done what they were designed to do.

Cedric approached quietly, noticing the pensive look on her face. "You all right?" he asked gently.

She nodded, eyes still on the horizon. "I'm just thinking about guardianship. The gargoyles—twisted as they were by old wards—embodied a duty to defend precious knowledge. In a way, it parallels our oath to defend Stonehaven from the Nexus. We do what must be done, even if it costs us dearly."

Cedric followed her gaze to the dark ravine. "Yes. We have a duty, too. Our fight is for something bigger than ourselves—so that future generations can live without the Nexus's shadow. The gargoyles fought to keep knowledge sealed. We fight to wield that knowledge for a better world."

A faint smile curved Elara's lips. "That's a comforting way to see it. Guardians, each in our own manner."

Morning greeted them with golden sunlight and a clearer sense of purpose. The texts from the Arcadium confirmed how the four elemental relics needed to be arranged for the Song. Two they already had—the Wyvern's scale for fire, and the Behemoth's disc for earth. The library's final tome identified the others: a pearl containing oceanic essence, and an amulet channeled by divine light. Each relic corresponded to a facet of Stonehaven's essence. Only by uniting them under the Song's incantation could the Shadow Nexus be cleansed.

Thalion explained the next moves as they broke camp. "We head for the regions where rumor says these relics might lie—coastal temples for the Pearl of Tides, perhaps a skyward fortress or storm-lashed mountain for the Celestial Air Amulet.

Elara hefted her shield. "One by one, we gather them, just as we overcame the Wyvern and the Behemoth. Only this time, we have far better guidance."

Mira patted the sealed scroll case containing the Arcadium's translations. "And if we need more details, we have them here, thanks to that final tome. The gargoyles' guardianship ironically ensures we can now free Stonehaven."

Cedric smoothed a hand over his horse's mane. "We'll ride. The Nexus's corruption grows daily. But with each relic, we gain the power to push back. The gargoyle guardians couldn't stop us—and neither will the next challenges."

They mounted up, turning one last time to the ravine. The illusions swirled with the morning breeze, half concealing the crevice. If any future explorers arrived, they might again face the library's wards—though the fiercest gargoyles now lay shattered. Still, the knowledge gleaned was safe in the heroes' hands, and that knowledge, in turn, could save countless lives.

Thalion touched the brim of his hood in a quiet farewell gesture. "May the Arcadium rest undisturbed again. One day, Stonehaven might rebuild these archives and honor the guardians for their loyal watch."

Mira's eyes lingered on the fissure. "I hope so. For now, let's ensure the Nexus can't threaten any library—nor any living soul—ever again."

With that, they urged their horses onward, leaving behind the haunted hush of the ancient halls. The farmland awaited, and beyond it, unknown lands where storm-cast spires and sunken altars might guard the remaining relics. Each hero felt the weight of the new texts in their pack—tangible proof of victory over the gargoyle guardians. Their combined abilities had carried them through yet another trial, forging an unbreakable bond.

As they rode under a brilliant sky, the significance of the Arcadium's secrets settled on their shoulders. No longer were they guessing at the Song's structure or the relic alignment. Now they possessed a complete blueprint for the final purification ritual. The library's knowledge, fiercely protected and nearly lost, would tip the scales in Stonehaven's favor.

In quiet reflection, Cedric recognized how each challenge—ghosts, wyvern, vampires, behemoth, gargoyles—had shaped their unity and skill.

Elara silently thanked the Goddess of Dawn for guiding them through such perilous battles. Thalion mentally rehearsed the newly revealed aspects of the Song, plotting how to manage the arcane energies. Mira felt an uplifting surge of confidence that no hidden terror could stop them from unveiling the next relic or finishing the quest.

The library had not yielded its secrets easily; the stone guardians tested their strategy, synergy, and grit. But in the end, the heroes' resilience overcame every stony claw and spear. Now armed with the final tome's revelations, they looked toward the horizon with renewed hope. Stonehaven's future no longer hinged on rumor or half-remembered lore. They had the map and the instructions for the ultimate confrontation.

Each step their horses took echoed the vow they carried: to use this knowledge only for good, to shield their world from the Nexus's darkness, and to honor the gargoyle guardians' testament of loyalty by ensuring that knowledge once kept hidden would be wielded to bring lasting peace.

Thus, with the Arcadium's secrets in hand—and no stony sentinels left to bar their path—Sir Cedric, Lady Elara, Thalion, and Mira galloped onward, hearts set on a destiny that once seemed impossible. Victory over the gargoyles had secured more than just a momentary triumph; it had secured the final advantage they needed in the war against the Shadow Nexus. Though many trials remained, they rode on with unwavering purpose, the Song of Severance shaping in their minds, and the dawn of a free Stonehaven gleaming on the horizon.

11

CROSSING THE BLOOD RIVER

A somber hush settled over the late afternoon sky as Sir Cedric, Lady Elara, Thalion, and Mira ventured deeper into Stonehaven's northern outskirts. In the distance rose a line of mountains wreathed in eerie clouds—beyond them, the haunting echoes of the Shadow Nexus pulsed through the land like a distant heartbeat. Armed with new knowledge from the Arcadium's ancient tomes, the party had grown increasingly certain of their destination. Yet an imposing obstacle loomed ahead: the Blood River, infamous for its crimson waters and the multitude of dangers lurking beneath its dark surface.

According to local legends gathered on their journey, the Blood River derived its name from the iron-rich soil upstream—or, as some insisted, from the countless battles once waged along its banks, staining the current with a permanent ruddy hue. Whichever story held truth, one fact remained: crossing the Blood River was perilous. The swirling waters were said to harbor deadly water spirits who lured travelers to watery graves, while half-amphibious trolls thrived in its marshy outskirts, attacking anyone rash enough to attempt passage.

Despite these warnings, the heroes had no choice. The map and their newly deciphered clues about the elemental relics indicated a path leading toward the river's far bank.

Only by reaching the other side could they follow the leylines that would guide them ever closer to the Shadow Nexus's heart.

The sun neared the horizon when they arrived at a vantage point overlooking the valley below. At its center snaked a broad, slow-moving river that appeared almost black in the waning light. But as the sun's dying rays caught the surface, glints of red shimmered, confirming the rumors of water tinted like old blood. A chill wind rustled the reeds at the river's edge.

Cedric drew rein, scanning the winding watercourse for signs of a ford or bridge. "It's as foreboding as the rumors say. But there must be a way across."

Elara, riding up beside him, crinkled her brow. "Even at this distance, I can sense a strange aura. The water holds an unwholesome energy—like a residue of hatred or anguish. We should expect more than just rapids."

Thalion and Mira brought their horses alongside. Thalion swept his staff out, letting a faint detection spell ripple through the air. "I feel it, too. The currents are laced with minor curses, and clusters of unstable magic swirl beneath. We'll have to be extremely careful—any misstep could pull us under or unleash something malignant."

Mira nodded solemnly. "We can't risk searching too far up or downstream for a safer crossing. According to the Arcadium's references, the path to the next relic site lies directly east from here. We have to cross somewhere close by or risk losing days—and the Shadow Nexus grows stronger each passing moment."

Cedric turned to the group. "Agreed. Let's set up camp here at the overlook for the night. At first light, we'll scout the river's edge and find the best spot to attempt a crossing."

Elara glanced at the darkening sky, worry in her gaze. "Yes—though something tells me even daylight won't banish all the threats hidden in these waters."

Nevertheless, they dismounted and began making preparations for a makeshift camp. The ground near the ridge was relatively solid, offering a safe vantage to watch for prowling creatures. Each hero felt the intangible weight of the coming trial—like an unspoken tension that teased the edges of their thoughts.

After gathering firewood from a nearby copse of twisted trees, they lit a small, smokeless flame in a sheltered hollow. They shared a quiet supper of bread, dried meat, and a handful of bitter berries found along the path. The gloom pressed in as the sun sank fully, leaving a sky studded with stars that flickered warily behind scudding clouds.

Cedric, taking first watch, stood at the ridge's edge, scanning the silent valley. The Blood River glistened in the moonlight, an unearthly scarlet sheen visible now that darkness had truly fallen. Occasionally, faint flickers of movement broke the water's surface—ripples hinting at creatures stirring below. Once, a shape reminiscent of a tall, hunched figure prowled the muddy bank, sniffing at the water before vanishing into reeds.

Behind him, Elara dozed in her bedroll, shield close at hand. Thalion and Mira sat together, quietly reviewing notes on their next objectives: the relics they still needed, and partial verses of the Song of Severance they hoped to fully realize. Every so often, Mira would pause in reading to glance at Thalion, seeking his confirmation on a line's meaning. The hush of their conversation underscored the night's watchful stillness.

Eventually, Thalion relieved Cedric for the middle watch. Cedric settled down to rest, though sleep came fitfully. The stench of the river wafted in the breeze, acrid and metallic, as though reminding them that tomorrow's crossing would be fraught with peril. By the time dawn arrived, each member of the group felt an undercurrent of tension thrumming through their bones.

Morning brought a dreary, gray sky, as though the sun hesitated to shed light on the ominous river. Still, the heroes packed up and carefully led their horses down from the overlook, picking a route that offered some cover in the sparse woods. Gradually, they reached the floodplain—a wide stretch of damp earth, pocked with shallow pools reflecting rust-colored water. The stench grew stronger, reminiscent of wet metal.

Elara let her mare pause at the edge of the floodplain. "We might not find a proper ford if the current is too strong. We should keep an eye out for trolls. They often lair in muddy hollows near rivers."

Thalion dismounted, staff in hand, eyes narrowed. "I sense a cluster of negative energy near the water's edge, likely drawing in lesser fiends or restless spirits. If we can find a stable crossing, perhaps a shallow stretch, we'll still have to ward off these influences."

Mira sighed. "And no telling how deep the main channel runs or what lurks there."

They pressed on, weaving among clumps of cattails and half-dead reeds. The ground squelched underfoot, threatening to mire their horses' hooves in suctioning mud. At one point, Cedric's horse stumbled, nearly toppling him. He cursed softly, guiding the beast onto slightly firmer terrain. The atmosphere felt oppressive, each breath tinged with the faint tang of decay.

Eventually, they emerged from the reeds onto a relatively open bank. The Blood River stretched before them, wider than expected, its surface reflecting a dull copper hue. In places, small eddies formed, swirling with an oily sheen. A chill breeze rippled the water, stirring the slightest current, though the flow was uncertain—here slow, there surprisingly swift.

Cedric panned his gaze along the bank. "If we try to swim with the horses, we risk being caught in undercurrents. A raft or boat might help, but do we have time to build or find one?"

Elara shook her head. "We don't see any sign of a ferry or crossing post. If local settlements existed, they've likely abandoned this place long ago. We'll have to improvise."

Mira tapped her staff on the ground. "We can attempt partial bridging with magic. Thalion and I might freeze some sections or create stepping-stone illusions. But the river is large—our spells might fail before we cross fully."

From behind them, the horses snorted uneasily, ears flicking. An unnatural hush cloaked the muddy shore, disturbed only by the sluggish gurgle of the water. Then a faint splash echoed, coming from somewhere around a bend in the reed-choked bank.

A low, guttural croak sounded, followed by a second. Cedric raised a cautionary hand, gesturing for silence. The party drew weapons or prepared spells. Slowly, they advanced toward the bend, weaving through waist-high reeds. The smell of stagnant water and rotting vegetation intensified.

Suddenly, two hulking figures lurched into view, amphibian-like trolls with coarse, warty skin tinted a sickly green. Each stood nearly eight feet tall, stooped forward, long arms ending in webbed claws. Their yellowish eyes gleamed with crude cunning, and thick drool dripped from their tusked mouths. One troll hefted a crude club made from a gnarled tree root, while the other clutched a half-eaten fish in one claw, glaring at the intruders.

With a guttural snarl, the first troll pounded its chest. The second troll joined in, gnashing its teeth. They bellowed, charging across the soggy bank with surprising speed, mud spraying from their webbed feet.

"Defensive positions!" Cedric shouted, stepping forward with shield raised. Elara mirrored him on the opposite flank, while Thalion and Mira hung back, ready to unleash spells.

The first troll swung its makeshift club overhead, aiming to crush Cedric. He blocked with a clang, the impact jarring his arm. Before the troll could recover, Cedric slashed the beast's thick forearm, drawing a spurt of dark, brackish blood. It roared in pain, swinging wildly in retaliation.

Elara engaged the second troll, ducking under a snapping maw. She bashed the creature's ribs with her shield, releasing a burst of holy energy. The troll snarled, stumbling backward but quickly regaining its footing. Saliva dripped from its jaws as it lunged again, arms flailing.

Mira quickly chanted an incantation, weaving arcs of frost that coalesced into shards. She launched them toward the troll fighting Elara, aiming for its legs to slow its charge. The icy spikes embedded in the troll's calf, provoking a guttural cry. Meanwhile, Thalion conjured a stinging barrage of arcane missiles at the troll assaulting Cedric, peppering its backside and drawing its attention away from Cedric's flank.

Amid the swirling mud and frantic grunts, the trolls fought with primal ferocity. Despite their lumbersome appearance, they moved unpredictably, lunging with jaws and swiping with claws. The watery terrain only aided them, allowing them to shift weight in slick maneuvers that threatened to topple the heroes.

Sensing the disadvantage of fighting in the mud, Cedric signaled the group. "We need firmer ground! Pull back, lure them out of the reeds!"

He feinted a retreat, stepping backward onto a patch of gravel near the river's bank. The troll followed, snarling, dragging its club with sticky slaps. Elara sidestepped the second troll's lunge, retreating similarly. Thalion and Mira fired a coordinated volley of magical blasts, giving Elara space to maneuver. Then they, too, fell back onto drier land.

The trolls, eager for a kill, pursued recklessly. Upon reaching the gravel patch, the beasts found themselves with less advantage—no longer able to sink into the mud for stability. Cedric seized the moment, pivoting around the first troll's slow overhead swing. His sword arced, cutting deeply into the beast's flank. It howled, staggering, blackish blood splashing onto the rocks.

Elara thrust her sword into the second troll's thigh, then bashed its torso with her shield. A burst of divine energy flared, causing the troll's eyes to roll back. It reeled, unsteady. Thalion aimed a final arcane bolt at its exposed back, and Mira added a shock of conjured lightning to the barrage. The combined impact knocked the troll flat, writhing on the gravel.

Cedric finished off the first troll with a precise slash across its throat, then dashed to help Elara. She had already pinned the second troll under her shield, pressing the blade to its neck. With a violent snarl, the creature tried to wrench free, but was too weakened by spells and wounds. Elara drove the blade home, ending its thrashing with a guttural shudder.

When both trolls lay still, the party exhaled, panting. The brackish smell of troll blood clung to the damp air, intensifying the river's foul tang. Elara withdrew her sword, face etched with effort.

"That was close," Mira muttered, wiping sweat from her brow. "They weren't subtle, but in this terrain, they had the advantage."

Cedric nodded, sheathing his sword. "Good job, everyone. Now we can keep an eye out for more. Trolls rarely hunt alone, but these might have been a small scouting pair."

Thalion rested on his staff. "Let's hope so. The last thing we need is a whole tribe chasing us. Shall we keep moving along the bank to find a crossing spot before more show up?"

They agreed and resumed their search. The ground gradually transitioned from muddy reed beds to rocky banks, giving glimpses of deeper water swirling ominously.

Occasional glimpses of fish tails or scaly shapes broke the surface, vanishing almost as soon as they appeared. Water spirits, perhaps, waiting for unwary travelers to step too close.

As midday sun filtered through a hazy overcast sky, the group located a narrow bend where the river's width was somewhat reduced. Boulders jutted from the current, forming stepping stones that might be used to cross. The water between them churned with a reddish foam, hinting at strong undercurrents.

Cedric eyed the boulders warily. "We might leap from rock to rock, but it'll be risky. One slip and we're swept away."

Elara frowned, patting her horse's flank. "And what about our mounts? They can't just hop across these stones. We'll need an alternative for them."

Thalion crouched near the water, swirling a hand through the crimson fluid. He shuddered at the cold that bit into his fingertips. "I sense spirits in the water—restless shapes flitting beneath the surface. They might be akin to nymphs twisted by corruption. If we force a crossing, they might lash out."

Mira tapped her staff lightly. "We could try an ice bridge or partial frost path for the horses. I'd have to focus continually to keep it stable against the currents, and that might attract the spirits. But it's an option."

Cedric considered. "Alternatively, we can try conjuring illusions to distract the spirits while we cross. But illusions alone won't carry the horses over."

Elara sighed. "If we had more time, we could build a raft. But building one strong enough for us and the horses might take days we don't have."

They deliberated for a tense few minutes, scanning the water and listening to its eerie lap against the rocks. In the end, a plan emerged: Mira and Thalion would collaborate on a combination of frost bridging and protective wards, forming a temporary crossing wide enough for the horses to walk single-file. Meanwhile, Cedric and Elara would stand guard on the ice, ready to repel water spirits or other threats.

It was a gamble—the swirling negative energy might destabilize the spell at any moment. But short of finding a miracle ferry, it was their best shot.

Thalion and Mira selected a relatively calm stretch of the narrow bend to begin their work. Horses and gear were set to one side, ready to move as soon as the path was stable. The mages stood at the river's edge, calling upon their combined knowledge. Mira summoned intense cold from the elemental plane, causing a thin layer of ice to crystallize outward from the bank. Thalion layered arcane wards that latched onto the swirling currents, funneling them away from the forming ice. Slowly, meter by meter, a sheet of frosty surface extended across the river.

The water hissed and steamed at the edges, as if refusing to freeze. Unseen shapes beneath the surface stirred, causing ripples that rattled the fragile ice. Thalion grit his teeth, fortifying the wards to reduce turbulence.

Cedric and Elara kept vigilant watch. Elara felt tingles of dread skitter along her skin, as if malevolent eyes watched from beneath. Once, a pale face or mask-like visage seemed to drift near the edge of the ice, only to vanish when she turned. Water spirits indeed. She clenched her sword, muttering a quiet prayer for protection.

Gradually, the ice sheet thickened. Mira, brow beaded with sweat, guided the shaping with precise gestures, forming a corridor wide enough for horses. Thalion erected a faint shimmering field along the path's edges, hoping to keep the water spirits at bay. After nearly half an hour, the frosty bridge spanned the river. It quivered under the swirl of red-tinged waters, yet it held.

"All right," Mira breathed, voice trembling with exertion. "We must move now. I can't guarantee how long it'll stay."

Cedric led his horse onto the ice first, testing each step. The bridge creaked ominously, but held his weight. Next came Elara, guiding her mare. Thalion and Mira followed, each controlling the spells that kept the ice from fracturing. The party moved slowly, forming a line. One by one, they advanced across the uncertain surface toward the far bank.

Midway over, the ice buckled slightly. Tension rippled down the group. Cedric patted his horse, calming it as it neighed in fear. Up ahead, Elara's mare danced anxiously, nearly slipping. She managed to steady the animal with gentle murmurs and a firm hand.

Suddenly, the water churned beside them. A ghostly figure rose from the depths—a water spirit with elongated limbs and flowing hair of kelp. Its eyes glowed an eerie green. With a haunting wail, it lunged at Elara's horse, spectral claws reaching to drag the mount under.

"Spirits attacking!" Elara cried, wrenching her shield up. The spirit's half-corporeal form clashed with divine light, hissing in ephemeral agony. Yet it did not vanish, swirling around the shield's edge to rake at the mare's flank. The horse kicked, nearly toppling Elara on the slippery ice.

Cedric rushed to help, slashing at the spirit with his sword. The blade passed through the watery form, scattering droplets. The spirit shrieked, recoiling. Another swirl of water parted near Thalion, revealing a second spirit that clawed at the ice's underside. Thalion struggled to maintain the wards, weaving a defensive swirl of magic to repel the intrusion.

Mira halted, staff raised. She conjured a pulse of arcane light that spread across the ice, momentarily solidifying the watery spirits into vaguely humanoid shapes. Their ephemeral forms struggled, pinned by shimmering mana. But as soon as Mira wavered, the spirits began slipping free, howling in alien tones.

To complicate matters, a roar sounded from behind—two more trolls emerged on the near bank, drawn by the commotion. They bellowed, charging the ice from behind, thick feet pounding. The fragile bridge trembled under the added weight. Cedric glanced back, fear spiking. If the trolls stomped onto the bridge, it might collapse entirely.

"Move, move, move!" he shouted. "We have to reach the far side before they overtake us."

Elara urged her horse forward, still fending off the water spirit. Thalion tried to multitask, fortifying the ice path while launching a searing bolt at the trolls. The bolt scorched one beast's shoulder, slowing it. The other troll, however, bounded onto the ice, snarling. Its first few steps cracked the surface. Water seeped up, forming treacherous puddles underfoot.

Mira redirected her energies, freezing the cracks as fast as she could. Her staff glowed with intense cold, lines of frost racing to patch holes. But the shifting weight of trolls, horses, and heroes on a magical ice crossing was near catastrophic.

"We'll hold them off!" Cedric roared, turning to intercept the lead troll. Elara nodded, dismounting her mare to stand beside him. They braced themselves, shield and sword at the ready. The troll lumbered forward, club raised. With coordinated skill, Cedric and Elara met the beast's swing. Cedric blocked high, Elara slashed low, cutting the troll's shin. It yowled, flailing, but the ice gave way beneath its thrashing foot, sending the troll stumbling into water up to its thigh.

Meanwhile, Thalion and Mira pressed on with the horses. The far bank was mere yards away. Yet water spirits converged on them, swirling beneath the surface. One spirit lunged up, trying to grab Thalion's horse's legs. He unleashed a thunderous clap of magic, blasting the spirit apart in a flurry of steam. Another spirit targeted Mira's mount, shrieking with watery malice. Mira cast a protective bubble around the horse's hooves, repelling the spirit's grasp. The mount whinnied in terror, but kept moving.

At last, Thalion and Mira reached the far bank, coaxing the horses onto solid ground. They spun around to see Cedric and Elara still battling the half-submerged troll, plus another troll at the edge of the ice. The path looked dangerously thin, cracks radiating across it. Water churned, water spirits lurking for any chance to strike.

"Go!" Cedric shouted across the distance. "We'll meet you on shore—just keep the path stable if you can!"

Thalion and Mira exchanged determined looks. Mira steadied her staff, feeding more icy energy into the bridge's weak points, while Thalion conjured a swirling barrier around Cedric and Elara, hopefully to guard them from spirit assaults. But maintaining such wards from a distance was tenuous.

Elara and Cedric worked in tandem, pressing the wounded troll further into the water. The beast howled, struggling to regain footing. Its companion on the bank roared, about to rush onto the ice, when a sudden crack signaled the approach of total collapse. Sensing danger, that second troll halted, uncertain. Seeing no easy meal, it retreated with a guttural snarl, leaving its flailing ally behind.

Sensing its doom, the submerged troll gave one last swing of the club. Cedric dodged, slashing across the beast's chest. Elara hammered it with her shield, a burst of holy light forcing it back. Ice splintered beneath the troll's immense weight. With a final wail, it sank into the swirling crimson water. The surface gurgled and churned, then stilled, leaving only a few bubbles.

No time to celebrate. The ice bridge's center was collapsing. Elara and Cedric sprinted for the far side, the ground cracking behind them. Seeing their desperate run, Thalion dropped his ward, focusing everything on reinforcing the final stretch. Mira conjured a wide patch of fresh ice near the bank, bridging the worst gaps.

Just as the middle section collapsed in a swirl of red water, Cedric and Elara leapt onto Mira's newly formed patch, slipping but staying upright. They charged the last few yards, practically diving onto the far bank as the ice behind them shattered and sank into the swirling current.

In a rush of breath, they made it. Water splashed the bank, but the heroes were safely on solid land. Thalion and Mira released the spells, letting the remnants of the ice bridge dissolve. The Blood River's current swept away shattered chunks, leaving a calm surface that belied the chaos moments before.

For a long moment, no one spoke, each grappling with the adrenaline spike. The horses stood trembling, ears pinned, their flanks lathered with sweat. Cedric rested his hands on his knees, panting. Elara dropped her shield arm, wincing at the bruise forming under her armor. Thalion sank onto a boulder, staff across his lap, chest heaving. Mira, too, was pale, staff trembling in her grip as the last vestiges of frost magic ebbed.

Finally, Cedric found his voice. "That... was too close." He gave a bitter laugh, eyes flicking to the river's swirling red waters. "But we made it. The trolls, the spirits—we left them behind."

Elara knelt, offering a silent prayer of thanks. "Any second later, and we'd be swimming in that cursed flow. Let's not do that again."

Mira exhaled a shaky chuckle. "If we have to cross on the return journey, maybe we'll find a better route. Or better yet, we'll be done with the Nexus so thoroughly that the river's corruption is lifted."

Thalion nodded gravely. "One trial at a time. But we proved our synergy again—overcoming not just monstrous foes, but also the environment itself. That's a good omen for the battles to come."

They found a drier patch of ground sheltered by low cliffs, perfect for a brief rest. The group unsaddled the horses, letting them graze on sparse tufts of grass while Elara channeled minor healing prayers to soothe bruises and cuts. The tension in the air began to lessen, though the distant stench of the river lingered.

Mira broke the silence. "So... we did it. The Blood River is behind us. Next step: following the tapestry's runes. We should be back on track to find the next relic, correct?"

Thalion retrieved the partial map from his satchel, cross-referencing. "Yes. The Arcadium's notes indicated relic sites further east. Our path remains. This crossing was the last major natural barrier before the foothills leading to the—" He scanned the parchment. "—the Labrynthian Mountains, if I'm not mistaken."

Cedric helped her pack gear onto the horses again. "Then let's gather ourselves. Once we've recovered, we press on. The trolls and water spirits will think twice before pursuing us across the broken ice, and we can't give the Nexus any more time to grow."

For the next hour, they took turns washing mud from boots and armor in a small spring trickling down the cliff. Cedric and Elara spoke quietly about their coordination in the troll fight, marveling at how far they'd come from their earliest battles. Thalion double-checked the wards on their supplies, ensuring no leftover curses from the river latched onto them. Mira sat with the horses, gently stroking their manes and murmuring soothing words, her gaze drifting occasionally to the ominous flow behind them.

Elara eventually joined Mira, placing a hand on the mare's flank. "I couldn't have stabilized that ice bridge alone," Elara said softly. "Your arcane control was flawless, even under attack."

Mira smiled, color returning to her cheeks. "It was a team effort. If Cedric and you hadn't kept the trolls busy, or Thalion managed the swirling currents, the whole attempt would've failed."

Elara nodded, admiration clear in her eyes. "We rely on each other now, in ways I never imagined when we started this quest. It feels... right."

Mira's smile widened. "And necessary. The tasks ahead demand that synergy. The Blood River was just another test."

Once sufficiently rested, they broke camp, leading horses away from the river's edge. The land on the eastern side felt marginally healthier, though pockets of withered shrubs hinted that the corruption still reached this region. They stuck to higher ground, avoiding boggy hollows that might conceal more trolls or twisted creatures.

Occasionally, they glimpsed the Blood River behind them, meandering in a wide loop. The water's crimson sheen under the midday sun looked almost surreal, as if an eternal sunset glowed from beneath. Yet the group pressed forward, relieved to have left that malevolent crossing behind.

After a few hours' ride, the terrain rose into gentle hills. From a vantage on one such slope, they paused to gaze back at the route they had conquered. The river's dull red line cut the landscape like a wound. Memories of swirling spirits and bestial roars weighed on them, but a sense of triumph overshadowed the dread.

"Let us hope the locals find a safer crossing—or avoid it altogether," Cedric remarked, turning his horse forward.

"No one should attempt what we just did without considerable power."

Elara agreed softly. "And may the trolls think twice before harassing travelers. We left enough warning in the mud."

Thalion closed the map, satisfied with their heading. "Next objective: following these hilly trails east toward the rumored Labrynthian Mountains or beyond. That's where we suspect one of the relics tied to air and the celestial might be."

Mira nodded, expression brightening with new resolve. "Onward, then. We overcame the Blood River's horrors. We can handle the next challenge."

They urged their horses onward, leaving the crimson shore behind in exchange for rolling meadows. Despite the gloom that haunted the horizon, their hearts felt lighter, knowing they had conquered a crucial milestone on the journey to halt the Shadow Nexus.

By evening, they found a suitable spot to camp at the base of a stony ridge, safe from prying eyes. The land here carried faint signs of life—birdsong in the distance, small rodents scurrying among rocks. Yet an underlying tension still clung to the air, an unspoken reminder of the Nexus's far-reaching corruption.

After dinner, they gathered around a modest fire. Conversation drifted naturally to the day's harrowing crossing. Mira recounted her heart-in-throat moment when the water spirit tried to drag Elara's horse beneath. Thalion described how the swirling energies nearly unraveled their ice bridge from below. Cedric recalled how he and Elara had tackled the trolls on the crumbling surface. Each anecdote underscored their synergy—none of them could have survived alone.

Elara's voice took a reflective tone. "We've faced illusions, gargoyles, monstrous beasts, but crossing that cursed river was a different sort of test. It demanded more than combat skill—it required trust and coordination in a chaotic environment."

Thalion lifted an eyebrow. "A microcosm of what we'll face at the Nexus itself. The environment there will be twisted, filled with horrors we can't foresee. We'll need to adapt, just like we did today."

Cedric gazed at his sword, the edge glinting in the firelight. "At least each trial strengthens our bond. After the Blood River, I feel a renewed sense that we can overcome whatever stands in our path."

Mira's lips curved into a gentle smile. "Agreed. We stand together, or we don't stand at all."

Night settled in, stars emerging in a clear tapestry overhead. Cedric took first watch again, pacing quietly around the camp's perimeter. Thoughts of the crossing replayed in his mind—the moment the ice nearly gave way, the troll's claws raking at them, the water spirit's ephemeral grip. He felt gratitude for Elara's unwavering shield, Thalion's spells, Mira's ice. Without any one of them, he might be drowned or battered to death under crimson waves.

Meanwhile, Elara rested but found her mind drifting to a silent prayer. She prayed for the souls lost in the Blood River, for the trolls who had died violently, and for the water spirits who once might have been peaceful dwellers, now corrupted by the Nexus's taint. A wave of sorrow stirred her heart, yet she reminded herself that forging forward was the only way to end this cycle of corruption.

Thalion dozed, staff cradled in his arms. His dreams flickered with images of swirling water and broken illusions, but also glimpses of the relics yet to claim. In his half-sleep, he orchestrated potential spells for forging safe passages across future hazards.

Mira, curled near the fire, was lulled to uneasy rest, her staff close by. She half-dreamed of forging a grand, permanent bridge of shimmering frost across the Blood River so no traveler would fear it again. A future vision, perhaps, if the Shadow Nexus were defeated and Stonehaven began to heal.

Morning arrived with a gentle light, the air crisp. The party rose, grateful for a quiet night. Over a quick breakfast, they solidified their next steps. Thalion cross-checked the tapestry's runes, confirming they needed to head northeast. The Stormcall Plateau's rumored location lay about a day's ride away—though the path meandered through craggy hills and ravines.

They broke camp, setting out with renewed vigor. While the memory of the Blood River still weighed in their thoughts, it also fueled them with a sense of accomplishment. Surviving that crossing proved they could handle even the most perilous environments. Now they carried that confidence onward.

The terrain gradually ascended, the meadows giving way to uneven rocky slopes. The horses, well-rested, navigated carefully, mindful of loose stones. From higher vantage points, they glimpsed the scarlet line of the Blood

River behind them, though the distance softened its ominous presence.

Elara paused at one lookout, turning her head. "I can't sense that dark aura as strongly now. We've truly left the river's influence behind."

Cedric reined in beside her. "Yes, but the Nexus is still out there, somewhere ahead. Each step forward is a step into deeper corruption."

Mira joined them. "And each step is necessary. At least our crossing proved we can overcome the monstrous and the arcane. Let's keep pressing on."

Not long after midday, they encountered a ragged band of survivors traveling southward—a mix of farmers and itinerant traders who had escaped the region's northern edges. Their clothing was torn, faces marked by exhaustion and fear. Upon spotting the armed heroes, the survivors approached warily.

A woman with disheveled hair stepped forward, clutching a small child. "Please... are you travelers? Warriors? We were driven from our hamlet by rampaging trolls. We fled east but found the Blood River. We... we don't know where to go."

Elara dismounted gently, offering a comforting nod. "We are on a quest to cleanse the source of these monsters. The river is behind us, but it's perilous. I'm sorry for your losses."

Cedric rummaged through his supplies, offering some rations. "There might be safety if you head southwest, toward the capital's outskirts. The roads are more guarded there."

The woman thanked them, eyes brimming with gratitude. Others stepped forward, receiving minor healing from Elara. Mira explained how the group had crossed the Blood River on an ice bridge, cautioning the refugees not to attempt it alone.

A thin man, presumably a guide for the group, sighed. "We can't face that river or the trolls. Thank you. We'll try the southwest route."

In parting, the survivors offered a token of thanks: a weather-worn amulet carved with a protective sigil. "An old charm," the woman explained. "Might bring you luck."

Though not magical, it was a heartfelt gesture. The party accepted it, hearts heavy with the knowledge that more innocents were displaced by the Nexus's creeping chaos. If nothing else, it reinforced their mission to press on.

As the day wore on, the hills steepened, the path winding among jagged outcrops. Occasional gusts of wind rippled across the grass, carrying hints of a storm forming beyond the far peaks—a harbinger, perhaps, of the next trial. The Blood River fiasco had shown them how the land's corruption extended not just to monstrous creatures but to the environment itself, twisting nature into new hazards.

Atop a small rise, they decided to rest their horses. Cedric gazed out at the horizon, where dark clouds gathered. "Stormcall Plateau might live up to its name. We should prepare for severe weather, or worse."

Thalion consulted the partial notes referencing the place. "If the plateau indeed holds the 'Orb of Tempests'— the relic representing air—it's likely the storms are unnatural, amplified by the Nexus's energies."

Mira's eyes shone. "We overcame the Blood River. We can face stormy heights if it grants us the relic we need."

Elara gave an encouraging nod. "Yes. Every challenge so far has tested us, but also strengthened us. Let's see this through."

They pressed on. Memories of crossing the crimson waters lingered, reminding them of their synergy, their refusal to let fear break their resolve. The synergy they had displayed—Mira's ice, Thalion's wards, Elara's shield, Cedric's steel—served as a model for the battles ahead. No matter the trolls or spirits, illusions or gargoyles, they would prevail.

Near sunset, they made camp at the foot of a stony ridge leading into the mountains. The sky to the northeast crackled with distant lightning, soft rumbles echoing. While Thalion and Mira carefully studied the spells they might need for storm-charged foes, Cedric and Elara prepared a modest meal. The talk around the fire drifted to the final confrontation they all knew was coming.

Cedric polished his sword, reflecting on how crossing the Blood River had been a microcosm of their entire quest: pushing onward despite monstrous adversaries, trusting magic and faith to overcome nature's cruelty. "Someday," he mused, "the Blood River might run clear if we truly rid the land of the Nexus's corruption."

Elara, stirring a small pot of stew, nodded. "And children will hear of it only in stories, never experiencing that horror themselves. That's the future we're fighting for."

Thalion, unrolling a map, gazed at them. "When we gather all relics and complete the Song of Severance, maybe this entire region, from the Behemoth's wasteland to the

Blood River, can heal. Nature has a remarkable capacity to recover if the source of corruption is removed."

Mira caught a spark of hope in her eyes. "I want to see that day—to revisit these places and find them teeming with life, not plagued by monsters or twisted energies."

They sat quietly, letting the hush of the evening envelop them. Despite the looming storm overhead, they felt a glow of optimism. The success at the Blood River, as grueling as it was, demonstrated how far they'd come.

Dawn arrived with a rolling thunder off in the distant peaks. Yet no matter the gathering storms, the heroes rose undaunted, checking gear and ensuring the horses were ready for mountainous paths. The crossing of the Blood River lay behind them—both a badge of their synergy and a testament to the challenges they would face again.

As they rode out from their final campsite near the river's shadow, each member of the group took one last glance back. The crimson waters receded into the landscape, a silent witness to the realm's suffering. Yet the memory of trolls, water spirits, and the ice bridge that almost collapsed forged a new layer of confidence in their bond.

They spurred their horses onward, hearts braced for the next trial: the Stormcall Plateau awaited, its hidden relic calling them. High winds would test them, lightning would threaten them, and perhaps new creatures would stand guard. But with the synergy proven by crossing the Blood River, no obstacle seemed insurmountable.

In the end, the Blood River served as both crucible and prophecy—showing them that if they could traverse crimson waters teeming with monstrous foes and unearthly spirits, they could face the even greater horrors that loomed.

Their quest demanded nothing less than full unity of mind, body, and soul.

By midday, the river's banks were a distant memory, left behind in the rolling hills. The path ahead was uncertain, but each hero felt emboldened. The trials they overcame had taught them that every step, no matter how perilous, brought them closer to purifying Stonehaven from the Shadow Nexus's malignant grip.

Thus, with dusk approaching once more, they steered their mounts up stony slopes, forging toward the storm-lashed horizon. There, amid the thunder and swirling skies, they hoped to retrieve the next relic on their list. United by the crossing of the Blood River—and all the battles and bonds that shaped them—they rode with unshakable determination, ready for the next chapter of their grand, unwavering pursuit.

12

THE MANTICORE'S DEN

A pall of silence hung over the stony ridges east of the Blood River. It was not the hush of peace, but of anticipation—a tense stillness that preceded the next phase of the heroes' journey. Sir Cedric, Lady Elara, Thalion, and Mira had only just emerged from the perilous crossing of the crimson waters, where ravenous trolls and malevolent water spirits tested their unity. The triumph of surviving that ordeal still rang in their hearts, but each knew that the road ahead promised no reprieve. The faint, lingering dread in the air suggested something far more dangerous lurked beyond the horizon.

For half a day now, they had advanced into a realm of craggy outcrops and scattered foothills. The remnants of farmland behind them grew sparse, replaced by rocky slopes that climbed toward a chain of higher mountains. Sparse grasses clung to the soil, eking out life among the stones. Gusts of wind rifled across the ground, carrying the taste of dust and a subtle metallic tang that reminded them uncomfortably of the Blood River's acrid scent.

"It's unsettling," Mira observed, guiding her horse around a cluster of broken boulders. "Almost as if the land itself is wary of our presence."

Elara nodded, scanning the high ridges. "Or wary of whatever calls this place home. We've heard rumors of a

Manticore in these parts—if it's as cunning as the stories say, we should expect a challenge unlike the trolls or water spirits."

Cedric, riding at the front, instinctively kept a hand near his sword's hilt. "Manticores are no common monsters. They combine the ferocity of a lion, the venomous sting of a scorpion, and the wings of a bat or dragon—each part lethal in its own right. Locals say the beast hunts travelers with ruthless intelligence."

Thalion, who rode last, was lost in thought. The pages salvaged from the Arcadium library indicated that somewhere in these ridges lay a key artifact—one that could enhance their magical abilities. The text spoke only vaguely of a "gem of transference," an object rumored to amplify the wielder's arcane potential, but it was also rumored to be guarded by a proud and territorial creature. The library scrolls had not named the Manticore outright, but local whispers and the group's pieced-together knowledge pointed to the same conclusion: the Manticore had claimed the artifact as part of its hoard, and any who sought it would face the beast's wrath.

After cresting a low ridge, they found themselves overlooking a broad swath of uneven ground. Sharp pillars of rock jutted up, casting long shadows in the mid-afternoon sun. It was a terrain of labyrinthine pockets where a large predator could hide, waiting to ambush. Cedric signaled for them to dismount, figuring that quiet footfalls might serve them better than the clatter of hooves.

Tethering their horses in a small cluster of scrub, the heroes proceeded on foot. Elara carried her shield, eyes narrowed. Thalion kept his staff close, scanning every dark crevice for magical residue. Mira walked slightly behind Thalion, staff at the ready for a quick spell if needed. Cedric led, sword partly drawn from its scabbard in case of a sudden attack.

They advanced warily, the dusty ground crackling under their boots. A few scattered bones—likely remnants of some unfortunate creature—lay bleached in the sun near the base of a tall spire. The sight prompted an uneasy pang in Mira's stomach. She recalled that Manticores favored devouring prey in open areas, leaving remains to deter intruders.

"I don't like this," she murmured, pressing a hand to her staff. "Feels like every rock could be hiding a pair of wings and claws."

Cedric paused near a jutting boulder, scanning the sky. "A Manticore might come at us from above if it spots us. Let's find higher ground ourselves, see if we can spot any signs of a lair."

Elara pointed to a winding path that led between two tall rock formations. "That pass might give us a vantage over this valley. If we can locate any cave entrances or fresh kill sites, we'll know we're close."

Steeling themselves, they followed the passage into the deeper recesses of the rocky landscape, each sense strained for the faintest echo of wingbeats, a distant roar, or the slithering rattle of a scorpion-like tail.

Before long, they spotted fresh markings that suggested they neared a predator's domain: deep claw gouges on the stone walls, as though a powerful creature had launched itself into flight. Tufts of fur, coarse and golden-brown, clung to jagged edges. The unmistakable musk of a large carnivore hung in the air, prompting Cedric to slow his pace. Elara ran her gloved fingers along the gouges, brow furrowed.

"These are quite recent," she said softly. "A day or two at most. The Manticore must be nearby."

Thalion nodded, conjuring a faint detection spell. "There is a residue of arcane energy. Manticores sometimes exude magical traces, especially those that have come into contact with potent relics."

Mira shivered. "Meaning it could be even stronger than usual, if it's been guarding a gem that amplifies magical energies."

They pressed on, each mindful that a single lapse in attention could be their last. The path sloped upward, curving around a rocky protrusion. A warm breeze gusted, carrying the faint stench of decaying meat. The group exchanged glances, treading more carefully. Manticores often stored prey remains near their lairs to mark territory or feed over multiple days.

Eventually, the path opened onto a broad shelf of rock. The sweeping view allowed them to see the ridges and canyons stretching in every direction. Jagged shadows danced under the shifting sun. At the far end of the shelf, a dark opening yawned—a cave mouth, half-shrouded in shadow. In front of it lay scattered bones of various creatures, large and small, heaped near a cracked boulder. The smell of death clung to the air.

"That has to be the lair," Cedric murmured, pointing to the cave. "No other predator piles bones like that."

Elara grimaced at the sight. "The Manticore must roost there, returning from hunts to feed. The artifact we seek is likely inside, or close by."

Thalion's expression grew thoughtful. "We could attempt to lure it out rather than face it in the confines of a cave. Manticores, being proud, might respond to a challenge."

Mira fidgeted, scanning the ledges above. "If it has wings, it might just circle overhead. We risk being pinned on this ledge if it attacks from the sky. Still, confronting it out here may be better than a cramped tunnel."

They weighed options quickly. Venturing into the cave blind was risky, but so was waiting in the open. The sun was now at a late-afternoon angle, leaving them limited daylight to act. If nighttime came, the advantage might shift even more to the beast, which likely saw well in the dark.

"Let's try a direct approach, but carefully," Cedric decided at last. "We'll approach the cave entrance, see if we can draw it out. If it remains inside, we might have to force a confrontation in its lair. Stay together and watch the skies."

Nodding in agreement, the four heroes quietly spread out in a semi-circle, stepping over the grim bones. The hush was profound, broken only by the scratch of gravel underfoot. Elara clutched her shield, heart pounding. She prayed silently for the courage to face the monstrous foe. This was no mindless troll or easily-distracted ghost—this was a cunning, dangerous predator known for trickery and lethal cunning.

They approached the cave mouth. A faint, fetid breeze wafted from within, carrying the tang of old blood. The gloom inside obscured details, but they could make out scattered debris—more bones, battered crates, possibly belongings from unfortunate travelers. The Manticore evidently hoarded not just a potential relic but also trophies from kills.

"We can't see the back," Mira whispered, staff raised. A faint orb of magical light glimmered at the staff's tip, illuminating the first few yards of stone floor. No sign of the beast yet. "Should we call out, or—?"

A low, rumbling snarl echoed, cutting her short. The sound emerged from somewhere deeper in the cave, reverberating across the stony walls. Then came a voice— raspy, yet disturbingly articulate:

"Who dares defile my den? Speak, fools."

Elara stiffened. The Manticore could speak. The legends were true. Cedric raised his voice, steel in his tone. "We come for a relic you guard. Surrender it, and we'll leave you unharmed."

A scornful laugh rattled the cave. "Surrender? To intruders? My domain... my trophy... I will not yield." The echoing voice dripped with arrogance.

Thalion frowned. "We want no quarrel, but we must have that gem. The Nexus threatens all of Stonehaven, including your hunting grounds."

A slow hiss. Then the Manticore stepped into view at the edge of the torchlight. It was a magnificent yet menacing sight: the body of a lion, sleek muscles rippling under tawny fur, a scorpion's tail arching overhead with a gleaming stinger, and a pair of leathery wings half-unfurled. Its face bore a twisted parody of human-like features—piercing eyes and a mouth that curved in a mocking grin. Draped over its forelegs was a faint shimmering chain from which hung a crystal orb, faintly pulsing with arcs of power.

"Fools," the Manticore sneered. "No threat touches me here. My jaws, my sting, and my cunning suffice to crush any who approach. Turn back and live, or press forward and die."

Cedric exchanged a glance with Elara, who nodded. "We cannot retreat," he said, taking a step forward. "Stonehaven's fate depends on that relic."

A low growl rumbled from the beast. "Then your fate is sealed." With a snap of its wings, the Manticore surged forward, clearing the cave threshold in a single bound. Dust and bones scattered as it launched itself onto the rocky shelf outside, eyes blazing with predatory glee. The confrontation began in earnest.

Cedric leapt aside as the Manticore's claws raked the ground where he stood. Elara moved in quickly, shield raised, sword angled. The beast snarled, scorpion tail poised overhead to strike. In the open air, its wings beat to keep it agile, a swirl of dust forming at every powerful thrust. Its leonine face twisted with a savage grin.

With shocking swiftness, the Manticore swung its tail at Elara, the stinger glinting in the dying sunlight. She blocked with her shield, but the blow was heavy, staggering her. The tail snapped back, spitting a droplet of venom onto the ground, sizzling in a faint hiss. Had that stinger connected, the outcome would be dire.

Mira and Thalion fell back to unleash spells. Thalion chanted an incantation, sending a volley of crackling arcs at the beast. The Manticore snarled, twisting mid-lunge so that only the periphery of the lightning collided with its flank. It let out a sharp hiss, a mixture of pain and anger, but swiftly retaliated by whipping its tail upward, firing a barrage of sharp spines from just below the stinger tip. Like barbed projectiles, they rained down on Thalion and Mira. They scrambled behind a rock outcrop, the spines clattering off stone.

"This creature's not just brute force—it has range," Mira gasped, staff ready for a counter-spell. "We must keep moving or be skewered."

Cedric circled from the side, slashing at the Manticore's hind leg. The beast sprang away, pivoting with alarming grace. Its eyes, filled with an unsettling intelligence, tracked every move of the group, prepared to exploit the slightest gap. Elara advanced, shield shimmering with divine energy, drawing the Manticore's attention. The beast roared, lunging once more at her shield, claws screeching on the metal.

"Distract it for me," Thalion called, starting a complex spell. Cedric nodded, feinting in with repeated sword jabs. The Manticore swiped and hissed, scorpion tail slashing overhead in an attempt to catch Cedric off guard. But Cedric kept his shield angled, blocking tail strikes. Each parried blow sent shockwaves through his arm.

Elara took the opening to deliver a slash across the Manticore's side. A spatter of dark blood emerged, drawing a furious roar. In retaliation, the beast whipped around, tail darting like a serpent. The stinger grazed Elara's armor, scraping off the metal plating but failing to penetrate. She stumbled back with a gasp, heart pounding at the near miss.

As the Manticore reeled from Elara's strike, Thalion unleashed a binding spell. Glowing runes spiraled around the beast's paws and tail, seeking to restrain its movements.

The Manticore roared, thrashing its wings to remain mobile. Stone chips skittered as it fought the magical bindings, tail thrashing. For a moment, it seemed pinned.

"Now!" Thalion barked, beads of sweat on his brow from maintaining the spell.

Mira sprang up from behind cover, staff flaring with conjured frost. She aimed at the Manticore's wings, loosing a barrage of icy shards meant to cripple its flight. The shards impacted with sharp *cracks*, freezing portions of the leathery membranes. The Manticore howled, eyes blazing with fury. Desperate to break free, it flailed, claws rending the rock beneath.

Cedric capitalized on the opening, charging in with a heavy slash at the creature's flank. Metal bit into fur and hide, eliciting a visceral snarl. Elara joined, striking from the opposite side. The beast, pinned by Thalion's magic, reeled under the combined assault.

But even constrained, the Manticore proved formidable. Mustering all its strength, it shattered the binding runes with a roar. Thalion staggered from the backlash, nearly dropping his staff. Freed, the beast lashed out in a frenzy. Its stinger shot forward, forcing Cedric to backpedal. Meanwhile, it swung its claws at Elara, who managed to brace with her shield—but the force hurled her sideways, crashing near the cave mouth.

Mira tried to renew her frost barrage, but the Manticore bellowed and pivoted, launching a fresh volley of tail spines. Mira had to dive behind a rock to avoid being skewered. For a heartbeat, the group fell into disarray. The Manticore's cunning exploit had opened a gap in their formation. Sensing advantage, it flapped its wings powerfully, lofting itself a few feet above the rocky shelf. From this vantage, it could strike at will with its stinger or pounce on any isolated hero.

Cedric grimaced, heart hammering. The creature's size and agility were staggering, and its scorpion tail added a deadly range. "Regroup!" he shouted, motioning to gather near Elara. She pushed herself up, bruised but not broken.

In that moment, the Manticore's leonine face twisted into a sneer. "Intruders, you amuse me," it hissed, voice resonant despite heavy breaths. "But your end is nigh."

The Manticore hovered, each flap stirring dust. Thalion and Mira crouched side-by-side, each preparing a fresh incantation. Elara and Cedric formed a defensive line in front of them. The beast snarled and dove at them, tail poised to impale. Elara raised her shield, summoning a burst of holy radiance that flashed in the Manticore's eyes. Momentarily blinded, the creature veered aside mid-attack, wings beating frantically to avoid slamming into the ground.

Cedric lunged, sword slicing at the Manticore's wing joint. He felt the blade bite flesh. The beast screeched in real pain, rearing back. Blood darkened the creature's fur around the wing base, restricting its flight. Sensing vulnerability, Cedric pressed the advantage, but the Manticore clawed at him with savage force, forcing him to retreat lest he be disemboweled.

"You will pay for that!" the Manticore roared, panting, fury dancing in its amber eyes.

Mira cast a swirling gust of wind, destabilizing the Manticore's battered wing. At the same time, Thalion seized the chance to craft a more potent arcane snare. Threads of shimmering light laced around the beast's forelimbs and tail. With the wing compromised, the Manticore couldn't fully lift off, and Thalion's ensnaring magic took hold more firmly. The creature spat in rage, thrashing as the web tightened.

Elara dashed in, shield locked forward, sword ready for a decisive blow. The Manticore bared its fangs, lashing tail in a desperate bid to land a venomous strike on her. She feinted left, then pivoted, forcing the tail to miss wide. Cedric, pivoting to the creature's other side, delivered a punishing slash near the beast's hindquarter. Another pained roar split the air.

For a heartbeat, the Manticore's eyes flicked in desperation to the cave behind it, as though contemplating retreat. But the binding spells and battered wing made a swift escape improbable. The beast let out a thunderous growl, stinger darting wildly. It was cornered, its cunning overshadowed by the heroes' teamwork.

Sensing the Manticore's weakening state, Cedric summoned all his courage, stepping in close. The scorpion tail lunged, but Elara intercepted with her shield, the stinger glancing off in a shower of sparks. Cedric lunged low, driving his sword into the creature's side. The Manticore howled, agony etched across its half-human, half-feline features.

At the same moment, Thalion channeled a burst of arcane force directly at the Manticore's chest. The beast staggered backward, pinned in place by the combined assault. Mira thrust her staff forward, releasing a concentrated bolt of frost into the crackling arcane vortex. The swirling energies collided, freezing and shattering the

Manticore's last defenses. Its roars grew desperate, each breath labored.

Elara raised her sword, emboldened by a flare of holy light. She drove it down with precision into the beast's shoulder, aiming for the heart. The Manticore gasped, fangs bared in a final snarl. Its tail fell limp, stinger scraping the rock. Eyes that once gleamed with malevolent brilliance dulled, and its mighty form collapsed to the ground, stirring dust in one last violent exhalation.

For a stunned moment, no one moved. The only sounds were their ragged breaths and the quiet rattle of rubble settling. Then Elara withdrew her blade, staggering back. The Manticore lay motionless, a once-terrifying guardian felled by the synergy of the four companions.

Mira exhaled, tears pricking her eyes—relief mingled with the sorrow of slaying such a magnificent, if deadly, creature. Cedric pressed a hand to his side, wincing at bruises. Thalion, staff trembling from spellcasting exertion, bent over to collect himself. Elara knelt, murmuring a soft prayer, whether for gratitude or in acknowledgment of the beast's end none could say.

They had triumphed, albeit at a cost in physical toll. But the prize was within reach: the artifact the Manticore had fiercely guarded.

A glimmer caught Mira's eye as she steadied herself. Draped on a chain around the Manticore's neck was a polished gemstone, large as a child's fist, swirling with faint arcs of color. Even now, after the beast's death, the gem pulsed like a miniature star enclosed in crystal. Carefully, Mira unhooked the chain from the corpse, cringing slightly as she touched the dark, matted fur.

She cradled the gem in her hands, feeling a subtle warmth. Tiny sparks of energy danced within. A hush fell as Thalion, Cedric, and Elara gathered. "This must be it," Mira breathed. "The relic that amplifies magical ability. You can almost taste the arcane aura."

Thalion extended a cautious hand. "Let me sense it." Mira passed him the gem. The moment it touched his palm, a soft hum reverberated in the air, as though the gem recognized a practitioner of magic. Thalion closed his eyes, lips parting in surprise. "Incredible... It's not malevolent. More like a conduit that augments spells, channels energies with greater efficiency. I can see why the Manticore guarded it so fiercely."

Cedric eyed the gem warily. "Will it bind to one of you, or can we all benefit?"

Elara stepped closer, feeling its radiance. "The texts implied a shared synergy. If it's used correctly, it might enhance not just arcane spells but also the divine or martial powers we channel. A universal amplifier, so to speak."

Mira nodded, still awestruck. "We must handle it carefully. Such power can corrupt if misused. But if we direct it toward cleansing the Shadow Nexus, it might tip the scales in our favor."

They shared silent agreement. The relic, once a dangerous creature's prized trophy, now belonged to them. This item, gleaned from the Arcadium's references, formed another stepping stone toward the final confrontation with the Nexus. With cautious reverence, Thalion produced a protective pouch and placed the gem inside, ensuring it was shielded from random surges.

At last, they turned from the Manticore's lifeless form. The final rays of the sun draped the rocky shelf in orange light. The day had been long and brutal, but the outcome was pivotal: not only did they remove a lethal predator from Stonehaven's frontier, they also secured a tool that might help them save the entire realm.

The group retreated a short distance to rest. While Cedric scouted the cave to ensure no other threats lurked, Elara examined the few battered crates near the entrance. Most were empty or held mundane debris—pieces of cloth, tarnished utensils. None matched the potency of the gem. The Manticore had clearly singled out the artifact as its greatest treasure.

Meanwhile, Thalion and Mira conferred about ways to safely tap the gem's power. Their hushed conversation focused on wards, focusing crystals, and shared incantations. More than once, Mira's excitement bubbled over, imagining the spells they could cast to defend against the Nexus's minions. Thalion tempered her enthusiasm with caution: "Power is a tool that can cut both ways. We must remain vigilant."

When Cedric emerged from the cave, he reported no further signs of living foes, but the lair stank of decaying carcasses, and the interior was cramped. They agreed to set up a separate camp under the open sky rather than remain in the lair's foul air.

Dusk settled. They found a flat rock plateau near a high vantage point. With the Manticore vanquished, the immediate danger lifted. Yet a certain solemnity prevailed; in slaying the proud creature, they felt a pang of regret. Manticores, while fierce and often malevolent, were also a part of Stonehaven's tapestry—beings shaped by the land's magic. But with an artifact of such power at stake, conflict had been inevitable.

Elara prepared a gentle healing prayer for everyone's bruises. Cedric cleaned his blade, caked with dried Manticore blood. Thalion carefully tested small energy flows from the gem, weaving them into harmless illusions to see how stable it was. Mira assisted, scribbling notes about how the gem might expand their repertoire.

Over a modest dinner, they spoke in low voices about the next steps. The gem might amplify Thalion's arcane wards, Mira's frost magic, Elara's divine blessings, or even Cedric's runic sword strikes. If harnessed properly, they could each benefit. The synergy that had seen them through ghosts, wyverns, gargoyles, trolls, water spirits, and now a Manticore, might reach new heights.

Morning dawned with a crisp clarity, the sky brightening over the ridges that had witnessed their fierce battle. The heroes awoke reinvigorated, as though the victory imparted an extra spark of confidence. The gem's subtle resonance pulsed from Thalion's pouch, a reminder of their newly acquired power.

Mira tested a minor cantrip, letting a swirl of frost dance around her hand. The ease with which she conjured it felt startling. "It's almost as if the gem's presence is smoothing out the arcane flow," she exclaimed softly.

Elara, practicing a quick invocation of healing, also noticed a heightened sense of divine connection. Even Cedric found a small difference in how his runic sword resonated when channeling a protective ward. The

Manticore's trophy was indeed an amplifier—an invaluable asset for their quest.

They mounted their horses, carefully stowing gear. Though battered from countless battles, each hero sensed a new wellspring of hope. Time pressed them onward: the Nexus's corruption spread daily, and the final confrontation loomed closer. They needed every advantage—this artifact most of all.

Pausing at the rocky shelf that overlooked the Manticore's cave, they cast one last glance at the silent lair. No further signs of movement. The proud beast's dominion ended in its final roar, leaving behind only bones, trophies, and the relic it had so adamantly guarded.

Cedric spoke quietly: "If not for our synergy, we might've fallen. The Manticore was cunning, strong... a reflection of the dangers we'll face at the Nexus."

Elara placed a comforting hand on his shoulder. "We overcame it together. May that remain our strength."

Thalion guided his mount to the front. "Onward, then. The land beyond these ridges leads us closer to the heart of corruption. With the gem, we stand a better chance."

Mira smiled, the morning sun catching her hair. "We've conquered gargoyles, trolls, a Manticore—fear won't stop us now."

And so, with the brilliance of a new dawn at their backs, they set forth, forging deeper into Stonehaven's untamed frontier. The Manticore's Den lay behind them, a testament to their unwavering bond. Each hero rode with renewed resolve, the artifact's subtle hum reminding them that all obstacles—no matter how fearsome—could be conquered by unity of purpose and the determination to save their realm.

They pressed on, away from the rocky domain of the fallen beast, carrying victory and the precious gem that promised enhanced magic. The next stage of their quest beckoned, and though the horizon remained fraught with shadows, the heroes advanced with a spark of hope. For they now bore more than just blade, staff, shield, and prayer—they also bore the power once coveted by a legendary Manticore, a boon that might tip the scales in the final showdown against the encroaching darkness.

13

THE VAMPIRE LORD

The wind whispered ominously through the barren trees as Sir Cedric, Lady Elara, Thalion, and Mira rode along an overgrown path toward a land steeped in twilight. Ever since crossing the Blood River and besting the fearsome Manticore, the heroes had journeyed closer to the heart of Stonehaven's darkness. Though they had claimed an artifact rumored to bolster their magic, new warnings reached them at each village they passed—rumors of a powerful Vampire Lord orchestrating vicious raids on remote hamlets and travelers.

Word of these nightmarish attacks disturbed the group. Tales told of entire farmsteads drained of life, villagers enthralled by undead charms, and roving packs of lesser vampires preying under the Vampire Lord's orders. Many whispered that this ancient being was consolidating power, sowing terror across the land, and perhaps even forging alliances with other monstrous forces. If so, it threatened to derail the heroes' mission to reach the Shadow Nexus before it fully awakened. They had to act.

Now, in the dim glow of an overcast dusk, the party approached a dreary region where the Vampire Lord's domain reportedly began. Thalion guided his horse to a standstill at the crest of a small rise, peering down at the valley. Rolling fog concealed much of the lower ground, but faint torchlight flickered from crumbling towers in the distance. Rumor said that was the seat of the vampire's power: an abandoned castle perched on a cliff, its once-proud walls now consumed by creeping vines and forbidding gloom.

"Elara," Cedric murmured, glancing at her as she halted alongside him. "Are you sensing anything from your divine powers?"

Elara closed her eyes, letting the crisp evening air brush across her face. The faint hum of her goddess's presence stirred within her chest. "It's... oppressive," she said softly. "The deeper we go, the more I feel an unholy chill, a distortion that repels the Light. This domain is steeped in blood magic, a perversion of life energy."

Mira wrapped her cloak tighter. "From the refugees' accounts, the Vampire Lord has enthralled lesser vampires and cultists to do his bidding. We'll likely face more than just one undead master."

Thalion nodded, tapping the pommel of his staff. "Agreed. Our infiltration must be precise. We can't wade into a swarm of undead. Perhaps stealth or subterfuge can get us close enough to confront the lord himself."

Cedric cast his gaze to the distant silhouette of the broken castle walls. "Once we eliminate the Vampire Lord, the undead scourge should be disrupted. The scrolls from the Arcadium mention that powerful vampire progenitors hold thralls in their iron will. Destroy the master, and the thralls may break free or become disorganized."

Elara's hand settled on the hilt of her sword. "Then we have our plan: we infiltrate the lair, find the Vampire Lord, and vanquish him. My powers can strike at his very essence—if we can get close enough."

At this, they exchanged determined nods. Night fell swiftly, and they knew vampires favored the darkness. All the more reason to strike swiftly, or else face an army of nocturnal monsters on their home turf.

They made camp in a nearby copse of twisted pine, waiting until the full blanket of night cloaked the land. Past midnight, under a waning moon, the group quietly advanced toward the looming fortress. It rose from a rocky cliff like a black fang, battered stone ramparts jutting out precariously. A moat of stagnant water, greenish with algae, surrounded the outer wall. No drawbridge lowered, but a crumbled section of the rampart near the southwestern corner offered a potential entrance.

Cedric led the way, creeping along overgrown footpaths that once formed a respectable road. Now thorny vines and gnarled roots marred every step. The hush of the night weighed heavily, broken only by distant hoots of nocturnal birds and the soft scuttling of nocturnal vermin.

At the moat's edge, they halted, scanning for sentries. Thalion pulled forth a faint detection spell, whispering incantations. A moment later, his eyes flicked open. "Vampire spawn patrol the walls, three or four at least. They're spaced out, probably relying on their enhanced night vision. We should slip in where the wall collapses."

Mira nodded, peering at the broken parapets. She let out a soft breath. "We can't just walk across the moat. Even if it's shallow, the spawn might spot us. Let me conjure a minor illusion to distract them."

She raised her staff, weaving illusions along the southern approach. Far down the perimeter, a faint glow appeared—a phantom figure moving along the opposite stretch of the wall. The idea was to draw the spawn's attention away from the southwestern breach. Seconds later, distant forms skittered along the battlements, focusing on the illusory figure.

At Cedric's signal, the four heroes carefully forded a narrow section of the moat. The water was murky and foul, reaching up to their knees, but they pressed forward with minimal splashing. In the darkness, the reek of decay nearly choked them. Elara silently prayed for purification, but stealth took priority over cleansing the moat's filth.

They scrambled up the crumbled stones to enter the fortress courtyard. Inside, the place reeked of neglect and rot. Broken statues, rusted portcullis chains, and heaps of rubble littered the space. No sign of immediate guards, but the tension in the air was palpable. Something twisted and malignant slithered through these halls—an unseen presence that made every hair prickle.

"We need to find the central keep," Thalion whispered, scanning the courtyard's multiple archways. "If the Vampire Lord holds court, it'll be in the main hall or a throne room deeper inside."

Elara clutched her shield, glowing faintly with her goddess's blessing. "I'll sense any strong undead presence if we draw near. Let's move carefully."

They advanced under collapsed archways, stepping over rotted carpets and shattered furniture. The architecture hinted at a once-glorious fortress with high, vaulted ceilings and grand corridors. Now, a film of dust and a stench of grave rot pervaded everything. Occasional squeaks of bats or scuttling rats echoed. Tapestries torn to ribbons hung in tatters. Indeed, the keep reeked of centuries of ruin, resurrected into a den of undead malice.

At length, they reached a grand hallway lined with shattered pillars. Faint torchlight flickered ahead—signs of occupancy. Cedric raised a hand, halting them. They crouched behind a toppled column, listening. From beyond a half-broken double door, voices hissed in low, guttural tones. Moments later, the door opened, and two vampire spawn emerged: gaunt figures with pallid skin, glowing eyes, and elongated fangs. Each wore ragged finery, perhaps from ages past, their movements graceful yet predatory.

Unaware of the heroes, the spawn conversed in hushed snarls. "The Master grows impatient—he demands new blood for the rites," one hissed, glancing around. "I shall patrol the walls again. The other intruders must not slip by."

The second spawn nodded. "Yes, we must remain vigilant. The Master's wrath is worse than any dawn's light. If only these rumors of meddling adventurers are false..."

Cedric tensed, exchanging a glance with Elara. They had to act now or risk more reinforcements being summoned. With a silent nod, they ambushed. Cedric lunged from cover, slashing at the nearest spawn. Elara sprang forward, shield leading. The spawn recoiled in shock, but quickly recovered, hissing in fury as it parried Cedric's blade with unnatural speed.

The second spawn wheeled, only to find Thalion and Mira unleashing spells. Thalion conjured arcs of bright green energy that slammed into the vampire's flank, while Mira hurled a burst of frost shards. The spawn shrieked as ice crackled across its chest. Yet vampire spawn were tough, resistant to many lesser magics. The creature tore free, eyes ablaze with hatred.

Cedric dueled the first spawn. Each swing of his sword was met by the spawn's clawed hands or a preternaturally fast dodge. Still, he pressed the advantage, remembering that vampires were vulnerable to holy energies. "Elara!" he called. "Light—help me!"

Elara invoked her goddess, channeling a burst of divine radiance around her shield. The spawn fighting Cedric screeched as the glow scorched its undead flesh. Panicked, it swiped wildly, forcing Cedric back, but left itself open for a finishing blow. Elara struck with her sword, severing the spawn's head in a single, clean motion. The creature's body disintegrated into ash, a faint, anguished wail echoing as it crumbled.

The second spawn rushed Thalion and Mira, ignoring its half-frozen limbs. Thalion blocked a vicious claw swipe with a hasty ward, but the impact shattered the magical barrier. The spawn lunged for his throat. At the last second, Mira cast a wave of arcing lightning, jolting the vampire backward. Snarling, it prepared to lunge again, but Cedric dashed in from the side, striking with a downward slash. The spawn hissed, wounded. In a final synergy, Thalion conjured a holy-laced flame—an echo of Elara's radiance—and directed it onto the spawn. Screaming, it too disintegrated into black ash.

Silence fell. The corridor reeked of charred undead. Elara breathed heavily, stepping over the ashes. "We can't risk extended fights like that. They'll raise the alarm."

Thalion nodded, wiping sweat from his brow. "We move swiftly now. The Vampire Lord likely awaits in the central chambers."

Pushing past the door the spawn had emerged from, they entered a wide corridor lit by flickering torches in rusted sconces. Shadows danced on tattered murals depicting medieval glories twisted into scenes of blood rituals. The air was cold enough to fog their breath. An unsettling quiet replaced the hiss of combat, intensifying the sense of stepping into a tomb.

A grand staircase rose to the second floor, presumably leading to the lord's private chambers. Yet Lady Elara paused, focusing. "I sense a stronger undead presence below," she whispered, pointing to a side hall that descended into gloom. "He might dwell in crypts beneath the keep. Vampires often prefer such lairs for their coffins, away from sunlight."

Cedric's jaw set. "Into the crypts, then. Everyone remain vigilant."

They descended a spiral stair that plunged into a sublevel. The stone steps, damp and coated in moss, wound down for what felt like ages, the air growing stale and oppressive. At intervals, carved niches held skeletal remains or decaying candelabras. By the time they reached the bottom, only the faint glow of Mira's staff and Elara's shield guided them.

A heavy door barred their way, etched with arcane runes. Thalion examined it, brow furrowing. "A warded barrier. The Vampire Lord must have sealed his innermost sanctum."

Elara raised her shield, letting divine energy radiate. The runes flickered, resisting. Mira joined in, weaving a subtle dispel to counter the vampiric sigils. With a final push, Cedric used physical force to break the rusted hinges. The door groaned open, revealing a wide, vaulted crypt beyond. Stalactites dripped from a high ceiling, and rows of ancient sarcophagi lined the walls. At the far end stood a dais where a black throne loomed, lit by guttering torches of eerie blue flame.

Seated upon that throne was the Vampire Lord: tall, slender, draped in dark finery. His features were sharp, pallid, and regal—eyes glowing crimson with dark amusement. A single black chalice rested in his pale hands, from which he sipped languidly as if unbothered by their intrusion.

"All this fuss," he purred, voice echoing smoothly in the crypt. "Four mortal meddlers come to challenge me. How quaint."

A circle of lesser vampires and thralls ringed the dais— some armed with swords, others baring fangs and claws. The heroes braced themselves. Cedric gripped his sword, whispering to Elara, "We must engage quickly. If we're swarmed, it's over."

Elara nodded, shield gleaming with a holy aura. "I'll focus on the Lord. You handle the spawn. Once he's weakened, I can deliver a decisive strike."

Mira readied a frost-laden incantation, and Thalion summoned arcs of crackling arcane power around his staff. The Vampire Lord raised an eyebrow, draining the last of his chalice. "Come, then," he invited, tone dripping with disdain. "Let me taste your lifeblood or your despair. Either shall suffice."

With that, the thralls lunged, half a dozen in total. Some wore battered armor, others only tattered cloaks, but each moved with undead agility. Their eyes glowed with the Lord's will. Cedric dashed forward, parrying the first thrall's blade with a clash of steel. Elara followed, shield-bashing a second thrall, knocking it aside. Thalion unleashed a volley of arcane bolts that battered two more thralls, while Mira conjured swirling frost, hampering their movements.

The Vampire Lord watched, unmoving from his throne, as if relishing the spectacle. But when two thralls fell to Elara's radiant sword, he sighed theatrically. "Incompetent. Very well—I shall handle this personally." He rose, smoothing his velvet coat with an air of aristocratic annoyance.

In a single blurred motion, the lord appeared behind Thalion, fangs bared. Before Thalion could react, the vampire struck with inhuman speed, slamming him into a sarcophagus. Cedric whirled, trying to intervene, but the lord darted away, reappearing near Mira. She barely blocked his claw with a hastily cast shield. The impact shattered her protective spell, sending arcs of magical feedback stinging her skin.

The beast's cunning was evident: he used illusions, vanishing into swirling shadows, then striking from unexpected angles. Each time Cedric or Elara lashed out, he slipped away, laughing. The thralls continued to harass them, though more fell to the group's synergy. Soon, only a couple of thralls remained, but the Vampire Lord himself was the real threat.

"Elara, we must corner him," Cedric hissed, gritting his teeth after the vampire delivered a rapid slash that left a gash in his armor. "We can't let him keep darting around."

Elara nodded, eyes alight with unwavering resolve. She lifted her sword, channeling her goddess's power, causing the blade to radiate a brilliant glow. "This will draw him out. Vampires despise the holy radiance."

Indeed, the lord hissed as the brightness intensified, retreating a few steps behind a pillar. Elara advanced, heart pounding. With every step, she amplified the light, creating an aura that burned undead flesh. The vampire glowered, covering his face with one pale arm. "You dare use that vile glare in my domain?!" he snarled.

Thalion, regaining his footing, added an arcane barrier around Elara to protect her from the lord's illusions. Mira threw a hail of frosty bolts at the vampire's feet, limiting his movement. Cedric flanked, ensuring the vampire couldn't simply vanish behind illusions once again.

Forced into a smaller space, the lord's arrogance shifted to fury. He lunged at Elara, claws extended. She braced with her shield, parrying his strike. Their faces were inches apart—her gaze unwavering, his eyes blazing with ancient hatred. "Your Light is a poison," he spat, voice trembling with centuries of scorn. "I shall extinguish it!"

He hammered her shield with unnatural strength, nearly knocking her aside. Cedric tried to slash the lord's flank, but with uncanny speed, the vampire caught Cedric's blade mid-swing. Metal screeched. The lord's grin returned. "You mortals amuse me."

Then, with a sudden burst of savage might, he hurled Cedric away, throwing him across a row of coffins. Elara gasped, stepping forward to shield Cedric's vulnerable form. The lord seized that moment, lashing out with a lethal claw at her exposed side. The blow rattled her, denting her cuirass. She staggered, breath driven from her lungs. The vampire closed in for the kill, fangs glinting in the torchlight.

Summoning every shred of will, Elara raised her shield and sword again, refusing to yield. The vampire's eyes widened in mocking surprise. "Persistent insect," he sneered, thrusting his claw once more. She dodged left, slicing across his forearm. A shower of black blood spattered, accompanied by a hiss of genuine pain.

"How dare you!" the lord roared, reeling back. "I have ruled these lands for centuries—no mortal woman shall stand against me!"

Elara's voice rang out, echoing across the crypt: "By the grace of my goddess, I stand for the living—for those you have terrorized. This ends now!"

She channeled a brilliant surge of holy power from deep within. The goddess's presence flared in her heart, traveling down her arm into the sword, which shone with a near-blinding radiance. The vampire recoiled, cursing, covering his face with his cape. The thralls that remained shrank away, howling in terror. Even Cedric, Thalion, and Mira felt the wave of warmth pulse outward in a flood of divine might.

Driven by that power, Elara advanced. Each step forced the vampire to retreat, his bravado faltering. Furious, he attempted illusions—shadows swirling to obscure him—but the holy light pierced them. He tried to transform into mist, a classic vampire escape, but the radiant aura disrupted his shape, forcing him back to corporeal form. Snarling in desperation, he launched a final frenzy of claws and fangs at Elara.

But the champion of the Light stood firm. Shield up, sword angled, she parried each frenzied strike, step by step pushing him back to the dais. The lord let out a strangled shriek as her sword slashed across his chest, burning with holy brilliance that seared undead flesh. His once-arrogant sneer contorted into agony.

At last, pinned against his own throne, the Vampire Lord stared into Elara's resolute eyes. The flames of the torches danced on her battered armor and shield, casting flickering halos. "You… will never… extinguish the darkness," he spat, blood trickling from his mouth.

Elara raised her blade high. "The Light of life endures," she proclaimed, voice echoing off the crypt walls. She drove the sword down, a surge of divine energy coursing through steel. The vampire's screech reverberated in the crypt as her sword pierced his heart. A brilliant flash of radiance engulfed his form, every shadow screaming in silent torment.

When the blaze subsided, the lord's body crumbled into ash, drifting away on an unseen breeze. A hush followed, the last echoes of his shriek fading into the crypt's recesses. Elara knelt, trembling from the exertion and the magnitude of the holy power she had wielded.

For a moment, no one spoke. Then Cedric limped forward, bruised but alive, offering Elara a supportive arm. She rose, leaning on his shield in exhaustion. Thalion and Mira stood nearby, surveying the aftermath. The remaining thralls—what few had not perished—had fled or crumpled to the ground, free of the Vampire Lord's domineering will. They twitched in confusion or scurried away into the darkness, no longer a cohesive threat.

"Well done," Thalion said quietly, staff still aglow with faint protective wards. He looked around, noticing how the once-suffocating aura of the crypt had lifted. "With the lord's death, the darkest enchantments are unraveling."

Mira approached, eyes lingering on the ash that once comprised the vampire's form. "All those rumors of brutal attacks... He orchestrated them. So many lost their lives. Now, at least, no more will fall victim to his cruelty."

Elara exhaled unsteadily, nodding. "The realm is safer." She glanced at the others. "This victory belongs to us all. But the goddess's grace gave me the strength to deliver the final blow."

Cedric gently squeezed her shoulder. "We fight as one. You finished it, yes, but your courage and our synergy made the difference. Now, the people oppressed by this fiend can begin to heal."

They took a moment to catch their breath, rummaging around the dais for any notes or items that might reveal further conspiracies. The Vampire Lord's throne area contained a small chest of curios—rings, jewels, possibly tributes from enthralled villages. None radiated the same malignant power as the lord. However, Thalion discovered a sealed scroll with arcane glyphs hinting at communications with other dark forces. He pocketed it, suspecting the Shadow Nexus might have enticed the vampire into alliance.

Emerging from the crypt was both a physical and emotional release. The courtyard, though still littered with remnants of undead activity, felt less oppressive. Dawn was breaking outside, faint rays of sun cresting the eastern horizon. As the heroes climbed the spiral stair, the gloom receded, replaced by the promise of a new day. The freshly fallen thralls scattered or turned to ash under the rising sunlight, leaving the castle quiet.

Once in the main courtyard, they took stock. Their bodies ached—Elara's arms from channeling so much divine energy, Cedric's from heavy sword blows, Thalion's from arcane exertion, and Mira's from repeated frost spells. Yet each wore a subtle smile of relief. The Vampire Lord was no more, and a major threat to Stonehaven had been vanquished.

"We should see if any villagers remain imprisoned," Elara said. "He might have kept them as a food source or thralls."

They scoured the fortress briefly, checking dank cells and makeshift quarters. A handful of pale, emaciated captives were found, too weak to stand. Some thralls cowered in corners, freed from the lord's mental hold but still confused. Elara, Thalion, and Mira offered what healing and clarity they could, while Cedric secured an exit path. Grateful, the survivors wept, scarcely believing the tyrant who terrorized them for months was truly gone.

Soon, the group escorted them outside, urging them to seek shelter in the nearest villages. The once-dreaded castle no longer exuded the same lethal aura. Shadows receded as the morning sun climbed. Cedric stared at the blackened windows overhead, imagining the centuries the lord must have spent weaving terror from within these walls. Their swift infiltration had torn that legacy apart.

They lingered a short while in the courtyard, helping the rescued souls gather enough strength to depart. Some took up meager possessions, others simply fled. The heroes gave them directions to safer territories. One older woman, trembling, approached Elara. "I prayed each night for a champion to end this nightmare. You are an angel of mercy, my lady. May the Light bless you."

Blushing, Elara bowed her head. "I'm only a servant of the Light, ma'am. Thank you—go in peace."

When at last the fortress lay still, the heroes reconvened near the battered gate. Each turned pensive. The crypt, once a nest of evil, was purified by Elara's divine might. Thalion said quietly, "We must keep pressing on to the Shadow Nexus. The Vampire Lord's downfall will free many lands from fear. But the ultimate threat remains."

Mira rubbed her arms, recalling the final shriek of the vampire. "He mentioned the darkness not being extinguished—almost like a final curse. We can't be complacent. The Nexus still looms, possibly forging new allies among other monsters."

Cedric nodded. "We'll face them, no matter how many. The people deserve safety."

Elara exhaled, gazing at the sky where crows circled overhead. "Yes. Perhaps this victory sends a message. If any monstrous tyrant hopes to conspire with the Nexus, they know we are out here, dismantling their plans."

Together, they departed the castle grounds, guiding those villagers who could walk. The grim spires stood behind them, an empty shell. The smell of death clung to the place, but it no longer menaced travelers. By midday, they reached a small crossroad, letting the refugees continue west. The group pressed east, resuming their quest with a lighter burden. The Vampire Lord's demise was a step closer to cleansing Stonehaven entirely.

In the following days, they passed through smaller settlements, relaying news that the dreaded Vampire Lord had been slain. Reactions ranged from stunned disbelief to cautious celebration. A few traveling merchants praised the heroes for restoring hope to regions long overshadowed by dread. Even in places untouched by the vampire's direct attacks, the rumor of his downfall spread quickly, stirring a sense that Stonehaven might yet be saved from the festering darkness.

Yet the heroes didn't linger for accolades. Their mission called them onward, to chase leads from the Arcadium's scrolls about other relics needed for the Song of Severance. Still, the memory of the vampire's lair and the dramatic showdown lingered in each companion's mind. Cedric and Elara found renewed confidence in their combined martial and divine prowess. Thalion and Mira marveled at how Elara's holy surge had shattered the undead's illusions, a testament to their synergy.

Even the artifacts they already possessed—like the Manticore's gem that enhanced magical potential—seemed to hum with added vigor after the confrontation. The relic recognized a new triumph, or so Thalion theorized. The swirling energies within the gem felt more stable, as if each victory over darkness honed their collective might.

In quieter moments around evening campfires, they recalled the Vampire Lord's final words. Some part of him had believed the darkness was eternal. But Elara's unwavering faith proved otherwise—that the Light, championed by righteous hearts, could banish even centuries-old evils. Now, with the undead tyrant gone, roads reopened, villages breathed freer, and one more obstacle to halting the Shadow Nexus had been removed.

A few days on the road after leaving the vampire's domain, the party found a serene glade to camp in. Under the canopy of tall oaks and a starry sky, they settled for the night. A mild breeze carried the scent of wildflowers, a refreshing contrast to the crypt's stale air. While Thalion and Mira poured over scrolls to chart their next route, Cedric set about maintaining the group's armor and weapons. Elara slipped away from the fire, letting the hush of the forest envelop her.

She knelt at a small clearing beside a trickling brook, shield resting at her side. Placing a hand over her heart, she closed her eyes. The memory of the Vampire Lord's final moments flashed in her mind—the triumphant surge of divine power, the anguished roar, the ashes carried on a silent breeze. Guilt mingled with relief, as she prayed for the souls lost to his cruelty and asked her goddess for continued guidance.

When she rose, she sensed a presence behind her. Turning, she found Cedric. He gave a reassuring smile, stepping gently onto the grass. "Didn't mean to disturb you," he said softly.

She shook her head. "It's fine. I was just... reflecting."

He nodded, coming closer. "I've never seen such pure radiance as you summoned against the vampire. It was incredible—and terrifying, in a way. But it saved us all."

Elara lowered her gaze. "Sometimes I fear that channeling such potent divine force could burn me out. But

I must trust the goddess to protect me while I do her work. The land depends on our strength."

Cedric placed a comforting hand on her shoulder. "We stand behind you, Elara. As you stand behind us. That synergy is our greatest weapon."

She smiled, warmth filling her chest. "Thank you, Cedric. Let's continue onward, for Stonehaven's sake."

They returned to camp, where Thalion and Mira had laid out a short-term plan. Next, they'd venture to a mountainous region rumored to host another relic site, possibly linked to ancient altars that once sealed the Shadow Nexus eons ago. Freed from the Vampire Lord's shadow, the group could travel more swiftly—no longer needing to fear undead patrols. The final confrontation with the Nexus still beckoned, but each step forward felt lighter after removing such a potent threat.

On their last evening in the vampire's domain, they quietly reaffirmed their quest. Cedric, steel in his voice, said: "We've dealt a major blow to the darkness. But the Nexus will not rest. We cannot slacken either."

Elara gazed around the circle, her eyes reflecting the firelight. "No. We must keep forging on. My vow to protect the weak stands until the Shadow Nexus is banished. Our battles so far proved we can do this."

Thalion tucked away a final reference scroll. "I suspect we'll face more vile creatures who see the Nexus as a path to power. Let's ensure they meet the same fate as the Vampire Lord."

Mira, stirring the embers, nodded. "And in doing so, we'll collect the relics needed for the ultimate purification.

Stonehaven will see a sunrise free of monsters. That is my hope."

Thus, their vigil ended with renewed resolution. They had infiltrated the lair of a dreadful Vampire Lord, orchestrator of countless atrocities, and ended his reign. Lady Elara's divine power, backed by the synergy of her companions, had shattered the vampire's dark ambitions. While greater horrors might still lie ahead—colossal beasts, twisted sorceries, or the Nexus's final shape—this victory stood as proof that no darkness was insurmountable.

Morning dawned bright, the sun's rays illuminating the once-gloomy terrain. As the party rode out from the region, villagers they encountered offered heartfelt thanks for the end of the vampire's terror. The presence of travelers on the roads began to pick up, merchants tentatively resuming routes once feared cursed. Indeed, the group's passage was met with cautious smiles, a flicker of hope lighting the eyes of townsfolk who had lived in dread for too long.

Though none proclaimed themselves heroes, each companion felt a quiet pride. One by one, they recognized how crucial their bond was. The illusions that once tested them, the gargoyle guardians, the monstrous beasts, the cunning Manticore, and now a Vampire Lord—none had been a match for their unity. This was not blind optimism, but the confidence born of repeated trials, each forging them stronger.

In time, the land behind them grew distant, and fresh landscapes beckoned. The swirling storms and mountain passes that lay ahead whispered of the next relic's location. Their immediate foes might be subdued, but the grand threat—the Shadow Nexus—still churned with malevolent promise. The group pressed on, each day weaving them tighter as a fellowship, each step carrying them closer to the final destiny that awaited.

Elara led a short prayer at midday, praising the goddess for their victory over the Vampire Lord and asking for continued guidance. Cedric, Thalion, and Mira bowed heads in respectful unity. When the prayer concluded, Thalion produced the gem from the Manticore's Den, remarking how it seemed more stable than ever. The group decided to begin experimental usage of its enhancements in sparing increments, ensuring they harnessed the relic's potential without succumbing to overreach.

And so the chapter of the Vampire Lord drew to a close—a potent demonstration that even the ancient undead, boasting centuries of tyranny, fell before the determined stand of mortal hearts bound by courage and faith. Lady Elara's triumph was a beacon of what was possible, a reaffirmation that the Light could flourish in even the darkest corners of Stonehaven.

Within the charred and cold crypt, dust motes danced in solitary beams of sunlight creeping through the broken castle windows. Ashes on the dais stirred in a faint draft, marking the exact spot where the Vampire Lord perished. The oppressive gloom that once choked every corridor had diminished; undead thralls, freed from compulsion, stumbled aimlessly or sought redemption beyond the ruined walls. Some might find ways to repent for their coerced crimes, others might wander as lost souls. But the seat of the vampire's power was shattered, leaving a vacuum that nature would eventually reclaim.

Far across Stonehaven, word spread swiftly: "The Vampire Lord has fallen." While some disbelieved, many breathed relief, sensing a shift in the winds. Farmers resumed plowing fields once left fallow. Traders reopened routes, no longer dreading an ambush by undead minions. Knights and guards found morale lifted, turning their attention to other threats. The clarion call of hope resounded in hearts that had known only fear.

Yet the Shadow Nexus loomed still. The relic hunts, the forging of the Song of Severance, and the culminating battle with the ancient source of corruption all waited on the heroes' horizon. They carried on, spurred by the knowledge that each foe bested, each relic claimed, each life saved brought them closer to preserving Stonehaven's future. The Vampire Lord's defeat was a chapter in that saga—a vital victory that proved even the highest lord of darkness would crumble when faced with resolute unity and the blessing of the Light.

And in the days to come, Lady Elara's name, alongside those of Cedric, Thalion, and Mira, would be spoken with admiration among the liberated hamlets. Their infiltration of the vampire's lair and Elara's decisive blow against the lord would become a story of defiance, a living testament to the unstoppable power of courage and faith. With hearts steadfast, the four companions rode onward, forging the next steps in their epic quest, guided by a dawn that shone just a little brighter across the land once steeped in midnight shadows.

14

LICH'S FORTRESS

A biting wind swept across the ash-gray plains as Sir Cedric, Lady Elara, Thalion, and Mira pressed onward, guided by the faint threads of dark magic that pulsed through the land. In the days since vanquishing the Vampire Lord and liberating countless souls from his nocturnal terror, the heroes had pushed deeper into Stonehaven's most forsaken territories, following cryptic markers gleaned from the Arcadium's references. These texts had pointed to a towering fortress of gloom, ruled by a cunning Lich whose mastery over death rivaled even the darkest legends of old. Rumor claimed that this necromancer commanded vast undead armies and was amassing power in preparation for the Shadow Nexus's return. Now, the group's most urgent mission was clear: eliminate the Lich and disrupt his plans before he fully harnessed the Nexus's corruption.

Yet no words could have prepared them for the harsh, desolate landscape they now traversed. The ground was arid and cracked, riddled with fissures that bled foul-smelling vapors. Ragged hills and crumbling rocks lined the horizon, each formation suggesting some ancient cataclysm or unholy influence. The sun, low on the horizon despite it being midday, cast a dim light through a veil of blackened clouds. Occasionally, a swirl of dust spun across the plains, scattering brittle bones and scraps of rotted cloth—remnants of past battles or hapless wanderers. Even the wind seemed reluctant to linger, howling its lament and fleeing toward distant mountains.

Elara, mounted on her trusted mare, felt her heart grow heavier with every mile. The faint warmth of her goddess's blessing flickered inside her chest, as though stifled by an oppressive shroud. She glanced at Cedric, who rode ahead, tense and vigilant. "I can feel it," she murmured, voice subdued. "An aura of death saturates this land. Whatever the Lich is planning, it's warping everything around his domain."

Cedric nodded solemnly, scanning the horizon with keen eyes. "Our latest informants said an army of undead patrol the fortress perimeter, harassing travelers and abducting stragglers to feed the Lich's rituals. If half the rumors are true, we face a legion that outnumbers any we've seen so far."

From behind them, Thalion lifted his staff, letting a subtle detection spell ripple out. His brow furrowed. "I sense the faint echoes of necromantic wards—intermittent pulses resonating through the leylines. The fortress must be near. Possibly shielded by illusions or cloaked by swirling negative energy. Still, we're on the right track."

Mira, feeling the subtle hum of the Manticore's gem in her pouch—a relic they claimed that amplified their magic—let out a measured breath. "At least we have new powers at our disposal. We'll need every advantage. A Lich is no ordinary necromancer—he's likely centuries old, driven by an unending thirst for forbidden knowledge."

No one refuted her words. They all understood that the Lich's threat stood on par with, or perhaps even surpassed, the challenges they had already overcome: ghosts, gargoyles, monstrous beasts, a cunning Manticore, and a Vampire Lord. Yet each victory, each relic discovered, each synergy forged, had fortified them for the final confrontation with the Shadow Nexus. Taking down the Lich was essential to dismantling the looming catastrophe. Should the necromancer fully ally with or empower the Nexus, Stonehaven would stand little chance.

As twilight approached, a grim sight emerged on the skyline: a procession of undead figures trudged across the plains, heading toward a tall ridge in the distance. Their silhouettes were skeletal or decaying, some hunched, others in ragged armor, all marching in unnerving silence. From this vantage, it was difficult to count them—dozens, perhaps hundreds—shuffling in a loose formation that vanished behind the ridge.

Cedric reined in his horse, urging the others to duck behind a rocky outcrop. "We can't fight that many head-on," he whispered. "We should let them pass, then see if we can follow their route. Likely they're heading back to the fortress."

Elara agreed, brow furrowed. "If we follow discreetly, we might confirm the entrance or get a sense of the fortress's defenses. Fighting an entire undead brigade in the open would be suicide."

Thalion guided them to a narrow depression in the ground, where they concealed themselves and the horses behind jagged boulders. From there, they watched the undead column pass. The creatures carried crude weapons, battered shields, or rusted pikes. Some wore the remnants of once-proud house banners, now tattered and smeared with grime. Their hollow eyes glowed faintly in the gathering dusk. Leading them was a figure in dark robes, tall and gaunt, presumably a lich's acolyte or a higher-ranking undead knight. It strode with an eerie grace, the hush of a black staff tapping on stone with each step. No mortal heartbeat or living breath accompanied them, only the scraping of bones and metal in the dying light.

The group crouched low, hearts pounding. One misstep, one whispered breath too loudly, and the undead might discover them. Yet fortune favored them. The column continued without pause, presumably blinded by the swirling negativity that only recognized orders from their master. In minutes, the undead ranks disappeared beyond the ridge.

"By the Light," murmured Elara, standing once the last skeleton vanished. "That's a full battalion. The Lich is fielding an army."

Mira exhaled, eyes wide. "If that's just one patrol or supply line, the fortress must be crawling with undead minions. We'll need cunning to breach it."

Cedric nodded, gazing at the ridge. "We follow them at a safe distance. Once we see the fortress layout, we'll plan our assault."

Thus, as night fully wrapped the plains in gloom, they led their horses carefully after the undead tracks, each step weighed with caution. The possibility of an entire legion within the fortress spurred a deeper sense of urgency.

For hours, they tailed the undead from afar, stopping whenever the column paused or scanning for wandering sentinels. At times, the path veered close to cracked ravines where putrid mist rose from below. The night air grew colder, laced with the stench of grave soil. The presence of necromantic wards prickled at their senses, and Elara found her divine aura flickering in discomfort at the pervasive unholy energy.

Finally, near midnight, the terrain opened into a vast, rocky basin. At its center towered the Lich's Fortress: a colossal stronghold hewn from obsidian-black stone, bristling with jagged ramparts. At each corner rose spires shaped like elongated skulls, their hollow eyes flickering with eerie purple flames. Strange runic pylons dotted the fortress's outer walls, clearly fueling protective wards or necromantic spells that shielded it from external siege.

Above the fortress, the sky churned with unnatural storm clouds tinted greenish-brown, occasionally crackling with arcs of sickly lightning. The entire citadel seemed drenched in gloom, as though reality itself bent under the Lich's dominion. Torchlight—if such a vile light could be called that—glimmered along the parapets. From their vantage point behind a ridge, the heroes could just make out scattered groups of undead patrolling the perimeter: skeleton archers, zombies laden with rusted pikes, wights or ghouls slinking in the shadows.

Cedric swallowed hard, the sight both terrifying and awe-inspiring. "That's not a mere fortress—it's a bastion of necromancy. The Lich must have been preparing it for a long time."

Thalion's eyes were drawn to the runic pylons. "He's harnessing negative energy from the land, forming a barrier that likely repels direct assault. We can't just rush the gates—dark wards of that magnitude would annihilate us."

Mira frowned. "Could we dispel them? Or at least create an opening?"

Elara, shield slung on her back, touched the hilt of her sword. "We'll need a plan. Taking down the wards from the inside might be the only way. Possibly the Lich has a phylactery—some object storing his essence. Destroying that is key to permanently ending his reign."

Cedric nodded. "We recall from the Arcadium texts that a Lich's phylactery is essential to its immortality. Without smashing it, the Lich can resurrect. We must search for it once inside."

They slid down behind a rocky berm to discuss next steps. From the vantage, it was clear the fortress had a massive iron gate flanked by spiked towers. A moat of black sludge circled part of the outer wall. The undead patrolled in pairs or small squads. Meanwhile, the wards flickered, forming a faint aura overhead. Storm clouds overhead churned, occasionally letting out a low rumble of unnatural thunder.

Quietly, they reconvened around a small lamp, shielded by a cloak to avoid detection. Thalion sketched an approximation of the fortress layout on a scrap of parchment, adding notes on patrol patterns gleaned from their observation. "It seems most undead converge around that main gate and the southern tower. The wards are anchored by pylons along the outer wall and likely a main nexus stone within the central keep."

Elara tapped a point near the east wall. "That area seems less patrolled. If we scale those rocks, we might slip over the ramparts. But we must still bypass or sabotage the wards. My divine aura alone might trigger an alert if the wards react to holy energy."

Mira considered. "I can cast illusions to cloak us from watchful eyes, but illusions won't block necromantic detection spells. We may need a direct approach to sabotage at least one pylon, opening a gap in the wards."

Cedric mulled over the scale of the undead. "Once we're inside, the Lich's minions will swarm us if alarmed. We'll have to move fast, disabling wards, locating the Lich's throne room or crypt, and destroying him—phylactery and all—before we're overwhelmed."

A hush fell. The fortress looked impregnable, with no shortage of horrors within. Yet each hero remembered how they had triumphed over monstrous legions before. Their synergy and the relics they possessed—like the Manticore gem—gave them new heights of power. The looming question: would it be enough?

Elara broke the silence. "We must. If the Lich cements his bond with the Shadow Nexus, entire armies of undead could sweep Stonehaven, devouring towns from within. This fortress is a keystone. Breaking it is essential to the Song of Severance's success."

Thalion's expression hardened. "Then let us plan the infiltration for tomorrow night. We can rest now, gather strength, confirm patrol timings. Under cover of darkness, we strike."

Cedric agreed. "We'll remain hidden till then, out of range of any scouts. Once we breach the walls, we move swiftly. No half-measures. We slay the Lich, break his phylactery, and free this land from another powerful servant of darkness."

They shared final words and set a watch rotation for the night. While the fortress loomed ominously under flickers of cursed lightning, the group huddled in their modest shelter behind boulders. Anxiety and determination warred in their hearts—by tomorrow, they would be inside the stronghold of a necromantic overlord. The outcome might shape Stonehaven's fate.

Dawn arrived cold and gray, offering meager warmth. The fortress remained a brooding silhouette, its undead inhabitants no doubt less hindered by daylight than typical vampires. Still, many forms slunk into subterranean tunnels for rest, replaced by skeletal archers or lesser wights patrolling the battlements. For the heroes, the day was spent observing from afar, memorizing patrol routes, and finalizing infiltration details. They discovered the eastern wall was indeed poorly monitored, especially near a collapsed section. But wards still shimmered overhead, requiring a cunning approach to neutralize them.

Elara took the time to center herself, chanting quiet devotions for fortitude. Cedric methodically checked each weapon, retying straps and polishing edges. Thalion prepared specific spells for ward disruption, layering illusions and arcane signals that might mask the group's presence. Mira practiced conjuring subtle illusions of drifting fog, hoping to cloak them from watchtowers.

Night returned, thick clouds masking the moon. A few sputtering torches lined the fortress walls, barely cutting through the gloom. This was the hour of the undead—yet ironically, it was also the best time for infiltration. The heroes crept forward, leaving their horses tethered behind a rocky bluff at a safe distance. Each step across the plain felt momentous. The wind hissed across the lifeless ground, as if protesting their bold plan.

Under cover of darkness, they reached the fortress's east side. Up close, the wall soared high, composed of black stone etched with necromantic runes. The faint aura of wards crackled near the top, forming a web of negative energy. Elara grimaced at the tingling sensation. This was no petty hex—the Lich's magic was formidable.

Thalion placed a hand on the wall, quietly chanting. A small portion of the wards flickered, allowing a fleeting gap. "Go," he whispered, sweat beading his brow. "I can't hold this void patch for long."

Swiftly, Cedric and Elara scaled the crumbling stones, using cracks and protrusions for grips. Above them, skeleton archers paced the parapet. Mira extended illusions of shifting shadows, dampening the group's silhouette. Thalion followed last, staff strapped to his back for freer climbing. The wards crackled again, but Thalion's disruption held just enough that the group could slip through without triggering an alarm.

Moments later, they dropped onto the rampart walkway. The stone was cold, stained with old blood. Two skeleton archers patrolled nearby. Before they could rattle a warning, Cedric lunged, slicing one's spine with a silent blow. Elara bashed the other with her shield, sending it tumbling off the wall. The bones shattered on the courtyard below with a hollow clatter.

The group froze, hearts pounding. Had the noise alerted others? No immediate shouts rose. The swirling gloom made it difficult for watchers on distant towers to notice such a quick scuffle. They shared relieved nods, then advanced along the battlement.

Beneath them, the courtyard teemed with undead: skeleton footmen, zombies dragging battered weapons, a scattering of wights or ghoul-like figures patrolling the gate. Opposite the courtyard lay the central keep, a massive structure with turrets brimming in necromantic effigy. Between them and the keep's door stretched a yard of open space. Another pylon crackled with runes near the door, presumably a key anchor for the fortress wards.

Mira spotted a narrower walkway leading to a side turret that jutted from the keep's flank. "Maybe we can enter from that turret. It seems less guarded."

Thalion peered over the edge. "Yes, and see that pylon below? If we sabotage it, a chunk of the wards might collapse, giving us freer movement inside the keep. Otherwise, we risk setting off every alarm if we just waltz into the main hall."

They crept across the parapet, dispatching a skeleton sentry with silent teamwork. Thalion used illusions to hide the remains. Soon, they reached a small balcony overlooking the pylon. Twisting wires of necrotic energy connected the pylon to the fortress's upper spires. The hum of dark magic vibrated in their chests.

Elara and Cedric posted guard while Mira and Thalion descended a short flight of stairs that led to the pylon's platform. The device stood roughly ten feet tall, shaped like a twisted obelisk. Inscribed runes glowed with a sickly purple, streaming arcs of negative energy up toward the sky.

Two skeleton mages hovered near it, chanting a low droning. Possibly they maintained the pylon's function.

Mira locked eyes with Thalion. They had to act fast and quietly. Thalion conjured a small orb of shimmering darkness, an anti-magic sphere that he gently placed around one skeleton mage. Confused, the undead creature faltered, its chanting disrupted, and within seconds it collapsed as the necromantic tether fueling its existence dissolved. The second mage noticed, turning with a silent snarl to fling a wave of dark fire at Thalion. Mira reacted instantly, conjuring a barrier of frost that neutralized the flame. Cedric leapt from above, stabbing his sword through the mage's spine. It collapsed in a heap, dissipating into dust.

Now at the base of the pylon, Thalion and Mira studied the runes, carefully weaving a dispelling pattern. Elara stood watch, scanning for additional guards. The pylon crackled, resisting their intrusion. Mira's staff flared as she wrestled with the swirling energies. "It's strong—like tangling with a living entity of pure negative force."

Thalion exhaled, continuing the incantation. "We don't need to destroy it entirely. Just sever its link to the fortress wards for a few minutes. That'll keep the alarm silent until we're inside."

With concentrated effort, they etched runic lines in the air. The pylon's hum grew volatile, arcs of purple lightning flickering. Then, with a final pulse, the negative energy sputtered. The pylon's glow dimmed, its connection to the upper spires temporarily severed. A wave of magical backlash rippled outward, but Mira and Thalion stabilized themselves with a protective shield. The courtyard beyond remained eerily calm, the undead oblivious to the subtle sabotage.

Mira gave a shaky grin. "It's done. The wards are partially down. We have a window."

Elara allowed herself a small smile in relief. "Excellent. Let's get to the keep. If we can find the Lich's phylactery and then confront him, we'll cripple this entire army."

They backtracked to the balcony, slipping along the ramparts until they reached a side turret that connected to the main keep's upper level. A rickety wooden door blocked the way. Cedric eased it open with minimal sound, peering into a spiral stair of dusty stone. The faint smell of decay wafted out, typical of this fortress's many halls.

Down the narrow stair, they proceeded with caution. Occasionally, they passed doorways leading to side chambers, some sealed, others ajar revealing storage rooms of rotting supplies or cluttered armories for undead soldiers. Groans and soft shuffling echoed behind certain doors, indicating more animated corpses on standby. But the party's priority lay deeper, presumably in the core of the keep, where the Lich himself would dwell.

Elara's holy sense prickled. Each step downward heightened the aura of necromancy saturating the corridors. "He's near. The Lich must be weaving spells in the fortress's heart. I can almost taste the corruption."

Thalion stifled a shudder. "We must remain stealthy. If we break stealth now, the entire undead legion might converge on us. Let's find his workshop or throne room—wherever he exerts the strongest control."

Mira took point, illusions at the ready, blending their silhouettes with the gloom. They skirted past a half-collapsed corridor, stepping around piles of dusty tomes and broken candelabras. Here and there, lesser undead dozed or stood idle, waiting for the Lich's command. The group carefully avoided making noise.

Yet at a T-junction, a skeletal guard equipped with a rusted halberd spotted them. It rattled a silent alarm, raising its weapon. Before it could strike or call others, Cedric lunged. The skeleton attempted to block, but Elara's shield followed, shattering the undead's collarbone. The rest of the skeleton collapsed in a jangle of bones. They hurried on, mindful that even this small scuffle might draw attention.

Eventually, they reached a grand corridor lined with statues of robed figures. Each statue's face was carved into a leering skull. The stench of sulfur and rotten incense choked the air. At the far end, a pair of ornate doors, inlaid with monstrous reliefs, stood ajar—beyond them flickered the flickering glow of greenish torches. Whispers of chanting leaked out, echoing with unnatural resonance. The Lich's presence felt overwhelming here, like a tangible weight pressing on their souls.

Cedric halted the group behind the last statue. "This must be it—the Lich's main hall or ritual chamber. Are we ready?"

Elara set her shield and sword, a fierce glow shimmering around her. "No turning back. If we slay him here, we deliver a mortal blow to the undead armies and keep the Nexus from gaining his support."

Thalion and Mira adjusted grips on staff and illusions. "We'll do our part to hold off minions and disrupt his spells," Thalion assured, steeling himself. "Elara, your divine power is key to unraveling his unholy wards. Cedric, you anchor the frontline. Let's end this."

Mira conjured a minor veil to obscure them as they approached. Step by step, they entered the chamber. The scene inside was grim: a vaulted hall, once grand, now twisted by necromancy. Rows of columns soared overhead, each carved with macabre runes. At the center, a circular dais glowed with a sickly green effulgence, swirling with ghostly shapes. Atop the dais stood the Lich: a tall, skeletal figure draped in tattered robes embroidered with arcane symbols. Dark pits for eyes flickered with malevolent brilliance. In one bony hand, he clutched a staff crowned by a skull. In the other, he cradled a black phylactery, shaped like an ornate box or reliquary that pulsed with negative force.

Around him, half a dozen undead knights waited, silent sentinels with eyes burning in the gloom. The Lich's chanting reverberated in the chamber, weaving necromantic energies into a swirling vortex overhead, presumably fueling the fortress wards or forging new horrors. The entire hall stank of dust, tomb rot, and old spellcraft.

At first, the Lich did not notice the intruders, his chanting too intense. But one undead knight turned with a hollow rasp, pointing a rusted sword at the heroes. The Lich's chanting ceased abruptly. He twisted his skull-like head, lips curling back from blackened teeth in a silent hiss of outrage.

"So," the Lich croaked, voice echoing with centuries of disdain. "You are the meddlers who silenced my vampire lieutenant. I sense your stench of living flesh even in my sanctum. How... unfortunate for you."

Elara moved to the forefront, shield shining. "Your reign ends here, necromancer. Stonehaven's people will not be enslaved by your undead legions. Surrender the phylactery, or face final destruction."

The Lich let out a soundless laugh that pulsed through the group's minds, more telepathic than vocal. "Arrogance. I have transcended mortal shackles. My armies spread across these lands by the day, fueling the Shadow Nexus with countless souls. You shall not bar my ascension."

With a wave of his staff, the dais flared in greenish light. The undead knights advanced in rigid unison, swords raised, eyes gleaming with cold malice. At the same moment, shadowy apparitions peeled from the air, swirling near the group. A half-dozen specters, each moaning faintly, rose to join the knights.

Cedric tightened his grip, stepping forward. "Elara, focus on the Lich. We'll handle his guardians. Thalion, Mira—keep that phylactery in sight. If we can break it, he's vulnerable."

The Lich sneered, drifting from the dais with effortless grace, the phylactery clutched protectively to his chest. "You presume to challenge me in my domain? Fall, mortals, and rise as my thralls!"

The knights charged. Cedric met them head-on, sword crashing against rusted blades. Sparks flew, reverberations numbing his arms. Elara faced two knights simultaneously, her shield flaring with divine wrath that scorched their undead bones. Meanwhile, Thalion launched arcane bolts at the swirling specters, and Mira conjured frost blasts to hamper the knights' movements. Wails of restless souls filled the air, swirling with each blow.

All the while, the Lich circled the dais, chanting dark incantations to strengthen his minions. Each time Elara's holy aura struck a knight, the Lich hissed, weaving a counterspell to blunt her power. Every step the heroes took forward was met with necrotic blasts that sizzled around them. The dais itself pulsed ominously, resonating with the fortress's wards.

Despite the onslaught, the heroes advanced with practiced synergy. Cedric deflected a knight's overhead strike, pivoting to cleave its spine. The skeleton collapsed in a jangle of armor. Elara bashed another knight's helmet, divine light fracturing its skull in a burst of dust. Thalion's staff flared, unleashing a swirling cyclone that entrapped two specters, dispersing their forms in a cacophony of shrieks. Mira targeted the final knight with precision frost shards, freezing it mid-swing until Cedric shattered it with a swift blow.

Freed from the guardians, they turned to confront the Lich directly. He hovered at the dais, dark robes billowing, staff raised. His phylactery glowed with frantic pulses, as though funneling necromantic power into him. "Impressive. But I am eternal," he spat, loosing a wave of crackling death magic that rippled across the chamber.

The wave struck the heroes, each feeling a chill sapping their vitality. Elara cried out, shield struggling to block the brunt. Thalion's illusions fizzled, Mira's conjured frost evaporated as negative energy clashed with it. Cedric felt his knees buckle under the crushing aura. In that moment, the Lich laughed silently, a cosmic mockery of life.

"Bow to me," his voice boomed telepathically, "and I shall grant you oblivion swiftly."

But the group refused. Thalion mustered a shining arcane barrier, buffering the death wave. Mira reignited her staff with the Manticore gem's augmented power, weaving a mirror of protective frost that helped mitigate the necromantic drain. Cedric forced himself upright, heart pounding, while Elara pressed a hand to her chest, summoning the goddess's strength to restore a measure of health.

The Lich's glowing eyes flicked between them, calculating. "You think yourself worthy of the relic's might? Even your holy champion shall yield." His skeletal jaws parted in a silent snarl. Another surge of corruption blasted from the dais, rattling the columns, threatening to collapse the chamber around them.

Elara advanced, brandishing her shield, the symbol of her faith blazing in white-gold. "Your tyranny ends here, necromancer!" She swung her sword, channeling beams of searing radiance that arced across the dais. The Lich's staff intercepted, swirling darkness deflecting part of the assault. Where the light touched his bony form, sizzling cracks erupted, yet he persisted, fueled by the phylactery's endless well of dark magic.

Cedric took advantage of the distraction, rushing from the flank. With adrenaline surging, he landed a slash on the Lich's ribcage. But the blow skittered off a magical barrier layered over the lich's bones. The creature hissed, twisting with unholy speed. In a flash, bony talons raked across Cedric's breastplate, sending him sprawling.

Mira moved to help, launching a concentrated frost beam at the Lich's staff. The staff iced over momentarily, hindering the Lich's grip. He responded by snarling an incantation, releasing a pulse of black fire that threatened to engulf Mira. Thalion reacted, shaping a protective shell around her. The black flames hammered the shield, roaring with necrotic intensity. Despite the shield's protection, the force knocked both Mira and Thalion backward.

Elara alone remained close to the dais, locked in a furious exchange with the Lich. Radiant arcs clashed with ghostly shadows. Each strike from her sword chipped away at his wards, but each counter from the Lich sapped her vigor, draining warmth from her limbs. She stumbled, nearly succumbing to the searing cold of undeath.

But the group's synergy was unstoppable: Cedric returned to the fight, challenging the Lich from behind. Thalion, reeling, cast illusions that distorted the Lich's perspective, forcing him to divide his focus. Mira harnessed the gem's amplified frost, summoning a ring of ice around the dais that restricted the Lich's movement. The necromancer reeled, staff lashing out in desperation, but each second, the circle tightened.

"Your eternity ends now," Elara declared, voice resonating with unwavering conviction. She lunged, sword shining with the pure brilliance of her goddess.

Sensing defeat, the Lich bellowed an inhuman screech, swirling shadows around himself. Bones jutted from the dais as necromantic constructs tried to shield him. But it was too late—Elara's divine blow sliced through the constructs. The Lich's wards cracked, exposing his skeletal torso. Cedric capitalized, delivering a punishing slash that severed the Lich's left arm. Black ichor spattered across the dais.

Snarling, the Lich clutched the phylactery, attempting to channel its essence to resurrect or regenerate. "I cannot fall," came his telepathic roar, echoing with centuries of obsessions. "I have transcended death!"

Yet Thalion recognized the crucial moment. "The phylactery! Strike it!" he shouted.

Mira lunged forward, staff raised, conjuring an icy spike aimed at the phylactery's chain. The force shattered the chain, sending the black box tumbling from the Lich's grasp. It clattered onto the dais, the swirl of negative energy around it flickering in disarray.

"NO!" the Lich howled, diving for the phylactery with his remaining hand. But Cedric's blade barred his path. Meanwhile, Elara stomped her boot atop the box, channeling a burst of holy light directly into it. The relic hissed, arcs of necromantic energy thrashing. The Lich screamed, convulsing as a portion of his soul tether was forcibly severed. The dais cracked, chunks of stone rising in a telekinetic frenzy.

Elara pressed harder, ignoring the howling vortex. With a final, decisive surge of faith, she crushed the phylactery under her heel, sword plunging through its cursed shell. A cataclysmic shriek tore through the crypt—both from the Lich and the relic—before the phylactery imploded in a burst of black shards. Shadows dissipated, negative energy collapsed in on itself, and the Lich shrank back, howling in agony as his immortality anchor was destroyed.

Robbed of the phylactery's protection, the Lich's wards disintegrated. His bones rattled, cracking from the inside.

He swiped once at Elara, only to have Cedric thrust his sword through the necromancer's chest. The Lich's jaw fell open, an unheard scream contorting his bony visage. Holy light and arcane power from the group flooded him, severing the necromantic bonds that held his form together.

"I—am—eternal—" he gasped telepathically, but the words carried no conviction anymore. As the last threads of negative energy fizzled, the Lich's skeleton collapsed piece by piece, dissolving into ash. No shriek, no dramatic roar— just a final, hollow clatter as centuries of unholy existence ended in a quiet puff of dust on the dais.

At once, the swirling storm overhead vanished. The necromantic glow infusing the fortress flickered out. All around, the moaning of undead foot soldiers ceased or turned to panicked howls as their link to the master severed. Freed from the Lich's absolute control, many undead crumpled, inert. Others wandered aimlessly, shells without purpose. The heroes stared in awe, hearts hammering, as the chamber brightened with flickers of normal torchlight. Without the Lich's oppressive aura, the fortress felt markedly less suffocating.

Elara stumbled to her knees, panting from the divine energy she had channeled to crush the phylactery. Cedric knelt beside her, checking for injuries. Thalion and Mira caught up, breathing heavily. The dais was a wreck of shattered stone and black shards. No sign remained of the once-infamous necromancer, aside from a scattering of broken bones.

"It's done," Thalion whispered, voice hoarse. "The Lich is gone for good. Without a phylactery, he cannot return."

Mira sank onto a fallen column, hugging her staff. "And his undead armies... likely in total disarray now. Stonehaven is safe from his threat."

Elara closed her eyes, murmuring a prayer of thanks. The swirling darkness in her chest eased, replaced by the goddess's gentle warmth. "Another piece of the Nexus's foul puzzle removed," she said softly. "We stand a step closer to cleansing the realm."

Exiting the fortress proved far easier with the Lich's demise. Most undead had collapsed or devolved into chaotic states, and any pockets of resistance were swiftly dispatched. The heroes emerged into the courtyard as the first hints of dawn touched the fortress walls, revealing the staggering scale of the once-thriving undead legion—now broken, left to gather dust on the cold stone. Freed thralls, if any, had fled or dissolved. The fortress, once a hub of necromantic activity, lay silent.

They made their way outside, crossing the moat with no more monstrous interventions. Dawn light bathed them in a soft glow, a stark contrast to the dreadful gloom they had endured within. Pausing on a windswept rise, they looked back at the fortress spires, each black tower crowned by the dissipating gloom. No swirling clouds of malice remained overhead. The wards, shattered, allowed sunlight to break across the ramparts.

Elara let out a breath of mingled relief and sorrow. "So much death. So many horrors. But at least no more souls will fall victim here."

Cedric laid a supportive hand on her shoulder. "We did what we had to do. The Lich's corruption was a direct threat to the entire realm."

Thalion and Mira joined them, both worn. The Manticore gem still hummed softly, acknowledging the massive wave of necromantic disruption just undone by their efforts. If the Vampire Lord's fall had signaled a turning point for Stonehaven's people, the Lich's demise might signal an even greater shift, crippling a major pillar of the Nexus's allied dark forces.

They trudged away from the fortress, retrieving their horses from the hidden camp. The animals whinnied, sensing the lighter atmosphere—no longer reeking of necromantic pulses. The group mounted up, guiding their steeds across the bleak plains. Rays of morning sunlight caught on armor and cloak, a testament to the heroes' unbroken spirit.

They rode in weary silence, each privately reliving the battle's crucial moments. How the Lich had nearly overwhelmed them with his foul spells. How the phylactery's destruction brought a final end to centuries of necromantic tyranny. Cedric recalled the Manticore gem flaring at key points, subtly boosting their magical synergy. Elara recalled the goddess's power coursing through her arms, magnified by the unwavering resolve of her companions. Thalion thought of the illusions and wards they deftly circumvented. Mira found hope in how effectively they had dismantled a fortress that once harbored an entire undead legion.

At midday, they paused to make camp near a shallow creek. The land here was only marginally less grim, but the presence of running water and a trickle of greenery felt like an oasis after the fortress's gloom. Thalion cleaned a small cut on his arm, courtesy of a skeleton's slash. Cedric unrolled a bandage around a bruised shoulder. Elara performed gentle healing prayers to ease stiffness from channeling so much holy power. Mira took stock of their supplies, concluding they had enough for a few days before needing to restock at any surviving settlement.

"Word will spread fast," Cedric remarked while refilling a waterskin. "Villagers or scouts will notice the fortress's wards gone, the undead army collapsed. They'll celebrate, or investigate the ruins."

Elara nodded. "That's good. Let them claim the fortress, bury the dead, and ensure no stray necromancers reanimate the remains."

Thalion settled by the small campfire, rummaging through the Arcadium texts. "We should also record how we overcame the Lich—notes on destroying the phylactery, the wards we disabled. This knowledge might help future generations if necromancers arise again."

Mira, half-listening, smiled. "Another vile threat undone. Another ally of the Nexus neutralized. Soon, the path to the final confrontation stands clearer."

They agreed. The Nexus's hold on Stonehaven weakened each time they thwarted one of its prospective pawns. Between the Vampire Lord and now the Lich, two major pillars of darkness had fallen. Of course, the ultimate challenge—facing the Nexus itself—remained. But each victory, each relic discovered, each synergy refined, brought them closer to halting the apocalypse.

Continuing east, they traveled for days across barren hills, gradually entering regions less scarred by necromancy. Sparse grass resumed, small creatures scurried in the underbrush, signs that nature might reclaim what the Lich had corrupted. They rested in hollows protected from the wind, forging deeper bonds in nightly discussions about the final relic hunts and the nearing showdown with the Shadow Nexus.

Elara often woke at dawn to pray, the sunlight easing her memories of that silent crypt, the Lich's menacing silhouette, and the final crash of the phylactery. She sensed the goddess's approval. Meanwhile, Cedric sharpened his sword meticulously, forging steel that would soon face even deadlier foes. Thalion and Mira took turns experimenting with spells using the Manticore gem, perfecting synergy that could unleash devastating blasts if needed.

One evening, they crossed paths with a small caravan of travelers who had heard rumors of an "undead fortress collapsing" just days prior. When the group admitted partial responsibility, the travelers expressed profound gratitude, offering the heroes fresh produce and praising their courage. Word indeed spread quickly, re-igniting hope across the frontier.

Mira accepted the thanks graciously, but her gaze remained on the horizon. "We appreciate your kindness," she told them, "but our quest isn't over. The darkness that birthed the Lich still festers. Keep watch for strange signs and spread word that we'll do all we can."

At last, they neared a transitional zone: the rugged highlands gave way to rolling moors dotted with ancient ruins. The day's travel was calm, offering a chance to reflect. In the afternoon sun, they paused on a windswept hill, scanning the moors for any sign of the next relic site. The Arcadium's notes hinted that a final relic might lie in distant ruins or a mountain temple, all tying into the Song of Severance that would end the Shadow Nexus.

Elara turned to Cedric, voice thoughtful. "You know, each major threat we've vanquished—be it the Manticore, the Vampire Lord, or this Lich—has tested a different facet of our strength. Yet we keep triumphing, forging a path to the Nexus."

Cedric nodded with a subdued smile. "I've never felt so certain of a cause. The land depends on our synergy. Our victories prove we're not powerless against ancient evils."

Thalion parted his cloak, retrieving the battered map and scribbles from the Arcadium. "Our next step, if these notes are correct, is to cross another region known for fierce storms or labyrinthine canyons, seeking a hidden shrine. The Lich's fortress was likely the last major necromantic stronghold in our path."

Mira studied the Manticore gem as it faintly gleamed. "The road is still perilous. We must remain cautious. But we're united. If we overcame a legion of undead and destroyed an immortal necromancer, we can face what's next."

They set up a small campsite on that hill, the evening sky streaked with embers of orange and purple. The triumph over the Lich warmed their hearts, a reassurance that no matter how daunting the Shadow Nexus's allies, they could be felled by unwavering unity and the will to protect Stonehaven.

That night, conversation drifted from memory to memory: crossing the Blood River, the Manticore's deadly cunning, the Vampire Lord's final shriek, the forging of synergy that allowed them to keep advancing. Now, the

Lich's downfall was another storied chapter, one that would echo in legends of how mortals tamed the black arts to free a kingdom. Yet each recalled how close they'd come to disaster. The necromantic blasts, the Lich's illusions, the phylactery that nearly shielded him forever. They had been seconds from overwhelming doom if not for Elara's unwavering faith and the group's quick thinking.

"I still see his eyes when I close mine," Elara admitted softly, gazing into the campfire. "The emptiness there was so... ancient. As if he had abandoned every trace of humanity centuries ago."

Cedric gently took her hand. "That emptiness was his downfall. He underestimated your compassion, your devotion to the Light, and our willingness to fight for life."

Thalion poked at the fire, nodding. "He also underestimated that we'd discover his phylactery. Without that artifact destroyed, he would have risen again. We must remain vigilant in future battles—other necromancers or monstrous foes might have similar anchors."

Mira quietly closed her eyes, recalling the swirling arcs of negative energy that battered them in that final chamber. "The Shadow Nexus lost a powerful ally. But it remains, forging or corrupting new servants. We can't let relief turn to complacency. Tomorrow, we press on."

They concluded the night with a renewed vow to see this quest through. Sleep found them in quiet intervals. Cedric kept watch, scanning the moors under the moon's silver glow. The fortress's memory loomed in his mind like a grim testament to how far they had come, and how far they still must go.

At dawn, the group rose, invigorated by a sense of closure from the fortress. The moors stretched ahead, dotted with crumbling monoliths or cairns that whispered of ancient civilizations. Birds chirped softly, returning life to an area once overshadowed by necromantic threat. As they mounted up, the horses trotted with a renewed spring, perhaps sensing that the immediate darkness was lifted.

Along the journey, the party encountered a few scattered travelers—hunters, merchants, pilgrims—each relieved to hear that the Lich's fortress had fallen. Some shared local updates: sightings of half-rotted undead wandering aimlessly, presumably leftover minions that lost purpose once their master perished. Others offered thanks or supplies, grateful that a new dawn of safety might blossom.

Elara found these encounters bittersweet. Each expression of relief reminded her of the countless lives impacted by the Lich's cruelty. She prayed her goddess might guide those still haunted by nightmares. Cedric, for his part, reassured them that no new necromancer would claim the fortress, not while the four heroes roamed Stonehaven's darkest corners, unraveling the Nexus's allies one by one.

"We carry on," Thalion would say, checking the map. "The final confrontation with the Nexus draws closer with each day. The land recovers step by step."

Mira nodded, letting her staff glean subtle energies from the environment. "I can't wait to see Stonehaven fully healed, no more vampire lords or lich kings terrorizing villages. Just peace... and the vibrant life that once flourished."

Within them, each carried a sense that their next challenge might be even more perilous, for the Shadow Nexus was not idle. Yet each victory, each step, each relic, and each synergy chipped away at the ancient evil's foothold. The Lich's fortress stood as the latest testament that no dark throne was insurmountable.

Onward they rode, the plains and moors sliding beneath the hooves of their horses, the wind scattering the last vestiges of gloom. The confrontation at the Lich's stronghold weighed in their memories, a fierce testament to courage, cunning, and the unwavering power of hope. When next they faced monstrous hordes or twisted sorcery, they would recall how a fortress bristling with undead legions and overshadowed by centuries of necromancy fell to four determined souls working in harmony.

In the coming weeks, they would seek out the last relics needed to perform the Song of Severance—a ritual that promised to sever the Shadow Nexus from the mortal plane. Past experiences had shown them that each relic lay guarded by monstrous keepers, cunning warlocks, or formidable wards. Yet the heroes advanced with unwavering faith, carrying the momentum of triumph.

Because once they had entered the Lich's domain, faced its horrors, destroyed the undead armies, and shattered the necromancer's phylactery, they proved that even the strongest outpost of darkness could not withstand their combined might. The future battles might be grander, the stakes higher, but their synergy and the relics they amassed forged an unbreakable path forward.

Thus ended the chapter of the Lich's fortress, a turning point in Stonehaven's fate. The realm's people felt the weight lift, villages ceasing to cower under the necromancer's looming threat, roads reopening, trade resuming, families reuniting. Word of the Lich's downfall would race across the land, a clarion call that hope still burned bright.

And so the four heroes—Sir Cedric, Lady Elara, Thalion, and Mira—continued east, guided by a map of half-forgotten shrines and ancient altars. The gem from the Manticore's Den pulsed in Mira's satchel, the blessings of Elara's goddess glowed in her shield, Thalion's staff thrummed with knowledge gleaned from the Arcadium, and Cedric's sword shone with steadfast resolution. Each carried an unspoken vow: no matter what horrors remained on the path to the Shadow Nexus, they would stand together, unwavering, until the final blow was struck and Stonehaven stood free of corruption's grasp forever.

15

SIEGE OF THE UNDEAD

Sir Cedric guided his horse down a gentle slope, the rising sun illuminating the plains ahead. Morning dew glistened on the grass, and a cool breeze stirred the open fields. Behind him rode Lady Elara upon her faithful mare, Thalion astride a lean horse more accustomed to swift travel than open war, and Mira perched on a skittish mount that picked its way around puddles left by the night's rain. Though they had savored only a brief respite since defeating an eastern Lich, their journey now led westward once more—grave rumors spoke of another undead threat: the fortress known as Vyndor's Bulwark under siege by a new necromantic commander.

They had encountered a half-starved messenger at a crossroads the day before. Between trembling fits, he described horrors clawing at the fortress walls, rotting soldiers commanded by a fearsome Lich, and defenders so exhausted that morale was stretched to its limits. Vyndor's Bulwark had long been a military stronghold with an extensive armory and thick stone ramparts, but according to the messenger, relentless assaults had battered the fortress for over a month. Skeletal warriors, wraiths, and even skeletal dragons prowled the perimeter, spewing foul necrotic breath and crumbling walls nightly.

Given Stonehaven's recent troubles with rising undead—animated by a greater power known as the Shadow Nexus—Cedric, Elara, Thalion, and Mira resolved to intervene. Their experiences with necromancers made them grimly certain that if this new Lich was allowed to fortify himself with an entire siege force, the surrounding region would be lost.

Progressing westward, they noted that villagers had abandoned farms and homesteads in haste. Crops lay half-harvested, cattle wandered untended, and shutters banged forlornly in the wind. Occasionally, they encountered disheveled refugees plodding in the opposite direction, laden with meager belongings. The sight of so many fleeing families painted a stark image of the devastation wrought by undead armies.

"It feels like the entire countryside is on the run," Mira murmured, drawing her cloak tighter as a chill wind rose. The gem in her staff glimmered faintly with each shift of light.

"Where the undead march, fear spreads faster than wildfire," Elara added, surveying the empty fields. "We must reach the fortress quickly. We'll give what aid we can."

Cedric tightened his jaw. "If the defenders have truly been under siege for a month, it's a miracle they haven't fallen."

Thalion brushed a strand of dark hair from his eyes. "Or the Lich in command might be savoring the siege. Some necromancers delight in slowly draining hope."

The possibility forced a chill silence among them. Prolonged sieges fueled dark sorcery by feeding on despair.

They hoped that if the Lich were playing such a sadistic game, there was still time to break his hold.

As midday approached, they passed grim reminders of the siege's intensity: battered skeletons rotting in ditches, blackened pools of undead ichor where a skirmish might have occurred, and broken crates likely from abandoned supply lines. By late afternoon, the land grew more rugged, with a chill in the air. Finally, Vyndor's Bulwark came into view: perched atop a stony rise, the fortress walls loomed beneath a leaden sky.

A wide moat, fed by a twisting stream, encircled most of the fortress. From afar, they saw small silhouettes along the ramparts—exhausted defenders, still repairing breaches and firing arrows at hordes of shambling skeletons. Towering among the undead were the horrifying forms of skeletal dragons: serpentine spines etched with glowing runes, each exhaling noxious fumes. Even from a distance, the sight made the heroes' stomachs clench.

They paused to take in the battlefield. A mass of undead encircled the fortress: skeleton foot soldiers in rusted armor, wraiths drifting ominously, and at least two skeletal dragons perched on nearby outcroppings of rock. Each dragon's rib cage glowed with sickly green necromantic light, roaring with a hollow, thunderous note that shook the ground.

"That many skeletal dragons..." Mira whispered. "I've never seen more than one at a time."

Thalion's eyes narrowed. "This Lich must be extremely powerful or extremely reckless, to command so many at once."

Elara, her cheeks paling at the dragon's roar, forced resolve into her voice. "We have to get inside the fortress. We can't let these defenders stand alone any longer."

Cedric raised a spyglass, scanning the walls. "The southern battlements are crumbled. The gates seem battered but still upright. We can't ride through the main siege lines without drawing the dragons' attention. Let's circle to a weaker flank and attempt a stealthy entry."

They guided their horses along a winding ridge, picking through boulders and rubble. As they drew closer, the stench of decay thickened: the unmistakable odor of undead, mingled with scorched wood and stagnant water. Occasionally, a patrol of skeletons or wights crossed their path, but the heroes hid behind rocks or used illusions cast by Thalion to mask themselves.

At last, they reached a segment of wall partially collapsed by bombardment. Thalion conjured illusions of swirling fog to confuse nearby skeleton archers, and Mira muffled the group's footfalls with a subtle cantrip. They dismounted, leaving their horses hidden in a rocky hollow.

In hushed unison, they climbed the broken stones. Weary faces peered over the ramparts—living soldiers who at first looked ready to fire. Then a clear voice shouted: "Hold your bolts! These are living allies!"

Ropes were swiftly lowered, and battered defenders helped haul them onto the rampart. The knights and footmen who greeted them looked gaunt, eyes ringed with sleepless hollows. Still, they found enough energy to offer a ragged cheer at the sight of reinforcements.

A knight in dented plate stepped forward, helm clipped at his waist. He wore the insignia of a captain. "I'm Captain Elys. By the gods, we've prayed for relief. Who are you?"

Cedric bowed. "Sir Cedric, Lady Elara, Thalion, and Mira at your service, Captain. We heard your fortress was under siege, and we've come to help."

Hope and fatigue warred on Elys's face. "You've arrived just in time—perhaps even a day later we'd have been overrun. The undead have hammered us daily, especially those cursed dragons. We can barely sleep for fear of night raids."

Elara scanned the courtyard below, where more soldiers labored to move debris and douse necrotic fires. "We'll do everything we can. How fares your food, water, and medical supplies?"

Elys rubbed his brow. "We're running low on everything. Most of our supply lines were cut off weeks ago. Worse yet, the Lich directing all this lurks somewhere in the surrounding hills, performing dark rites. My scouts haven't returned."

Mira's eyes glinted with determination. "Then we know what we must do: help you shore up defenses, find and eliminate the Lich, and break this siege."

A grim but resolute mood settled over the defenders once the newcomers' plan was shared. Elys wasted no time assigning the four heroes to areas most in need. Cedric led a small team of masons to reinforce gaps in the eastern wall, while Elara walked the ramparts, raising wards of divine light. Soldiers seemed to draw courage simply from her presence: battered archers stood straighter, and pike-bearers gripped their weapons with renewed resolve.

Meanwhile, Thalion and Mira consulted with the fortress mages—a weary cadre who'd been hurling spells for weeks. Together, they crafted illusions to conceal the fortress's weakest sections. Phantom fortifications projected over a southern breach, tricking undead into believing it intact. Whenever wights tested the area, they found only confusion and false stone. At nightfall, the illusions flickered to resemble fully staffed ramparts, further diverting attacks.

Despite these successes, the siege continued. Sometimes, a skeletal dragon would lurch into motion, drawing black breath to sweep across the walls. Defenders in its path would choke on necrotic fumes or collapse before the fortress mages retaliated with blasts of arcane fire. Though the dragons never fully breached the fortress, each of their passes inflicted casualties and a terror that weighed heavily on morale.

Yet the defenders held strong. There was a collective sense that help had finally arrived, rejuvenating their will to fight. Over meager rations of dried fruit and watered ale, knights and mages alike thanked the heroes for coming.

That night, the undead launched another major assault. From the ramparts, Cedric, Elara, Thalion, and Mira beheld a tide of skeletal soldiers marching in lockstep, led by wights whose eyes burned with necromantic power. Arrows from the fortress defenders rained down; ballista crews manned their war machines, their lines shaky but determined. Wraiths soared overhead, letting out piercing shrieks.

Elara's shield shone with divine luminescence, driving back a cluster of wraiths seeking to dive-bomb the walls. Behind her, Cedric commanded archers to concentrate fire on the wights. Each arrow struck bone with deadly force.

Meanwhile, Thalion conjured illusions of ghostly knights, distracting pockets of undead and luring them into kill zones. Mira blasted frosty cantrips at skeletal archers perched on ridges of rock.

On the eastern tower, a breach threatened to let a wave of skeletons inside. Cedric rushed there, leading a group of defenders in a countercharge. His blade, infused with protective wards, flared blue with each strike against undead bone, leaving behind blackened scorch marks. Elara arrived a heartbeat later, brandishing her shield to repel a wight that hurled necrotic bolts at her companions. Together, they cut through the skeleton ranks, scattering them back over the broken ramparts.

Below, fortress mages—buoyed by Thalion and Mira—launched magical salvos to clip the skeletal dragons whenever they swooped low. One dragon crashed near the moat, thrashing in confusion under illusions that made the ground appear to collapse beneath it. Another soared overhead, roaring, only to be bombarded by ballista bolts until it retreated.

For hours, the siege raged. When the undead finally pulled back, the fortress still stood—though battered anew. Casualties were carried to a courtyard designated as a triage station. Elara offered healing prayers to the grievously wounded, while Thalion lent illusions of calm scenes to soothe soldiers wracked by terror. Cedric and Mira oversaw disposal of undead corpses, ensuring no necromantic residue could reanimate them.

Near midnight, Captain Elys convened a war council in a cramped torchlit chamber. Cedric, Elara, Thalion, Mira, and a handful of the fortress's senior knights crowded around a table where a hastily drawn map displayed the surrounding hills and roads.

Elys tapped a quill against a marked ridge to the north. "We think the Lich resides here, commanding the siege. Some of my men made an attempt to scout the area. They vanished without sending word."

Thalion scrutinized the map. "If we strike at the Lich directly, the undead forces will lose their central command. The dragons might still pose a threat, but they'll be easier to deal with if the Lich's spells are disrupted."

Elara eyed the fortress layout. "But how do we leave without alerting the entire legion? The undead have us surrounded."

Mira brushed the dust from her staff's gleaming gem. "We create a diversion at dawn. If we can bait the horde to one section of the walls, a small team can slip out on the opposite side."

Elys nodded gravely. "Agreed. We're stretched thin, but we can stage a feint at the western gate, making them think we're attempting a breakout. Meanwhile, you four slip out the east sally port, moving under illusions and wards."

Cedric laid a hand on Elys's shoulder. "We won't be gone long. With luck, by midday we'll have silenced the Lich—and your fortress will be free."

Despite the dark circumstances, a flicker of hope lit the chamber. The defenders needed only to survive one more night, and once the Lich was slain, the undead might collapse altogether.

They retired briefly, grabbing fitful hours of rest. Each hero felt a throbbing ache in weary muscles and bruises from the night's battle. Still, they remained resolute. Before dawn, they reassembled in the fortress courtyard, where Captain Elys and a group of soldiers awaited them, ready to commence the diversion.

Thin gray light touched the fortress ramparts. Trumpets blared from the western gate, their echo reverberating across the courtyard. Shouts rose as Elys's men sallied forth, clashing spears and waving torches to project an illusion of a major offensive. Mira and Thalion contributed illusions of additional cavalry, stamping and snorting in the shadows. Undead masses lumbered toward the western walls, drawn by the commotion.

Simultaneously, Cedric, Elara, Thalion, and Mira slipped out through a postern gate on the eastern flank. They crept over debris fields, illusions cloaking them in drifting mists. The moat's rotted drawbridge on the eastern side stayed up, so they lowered themselves with ropes onto the moat's banks. Black water festered around their ankles. Still under cover of illusions, they slipped into a shallow ravine that wound behind the hills.

The sounds of clashing steel and unearthly shrieks drifted from the fortress. Each time a skeletal dragon roared, their hearts clenched with worry for the defenders. Yet they pressed on, knowing this was the only way to end the siege once and for all.

They moved swiftly through the ravine, stepping gingerly around skeleton patrols. Thalion masked them from watchful wraiths overhead by creating phantom silhouettes of undead, so to any onlooker, they simply appeared to be another group of shambling minions. Eventually, the ravine curved north toward rockier terrain.

The ground was pitted with craters, as though from repeated magical strikes.

After nearly an hour of tense progress, the fortress walls receded behind them. They paused in the shadow of a jagged cliff, hoping the diversion would still hold. Cedric counted them off in a soft voice: "One, two, three, four. All here. Let's keep moving."

A fresh roar from above cut him off. A skeletal dragon swooped across the eastern sky, scanning for intruders. Thalion quickly projected illusions of swirling shadows, disguising their figures among the rocks. The dragon circled once, then flew off with a final rattling shriek.

Mira let out a pent-up breath. "That was close."

Elara's gaze traveled the ridgeline. "We've still got to find the Lich. If the fortress's scouts were right, his ritual site is beyond this slope."

They pressed on, climbing gingerly where the earth turned slippery from recent rains. Necromantic energy felt palpable in the air—an almost electric hum that raised hairs on the back of their necks. Occasionally, they glimpsed skeletal footprints or strange runic carvings on rocks, as if the Lich had used them in a vile ceremony.

At last, they crested a ridge to behold a chilling tableau: a ring of tall standing stones, each carved with necromantic glyphs that pulsed sickly green. In the center hovered a gaunt figure draped in tattered black robes—unmistakably a Lich. Around him, legions of skeleton soldiers remained in eerie stillness, as if awaiting orders. Multiple wraiths floated near clusters of bone altars. At the edge of the ring crouched three skeletal dragons, each glowing with malignant life.

The largest dragon boasted swirling runes etched into its skull.

Cedric's breath caught in his throat. "How in the world have the fortress defenders held out so long?"

"Elara was right: the Lich might be toying with them," Thalion whispered. "Delighting in a slow and constant barrage."

Mira tightened her grip on her staff. "We take out the Lich first."

They needed a plan. Thalion proposed conjuring illusions on the far side of the plateau, forcing a portion of the skeletons—and maybe one dragon—to investigate. Mira would then unleash frost magic to contain the Lich's reaction, while Elara and Cedric rushed forward to strike the final blow.

Timing would be everything. This Lich was no novice: to command multiple skeletal dragons demanded potent, ancient necromancy. A single mistake could end in the heroes' swift demise.

Thalion crouched and released his illusions. Across the rocky slope, phantom cavalry appeared—a swirling mass of knights brandishing blazing torches. At once, the skeletons pivoted, forming rigid ranks to meet this "threat." A skeletal dragon spread its wings in agitation, letting loose a banshee-like roar.

Seizing the moment, Mira rose and extended her staff. A swirl of icy wind condensed, launching a frosty gale that battered the Lich. The robed figure spun around, green light searing the air as he shielded himself with necrotic wards. Even so, shards of ice dug into his bony frame.

Elara and Cedric charged in, weapons shining with the faint glow of divine wards. The Lich hissed, a guttural sound reverberating in their minds, and flung a volley of dark bolts. Elara's shield glowed, deflecting part of the impact, though she felt an icy sting sear her arm. Cedric dove low, sword biting into the Lich's torso, sending sparks of necrotic energy skittering across the ground.

Behind them, illusions shimmered as skeleton soldiers began to realize they were chasing phantoms. One skeletal dragon, tricked, clawed at empty air. Another turned, bellowing at the real intruders. It stomped forward, jaws gaping to spew necrotic breath. Thalion hastily conjured a shimmering barrier, deflecting the worst of the putrid haze.

The Lich rallied, unleashing roiling strands of black magic. Elara felt them coil around her, draining warmth from her body. She summoned divine light in a surge of determination, shattering the tendrils in a burst of golden radiance. Cedric pressed the advantage, slashing again across the Lich's chest. This time, the blow struck deeper. The Lich shrieked, flickers of green flame stuttering in its eyes.

A skeletal dragon lunged, tail lashing. Mira unleashed a wave of frost, freezing the beast's flank. It let out a fractured roar, staggering. Thalion hammered it with illusions of colossal stone pillars collapsing onto its head. Confused, it reeled. Meanwhile, skeleton soldiers converged on Cedric and Elara, attempting to shield their master. Elara's sword rang out in a brilliant arc, hacking through ranks of undead. Cedric's runic blade glowed with each strike, severing bone and vile sinew alike.

At last, the Lich spewed a final incantation, attempting to tear open a swirl of black winds. But Mira's staff glowed bright as she incanted a spell of arcane disruption, freezing the portal mid-creation. Elara seized that opening, lunging with her sword, which flared in divine brilliance. The blade sank through the Lich's rib cage, splintering bone. Cedric followed with a crushing blow from his runic sword, slicing across the creature's spine. The Lich reeled, mouth wide in a silent, enraged scream, until the necromantic flames in its sockets flickered and died. Its skeletal form clattered to the ground in a shower of black sparks.

A shudder ran through the undead legion. Skeleton soldiers froze in place, as though their animating magic had been abruptly severed. Wraiths let out high-pitched shrieks and dissolved into wisps of darkness. Two of the skeletal dragons collapsed with thunderous crashes, bones cracking into lifeless heaps. The largest dragon, staggering without the Lich's direct control, tried to take flight but slammed into the hillside, fractured ribs glowing with faltering green light. Moments later, it too stilled.

Panting, Cedric wrenched his sword free of the Lich's remains. Elara leaned on her shield, trembling from exhaustion. Thalion, illusions fading, collapsed to his knees, pressing a hand against the rocky ground. Mira stood beside him, breathing heavily, staff tip still brimming with leftover frost magic. They had done it—they had struck down the Lich.

Within the hour, the fortress defenders—led by Captain Elys—arrived on the ridge, guided by the heroes' signs. They gaped at the carnage: the toppled dragons, the standing stones that had pulsed with dark magic now lying inert. Weary but elated, Elys clapped Cedric on the back, tears of relief shining in his eyes.

"You've saved us," Elys said simply, voice shaking. "We would never have escaped that siege without you."

Word soon reached the remaining undead encircling the fortress, and many simply crumbled or wandered aimlessly. Defenders took advantage, driving out the last skeletons and wights. As the sun climbed higher, a sense of liberation spread through Vyndor's Bulwark. Fires were quenched, ramparts were cleared, and supply wagons reclaimed.

That evening, the fortress hosted a modest celebration in the courtyard. Though the cost in lives was heavy, the survivors' joy at being free from nightly terror was palpable. Soldiers lit torches, and even a few ragged minstrels played an upbeat tune. Elys insisted on holding a final war council to map out next steps.

"We must rebuild," Elys declared, standing near a table cluttered with reports of missing men and battered equipment. "The Shadow Nexus still looms over Stonehaven, but if we can hold the fortress, we can keep the western border safe."

Elara nodded. "We'll be moving on before long. But until then, we'll do what we can to shore up your walls."

The next day, after assisting with repairs and seeing that the worst wounds were tended, the four companions gathered in the keep's main hall. Soldiers and fortress staff milled about, offering thanks in hushed tones. Cedric caught sight of a child wrapped in a medic's cloak—the same boy whose father had fallen to a skeletal archer. The child looked up at him with tear-brimmed eyes, but there was gratitude there too.

Mira touched the child's shoulder gently, whispering a few comforting words. Elara finished distributing the last of her healing wards among the medics, while Thalion lent illusions to calm soldiers traumatized by wraith attacks.

That afternoon, a welcome lull fell upon the fortress. The battered war banners snapped in a gentler breeze, and the courtyard that had once been choked with undead was gradually restoring some semblance of normalcy. The stench of rot faded as pyres consumed the necromantic remains. Knights practiced in small groups, hoping to reclaim lost discipline.

In a quiet moment, Elys approached the heroes with deep gratitude. "I wish we could grant you proper rest," he said. "But your quest continues. And if our scouts' rumors prove true, there's already another threat on Stonehaven's eastern coast."

Cedric exchanged a glance with Elara. They all knew their mission was larger than any single fortress. While the Lich was defeated, the Shadow Nexus was not, and more abominations likely festered elsewhere.

"Let us confirm what we can about these rumors," Cedric said gently. "We'll leave at first light tomorrow."

Elys bowed, placing a hand over his heart. "Bless you all. Vyndor's Bulwark will never forget your valor."

That final night in the fortress was mercifully peaceful. No howling undead rattled the gates. No wraiths hovered overhead. The defenders slept in shifts, letting each other rest for more than a fleeting hour. In the keep's upper rooms, Cedric, Elara, Mira, and Thalion gathered for a simple supper, finishing the last bits of dried rations. Despite sore limbs and battered spirits, they felt a lightness of being that only came from triumph over impossible odds.

Elara set aside her half-eaten ration. "We should be proud. This fortress was minutes away from total collapse when we arrived."

Mira nodded. "Still, the Shadow Nexus is our true adversary. We topple one Lich, and another sprouts up somewhere else. We can't let Stonehaven suffocate under this tide of darkness."

Thalion tapped his staff lightly on the stone floor. "Agreed. The troglodyte sightings near the coastal temples may only be rumors, but we can't ignore them. And if a Hydra or sea monster has indeed been corrupted—"

Cedric exhaled. "Then we have our next task. The fortress here is safe now. Elys and his knights can handle the rest."

They drifted to their bunks, each mind abuzz with images of swirling necromantic magic, skeletal dragons collapsing into piles of bones, and the fortress's battered defenders cheering with new hope.

16

THE COASTAL TEMPLES

When the first hint of dawn lit the sky, Sir Cedric, Lady Elara, Thalion, and Mira rose, donned their gear, and made their final rounds through the fortress of Vyndor's Bulwark. Though the soldiers still bore the scars of the undead siege, a tangible hope permeated the halls—no skeletal dragons circled overhead, and the torrent of nightly assaults had finally ceased.

In the courtyard, they gathered their belongings, exchanging farewells with Captain Elys and a handful of knights who had assembled to see them off. Elys, lines of fatigue etched into his face, leaned on a pitted spear as he spoke.

"We're in your debt," he said, voice low but sincere. "Given time, we'll rebuild. But you've indicated you must push east—for reasons I can only guess relate to the Shadow Nexus?"

Cedric nodded. "Yes. Word reached us of a Hydra attacking the coastal temples. It may be linked to the same dark power we've fought here. If so, it must be stopped before it wreaks further havoc."

Elara swung onto her mare, shield secured across her back. Thalion checked his spellbook in a leather satchel, while Mira twirled her staff, verifying that the Manticore Gem was still embedded at its apex. As Cedric mounted, he grimaced at the tug of still-healing bruises beneath his armor.

Elys saluted. "May the gods guide you. This fortress will remain strong for Stonehaven. And if ever you need us, we'll answer."

Elara inclined her head in thanks. "Stay vigilant, Captain. Stonehaven depends on strongholds like yours standing firm."

With that, the four companions spurred their horses through the gates, into a brightening morning sky. Soldiers and civilians alike watched them depart with whispered blessings. Once on the open road, the group rode in thoughtful silence, each reflecting on the battle they had just won—and on the looming threat of a monstrous Hydra on the coast.

They followed faint roads eastward for hours, leaving behind farmland scarred by weeks of undead activity. Gradually, the terrain grew less cultivated, scattered with rocky outcroppings and patches of gnarled brush. A sharper tang of salt on the breeze signaled they were nearing the sea.

Along the way, they crossed paths with refugees— haggard folk fleeing coastal regions. One elderly man relayed how a "three-headed sea serpent" emerged from the tides at night, melting fishing vessels and docks with acidic breath. Another traveler, a young woman, described how the ancient Coastal Temples were half-sunken, desecrated by an "unholy Hydra" that seemed to part the waters at will. The accounts varied, but the common thread was a colossal creature far deadlier than any natural sea beast.

Elara frowned at each tale, glancing at Cedric. "The more we learn, the more it aligns with those Arcadium texts about corrupted sea creatures."

Cedric's mouth was a grim line. "If the Hydra is under the Shadow Nexus's influence, it might already be too powerful for any normal garrison to handle. We have to stop it—just like we ended the undead siege."

Mira tapped her staff lightly on the ground as they rode. "The Shadow Nexus can twist almost anything—lich-lords, troglodytes, skeletal dragons. Now a Hydra. It feels like we're racing from one disaster to another."

Thalion regarded her with a measured look. "Yet each victory we've gained chips away at the Nexus's grand design. Don't lose faith. In time, we can unravel its corruption."

By dusk, they reached a rolling marshland that sloped toward the sea. Reeds and cattails swayed in the shallows, and the air grew thick with brine. A few gulls circled overhead, their cries echoing above the open expanse of waterlogged earth. The surf pounded the distant shoreline, a reminder that they were drawing closer to Stonehaven's eastern coast.

They made camp on a small rise of dry land. A single oak tree offered meager shelter, its twisted branches stretching over their tents. As the moon rose, they dined on simple provisions—hardtack, jerky, and water. Elara pulled out a small map gleaned from Vyndor's Bulwark scouts.

"If the Hydra roams the coastal temples, it might be drawn to something sacred," she reasoned. "You remember those references to the Pearl of Tides?"

Cedric nodded. "Yes. A relic said to embody the ocean's blessing, possibly tied to the Song of Severance. If that

Hydra has seized or corrupted it, we'll have to reclaim it for Stonehaven's sake."

Thalion rummaged through his pack, withdrawing a battered tome. "Ancient records indicate the Coastal Temples were built around revered reefs. Each temple had wards protecting sacred relics. If those wards have fallen, and the Hydra claimed the Pearl, it explains why the beast is so unstoppable."

Mira's brow furrowed. "Then we'd better brace for more than just one monster. Corrupted water sprites, troglodytes—who knows what else lurks near the coastline?"

The four agreed to rest and begin their search in earnest at dawn. Fog drifted across the marsh, croaking frogs and rustling reeds forming a quiet lullaby. Though each hero felt worn from weeks of ceaseless battles, their determination pushed them onward. If the Shadow Nexus had indeed empowered a Hydra, they had no time to lose.

Dawn found them saddling up, the swamp teeming with unseen life. Frogs croaked, and waterfowl soared overhead as they followed an old fisherman's trail. The path became increasingly waterlogged, forcing them to pick careful steps around boggy patches. The tang of salt grew stronger, until midday revealed columns of broken stone looming over the horizon.

"There," Mira said, pointing with her staff. "The first sign of the Coastal Temples."

A battered stone arch jutted from a shallow lagoon, carvings worn by the relentless tides. Beyond it stretched the main complex: partially submerged courtyards, weathered columns, and scattered shrines. Robed figures—

likely temple acolytes—moved about, hauling debris or tending to the injured.

A guard in sea-green attire hailed them, relief obvious on his face. "Travelers! Please—tell me you've come to help. A Hydra is terrorizing these temples."

Cedric dismounted and introduced the group. "We've come from Vyndor's Bulwark, heard you were under attack. Show us what remains of your defenses."

Soon, a small knot of sages and mages gathered. An elderly woman in tattered wave-motif robes stepped forward, leaning on a coral-branch staff. "I am Sage Elder Kariel. This place was once sacred, but the Hydra has ravaged it. Worse yet, our waters feel tainted; we suspect a foul magic. Many fear it's related to this 'Shadow Nexus' we've heard rumors about."

Elara removed her helm, shaking out her hair. "We've fought undead under that same influence. If your Hydra's corrupted, we'll do what we can to stop it."

Kariel led them into a courtyard half-swamped by tidewater. Broken statues of sea deities lay toppled, and brackish pools covered mosaic floors. A haggard mage limped forward, salt crusting his hair. "I am Arven, one of the ward-keepers. We tried summoning protective barriers when the Hydra first attacked, but it tore through them as if they were parchment."

Mira studied the battered columns. "Has anyone seen a relic called the Pearl of Tides?"

Kariel and Arven exchanged uneasy glances. "Legends say the Pearl lay in our main altar, guarded by a benevolent spirit," Kariel explained softly. "But ever since the Hydra appeared, we've lost all trace of it. The beast might have taken it—or become its twisted new guardian."

Thalion's brow furrowed. "If a Hydra infused with that Pearl's power roams unchecked, it could be unstoppable."

Arven gestured toward the eastern coastline. "We believe it retreats to sea caves near the reefs. Troglodytes and corrupted water sprites also lurk in the nearby Marshland—likely drawn by the Hydra's power. Fishing villages are in ruin, and we can barely keep our own defenders alive."

Elara inhaled deeply, gaze flicking toward the horizon where storm-gray skies met the sea. "Then we have no choice but to face it. Any wards or knowledge you can share will help."

Kariel nodded, her voice trembling with earnestness. "We have a few shell-etched talismans left—minor charms to repel smaller swamp creatures. They won't stop the Hydra, but might ward off lesser threats."

She pressed a pouch of seashell wards into Cedric's hands. He thanked her. Over a hasty council in the temple's remains, they plotted their approach. The Hydra's lair presumably lay across an expanse called the Misty Marshland, a region choked with fog and troglodyte-infested pools. Only a partially submerged causeway, built ages ago by temple pilgrims, offered a direct path.

The next morning, the group set out, each carrying a seashell talisman. Around them, the temple's battered priests and acolytes watched with a mix of hope and sorrow. Pushing onward, the heroes skirted collapsed shrines and followed a winding trail until they reached the Misty Marshland—a realm of vine-wreathed cypress trees and stagnant pools. Heavy fog clung to the ground, obscuring gnarled roots and hidden sinkholes.

Their passage stirred the marsh's inhabitants. At first, shapes darted under the water—troglodytes, reptilian creatures with scaled hides and sharp teeth. Then, in a flurry of hisses, they emerged onto the slippery causeway with crude spears, eyes glinting with malevolent cunning.

Cedric held his sword defensively. "We mean no harm—" His words were cut short when a troglodyte lunged, spear aimed at his chest. He deflected the blow, pivoting to slash its shoulder.

Elara dismounted, shield raised. She bashed a second attacker, divine light coursing from her shield's rim. Meanwhile, Thalion conjured illusions of writhing serpents, distracting pockets of troglodytes and causing them to hiss and flinch. Mira unleashed a flurry of ice shards, freezing the marshy ground beneath the reptiles' feet.

The troglodytes attacked relentlessly, brandishing clubs and unleashing guttural cries to rally their kin. Yet the seashell wards glowed faintly, repelling some of the creatures with invisible force. Bit by bit, the heroes pushed forward. Several troglodytes, stunned by illusions or battered by frost, fell back into the swamp, croaking in alarm.

"That was too close," Mira panted, wiping sweat from her brow once they emerged from the densest section of troglodyte territory. "They're definitely more aggressive than normal."

"Corruption of the Shadow Nexus," Thalion muttered. "We'd best move quickly."

They pressed on, ignoring the watchful reptilian eyes gleaming from submerged hollows. About an hour later, the marshland gave way to drier ground along a rough shoreline. Mist parted, revealing a wide beach pockmarked with tide pools. Gulls circled overhead, and thick kelp blanketed the sands.

Yet fresh danger rose before they could catch their breath: water sprites, typically shy spirits of the shore, now corrupted by inky tendrils of darkness. With eerie shrieks, these half-translucent figures launched watery lashes and swirling bolts at the group. Elara barely deflected one aquatic whip with her shield, droplets splashing across her armor.

"Pull back from the pools!" Cedric yelled. "They're strongest in the water."

They regrouped on a patch of higher sand, Thalion conjuring illusions of blazing fires to disrupt the sprites' liquid forms. Mira cast a broad wave of frost, coating several sprites in ice. Elara shattered one with a shield strike, while Cedric sliced through another with a luminous arc of his runic blade. Hissing in confusion, the surviving water sprites fled to the tide's edge, glaring with black, corrupted eyes.

Elara pressed a hand to her chest, catching her breath. "If even these sprites are twisted, the Hydra must be unbelievably strong."

Mira nodded, sweat dampening her temple. "Which means the Pearl of Tides is likely fueling it. We have to end this at the source."

Guided by temple rumors, the group followed deep footprints along the beach—three-toed impressions the size of small tables. Giant claw marks led them to a cluster of sea caves carved into the cliffs. The tide lapped at cavern entrances, sending echoing booms through half-submerged passages. Within, they glimpsed battered pillars and broken altars. This, they surmised, was the Hydra's lair.

They tethered their horses in a sheltered cove to keep them safe. The monstrous footprints trailed into one cave mouth bigger than the rest. A briny stench wafted out, mingling with an acrid odor reminiscent of old fish and rot.

"This is it," Cedric murmured, hand tightening on his sword's hilt. "We'll have to fight it in its own domain. We've faced undead dragons, wights, and horrors beyond counting—let's hope we're up to the challenge of a sea-beast this size."

Elara's gaze swept over the battered shoreline. "The temple defenders are counting on us. Not to mention every coastal village in the region."

Thalion gave a slight nod, illusions dancing faintly around his staff. "Let's finalize the plan. If the Hydra wields acidic breath or watery blasts, we'll have to spread out. But remember: Hydra heads can regrow unless they're immediately cauterized. That means well-timed spells of flame."

Mira exhaled, recalling Elder Kariel's warnings. "One head at a time. Sever, then seal the stump. We can't let it transform into something even worse."

They entered the cavern with weapons ready, hearts pounding. Water droplets echoed from cracks overhead, and swirling greenish light hinted at some necromantic energy in the depths. Clusters of algae clung to half-collapsed shrines. Around the bend lay the final confrontation with the Hydra—a monstrous foe that might be linked to the Shadow Nexus itself.

For a moment, they paused near a battered maritime altar, broken shells and tide-worn carvings scattered on the floor. Each hero felt the weight of destiny settle over them. A single misstep could be fatal. Yet if they triumphed, the Coastal Temples would be freed from the Hydra's reign, and Stonehaven would claim one more crucial relic against the Shadow Nexus.

"Ready?" Cedric asked, voice hushed in the damp air.

Elara steadied her shield. "As I'll ever be."

Thalion's grip on his staff tightened, illusions flickering. "Let's end this."

Mira touched the Manticore Gem at her staff's apex. "For Stonehaven," she murmured.

With that, they advanced deeper into the lair, disappearing past walls slick with moisture and ruin. Soon, the Hydra's low, thunderous growl reverberated through the cavern, promising a brutal fight ahead. The heroes pressed on, fully aware that their next moments might shape the fate of the entire coastal region—and bring them one step closer to unraveling the Shadow Nexus itself.

17

THE HYDRA'S WRATH

A low, rolling growl echoed through the sea cave, rattling stone and bone alike. Sir Cedric, Lady Elara, Thalion, and Mira stood at the mouth of the cavern's inner chambers, each bracing for the impending onslaught. Behind them lay scattered remains of once-sacred maritime shrines—toppled statues of sea deities, shattered coral offerings, and half-crumbled altars now slick with algae. Ahead, the darkness teemed with the presence of a massive, three-headed Hydra, its thick scales glistening in the faint light filtering through rock fissures overhead.

The brackish water pooled around their boots as they crept forward. Somewhere deeper in the lair, an unseen tide surged, stirring the flooded passages. The rank odor of fish rot and acid stung the air, hinting at the beast's foul dominion over this domain. The Hydra's breath resonated like monstrous bellows, each exhalation reverberating against the cavern walls.

Elara's shield shimmered with a faint turquoise blessing granted by the Coastal Temples' sages. Cedric's runic longsword hummed in response to the primal energy swirling in the cave. Thalion's staff glowed at its carved tip, while Mira held her own staff ready, the Manticore Gem swirling with arcane potential. Each hero felt their pulse quicken as they stepped into the Hydra's line of sight.

All three Hydra heads swayed in reptilian unison. The left-most maw hissed, flicking out an acid-laced tongue. The center one emitted a deep, rumbling growl that spat flecks of foam on the cavern floor. The right head released a piercing shriek that sliced through the dank air like a knife. Each neck bristled with jagged spines, and a thick tail smashed the stone behind the creature, sending pebbles skittering.

Cedric raised his voice, though it shook with adrenaline. "Hydra! We're here for the Pearl of Tides. Surrender it, or.."

An enraged roar tore from all three throats, the sheer volume shaking the pillars overhead. Negotiation was futile. The Hydra launched itself forward, snapping its jaws inches from Cedric's chest. Elara interposed her shield, intercepting a wave of putrid breath that made her stomach lurch.

"Scatter!" she commanded, stepping sideways. Cedric dove in the opposite direction, while Thalion and Mira fanned out behind piles of broken stone. The Hydra's heads lashed out one by one, testing each hero's position. Stagnant water sloshed around its massive frame.

From behind a crumbled altar, Thalion began chanting, tiny motes of flame gathering at the tip of his staff. Summoning fire in this damp, salt-filled environment was tricky, but Elder Kariel's warning about Hydra regeneration left him no choice. Meanwhile, Mira unleashed illusions around the left-most head, conjuring phantom knights to draw its attention. The Hydra struck at these illusions, fangs clashing with empty air.

Elara dashed in, shield raised, to engage the center head. It lunged, jaws snapping so hard they sent tremors through her arm. She gritted her teeth and shoved back, forging a brief stalemate as the two forces strained against each other. She glimpsed a swirling green glow in the Hydra's throat, suggesting some acidic or watery blast was imminent.

Cedric took advantage of that moment. Circling behind, he slashed at the Hydra's flank, his runic sword lighting the gloom with pale-blue radiance. Scales nearly deflected the blow, but he carved a shallow cut that drew blackish blood. The left head hissed in pain, swinging around to spew a rancid jet of bile. Cedric ducked behind a column, droplets sizzling where they struck stone.

The group knew their goal: chop off each head and cauterize the stump before it could regrow. The Hydra's monstrous resilience made it tough to even land a decisive blow, and the environment favored the sea beast. Pools of water splashed around their ankles, and every step risked slipping on slime-coated rock.

Mira hurled a frost-lance at the Hydra's right neck, aiming to stiffen the scales. A sheen of ice formed, then melted almost instantly under the beast's thrashing heat. Still, it distracted the Hydra long enough for Cedric and Elara to reposition.

Thalion shouted above the din, "Focus on one head! Don't let them flank us!"

Elara nodded, raising her shield. "I'll draw the center! Cedric, target the left!"

They rushed in. The center head lunged for Elara, jaws parting wide. She angled her shield to deflect the bite upward, muscles straining. Meanwhile, Cedric darted forward, sword slicing across the Hydra's left neck. The blade bit deeper than before, spraying blackish gore. The Hydra shrieked and lashed its tail in fury, smashing a half-toppled statue to rubble.

Mira conjured illusions of raging fire at the Hydra's rear legs, hoping to confuse its tail movements. Through the chaos, Thalion at last gathered a stable flame in his hand— golden embers swirling like a miniature sun.

The left head reeled from Cedric's strike, blood oozing in rivulets. Seizing the moment, he slashed again, severing cartilage and sinew. The Hydra bellowed, thrashing violently. One more blow—and the head toppled with a wet thud onto the soaked cavern floor.

"Now!" Elara shouted, bracing against the center head's renewed assault.

Thalion hurled his orb of flame with pinpoint accuracy. The moment the severed head hit the ground, the magical fire flared across the open stump, sealing flesh and bone in a cauterizing blaze. Smoke rose in thick tendrils, along with the acrid stench of burnt scales.

The Hydra howled, retreating a few steps. With two heads left, it coiled in frenzied pain. Water splashed in heavy waves around its limbs. Yet no regrowth manifested. For the moment, that wound was sealed.

But the fight was far from over. The creature's remaining heads went berserk, snapping in different directions. One spat a spray of acid toward Mira. She scrambled behind a broken column but couldn't avoid all of it—searing droplets struck her arm, and she bit back a scream. Elara rushed to intercept the next strike, shield flaring with turquoise light to repel the acid.

Cedric pivoted for a second offensive. The Hydra's tail whipped around, crashing into him with punishing force. He flew backward, colliding with a jagged rock formation. Spots of light danced in his vision, and blood trickled down his brow. Through the haze, he saw the monster's center head coil back, eyes gleaming with savage intent.

Mira, panting, forced herself to stand despite the pain. She conjured illusions again, swirling ephemeral shapes to distract the center head. Thalion, staff in hand, concentrated on building a fresh orb of flame, though his breath came in ragged bursts. Summoning such power in this moisture-laden environment drained him quickly.

Elara skid across the cavern floor, water splashing at her ankles, trying to lure the Hydra's attention. But the beast pivoted on powerful haunches, baring fangs at Thalion as if sensing the source of the searing fire.

"Not this time," Elara muttered, ramming her shield into the Hydra's flank. The blow drew a snarl, and the creature swung one head toward her. She braced, stepping carefully to avoid stepping into a swirl of acidic water.

Cedric pushed himself upright, ignoring the dull ache in his ribs. "We can do this," he said under his breath, repositioning to flank again. If they could decapitate another head, they stood a real chance of ending the Hydra's reign.

Thalion inhaled sharply, mustering enough energy for a second flame spear. Meanwhile, Mira unleashed a concentrated arcane blast that struck the Hydra's right neck, momentarily staggering it. Cedric seized the opening, sword gleaming with runic power, and drove the blade deep into that same neck. Scales cracked and parted under the blow. Blood spattered his gauntlets.

The Hydra roared, trying to twist away, but Elara slammed into it from the side, shield glowing with righteous light. Teeth gnashed near her face, but she held her ground, giving Cedric the fraction of a second he needed to slice again. With a revolting rip, the Hydra's right head dropped onto the cavern floor. The beast's shriek reverberated to the cave ceiling, intensifying as the stump bled black ooze.

Without a moment's hesitation, Thalion cast the second flame spear onto the raw stump. Flames exploded, cauterizing the neck in a crackling blaze. Another wave of searing smoke stung their eyes. The Hydra reared back on its hind legs, the stumps of two heads smoldering. Cracks formed in the cave walls as it thrashed, tail lashing violently. Rocks pelted down, forcing the heroes to scramble aside.

Now only one head remained—the middle, overshadowed by wounds but no less furious. Acidic saliva dripped from its jaw, and necrotic energy flickered along the ridges of its spine. It glared at the four intruders who had maimed it so brutally.

The Hydra lunged in a blind frenzy. Its single remaining head whipped around at terrifying speed. Cedric managed to duck, but Mira—slowed by the pain in her arm—could not avoid the full force. The Hydra's jaws clamped around her lower leg, fangs sinking deep. She let out a piercing scream, staff clattering from her hands. Blood and blackish venom spilled across the Hydra's teeth.

"Mira!" Elara yelled, charging forward. She bashed the Hydra's jaw with her shield, forcing it to release Mira. The mage collapsed, leg punctured and twisted at an odd angle.

A sickly gray hue already spread across her skin near the bites.

Snarling, the Hydra tried to press its advantage, jaws snapping a breath away from Mira's fallen form. Thalion unleashed a shockwave of arcane force, battering the Hydra's skull to buy a few seconds. Elara dropped to her knees beside Mira, golden healing magic pouring from her hands to stanch the bleeding. But the venom had already invaded Mira's bloodstream, turning her face ashen.

Cedric felt a surge of rage and desperation. Sword in hand, he vaulted over a pile of debris, ignoring the sharp pain in his own ribs. "Elara, keep Mira safe!" he shouted.

He and Thalion converged on the beast's final head, determined to end this. The Hydra spat a last stream of vile acid, forcing Cedric to roll aside, sizzling rivulets running across the stone. Thalion flung illusions of roaring flames to distract the monster, swirling phantom shapes around its eyes. For a moment, it snapped blindly.

"Now!" Thalion commanded.

With a fierce battle cry, Cedric lunged under the Hydra's chin, runic blade thrusting upward. He felt flesh and bone yield in a grisly pop, the sword piercing the skull from below. The Hydra's shriek devolved into a wet gurgle as its body convulsed. Thalion flung one more flare of fire onto the stump, ensuring no regeneration could follow. The beast shuddered, tail slamming the ground one last time before slumping in a final collapse. Then, at last, the Hydra lay still, three severed stumps smoldering.

Elara and Thalion turned toward Mira. She clutched at her leg, face contorted in agony. "We need an antidote," Elara said, voice trembling as she pressed healing light to the wounds. "Hydra venom can kill within hours... or worse, corrupt the victim."

Mira whimpered, drifting in and out of consciousness. A streak of blackish tendrils snaked across her thigh, creeping steadily. Elara's magic could slow the bleeding, but the poison's spread was relentless.

Cedric's face went pale with alarm. "Is there anything in the temple ruins that can help?"

Thalion shook his head, conjuring a low-level healing cantrip to no avail. "Elder Kariel mentioned no cure if the Hydra's venom was empowered by dark magic. We may have to find an advanced alchemical remedy—something rare."

Elara blinked tears away, voice cracking. "We can't lose her, Cedric."

He swallowed, gripping Elara's shoulder. "We won't. We'll find a cure. But first, the Pearl—where is it?"

The Hydra's colossal body nearly blocked the cavern's depths. Picking their way past its bulk, Cedric and Thalion pressed forward. Water sloshed around their ankles, and the air reeked of blood and brine. Around a bend, they discovered a smaller side chamber partially flooded, where broken pillars rose from the murk. Atop a battered stone pedestal sat a magnificent pearl the size of a clenched fist, shimmering with oceanic light.

A subtle aura radiated from it, reminiscent of rolling tides. Even from a few paces away, Thalion sensed the relic's purity clashing with lingering necromantic corruption in the air. "This must be the Pearl of Tides," he whispered, placing a careful hand on it. Warmth pulsed through his palm.

Cedric retrieved a cloth pouch. "We'll need to get it cleansed in the temple courtyard. But we have no time to linger. Mira—"

Together, they hurried back. Elara knelt at Mira's side, hands slick with blood, tears on her cheeks. "She's fading. The venom is too potent."

Cedric placed the Pearl gently into his satchel, then knelt beside Mira, pressing a trembling hand to her brow. "Hold on. We're taking you somewhere safe." She managed a shaky nod, though her eyes fluttered.

Thalion exhaled. "If we can get back to the Coastal Temples, maybe they can stabilize her until we find the antidote. Hurry."

They lifted Mira carefully, ignoring their own exhaustion. Outside the cavern, a late-afternoon sun bathed the shoreline in wan gold. Salt air felt painfully refreshing after the stench of Hydra gore. Sage Elder Kariel and a few defenders had stood watch at a distance; they rushed forward the moment the heroes emerged, battered and grim.

Kariel's eyes widened at the sight of Mira's injury. "By the gods... you slew the Hydra?"

Elara nodded, her throat tight. "But it bit our friend. She's in dire need of a cure—Hydra venom."

With Kariel's assistance, they transported Mira back to the main temple courtyard. Word spread quickly of the Hydra's death, sparking both relief and worry among the battered acolytes. The Pearl of Tides, once believed lost, had been reclaimed. Yet one of its saviors now lay at death's door.

Temple healers placed Mira on a cot. While Elara and Thalion tried every healing spell they knew, Kariel and her acolytes prepared a purification pool for the Pearl, hoping to remove any leftover corruption. Together, they submerged the relic in salted water and blessed herbs, chanting incantations that swirled the water with soft turquoise light. Faint wisps of black energy lifted from the Pearl, dissolving into the air.

"It's cleansed," Kariel finally announced, cradling the shining orb. "The reef may heal, and the seas should calm now that the Hydra is gone."

Cedric took the Pearl, storing it safely in a reinforced chest. "Thank you, Elder. But we have no time to celebrate. Do you know of any cure for Hydra venom?"

Kariel bowed her head, voice trembling with sympathy. "Not in these ruins. It's said an old alchemist beyond the northern foothills might brew such antidotes. Many speak of it as legend—but it's the only rumor I know."

Cedric turned to his companions, desperation in his eyes. "We ride at dawn."

Elara hovered near Mira, who lay feverish, her leg swathed in bandages. "I'm not leaving her side," she murmured. "Not until we find this cure."

They spent the night in the temple's battered halls. Kariel and the surviving sages offered what prayers and herbs they could to slow the poison. Mira's breathing remained shallow, face pallid with pain. At times, her eyes opened just enough to see Thalion or Elara, and she managed a faint, reassuring smile—even as her leg took on a sickly gray hue.

Outside, a bittersweet celebration emerged among the temple defenders. They lit torches, sang a hymn to the ocean gods, and recounted how the Hydra's roar had ceased at last. For the first time in weeks, no monstrous shape stalked the beaches. Yet the heroes who had saved them could not rest easy while Mira's life hung in the balance.

When morning arrived, they wasted no time. With the Pearl of Tides locked away, Elara helped Mira onto a horse, tying her in place so she wouldn't fall if she lost consciousness. Thalion cast illusions to cloak their departure from any lurking threats, while Cedric organized supplies for a hard ride north.

Kariel and her acolytes lined the courtyard, offering blessings. One elder priestess draped a necklace of shells over Elara's shoulders, a final token of gratitude. "May the ocean's power guide you. And may the gods speed your friend's recovery."

Cedric bowed in thanks. "Without your help, none of this would be possible. But now we must go."

The four set off, leading a small retinue of defenders who escorted them beyond the immediate ruins. Once out on open roads, they spurred their horses to a brisk pace. Mira slumped against Elara, eyes half-lidded, beads of sweat tracking along her temple. Each jolt of the saddle elicited quiet groans. Elara offered steadying prayers, but the venom's corruption lingered like a shadow.

Thalion rode in silence, staff strapped to his back, mind racing through every potion formula he'd studied. Cedric's gaze flickered from the road to Mira and back again, jaw clenched. The Pearl of Tides pulsed in his bag—a symbol of success, but also a reminder of how quickly fortune could turn.

They pressed onward, mile after mile, determined to reach the alchemist's rumored abode before it was too late. The Shadow Nexus might have lost its Hydra champion on the coast, but its greater threat remained—and now threatened the life of one of their own. Each hoofbeat echoed Cedric's vow: They would save Mira, reclaim every lost relic, and shatter the Nexus's hold on Stonehaven. No monstrous venom or darkness would stop them from forging a dawn free of such horrors.

By midday, the temple defenders left them, turning back to help rebuild. The four heroes rode alone through a patchwork of marsh, farmland, and sparse woodland, an urgent sense of purpose driving them onward. Wind rattled the tops of slender pines, whispering of the journey yet to come. Here in Stonehaven's eastern reaches, the threat of bandits or roving monstrosities lingered on every deserted trail. But the real battle lay within Mira's bloodstream.

Nightfall brought them to a small clearing near a winding river. They made camp in sullen silence, Elara doing what she could to soothe Mira's fever. Thalion collected rare herbs from the riverbank, hoping to craft a rudimentary salve to slow the venom. Cedric stood watch, runic sword in hand, scanning the darkness for any sign of threat.

"We're close," he told himself quietly, as if repetition could will it into truth. "We have to be."

Lying still, Mira stirred in fever-dreams, mumbling disjointed words about illusions, hydras, and the cold emptiness of necromantic gloom. Elara dabbed her forehead with a damp cloth, tears slipping unnoticed down her cheeks. Thalion crushed the gathered herbs into a poultice, though he doubted its potency against Hydra venom. Cedric kept the fire stoked, an unspoken vow burning in his heart that they would do whatever necessary to make sure Mira had a cure before it was too late.

18

A RACE FOR THE CURE

A chill breeze wind swept across the small campsite where the four weary heroes gathered around the remnants of a smoldering fire. Clouds overhead broke into ragged edges, revealing the faint light of a waning moon that glimmered on dew-streaked grass. Sir Cedric, Lady Elara, Thalion, and Mira had traveled hastily northward from the coastal region where they had slain the three-headed Hydra. The group's reward for that monumental victory? The fourth relic—**the Pearl of Tides**—and a grievous wound that now threatened Mira's life.

Some distance away, the horses pawed at the ground and snorted softly, as though reflecting the tension that clung to the camp. Mira lay still on a bedroll, dark hair splayed across a rolled cloak. Her complexion had dulled to a pale gray, and thin lines of blackish discoloration traced veins around the bandaged bite on her calf. Though Elara's healing magic had slowed the venom's spread, it could not eradicate it.

Thalion, the scholarly elder mage, knelt beside Mira's form, murmuring a soft incantation under his breath. A haze of gentle light shimmered over her body, and for a moment, her breathing steadied. Once the glow faded, Thalion bowed his head. "Her heart grows weaker," he said softly, voice hoarse with long nights of worry. "We must find that alchemist's shop soon."

Across the fire's dying embers, Cedric crouched on one knee, running a hand over the runic inscriptions on his sword's hilt. "The rumors say it's near the Land of Giants, not far from a mountain pass. We can't waste any more time." He glanced at Lady Elara, who had just finished cleaning and reapplying salve to Mira's wound. "How is she?"

Elara's face tightened, the lines of fatigue etched deeper by her concern. "We're barely holding the poison at bay. She manages to stay conscious for moments, but the pain is... intense. My healing wards help with her suffering, but the toxin itself resists. If we don't get the proper antidote, I—I'm afraid she won't make it."

Quiet dread sank into the group. Mira, always the vibrant spark of arcane brilliance, now teetered on the edge of a fate too grim to contemplate. Even as the gloom of dawn gave way to the first hints of sunlight, the chill in the air felt heavier than any night shadow.

Determination lit in Cedric's eyes. "Then let's pack up. We'll ride as soon as it's light enough to see the path." He pushed upright, voice firm. "Ready your gear. If we ride hard, we can cover enough ground by midday."

Thalion gently laid a hand over Mira's brow, checking for fever. "The sages mentioned an old valley pass on the way north. If that's the correct path, we should confirm it quickly. Any detour might prove fatal."

Elara brushed away a stray tear and stood, her battered armor reflecting the faint morning glow. "Let's go, then," she said, softly but resolutely. "For Mira."

And so, they gathered what few supplies they had, doused the last of the embers, and carefully lifted Mira into her saddle, fastening her with rope and blankets so she wouldn't fall if she slipped unconscious. The group set off as the horizon turned gold, determined to outrun the looming threat of Hydra poison—and whatever else might stand in their way.

The next hours saw the quartet pressing onward across a landscape of rolling foothills and sparse pine groves. The coastal humidity had long faded, replaced by a crisp dryness that hinted at mountainous air. Thalion consulted half-remembered lore about the Land of Giants, sketched on a tattered map with runic notes scrawled in the margins.

They rode in silence for the most part, occasionally exchanging worried glances whenever Mira let out a pained groan. Elara rode beside her, an unwavering presence of gentle healing auras. Whenever the trail widened or the terrain leveled out, Elara took those moments to lay a hand on Mira's shoulder, letting the soft glow of her faith quell a fraction of the venom's agony.

Cedric led the way, scanning for hazards. He'd heard rumors that beyond these hills, bandits often preyed on travelers, and monstrous creatures roamed at times—though perhaps none as fearsome as the Hydra they had just slain. Reining in his horse on a slight crest, Cedric peered forward. The sun, climbing higher, revealed a series of jagged rock formations funneling into a narrow valley. Pine trees dotted the slopes, thickening toward a craggy pass.

"That must be the route," Cedric said. "We skirt the edge of the Land of Giants from there, if the stories are right."

Elara pulled alongside him, gazing at the imposing ridges that loomed. "Looks like a prime place for an ambush," she muttered. "But we have no choice. We can't go days around the mountains. Mira won't last that long."

Behind them, Thalion coaxed his horse forward, Mira's mount trailing. Despite the bright morning sun, the tension in the group never eased. Every step toward the pass felt like stepping into the jaws of a sleeping predator.

As the path narrowed, the travelers slowed. The horses whickered anxiously, hooves clattering on loose stones. The valley walls rose on both sides, an almost vertical climb of rocky outcroppings and spiny brush. Wind whistled through the gorge, echoing dissonant notes. Cedric motioned for silence, raising a hand. In the hush, a faint noise could be discerned—rustling movement on the cliffs above.

He glanced back at Elara, who gave a single nod, her shield lifting ever so slightly. Thalion gently patted his horse's neck, his staff angled for quick conjuring if needed. This place did indeed feel like the perfect spot for a trap.

They hadn't gone more than fifty yards into the valley when an eerie whistle cut through the air. Then another. And another.

Arrows.

Like a deadly rain, they streaked down from the cliffside, their fletching catching the sunlight. Cedric had only enough time to shout, "Shields!" before the volley descended upon them. With practiced reflexes, Elara yanked up her broad paladin shield, intercepting half a dozen arrows with a resonant clang. Cedric lifted his own shield—though smaller—managing to deflect two that would have found his chest.

"Ambush!" Thalion growled, pulling his horse behind a rocky bulge. He spotted movement up on the ridge: half-equine, half-human shapes sprinting among the boulders. **Centaurs.** He recognized the powerful flanks, the torso of a human archer, and the swift grace with which they navigated the uneven ground.

Mira, hazy with fever, barely stirred at the warning. An arrow glanced off Elara's shield with a spark, leaving Mira unharmed—if rattled.

"They're up there!" Cedric called, pointing with his sword. "We can't fight them easily at this range. Move, move!"

The group urged their horses to gallop, hooves thundering through the narrow pass. Another flurry of arrows rained down from the opposite slope. Cedric and Elara angled their shields overhead, forming a precarious roof of steel. Shafts clattered off the metal or wedged into wooden frames, the entire cacophony echoing around them.

"Thalion, illusions!" Elara shouted through gritted teeth, trying to keep her shield steady over Mira.

With one hand gripping his staff, Thalion twisted in the saddle. He spoke a sharp phrase in an arcane tongue, conjuring a shimmering distortion in the air above them. This partial illusion, a swirl of refracted light, confused the archers' line of sight. At once, half the arrows veered wide, landing with hollow thunks in the valley floor.

"Go!" Thalion barked, straining to maintain the spell. His illusions flickered in and out with the galloping motion of the horse, the concentration required nearly impossible in a full sprint.

Centaurs emerged to the valley's edge, their powerful equine bodies stamping dust clouds as they released arrow after arrow. Some bellowed war cries, while others remained unnervingly silent. The glimpses Cedric caught revealed strong, proud faces, brows knit in fierce concentration. *Why are they attacking us?* he wondered. The group had no quarrel with centaurs—nor had they trespassed on known centaur territory. But these savage hills were unpredictable.

"We're almost through!" Elara called, spotting a bend in the valley that broadened. Beyond lay a gentler slope leading out of arrow range. She pressed her heels into her horse's flanks, ignoring the arrows whistling overhead. One grazed her pauldron, leaving a gouge in the metal. Cedric grimaced as another arrow pinged off his helmet, jarring his vision.

Thalion hissed in pain as a stray arrow clipped his forearm, opening a shallow gash. The mage clenched his teeth, refusing to relinquish his illusions. Another volley whistled in, partially deflected by the swirling barrier of shimmering light.

Hooves pounding, the companions raced through the final stretch of the valley. At last, the narrow gorge opened onto a rocky plateau. The barrage of arrows slackened, the centaur archers ceasing fire once their targets were at the far edge of the valley. Whether they deemed further pursuit unwise or they simply guarded the pass was unclear. By the time the group slowed the horses to a canter, no additional arrows came.

Still, they didn't stop. Panic thrummed in each chest. Once they had put enough distance and boulders between themselves and the lethal vantage points, Cedric reined in. The others followed suit, hearts pounding, adrenaline surging.

Elara immediately turned to check on Mira. She still sat slumped in the saddle, eyes half-lidded. No arrow had found her, but the venom, combined with the chaotic ride, had taken a toll. The blankets tied around her had loosened, leaving her dangerously close to tipping. Elara eased her upright, mouth set in a grim line.

Cedric spun, scanning for any sign of pursuit. None. No clatter of hooves on stone, no war cries. Only the wide, empty plateau beneath a blazing midmorning sun.

"Why would centaurs ambush us like that?" Thalion panted, blood trickling from his wounded arm. "We had no conflict with them. They never even made demands."

Elara shook her head, lips pressed tight. "The land is rife with tensions. Maybe they see us as outsiders or blame humans for destruction. Or the Shadow Nexus's corruption might be affecting their territory. We can't know."

Cedric grimaced, pulling an arrow from his shield. "No time to dwell on it now. We have to keep moving. Let's see that arm, Thalion."

The mage nodded, gingerly offering his forearm. Elara poured a splash of water over the wound, cleaning away dust, then pressed a cloth bandage. A faint golden glow sealed the laceration enough to stanch bleeding, though not fully restore him. With that attended to, they turned their attention to Mira, checking if her condition had worsened during the frantic ride.

Her brow was damp with sweat, and she muttered something incoherent under her breath—possibly a spell or a name. Guilt pricked at all of them for having to jostle her so roughly through the valley, but no alternative existed. She needed the cure, or this desperate flight would be for nothing.

"All right," Cedric said quietly, trading looks with Elara and Thalion. "We survived the ambush. Let's go find this alchemy shop. It has to be near, if the map is correct."

They urged the horses forward once more, the next leg of their perilous journey unfolding under a harsh sun and stinging mountain wind.

By late afternoon, the terrain shifted from rocky plateau to gently rolling highlands. Thorny shrubs lined the route, and above them, tall pines swayed in the crisp breeze. The looming mountains to the northeast formed a jagged backdrop, rumored to be the outskirts of the Land of Giants. Even from a distance, the sheer scale of those peaks felt imposing.

Thalion's map led them to a faded signpost near a fork in the trail. Most of the lettering was worn away, but the etched outline of a mortar and pestle offered a clue: an alchemist's symbol. Hope stirred in Cedric's chest.

The sign pointed to a modest path winding down a slope toward a collection of ramshackle buildings nestled by a wide, placid stream. As they neared, the travelers caught sight of an old wooden arch over the lane, carved with the words: **WILLOWWICK CROSSING**. The scent of herbs hung faintly on the air, and smoke from several chimneys rose in curling plumes. A few goats and chickens roamed near the outskirts.

"Elara, how's Mira?" Cedric asked, glancing back.

Elara's gaze flicked to the bandaged wound. "She's still stable, but her breathing's shallow. Let's not delay."

The group pressed on, following the sound of a spinning watermill. Rounding a bend, they spotted the heart of Willowwick Crossing: a small cluster of humble timber-and-stone buildings along the stream. Among them stood a shop with a large mortar-and-pestle sign swinging overhead. Faded paint spelled out: **Harrow's Alchemy & Curatives**.

A wave of relief washed over them—if the legends were correct, this was indeed the place rumored to carry cures even for monstrous venoms. They wasted no time dismounting in front of the shop. Cedric gently lifted Mira from her saddle, her head lolling against his shoulder. Thalion quickly hopped off his horse, staff in hand, while Elara approached the door and gave a polite knock.

Almost immediately, a voice from inside called, "Come in, come in—if you've coin or need a salve, I've got it. Hurry, it's drafty out there!"

Elara pushed the door open, revealing a cluttered interior lit by rows of oil lamps. Shelves spilled over with clay jars, glass vials, dried herbs in bunches, and oddities pickled in solutions. The air teemed with pungent aromas—lavender, sulfur, mint, and countless other scents that blurred together.

Behind a narrow wooden counter stood a lanky figure with round spectacles perched on a hooked nose. Dressed in a patched apron, the individual looked half-scholar, half-tinkerer. A wave of bushy hair framed a deeply lined face.

He blinked at the group, eyes instantly narrowing on Mira's limp form.

"Hydra venom?" the alchemist asked bluntly, stepping around the counter with startling speed.

Elara sucked in a breath. "You... you can tell?"

He nodded grimly, placing a careful hand on Mira's arm. "Seen it thrice in my life. Twice was too late. Come, bring her to the back. I'll do what I can."

They followed him into a cramped but well-ordered workroom. Wooden tables were strewn with vials, mortar and pestle sets, and open tomes scrawled with formulas in spidery handwriting. The alchemist directed Cedric to lay Mira on a sturdy cot in the corner. She let out a faint whimper as he set her down.

"I'm Harrow," the shopkeeper said, bustling to a cabinet. "Specialize in potions, antidotes, and wards. And you four look like you've fought a war to get here." He rummaged through bottles until he found one with dark green liquid. "She's far gone. That leg wound's nearly turned black. A standard hydra venom cure might not suffice if the creature was... corrupted. Let's see."

He pried away Mira's bandages, wincing at the swirling black lines beneath her skin. The group's hearts sank at the sight of how widespread the venom had become. Harrow uncorked the bottle, letting out a pungent reek of bitter herbs, and dribbled a measure onto the wound.

Mira stirred, eyes flying open in sudden agony. "Nnngh!" She clenched her teeth, tears streaking her cheeks. Elara and Cedric had to hold her gently while Harrow examined the reaction.

The green fluid bubbled on contact with the flesh, hissing quietly, but the dark lines remained. The alchemist cursed under his breath. "As I feared. This hydra's poison is... enhanced. The standard brew won't purge it." He placed the bottle aside, rummaging deeper in a drawer. "I do have a stronger antidote—rare, complicated to brew, and extremely expensive. But it might work."

Thalion, still cradling his wounded arm, stepped forward. "Name your price," he said. "We'll pay. Our friend's life depends on it."

Harrow paused, a flicker of regret crossing his face. "Normally, I'd say two hundred gold pieces for the advanced hydra cure. But with how dire she is... let me see if I can adapt the formula without charging you a fortune. I don't fancy letting someone die on my watch." He busied himself with flasks, roots, and extracts lined up in neat rows.

Cedric exhaled a shaky breath. "Thank you, Master Harrow. We—" He hesitated. "We don't have that much gold, but we do have items for barter, plus some coin we've gathered along the way."

Harrow shook his head, already too absorbed in measuring precise amounts of thick, tar-like extract into a glass beaker. "Let's talk payment once I see if I can save your friend."

Elara clasped her hands, leaning over Mira with a gentle expression. "Hang on, Mira. Help's here."

Squeezing her eyes shut against the pain, Mira gave a slight nod, delirium swirling in her mind. For the first time in days, a glimmer of genuine hope fluttered in Elara's chest.

A tense hour followed, where Harrow painstakingly combined powders, liquids, and ground-up seeds. He heated the mixture over a small brazier, swirling it meticulously with a glass rod. The shop filled with an herbal tang so potent that Thalion fought the urge to sneeze. Periodically, the alchemist tasted a drop from the rod, grimacing or nodding as he adjusted the ratio of ingredients.

Meanwhile, Cedric and Elara hovered at Mira's side, occasionally wiping sweat from her brow. Thalion busied himself by scanning the shelves. The store boasted potions labeled for all manner of conditions: spider venom, giant wasp stings, undead curses, even something referencing "dragonfire toxin." The magnitude of Harrow's expertise was impressive.

At last, Harrow gave a triumphant huff. He extinguished the brazier and tilted the beaker, decanting a thick, dark-blue syrup into a small clay vial. "This is as potent as I can make it," he announced, wiping his forehead with a rag. "Given the corruption, I can't guarantee a miracle, but it's your best chance."

He knelt beside Mira, gently lifting her head. Elara propped her up. "Ready?" Harrow asked, glancing at Cedric for consent. Cedric nodded gravely.

With great care, Harrow poured a measured trickle of the thick remedy into Mira's mouth. The taste must have been awful, for she jerked and sputtered. Still, Harrow kept at it until she swallowed the dose. Then he dabbed the rest onto her wound, watching intently. A faint hiss emanated as it touched her skin, and Mira groaned softly.

For a moment, no one dared breathe. Then, as they watched, the blackish lines around the bite began to slow their creeping advance. The tension in the heroes' chests felt near to bursting. Mira's breathing remained shallow, but her face lost some of its ghastly pallor.

Harrow sat back on his heels, exhaling. "I think... it's working," he said in a subdued tone. "She'll need rest, maybe a full day or more, for the venom to flush out completely. And in the morning, I'll examine her again. If all goes well, the corruption should recede in about a day's time."

A wave of relief and exhaustion washed over the party, so palpable they nearly wept. Elara brushed a trembling hand over Mira's hair. Cedric thanked Harrow, voice rough with gratitude. Even Thalion managed a weary smile, sagging against the shelves to ease the ache in his arm.

The alchemist cleared his throat. "There's an inn next door, run by my cousin. Very modest, but there's a real bed for your friend. I assume you'll want separate rooms?"

Cedric nodded. "Yes, if possible."

Harrow rose, dusting off his apron. "I'll bring a few more potions. She might need them overnight. But that's enough alchemy for one day." He glanced at the group, a note of pity in his gaze. "You're all exhausted. Best get some proper rest."

They carried Mira—who was drifting in and out of consciousness—next door to the **Willowwick Inn**, a squat, single-story building with a thatched roof. The afternoon sun cast long shadows across the small yard, dotted with potted herbs. A kindly matron greeted them, clearly expecting their arrival, and led them to two rooms at the far end of a modest hallway.

Elara and Thalion helped settle Mira in one, propping her up on a straw-stuffed mattress. Cedric lingered by the door, scanning the space for any hazards—though it was plain, just a table, a single window, and a small basin of water. It felt as if they'd stumbled into the coziest place in the world after so many miles of hardship.

Between Harrow's antidote and Elara's healing presence, Mira's color improved slightly. Though still feverish, she no longer thrashed about from pain. She half-opened her eyes once, recognizing Cedric's silhouette. "Ced..." she murmured, voice raw. "Th-thank you for... saving me."

Cedric, lips curving into a faint smile, answered gently, "Thank Thalion, Elara, everyone... Just rest. You'll pull through."

She gave a small, fragile nod before slipping back into a fatigued sleep.

Outside the room, Thalion eased the door shut. "We should let her rest," he said softly, a mixture of relief and exhaustion etched on his features. "I'll stay nearby in case I need to conjure any wards."

Elara smoothed her hair. "I'll check in on her every half hour or so. If the venom flares up again, we'll call Harrow."

Cedric placed a hand on Thalion's shoulder. "You need rest too, old friend. That arrow wound is no joke. Let's find some food, get these cuts tended."

Thalion nodded, not bothering to hide how tired he felt. The day's frantic race, combined with the ambush, had drained them all. They meandered to the small common area of the inn, where the matron served stew and crusty bread. The warm aroma was both comforting and surreal after so much tension.

Night settled across Willowwick Crossing. The inn's handful of guests—two traveling merchants and a local farmer—retired to their rooms early. The hallway outside

Mira's door remained quiet, lit by a single lantern. Elara quietly tended Mira, wiping her brow, ensuring she drank water. Periodically, she recited soft prayers.

Cedric bunked in the second room with Thalion. Both men found sleep elusive. Despite bone-deep weariness, each time Cedric closed his eyes, he replayed the day's events: centaur arrows hissing by, Mira's pained face, the possibility of losing her. He prayed silently to any deity who might listen, just to keep his friend safe.

Eventually, near midnight, he dozed. The inn was hushed, the flicker of the lantern in the hall casting dancing shadows. Until—

Knock, knock.

Cedric stirred. The knock on their door sounded soft but insistent. He rubbed bleary eyes, crossing the room to open it.

Standing there in the dim corridor was Harrow, clutching a small satchel. He raised a finger to his lips. "I know it's late, but... I needed to talk to you." His voice was subdued, anxious.

Cedric beckoned him in. Thalion rose as well, lighting a candle. "Is something wrong with Mira?" Thalion asked, worry spiking.

Harrow shook his head. "No, she's stable for now. I checked with Lady Elara. She's asleep, resting peacefully." The alchemist sighed. "But I discovered something about the venom sample from her bandage. I think you should know."

Cedric tensed, dread coiling in his gut. "What is it?"

Harrow set the satchel on the small table. From inside, he produced a tiny glass vial containing a droplet of blackish sludge. It shimmered faintly in the candlelight, reminiscent of congealed oil with swirling purple undertones.

"This is more than hydra venom," Harrow explained, voice low. "It has distinct traces of what I can only call... *void essence*. I suspect it's from the Shadow Nexus you mentioned. This means your friend was essentially envenomed by a monstrous Hydra *and* corrupted magic. My antidote will save her from the hydra's poison, but the void essence remains... dangerous."

Thalion's gaze flicked to Cedric. The older mage's expression turned grim. "Could it linger in her system? Infect her with some form of dark magic?"

Harrow nodded slowly. "Yes, though it's dormant for now. I've never seen something quite like it. Typically, if the body recovers fully, it might purge the void essence on its own. However, if any seeds of corruption remain, it might resurface under stress or further exposure to dark energies."

Cedric's hand curled into a fist. "So she's in no immediate danger, but it's not a guaranteed fix," he murmured. "Can we do anything else?"

The alchemist pursed his lips, deep lines of thought crossing his brow. "There is a specialized purification ritual you might seek, though it's rare. A priest or paladin of formidable standing—someone with direct grace from a powerful deity—could banish lingering void corruption. Or an artifact aligned with pure light might suffice. If you have such contacts or relics, it could help ensure your friend is truly free of this taint."

Cedric and Thalion exchanged a meaningful glance. "We've heard rumors of an **Amulet of Light**, a relic of divine aspect that might be the last piece we need for a larger quest," Cedric explained, voice subdued. "We still don't know exactly where it is. But if it's as holy as the legends say, it might purge any leftover corruption."

Harrow studied their expressions, then nodded. "Well, if your quest leads you to a relic of pure light, that could solve it. Just keep an eye on her in the meantime. If she recovers well, the leftover void essence may remain dormant—only a hazard if she's subjected to strong negative magic again."

Cedric let out a slow breath. "Thank you for telling us, Harrow. And for... everything else."

The alchemist gathered his satchel. "I'm sorry I haven't better news. But at least your friend will survive the night. She's lucky to have companions like you." He gave them a tired smile, then slipped out into the corridor.

Thalion sank onto the edge of the bed, shoulders sagging. "One challenge ends, another begins," he murmured.

Cedric blew out the candle, mind spinning with the news. "We'll face it when the time comes. For now, let's pray Mira makes a full recovery and we can track down the Amulet of Divine Light. We owe her that much."

Despite the looming worry about void essence, a kernel of relief remained: Mira was alive, and Harrow's cure had done its job. That had to be enough for tonight.

The next day dawned bright, sunlight filtering through the small windows of the Willowwick Inn. Elara had maintained a vigil by Mira's bedside for much of the night, dozing in a chair in brief intervals. Soon after sunrise, Thalion and Cedric joined her to assess Mira's condition.

She was awake, propped against pillows. Though pale, she wore a tentative smile as she stirred from a light doze. The black streaks around her calf had receded significantly, leaving only faint bruises. When she attempted to speak, her voice came out scratchy, but steady enough to convey gratitude.

"I owe you everything," she whispered, blinking at the brightness. "Harrow says another day of rest, and I might be back on my feet."

Elara gently pressed a hand to Mira's forehead, gauging temperature. "Your fever's broken," she said, tears of relief gleaming in her eyes. "Thank the Light."

Mira winced as she shifted her injured leg. "Still hurts. But it's nothing like before. I... I felt that darkness in my blood. Like an anchor pulling me under." She exhaled shakily. "Now, it's... quiet."

Cedric exchanged a glance with Thalion, remembering Harrow's warning about lingering void essence. But now wasn't the time to fill her mind with dread. She needed calm and recovery.

He cleared his throat. "We'll stay as long as you need," he said, voice kind. "We have time to stock up on supplies. Harrow's shop might have potions for future emergencies, and the innkeeper here can provide a decent meal."

Mira nodded faintly. "Yes... I can walk soon enough, I promise." Her tone held a trace of the determined spark that once fueled her spells.

Elara squeezed her hand. "There's no rush. Our journey continues when you're well. We have the Pearl of Tides now. And we still have relics to find."

Late in the morning, Thalion visited Harrow's shop again, rummaging through racks of alchemical ingredients. Despite the arrow wound in his arm—now bandaged—he managed a stoic focus on the party's needs. Harrow offered them discounted prices, possibly out of goodwill after saving Mira. Thalion purchased healing potions, salves for traveling wounds, and a few single-use scrolls that might conjure illusions or protective wards.

Cedric arrived to trade items they had collected along their travels—rare monster parts from the Hydra, a few decorative stones from the labyrinth near the Minotaur clan, and a small chunk of the Wyvern scale (which they had carefully trimmed). Harrow marveled at these spoils, evidently pleased to study such curiosities. In return, he handed over specialized potions to help them endure extreme climates, in case they had to traverse scorching deserts or icy mountains in pursuit of the next relic.

Elara visited the local chapel in Willowwick Crossing, a humble structure with a worn wooden symbol of the Dawn. There, she prayed for Mira's continued healing and gave thanks for their survival. Though no high priest presided, the caretaker—a kindly old woman—welcomed Elara warmly, offering leftover bandages and simple blessings.

Mira stayed at the inn's modest lounge area, leaning on a crutch Harrow had fashioned from a stout piece of wood. She occasionally practiced minor illusions with her staff. Her leg throbbed if she put too much weight on it, but walking short distances was now possible. Despite this step toward normalcy, a faint tension haunted her eyes—some lingering anxiety that all was not entirely well inside her body. She tried to shake it off, focusing instead on how to help the group move forward.

That evening, the companions reconvened in the inn's small dining nook. They shared a meal of stewed vegetables, salted pork, and fresh bread. Over dinner, talk turned inevitably to next steps.

Seated around a sturdy wooden table, the four friends looked more like weary travelers than the heroic band rumored to have slain a Hydra. Cedric's eyes, though sharper now that they'd found respite, still harbored a flicker of worry whenever he glanced at Mira.

"So," Thalion began, pushing aside his empty bowl. "We have the Pearl of Tides, third relic in hand, along with the Wyvern scale and Behemoth disc. By the Arcadium's records, we still need the **Amulet of Divine Light** for air and the celestial to complete the set."

Mira rested the staff across her lap, absentmindedly tracing the swirl of starlit flecks in the Manticore gem at its tip. "The Song of Severance calls for all four elements—earth, fire, water, air, and a divine spark. If we truly want to banish the Shadow Nexus for good, we can't skip any." She paused, wincing as her leg cramped. Elara leaned over to support her, and Mira offered a grateful smile.

Cedric rubbed his chin. "From the rumors we've gathered, the **Amulet of Divine Light** might lie high up in the Labrynthian Mountains. But that's dangerously close to the Land of Giants. Could be a treacherous journey."

Elara nodded, pressing a cloth to Mira's forehead. "But it may be the final relic we need". We may need to consult someone like High Seer Malachai back at Stonehaven's capital for more direct clues on its possible location."

Mira frowned thoughtfully. "We risk letting the Shadow Nexus's influence spread in the meantime. Every day we linger, more monsters—like that Hydra—might warp. And we still have no idea if the centaur ambush was random or if they're also being corrupted." She sighed. "But after nearly dying, I... I don't want to leap into danger without a plan."

Cedric nodded, reaching out to place a reassuring hand atop hers. "We'll plan carefully. And we'll make sure you've recovered fully before we face giants or storms. The wise path is best now."

Quiet gratitude filled Mira's eyes. This was the fellowship that had carried her through so many trials. She mustered a gentle smile, returning Cedric's gesture by resting her other hand on his. "Thank you," she murmured.

Elara cleared her throat, guiding the conversation. "So what's immediate? We have supplies and healing potions. Mira needs at least one more night to convalesce, maybe two. Then we ride. Perhaps we circle back to Stonehaven's capital to consult High Seer Malachai about the Amulet's whereabouts. Or do we simply push north with the information we already have?"

Thalion considered, rubbing at the bandage on his forearm. "If the Amulet is indeed in the Labrynthian Mountains, we're not far from that region. Going back south to the capital might cost us weeks. But we do need every advantage. And Malachai might be the key to locating the Amulet quickly. A tough choice."

Cedric released a slow breath. "We'll let Mira decide once she's stronger. If she's up for traveling north, we do that. If not, we head to the capital and gather more intelligence."

A comfortable hush descended on the table, the warmth of their meal dulling the sharp edges of uncertainty. Outside the inn's windows, night thickened, stars pricking through a clear sky. They were safe here, for the moment—no Hydra, no centaur ambush, no swirling shadows. Only the faint glow of lanterns and the reassuring murmur of a village at rest.

When the group finally retired for the evening, they escorted Mira to her room. She insisted on walking with minimal help, testing her recovering leg. She managed a short shuffle, only wincing occasionally. Elara hovered behind her, ready to steady her if needed.

Upon reaching the modest bedroom, Mira sank onto the bed with a weary sigh. Elara left briefly to fetch a fresh bandage and check on supplies. Cedric lingered at the threshold, uncertain if Mira wanted more company or not. She looked up, meeting his gaze.

"You can come in," she said softly.

He stepped inside, carefully closing the door. The single lantern on the bedside table cast warm light across Mira's features, highlighting how drained she still was, yet how relieved. The tension from days of near-fatal crisis lingered, though now overshadowed by a quiet gratitude.

"How do you feel?" Cedric asked, settling on a small stool.

She shrugged, brushing a hand over her leg. "Honestly? Lucky. Even with the pain." A small, almost self-conscious laugh escaped her. "Never thought I'd say that about a hydra bite. But... I was so close to not making it."

Cedric's chest clenched. "I should have been faster to intervene. That monstrous head bit you—" He paused, swallowing the guilt.

Mira frowned. "No, none of that. You saved me, all of you. No regrets, Ced. Please."

He forced a smile, nodding. "All right. But next time we fight a multi-headed beast, I promise to watch your flank more closely."

That coaxed a genuine grin from her. She reached out, and he lightly took her hand. A gentle warmth passed between them, a reminder of the bond forged by so many shared perils and triumphs. For a moment, the swirling anxieties of relics, shadow threats, and uncertain futures lifted.

"Get some rest," Cedric whispered, releasing her hand. "Tomorrow we'll see how you're feeling. Then decide our next move. We—" He hesitated, thinking of Harrow's warning. "We might also want to find a way to fully purge any leftover corruption. But one step at a time."

She nodded, eyelids drooping with fatigue. "Thank you. Good night."

He offered a faint smile, snuffing the lantern, leaving only moonlight through the window. As he slipped out, Elara met him in the hall, holding fresh bandages. She peered inside, saw that Mira was nearly asleep, and softly shut the door again.

"She's doing better," Elara whispered, sounding both relieved and exhausted. Cedric put a hand on her shoulder in silent agreement. Together, they walked to their own respective rooms for what they hoped would be a peaceful night's slumber.

Morning arrived with a crispness in the air. The sun rose over the highland ridges, painting the Willowwick Crossing in soft pink and gold. Thin tendrils of mist clung to the stream behind the inn. The smell of fresh bread wafted from a kitchen window, mingling with the dew-kissed scent of herbs and pine.

Mira woke feeling unexpectedly refreshed. She still had a dull ache in her calf and general weakness, but the searing agony and fevers were gone. When she tested her weight on the leg, it hurt, yet she managed several steps without collapsing. Elara, who had quietly entered to check on her, broke into a pleased grin at the sight.

"You're walking," Elara said. "Not the fastest pace, but— look at you."

Mira tested another cautious step, leaning on the bedpost. "I think... I might be able to ride a horse again, though carefully," she said, voice laced with lingering amazement. "This cure was miraculous."

Elara guided her back to sit. "Slow progress," she advised, gently patting Mira's shoulder. "Harrow wants to do a final check, but it looks like you're almost out of the woods."

Downstairs in the inn's common room, Cedric and Thalion had already paid for another night's stay, planning to let Mira rest at least one more full day before traveling. Harrow arrived soon after, toting a small chest of tools and potions to give Mira a last examination. He listened to her heartbeat, inspected the bite wound, and nodded in satisfaction.

"Seems stable," Harrow pronounced, applying a final salve to reduce scarring. "I'd recommend you not engage in sword duels or strenuous rides for a couple of days, but with each passing hour, your body's eliminating the last toxins. Good."

Mira exhaled in relief. "Thank you. I owe you my life."

The alchemist shrugged, a faint flush coloring his cheeks. "Just doing my job. Glad the advanced formula worked. Please, be mindful of that 'void essence' component, though," he added in a lower tone, darting a glance at Cedric and Thalion. "I told them about it. Just, if you feel any darkness stirring, speak up."

Mira's expression grew pensive, but she nodded. "I will. Thank you for telling me."

With that, Harrow gave them some final potions—pain relief tonics, a mild stamina draught—and left them to their breakfast. The day felt strangely bright, as though a storm cloud had passed. Despite the uncertain future, the taste of hope was sweet.

By midday, Mira had ventured outside the inn on a slow walk, leaning on a walking staff. The others accompanied her, scanning the small settlement of Willowwick Crossing with fresh curiosity. It was hardly more than a handful of farmsteads, an herbal garden, and Harrow's shop plus the inn. But the villagers here greeted them with kind words and curious looks. Rumors had spread that these strangers fought a Hydra and survived.

Elara spent time near the stream, gathering her thoughts in silent prayer. Thalion browsed more of Harrow's curios, fascinated by a rare fungus said to glow in the presence of necromancy. Cedric carried out some routine maintenance on the horses, checking saddles and gear for the next leg of their journey. He kept glancing toward Mira, quietly marveling at how she was standing tall after days on the brink of death.

They reconvened in the inn's lounge by late afternoon, the day's last golden rays streaking across the wooden floor. Mira still felt fatigued, but the color in her cheeks had returned. A sense of renewed energy pulsed among them—the knowledge that they'd overcome a lethal setback, forging on with their quest.

"Tomorrow," Cedric said, addressing the group, "we depart. We have the Pearl of Tides safe in Thalion's pack. We also have new potions. And Mira can at least sit upright on her horse. The question remains: do we head to the Labrynthian Mountains for the Amulet of Divine Light or return to the capital for more guidance?"

Thalion studied the half-finished map on the table. "The Labrynthian Mountains are likely only a few days away, but it's known for savage storms, high winds, possibly even elemental creatures. Another big risk. The capital is a much longer ride south and east, though perhaps safer overall."

Elara glanced at Mira. "Your call. You're the one who nearly died. If you prefer a safer route, we'll do it."

Mira's brow furrowed. She flexed her recovering leg. A flicker of stubborn determination appeared in her eyes—like the old spark that lit her illusions. "We can't afford to slow down too much," she admitted. "I appreciate the caution, but the Shadow Nexus won't pause for us. Let's attempt to find the Amulet of Divine Light with the information we currently have. Then we'll have all four relics. After that, we can focus on finding the exact location of where the Shadow Nexus might be."

Cedric gave a half-smile, relief and admiration mingling. "You've always been brave, Mira. Just promise to speak up if you're pushing yourself too hard."

She nodded, returning his gaze. "I promise."

Thalion traced his finger along the route drawn in charcoal. "We follow the old caravan path into the Labrynthian Mountain region. Should avoid the direct territory of the Giants, but still, it's close. Let's keep an eye out for large footprints." His attempt at humor drew small chuckles from the group.

Elara leaned back in her chair, letting out a breath. "Agreed then. At sunrise tomorrow, we head north to the plateau."

And so, the next chapter of their odyssey was decided. They finished the evening in subdued celebration. The innkeeper served them honey cakes and spiced cider, a treat for travelers who seldom tasted real comfort. Outside, the night deepened over the tranquil crossing, as the swirl of stars mirrored the swirl of possibilities that lay ahead.

19

THE LAND OF GIANTS

A luminous morning sun broke over the high ridges surrounding Willowwick Crossing, painting the modest village in honey-gold light. In the humble upstairs hallway of the inn, Sir Cedric, Lady Elara, Thalion, and Mira gathered with renewed spirits. No longer limping or feverish, Mira stretched her leg experimentally, testing the range of motion that had been so compromised by the Hydra's venom. Relief shone on each companion's face—Mira, fully cured at last, stood with them, ready for the next step of their quest.

Elara passed a canteen of water to Mira, who accepted it with a grateful nod. "I feel like a new person," Mira said, voice brimming with quiet excitement. "I slept without pain for the first time since that Hydra bite."

Thalion, watching Mira closely calmly remarked. "Just promise not to push too hard on that leg," lips curving into a small smile. "We still don't know if any latent corruption might linger. But I trust your body's had enough rest to continue."

Mira tested a single step, satisfied that only a slight soreness remained. "I promise to be careful," she said, meeting Thalion's gaze. Then, turning to the broader group, she added, "We have to press on. The innkeeper's talk last night gave us new clues: the Labyrinthian Mountains, home to the rumored **Amulet Channeled by Divine Light**, lie beyond the Land of Giants."

Cedric's strong hand rested on the pommel of his runic sword as he glanced out a nearby window. The horizon to the north rose in stark, craggy silhouettes. "The Land of Giants," he mused, exhaling. "Our final stretch to find the artifact. If it truly is one of the last relics we need, then we're close to ending this journey—close to forging the final blow against the Shadow Nexus."

Elara fingered the phoenix sigil on her shield, eyes determined. "We can't delay. If the Land of Giants is as perilous as rumors say, best we tackle it with fresh bodies and minds." She tightened a strap on her gauntlet. "I just hope this relic is indeed the one we need. We've endured too many near-fatal battles to chase a false lead now."

Mira snatched her staff from where it leaned against the wall, testing its weight. "Let's gather our belongings and head out. Before nightfall, we can hopefully reach the first foothills of Giants' territory."

Thus agreed, the four companions filed downstairs into the inn's modest common room, where they made final farewells to the kindhearted innkeeper. After securing their horses and bidding thanks once more to Harrow—who stood outside his alchemy shop waving farewell—they rode northward. The Land of Giants awaited, a realm of colossal beasts, harsh terrain, and a monstrous Cyclops rumored to guard the only pass into the Labyrinthian Mountains. Yet, fear did not rule their hearts. Determination, tempered by close calls and renewed by friendship, carried them forth into the unknown.

The morning ride began in rolling highlands, the grass swaying in a crisp wind. Gradually, the environment shifted: The pines grew taller and denser, the hills steeper, and the air took on a wilder cast. By midday, rocky outcrops broke the horizon, flanked by meandering streams that had cut deep gorges over centuries. The terrain felt simultaneously grand and foreboding—a preview of the Land of Giants' reputed vastness.

Mira noted it first: a low, distant rumbling that might have been wind or an echo of far-off stampeding. She reined in her mare, brow creasing. "Listen," she said softly. "Does anyone else hear that?"

Cedric and Thalion paused, turning heads. The wind carried faint tremors that pulsed beneath the usual birdsong. Elara's knuckles tightened on her reins. "Could be anything," she murmured. "A geological rumble, or some massive creature plodding about."

From what the inn's patrons had shared, the Land of Giants was rife with colossal fauna. In addition to tales of a towering Cyclops, travelers spoke of monstrous bull-like creatures plated with seemingly impenetrable fur, thronging the grassy plains in small herds. Some were docile if unprovoked. Others, rumored to be "Giant Bull Gorgons," took great pleasure in stalking unwary travelers.

Thalion flipped open a thin field journal he kept strapped to his belt. He had scrawled rough sketches from local legends, trying to glean any weaknesses. "The Gorgon's fur—like living armor," he muttered, scanning his notes. "We'll need to find a vulnerable spot if we're forced to fight. Possibly the underbelly, or between the plates near the neck.

If it's truly a Gorgon, we'll have to watch for petrifying breath or some other vile trick."

Cedric's expression hardened. "This place is a hunter's paradise for monstrous beasts, it seems."

"Let's not let them turn us into prey," Mira said firmly.

They pressed on at a careful pace. The ground, spongy with thick grass, occasionally revealed footprints that dwarfed those of a normal bull. Each massive indentation spoke of weight and power beyond typical animals. The travelers exchanged uneasy looks but continued forward. They needed a direct route to the Labyrinthian Mountains, which the inn's lore insisted was guarded by a pass overshadowed by a Cyclops's lair. The plan was to cross this expanse quickly, hoping to avoid any unnecessary battles with the local giants.

Still, fate rarely heeded such hopes. By late afternoon, the travelers entered a rolling meadow where knee-high grass rippled in gentle waves. Towering pines and boulders flanked the meadow's perimeter. Overhead, broad clouds drifted, shading the land in shifting gray. The earlier faint rumblings seemed nearer, more rhythmic.

Clutching his reins, Cedric surveyed the meadow. "Something's out there," he murmured. "Stay sharp."

A hush fell. Even the wind seemed to pause, as if bracing for what came next.

It began as a tremor in the soil: a faint vibration that tickled the horses' hooves, causing them to tremble in an anxious alarm. The group halted. From behind a rocky rise, a shape emerged—larger than any normal bull. The creature stood nearly twelve feet tall at the shoulder, its hulking frame layered in thick, reddish fur that formed spiked ridges across its back. The fur itself shimmered, almost metallic in the slanted light. Sharp horns jutted forward, curved like scimitars.

A Giant Bull Gorgon.

The beast pawed the earth, exhaling a snort of hot breath that roiled the grass. Muscles rippled beneath its fur-armor. The eyes, dark and uncanny, glimmered with a predatory intelligence. Slowly, the Gorgon advanced, each step stomping an indentation in the ground. A low, rolling bellow emanated from its throat.

Elara exchanged a quick glance with Cedric, her shield rising. "We can't outrun that with the baggage we carry," she whispered. "We might have to stand our ground."

Mira tightened her grip on her staff, mindful of her newly healed leg. "If we can avoid killing it, maybe it'll leave us be." But the Gorgon's taut posture and pinned ears suggested otherwise.

Thalion's staff crackled with latent energy. "I'm not sure we have a choice."

Cedric nudged his horse forward a single pace, calling out in a firm voice, "We mean you no harm, beast. Let us pass in peace." The Gorgon responded with a thunderous snort, lowering its head in challenge.

A heartbeat later, the giant bull charged. It streaked across the meadow with terrifying speed for such a massive creature. Dirt and grass clods flew in its wake. The companions scattered, urging their horses aside, but the Gorgon adjusted its path, targeting Thalion's mount.

Hooves pounding, the bull bore down. Thalion cast a hasty illusion, surrounding the Gorgon's head with flickering lights. For an instant, the monster tossed its horns in confusion, but momentum carried it onward, slamming broadside into Thalion's steed. Horse and rider tumbled in a chaotic sprawl. Thalion's staff clattered free, rolling into the grass.

Elara spurred her mount forward, shield raised. "Over here!" she shouted, banging the shield to draw the Gorgon's attention away from Thalion. The beast pivoted with surprising agility, swinging its horned head at Elara's flank. She braced, but the impact hammered her shield, nearly unseating her. Metal shrieked as horns scraped the shield's face.

Cedric closed in from behind, runic sword flaring as he slashed the Gorgon's hindquarters. Sparks flew where blade met fur-armor. He cursed under his breath—its hide was far tougher than expected. Though the force of his strike cut some coarse fur, it barely penetrated the thick hide beneath.

Mira dismounted, unwilling to rely on horseback to cast complex spells. Planting her staff, she conjured a swirling orb of frost and wind, hurling it at the Gorgon's flank. The icy blast impacted with a resounding crack, and the Gorgon let out a pained bellow, its side momentarily rimed with frost. However, the monster's raging charge continued.

Thalion, dazed, scrambled up from the grass, bruised but unbroken. He snatched his staff, conjuring an arc of lightning that danced across the Gorgon's horns. The beast shuddered, momentarily disoriented. Spotting the opening, Cedric lunged in again, aiming a thrust at the unarmored eye area. The Gorgon jerked its head, and the blade glanced off the horn base instead. Another rumbling bellow erupted from its throat.

The bull spun, tail lashing, and reared on hind legs in a display of formidable strength. Its front hooves slammed down, cracking the ground. Elara narrowly guided her horse aside, heart hammering.

"We need a better angle," Thalion shouted. "Its neck or underbelly—only place not fully shielded by that fur."

Mira nodded, casting illusions to distract the Gorgon: shimmering forms of phantom archers took shape, flitting at the edges of the meadow. Snorting in confusion, the Gorgon hesitated, thrashing horns at the illusions.

Elara dismounted, hooking her reins on a nearby sapling. She moved in at a crouch, shield angled. "Cedric, go high; I'll go low!" she called. As the Gorgon shifted to swipe at the illusions, Elara dashed under its flank, jabbing her sword upward at the creature's belly. The blade found softer hide, drawing a spurt of hot blood. The Gorgon bellowed in rage, staggering to the side.

Seizing the moment, Cedric leaped onto a low boulder, then launched himself upward at the beast's thick neck. His runic sword stabbed down between the dense fur ridges near the top of the shoulder, sinking deeper than before. A guttural cry shook the air. Gorgon blood splattered Cedric's armor as the creature thrashed wildly, nearly throwing him off.

Thalion added another arc of lightning, while Mira channeled a burst of freezing wind at the Gorgon's back legs, hoping to hamper its movements. The bull buckled, staggering as ice formed around its hooves. Elara delivered a second thrust to the underbelly, pushing her blade in up to the hilt. At last, the giant creature's strength ebbed. With a final heaving snort, the Gorgon collapsed sideways, shaking the ground in a mini-earthquake.

Cedric rolled away just in time to avoid being crushed by the mass. A wave of dust and torn grass billowed across the meadow. For a heartbeat, the group stood still, panting as the Gorgon's final breath rattled in its throat. Then it lay still, thick fur flecked with frost and blood.

They regrouped. Horses paced nervously at the meadow's edge. Elara withdrew her blade from the creature's underside, her hands trembling from adrenaline. "We tried not to kill it," she whispered, half to herself, "but it gave us no choice."

Cedric nodded solemnly, wiping sweat from his brow. "At least we survived. Let's hope we don't encounter a whole herd of these."

Thalion, checking bruised ribs, forced a grim smile. "I suspect the rest might avoid us if they catch the scent of this. Gorgons are territorial, but hopefully we're through their domain."

Mira stepped closer, staff in hand, eyes flicking to the fallen beast. "At least it seemed unaffected by the Shadow Nexus—just an aggressive guardian of these lands. Still, it sets a tone for what else we might face."

No one argued. Together, they took a moment to calm the horses and bandage minor wounds. The late afternoon sun hung low, painting the grass in warm gold. Far off, thunderheads gathered near distant peaks, a reminder that giant storms were rumored to roam these skies in the form of monstrous thunderbirds.

They had defeated one giant beast. But bigger challenges soared overhead.

They continued north, traversing a shallow river where the Gorgon's blood rinsed from their boots and armor. As dusk approached, the land opened into a wide, rolling plain scattered with jagged stone columns. The final pass to the Labyrinthian Mountains lay somewhere beyond, guarded by the legendary Cyclops. Their plan was to press until nightfall, then find safe shelter. However, the wind carried ominous cries that stilled their hearts: **shrill screeches overhead**.

Thalion squinted at the darkening sky. "Thunderbirds," he murmured. "Look, there—wingspans huge enough to blot the sun."

Elara followed his gaze. Far above, three silhouettes circled, each shaped like a monstrous eagle with elongated tail feathers trailing like streaming banners. White arcs of flickering lightning crackled around their talons, glimpsed whenever their wings angled in the fiery glow of sunset. These were not mere birds of prey; they were apex predators rumored to conjure storms.

"They've spotted us," Cedric said, voice low. The thunderbirds glided in broad loops, still distant but clearly observing. "We should find cover—traveling under open sky invites an aerial attack."

Mira frowned, glancing around the mostly treeless plain. "Easier said than done. There's barely any forest or rocky overhang out here."

"Keep riding," Elara urged. "If they decide to swoop down, we can only scatter or attempt illusions. Or find a cave if we spot one."

They pressed on in a tense trot, scanning the horizon for any outcropping or cliff that could grant refuge. The thunderbirds soared closer, their screeches echoing across the plains, as though testing the travelers' resolve. Despite the distance, the flap of their immense wings stirred currents in the air, making the horses skittish.

Thalion muttered incantations under his breath, preparing illusions in case the birds dived. Cedric and Elara kept shields at the ready, though they were acutely aware a single shield might not stop the talons of a multi-ton avian. Mira tapped the ground with her staff, conjuring mild illusions of swirling mist. The half-fog might confuse the thunderbirds' initial approach, but only for a moment.

When the largest thunderbird—its feathers streaked with crackling white arcs—peeled off from the formation and dived, the group's blood ran cold. It angled downward at alarming speed, lightning dancing around its beak. Thalion hurled an illusion meant to distort the ground, but the giant eagle's keen eyes barely wavered.

Its screech rattled the travelers' teeth. A massive wingspan cast a looming shadow as it barreled toward Thalion's position. The mage cursed, spurring his horse to gallop. With a deft pivot, he conjured a protective barrier of swirling air. The thunderbird's talons slammed into the magical shield, sending sparks of lightning in every direction. The force nearly knocked Thalion from the saddle, but he clung to his horse's mane.

Meanwhile, Cedric and Elara circled around, swords out, unsure how to strike a creature so high above. The thunderbird's wings buffeted the area, kicking up grit and grass. Another screech, and it rose again, swirling overhead for a second pass.

Mira, eyes narrowed, unleashed a volley of frost-lances aimed at the bird's exposed underside. The shards glimmered in the twilight, but the thunderbird twisted nimbly, avoiding direct hits. One shard grazed a wing, eliciting an outraged squawk. Thunder rumbled in the clouds overhead, as though the creature's anger echoed in the sky.

Suddenly, the second thunderbird joined the attack, stooping at high velocity. Cedric braced. This new bird targeted him, talons extended. He raised his runic shield, the monstrous talons scraping with an ear-splitting screech that jarred his entire arm. Sparks of runic energy flared. The bird's momentum dragged Cedric sideways in the saddle, nearly toppling him. With an effort, he swung his sword upward, scoring a shallow cut on one talon. The thunderbird soared past, shrieking in fury.

"This is madness," Elara shouted over the gale. "We can't fight them in the open!"

In that moment, Mira cried out, pointing toward a line of jagged rocks near a sloping hill. "A cave entrance, I think!"

They spurred their horses in that direction, the thunderbirds wheeling overhead. The largest bird made a savage dive for Thalion once more—lightning crackled around its beak, threatening to discharge. Thalion yelped, urging his horse into a frantic sprint. The thunderbird swooped so low that he felt the static prickle across his shoulders. A fraction of a second's difference, and the bird's beak would have clamped around him. He narrowly avoided that lethal grasp. The creature's screech flayed the air, outraged at missing its prey.

Stumbling over rocky ground, the four riders half-galloped, half-scrambled to the mouth of a dark cave. Once inside, they dismounted, tugging the nervous horses after them. The thunderbirds soared overhead, talons and lightning searching for an opening. But the cave extended just far enough that the monstrous eagles could not maneuver inside. Furious shrieks echoed at the entrance.

Heart hammering, Cedric led his horse deeper into the shadows, calling quietly, "Everyone all right?"

Thalion gasped, "That was too close. I nearly got plucked off my horse like a field mouse." The mage's face was ashen, but a spark of relief lit his eyes.

Elara carefully patted her mount's flank, voice shaky. "The birds can't follow us in here. We should set up camp. They might linger outside for hours, hoping we come out. Better to wait."

Cedric nodded. "Agreed. We'll rest here until morning. With luck, they'll lose interest or be preoccupied by other prey. The pass is still a half day's ride away."

A thunderous screech from outside the cave reminded them how close they'd come to death. The travelers found a wider chamber within, out of immediate view from the entrance. The ceiling soared overhead, and a few stalactites glimmered faintly in the gloom. An underground stream trickled along one wall, providing water for the horses.

Mira rubbed her arms, trying to settle her nerves. "We faced a Hydra, a Gorgon, now thunderbirds... At least we're still breathing."

Thalion mustered a weary grin. "And we have to top it all off with a Cyclops, apparently."

Elara offered a reassuring pat on Mira's shoulder. "One trial at a time," she said gently.

Thus, with the thunderbirds' shrieks gradually receding outside, the companions prepared to pass the night in cautious vigil within the Land of Giants' caverns.

Deep in the cave, the companions assembled a small fire using dry kindling from their packs. The flickering light danced across stone walls, revealing layers of mineral deposits. Despite the presence of a narrow stream trickling at the rear, the environment felt surprisingly comfortable—cool but not frigid. Outside, the occasional screech or beating of colossal wings served as a menacing reminder.

They sat in a semicircle: Cedric, Elara, Thalion, and Mira. The horses stood tethered further back, chomping at oats. Tension still coiled in every muscle, but relief from the near misses set a faint sense of camaraderie over them. After a meal of dried fruit and salted jerky, they turned their thoughts to the next leg of the journey.

Mira leaned her staff against a rock, massaging her calf gingerly. "The pass to the Labyrinthian Mountains is rumored to be guarded by a Cyclops, right? The inn's rumor said it's the only direct route. Do we have any plan beyond hoping we can slip by?"

Elara's gaze flicked across the group. "Cyclopes are massive, but not always mindlessly hostile. Some are cunning, others easily provoked. The question is whether this one's actively blocking the path, or merely living there."

Cedric sighed. "Given our luck, it's likely a proud sentinel. The travelers called it the Gatekeeper of the Land of Giants. Must be used to challenging anyone who tries to pass. We might have to fight—unless we can reason with it or strike a bargain."

Thalion folded his arms, expression pensive. "Reason might be possible if it's less savage than these thunderbirds and Gorgons. But if it's fully corrupted by the Nexus... or simply territorial... we'll have no choice but to defeat it. Another epic battle."

Mira frowned. "Between the Hydra, Gorgon, and thunderbirds, I'd prefer a day without lethal confrontation. But if the only way to the mountains is through the Cyclops, so be it. We can't turn back. We need that Amulet of Divine Light to complete our quest."

Elara reached for her pack, producing a tattered map that combined local rumors with older Stonehavenn charts. She spread it on the cave floor, pointing to a rough depiction of the northern range. "Here," she said, indicating a narrow corridor in the mountains. "That's where we expect the pass to be. The question is, can we approach it in a stealthy manner, or must we go head-on?"

Cedric rubbed his chin. "Cyclops or not, it has only one eye. Illusions might help. Thalion or Mira could craft illusions to distract or mislead it, giving us an opening to slip by. Alternatively, if it demands single combat, maybe we can outsmart it."

The group nodded at the possibilities. Yet each idea held risk: illusions might fail if the Cyclops boasted keen senses or was used to trickery. Negotiation could falter if the Cyclops craved battle. A direct fight might sap their strength before climbing the treacherous mountains. The only certainty was that the pass was non-negotiable, if they wanted to reach the relic quickly.

Thalion passed a hand over his bruised ribs, wincing. "We'll see what tomorrow brings. If the thunderbirds remain outside, we'll have to slip away at first light. We can't ride in the open during daylight if they're circling. They'll spot us. We might need darkness to cross more safely."

Cedric considered the risk. "Traveling in darkness could help us avoid the birds, but hamper our approach to the Cyclops. Let's see if the thunderbirds are gone by dawn. If they remain, we move under cover of twilight. We can't just idle."

Elara brushed dust from her greaves. "Agreed. Now, let's rotate watch shifts. The thunderbirds could roost outside, or some other monster might wander in. We can't let our guard down."

Mira volunteered for a later watch, wanting time to rest her leg. Elara took first watch, and Thalion offered to join, though Cedric insisted on at least part of the shift to keep her company. Meanwhile, a sense of anxious excitement flickered among them: after so many trials, what may be one of the final relics seemed near. If the Land of Giants was the last barrier, they'd press on. No monstrous bull, thunderbird, or Cyclops would stand between them and the next crucial step toward banishing the Shadow Nexus.

Hours passed in the cave. The night outside gradually darkened to inky black. Occasional screeches from distant thunderbirds echoed, though they grew less frequent as time wore on. Likely the giant raptors had soared elsewhere, searching for easy prey. Inside, the group took turns dozing fitfully on bedrolls. The glow of the campfire dimmed to embers.

During the second watch, Thalion and Mira found themselves side by side near the cave entrance. The horse reins were looped around a jutting stalagmite, and they dozed with pinned ears, occasionally rustling at the faint outside noises. A swirl of moonlit air drifted in from the entrance, carrying a slight chill.

Mira fiddled absently with the Manticore gem affixed to her staff, the star-flecked swirl reflecting flickers of silver from the moonlight. Thalion gave her a sidelong glance. "How's the leg holding up?" he asked softly, mindful not to rouse the others.

"Better each day," she replied, rotating her ankle. She looked at him, expression turned serious. "I can't stop thinking of how close that thunderbird came to snatching you."

Thalion let out a short, rueful laugh. "Yes, well… I've never been so grateful for illusions and good horse reflexes. We can't keep flirting with death like this."

She nodded, quiet for a moment. "I'm also worried about what Harrow said. The void essence. Sometimes, when I cast illusions now, I feel a… dark twinge. Like an aftertaste in my magic." She exhaled shakily. "I'm trying to ignore it, but it lingers."

Concern etched Thalion's lined face. "If it grows, or if you sense any malevolent force stirring inside you, tell us immediately. We'll find a way to purify it—maybe with the relic we seek, or with a grand cleric's help."

Mira looked at the staff in her hands, features lit by faint moonlight. "I will. Thank you, Thalion."

They lapsed into companionable silence, the crackle of low-burning embers the only sound. Outside, a coyote-like howl rose and fell, a lonely note in the giant domain. The two mages kept vigil, each immersed in private thoughts of looming battles, monstrous guardians, and the far greater war against the Shadow Nexus.

Eventually, they roused Cedric for the next watch. The night slipped by uneventfully afterward, save for an occasional distant roar or screech that pricked the group's nerves. In the darkest hours, the thunderbirds seemed to have vanished. Whether that was a respite or the calm before another storm, no one could say.

Dawn tinted the cave mouth in soft pink and orange. Exhausted though they were, the companions woke with renewed determination. Horses were fed and saddled, weapons cleaned and readied. Elara checked the faint lines on Mira's leg, relieved to see no sign of further infection. Cedric scouted the cave entrance: the sky was clear, no thunderbirds in immediate sight.

"Well, we might have outrun the birds," he said, turning back. "Time to ride."

They emerged onto the plain under a vast, pale-blue morning sky. A gentle breeze ruffled the grasses; of the monstrous eagles, no sign. In the distance, the jagged form of a mountain range rose like a fortress wall, shadowed slopes hinting at hidden valleys. The rumored pass—Cyclops territory—awaited somewhere along those stony ridges.

They rode at a brisk pace, covering ground while the day was young. The horses, though tense from the prior day's ambushes, responded well to the group's careful guidance. Occasionally, a faint rumbling in the distance reminded them that giant creatures still roamed. Yet no immediate threat surfaced.

By late morning, the landscape changed. Boulders and rocky pillars jutted from the earth, some shaped by centuries of wind and rain. The group halted near a steep, winding slope that ascended toward a cliff face. Between two towering stone monoliths, a narrow gorge beckoned—likely the pass leading into the Labyrinthian Mountains.

Elara pressed a hand to her shield, gaze scanning the rocky outcrops. "If I were a Cyclops, that's where I'd stand guard—some vantage point in that gorge. Perfect spot to see intruders."

Thalion eyed the path, frowning. "We can't scale the mountains any other way; those cliffs look impassable. If the Cyclops is indeed the 'Gatekeeper,' we might have to confront it directly."

Mira closed her eyes briefly, steadying her nerves. "We've come this far. Let's see if it'll listen to reason. If not—" She hefted her staff. "We'll do what must be done."

Cedric nodded, tightening his grip on his reins. "We approach carefully. Illusions at the ready. Let's try parley first, see if it's more than a mindless brute."

With that, they urged their horses onward. Stone towers loomed on either side, the gorge narrowing with each yard. Shadows deepened, the temperature dropping in the gloom cast by steep cliff walls. A sense of foreboding sank in. The land felt ancient, scarred by eons of tectonic might—and the footfalls of giants.

An echoing growl reverberated across the rocks. The travelers exchanged wary glances. Up ahead, half-veiled by a protruding ledge, a colossal silhouette rose. Towering at least fifteen feet in height, the creature had a broad, muscular frame with limbs as thick as tree trunks. One massive eye dominated its face, glinting with savage intelligence. Ragged hair tumbled over its shoulders, and a patchwork of hide garments clung to its torso. In one giant hand, it gripped a rough-hewn club the size of a small tree trunk.

The Cyclops.

It stood like a living statue, gazing down at them with that singular, unblinking orb. A rumble akin to a low thunder built in its throat.

Cedric stopped his horse, heart thudding. He raised a hand in what he hoped was a universal gesture of peace. "Mighty Cyclops," he called, voice steady. "We're travelers seeking passage through this gorge to the Labyrinthian Mountains. We mean no harm. Will you let us pass?"

For a moment, the Cyclops simply stared, chest rising and falling like bellows. Then it snarled, baring yellowed teeth. The behemoth's single eye flashed with a feral gleam. Its lips curled into something that might have been a sneer or a grin. Slowly, it lifted the club, pointing it at the group like an accusation.

Elara's knuckles whitened on her shield. "Doesn't look welcoming," she whispered.

In a booming voice that made the stones vibrate, the Cyclops spoke in broken Stonehavenn. **"No pass. This land... MINE. You... leave."** It pounded its chest with a fist, the blow echoing like a drum.

Thalion tried reason. "We only need to cross the mountains to retrieve an artifact that can save our kingdom from a great evil. We won't stay—just let us through."

The Cyclops roared, stepping forward. The impact of its foot shook gravel loose from the canyon walls. "**You bring more war.**" It thrust a finger at them. "**I see men... kill beasts. Giants no trust men.**" The single eye glowed with fury. "**You... LEAVE. Or I CRUSH.**"

Cedric tensed. They had indeed slain a giant Gorgon, though in self-defense, and the thunderbirds might be considered giant creatures as well. Word or scent of that might have reached the Cyclops, fueling its hostility. The behemoth brandished the club. There was no sign of reason in that glare.

Elara swallowed. "We don't want to fight you, but we can't turn back. Please—"

The Cyclops let out a savage bellow, the meaning clear: negotiations ended. It stomped closer, swinging the club in a slow arc, daring them to stand ground. Rocks tumbled from overhead ledges. The horses whinnied in alarm.

Mira's eyes darted to Cedric. "No choice, is there?" she murmured, fear lacing her tone.

He gave a grim nod, drawing his sword. "We do what we must."

Thus, they prepared for the final confrontation in the Land of Giants—one last monstrous guardian blocking their path to the Labyrinthian Mountains.

Just as the Cyclops roared, the group realized full dark was close at hand. The gathering gloom made the gorge even more perilous. The Cyclops glared down at them from a vantage point, but it did not immediately charge. Perhaps it was content to intimidate them, or perhaps the night's approach dulled its aggression.

"It's nearly dusk," Thalion said under his breath. "If it attacks in these shadows, we'll be at a disadvantage."

Elara gritted her teeth. "Better we not engage in pitch darkness. The monster's likely adapted to cave life and nighttime hunts. We'd do well to retreat for now, find a hidden cave or outcropping to camp in, then face it at dawn."

Cedric studied the looming figure, who now simply watched them with menacing intent. "Agreed. We can't fight effectively in these conditions. Let's back off, slowly, and find shelter."

Carefully, the party reversed course, horses stepping nervously. The Cyclops remained on its ledge, brandishing the club but not pursuing. Likely it assumed they were retreating from its domain. By the time the travelers found a small side tunnel branching off the gorge, the sun's last rays had vanished. They crept inside, lighting torches to reveal a modest cavity. Not as large as the earlier cave, but enough to hide them from the Cyclops's vantage.

There, they built a small fire, bedding down in cautious hush. Outside, the night pressed close, the distant roar of the Cyclops occasionally echoing off canyon walls. A sense of tension weighed heavily. They'd faced monstrous foes, but a Cyclops was something else—a giant of cunning intelligence and unstoppable might.

As the flames crackled, the four friends formed a huddle. Maps lay scattered on a flat rock, and each took turns suggesting strategies. Thalion proposed illusions to lead the Cyclops astray, but Mira, still mindful of her healing leg, worried illusions alone might not fool a creature with heightened instincts. Cedric favored a direct approach: draw the Cyclops out, exploit its single eye. Elara suggested parley again, but the Cyclops's hostility might be unshakable.

In the end, they settled on a compromise: approach at first light, attempt illusions to divert the Cyclops, and if it refused to yield, strike fast at any vulnerable point. Thalion's magic could conjure decoy shapes to confuse it. Meanwhile, Mira would launch chilling or arcane blasts. Cedric and Elara would press the frontal assault—Elara's shield might block the club long enough for Cedric to blind or wound the Cyclops's eye.

"That's the best plan we have," Cedric murmured, eyes flicking to the dancing flame. "Let's pray it's enough."

Mira sighed, leaning against the cave wall. "At least we'll face it rested," she said softly.

Elara nodded. "Get some sleep, all of you. At dawn, we do what must be done."

Thus, amid the flickering shadows, they prepared for what was likely their final obstacle in the Land of Giants. The Cyclops's roars echoed in their dreams, a challenge and a warning, as the night wore on. Tomorrow would decide their fate: success leading them onward to the Labyrinthian Mountains, or defeat at the hands of a towering foe. Whatever came, they would face it together.

20

THE DEADLY PASSAGE

arm, golden light seeped into the narrow cave where Sir Cedric, Lady Elara, Thalion, and Mira had taken shelter. The shadows of dawn stretched across the stony walls, accompanied by a gentle draft that carried the faint smell of dewy grass and distant pine. After a tense and restless night—haunted by the roars of the Cyclops echoing in the canyon—the companions stirred from their makeshift beds, silent but determined.

Mira rubbed her eyes, yawning softly. Though fully cured of her venomous wound, she still felt the weight of the previous days' tribulations press on her shoulders. Elara offered her a hand, helping her stand. Cedric and Thalion worked quietly to bank the remnants of their tiny campfire, then checked the horses tethered near the cave's rear. The animals stirred anxiously, as if sensing the presence of a towering threat somewhere beyond the gloom.

Their eyes met, and each knew the unspoken truth: The Cyclops barred the sole, narrow passage into the Labyrinthian Mountains. If they could not bypass the giant, their entire quest to retrieve the last relic—the **Amulet Channeled by Divine Light**—would grind to a halt. More critically, so would Stonehaven's chance of defeating the Shadow Nexus.

Cedric, armor glinting in the early sun, clapped Thalion on the shoulder. "Well, old friend, how's the bruising?" he asked, voice low. Thalion had been thrown from his horse by the giant bull Gorgon in days past.

The mage shrugged, pressing a hand to his side. "Tender, but manageable," he murmured. "I've known worse. And after last night's partial rest, I'm ready as I'll ever be."

Mira stood near Elara, the morning glow revealing a flicker of anxiety in her eyes. "I keep remembering the Cyclops's roar," she admitted, recalling the thunderous challenge they had heard from the next canyon over. "If that monster truly stands nearly fifteen feet tall while *sitting*, I can't imagine how imposing it'll be when it rises to full height."

Elara, adjusting the straps on her shield, offered a reassuring nod. "We won't fight it if we can avoid it. We survived Gorgons and thunderbirds, but a Cyclops of that scale might be beyond us—especially if it's prepared to roll boulders onto us from above."

A heavy pause settled on the group. Each remembered seeing from afar how the Cyclops had neatly arranged boulders the size of cows in towering piles behind its perch. Clearly, it was prepared to hurl these missiles at intruders. Even a single boulder, crashing from those heights, could flatten them or their horses in an instant. Their only hope lay in subterfuge.

Cedric squared his shoulders, expression firm. "We agreed last night: we'll attempt to sneak past. A direct confrontation would be suicide. Let's finalize the plan."

No one disagreed. Hushed but resolute, the four heroes strode out of the cave and mounted their horses. Beyond the narrow canyon, the final pass leading to the Labyrinthian Mountains beckoned, shadowed by towering rock walls. The day was just beginning, the sun still low enough that elongated shadows might grant them a degree of cover. But it also meant the Cyclops would likely be fresh and alert—if indeed it kept a sentinel's watch.

They nudged their horses forward, hearts pounding in time with the distant rumble of wind through the canyons. Each was acutely aware that a single misstep might spell disaster.

It took less than an hour's ride to reach the vantage point where the Cyclops had appeared the previous day. The terrain rose in layered stone ledges, forming a makeshift amphitheater that overlooked a chokepoint in the cliffs. The path beyond, if the rumors were correct, twisted up and over the first ridge of the Labyrinthian Mountains— impossible to ascend without passing beneath the Cyclops's perch.

In the slanted light of morning, the four companions dared to peek from behind a tall boulder. There, in the distance, the massive figure of the Cyclops came into view. Even from hundreds of yards away, its bulk was unmistakable: a hulking humanoid shape with a single, huge eye set in a broad, weathered face. Tufts of coarse hair framed its skull, and enormous hands rested on thick knees. The creature sat on a narrow ledge carved into the rock wall, leaning back against a jagged stone formation. Spread out behind it were piles of boulders—each as large as a small cart or a cow, indeed. They lay in neat rows, as though carefully organized for easy rolling or hurling at unfortunate trespassers. Additionally, his club with the circumference of a good-sized tree lay beside him on the ledge.

A slow, rumbling exhalation reverberated across the canyon, suggesting the Cyclops was awake. Its single eye scanned the canyon below. The angle from which the heroes watched the giant gave them some measure of concealment, but that single watchful eye was terrifying in its intensity. If it spotted any movement on the path, it could lob a boulder with lethal precision.

Elara swallowed, lowering her voice to a whisper. "He's even bigger up close. Gods help us if we're found."

Cedric nodded. "We'll stick to the plan. We use the canyon's natural shadows and keep as low as possible. No speaking. Thalion and Mira, you both stand ready with illusions in case the Cyclops turns our way. We must keep it from noticing us."

Thalion let out a slow breath. "We'll need the horses to remain calm. Any sudden neigh or spook could alert the giant. Let's use the calming potions we acquired from Harrow."

Mira carefully retrieved two small vials from her saddlebag. They contained a mild herbal mixture designed to soothe equine nerves. She poured half a vial into a waterskin for Cedric's horse, half for Elara's, and repeated for Thalion's and her own. "Let's hope this keeps them quiet," she said, patting her mare's flank. "If the Cyclops hears a panicked whinny, we're done."

When all preparations were complete, they silently maneuvered into single file. Cedric led, Elara and Thalion followed, and Mira took the rear, ensuring illusions could cloak them if needed. The path wound close to the canyon floor beneath the Cyclops's ledge. With every step the horses took on gravel or loose rock, the travelers tensed, fearing the slightest sound would betray them.

Despite the tension coiled in their muscles, the heroes advanced with painstaking caution. The canyon's base was partially in shade, thanks to the angle of the morning sun. Sheer rock walls towered hundreds of feet above, forming a rugged labyrinth of overhangs, shallow caves, and protruding ledges. The Cyclops perched high overhead, scanning the expanse. Every few moments, the giant exhaled a rumbling breath or shifted its weight, causing bits of stone to crumble from the ledge.

Cedric led the group along the left side of the canyon, keeping close to the walls. The horses trod on patches of gravel, but thanks to Harrow's calming potions, they did so quietly. Now and then, a stone would clink against another, sending a soft echo up the cliff. Each time, the heroes froze, hearts pounding, eyes flicking upward. The Cyclops would shift, sniff the air, but so far, had not spotted them.

When they were a quarter of the way through the canyon, Thalion summoned a subtle illusion: waves of refracted light that distorted the silhouettes of the party against the rock face. From above, it would look like vague, shimmering shapes, easily mistakable for shifting shadows or heat haze. Mira, cradling her staff, remained ready to conjure a second illusion or an ice shield if needed. The strain of silent vigilance weighed on her mind, but she steeled her resolve, remembering everything hinged on slipping past unnoticed.

Another hundred yards. Sweat beaded on Cedric's brow. He signaled a halt, noticing a slight bend in the canyon ahead—here, the path veered closer to the Cyclops's vantage, leaving a narrower margin of shade to conceal them. The giant's single eye, scanning slowly, could spot them if they made too bold a move.

Elara pressed close, whispering so faintly her voice was barely audible. "The sun's angle is shifting. If we wait too long, we'll lose the shadow."

Cedric nodded. "We go now, but slowly. Thalion, Mira—keep illusions at full strength."

Thalion closed his eyes a moment, focusing. The shimmering haze around them intensified slightly. Mira, similarly, willed the air to distort, wrapping the party in subtle camouflage. They advanced, each horse picking its steps with eerie calm. Another rumbling snort from the Cyclops drifted down from the heights. The giant turned its head, scanning the lower canyon with that watchful eye. The heroes flattened themselves against the rock, hearts hammering.

A moment later, the Cyclops let out a bored grunt and shifted away, turning to rummage among the boulders behind it. Cedric risked an exhalation. They pressed onward, the canyon's bend gradually hiding them from the giant's direct line of sight. Relief surged.

But fate had other designs.

They were nearly beyond the Cyclops's vantage—a mere fifty yards more, and they would be fully out of line of sight. Perhaps they would have made it cleanly, had not a loose stone or echo caught the Cyclops's attention. From above, they heard a startled growl, as though the giant sensed something unusual. Shuffling footsteps rattled pebbles off the edge.

Cedric motioned for the group to freeze, illusions still swirling. Mira held her breath. Thalion gripped his staff, beads of perspiration on his forehead. Elara steadied her horse's muzzle to keep it from whinnying. The canyon fell silent. Then came the scrape of something large—stone against stone—like the Cyclops adjusting its seat among the boulders.

CRACK.

A thunderous cracking sound split the air. High above, on the ledge, the Cyclops jerked around, inadvertently dislodging a massive boulder from its neat stack. Time slowed for the travelers below. They glanced upward in horror to see a colossal rock—easily the size of a bull or small cart—teeter on the edge. Then, with a grinding lurch, it toppled over.

For a heartbeat, the Cyclops appeared almost surprised by its own blunder. The giant let out a sharp grunt and reached out a hand too late to grab the boulder. The huge stone plummeted off the ledge, bounding once against the cliff face, then spinning outward.

Directly below, the four heroes and their horses saw the boulder hurtling toward them. Instinct took over.

"Move!" Cedric shouted, voice echoing as they all spurred their mounts in separate directions. The illusions vanished in the scramble, replaced by raw, panicked flight. Gravel sprayed under the horses' hooves as they bolted, guided only by the riders' terrified commands.

The boulder, spinning and falling with lethal speed, crashed onto the canyon floor not ten yards from the group.

The impact rocked the ground, sending up a shockwave of dust and shattered stone. Fragments of rock whirled like shrapnel. A thunderous boom reverberated through the canyon, momentarily deafening.

Elara's horse reared with a shriek. She clung to the saddle, shield raised to protect them from flying debris. Cedric swerved, narrowly avoiding a chunk of stone the size of a man's head. Thalion, behind a smaller boulder, pressed himself flat, arms shielding his face. Mira, staff clenched, conjured a hasty barrier of frosty air that deflected several shards, though the force still knocked her sideways in the saddle.

Dust choked the air, obscuring sight. For several seconds, the world became a cacophony of crumbling rock and thunderous echoes. When the dust began to settle, Cedric coughed, blinking away tears. He spotted Elara's silhouette, horse trembling, just a few yards away. Thalion staggered to his feet, having fallen from his horse in the confusion. Mira pressed a hand to her forehead, wincing as she assessed bruises. Miraculously, none of them looked mortally wounded.

The boulder had missed the group by a razor-thin margin. Instead, it lay wedged into a new crater in the canyon floor, steam rising from the friction of its descent. Another foot or two, and the entire party would have been crushed.

Above them, the Cyclops roared in surprise and anger. Perhaps it sensed that it had nearly pinned intruders but remained uncertain of the outcome. Dust still swirled around the ledge, and the giant peered over the edge, searching. That single eye glowed with menace.

"Go, go!" Cedric rasped, motioning the others forward. Hiding now was useless; the illusions had dropped, and the Cyclops suspected something was down there. One more moment, and the monster might hurl another boulder—intentionally this time.

Scrambling, they mounted up—Thalion hoisting himself back onto his horse with Elara's help. Reins snapped. The group galloped down the canyon, hugging the left side, trusting the final bend would free them from the Cyclops's vantage. Another savage roar echoed behind them. Rocks tumbled. But no second boulder soared after them yet.

The canyon walls funneled them into a twisting corridor of stone. Hoofbeats thundered across the ground, hearts pounding with adrenaline. Dust from the fallen boulder still drifted in the wind, shimmering in stray beams of sunlight. Overhead, they heard the Cyclops's furious snarls. It was too large to give immediate pursuit, but if it found a path downward, the heroes knew they might still face mortal danger.

At last, they rounded the final bend. Beyond lay a more open pass—a winding trail that ascended into the lower slopes of the Labyrinthian Mountains. The air here felt crisper, the elevation more pronounced. Cedric drew his horse to a stop, half turning in the saddle, ensuring the others caught up. Mira arrived next, chest heaving, staff clutched close. Elara and Thalion followed, each scanning the rocky spires overhead for signs of pursuit.

No boulders rained down. The Cyclops's roars had faded to distant echoes. After a tense pause, the group realized the giant had not found a route to chase them.

Possibly it was stuck on its ledge, uncertain how to navigate the canyon's twists.

Collapsing in relief, Cedric slid off his horse. Thalion did the same, leaning heavily on his staff for support. They exchanged disbelieving stares. "We... made it?" Elara whispered, voice trembling between awe and exhaustion.

Mira exhaled shakily. "We did. That boulder nearly ended us, but we're through." She glanced back, suppressing a shudder at the thought of the Cyclops accidentally dealing them a lethal blow with a single slip of the wrist.

Cedric wiped sweat from his brow, eyes bright with gratitude. "We owe a piece of luck or fate. I can't believe that stone missed us." He paused, gazing up at the canyon walls. "If the Cyclops were truly aiming, we might not have been so lucky."

Elara tapped her shield, taking a moment to process their survival. "A single misstep, and we'd be flattened." She shook her head. "Let's not linger. The pass might still be within range if the Cyclops finds a vantage higher up."

Collecting themselves, the heroes remounted. Their horses, though rattled, obeyed. It was time to push onward—upward—into the Labyrinthian Mountains. The **Amulet Channeled by Divine Light**, supposedly lay hidden in an ancient temple or crypt somewhere in these peaks. Now that they had slipped past the monstrous guardian, the path opened before them.

But the journey was far from over.

They rode slowly up the winding trail, the canyon behind them shrinking into the distance. Each turn offered glimpses of distant valleys, shadowed canyons, and the faint line of the path they had just navigated. The Cyclops's ledge was no longer visible, hidden behind jagged outcrops. Now the companions could observe the broader panorama of mountains: soaring cliffs crowned by snow, ridges draped in pine forests, and high above, peaks that pierced the sky.

For a time, no one spoke. Their minds lingered on the near miss, hearts still pounding from the rush of fear and relief. Finally, Thalion broke the silence, voice echoing in the crisp air. "We faced a Hydra, a Gorgon, thunderbirds... and now a Cyclops. This land tests us at every turn."

Mira's gaze swept across the mountains. "Each test we pass seems to remind us how fragile life is. Yet we keep going, because we must."

Cedric guided his horse around a crumbling ledge. "The relic awaits," he said with quiet conviction. "And if we're to end the Shadow Nexus's threat, we can't fail now."

Elara nodded in solemn agreement. "I'd rather not think about how close we came to losing everything. But the gods favored us this day. Let's push on, find a safe place to camp higher up, and recover."

As they ascended, the temperature dropped. The sun climbed overhead, casting sharp shadows on the switchback path. Occasional bird calls echoed from the forested slopes, though none sounded like the thunderbirds' fierce shrieks. Once, they glimpsed a solitary eagle far above, a normal raptor. Relief washed over them at the mundane sight.

With each step, the Labyrinthian Mountains loomed closer. The party's thoughts turned to the next leg of their quest: locating the **Amulet of Divine Light**. Rumors suggested it might lie within a hidden temple or an old labyrinth carved into the mountains' core. None of them knew the precise location. They might have to search every ancient ruin, follow cryptic clues, or rely on local legend. But at least they had overcome the deadliest barrier to entry.

By late afternoon, they found a natural terrace halfway up a mountainside. A shallow stream trickled from a rocky outcrop, forming a small pool among moss-covered stones. Pine trees clustered here, offering shelter from biting winds. With the memory of the day's close call lingering, the heroes opted to make camp early, to gather strength for the next stage.

They dismounted, letting the horses drink at the pool's edge. Cedric tested the water's temperature, splashing his face. The chill shock woke him fully from the lingering daze of near-death. Elara and Thalion worked together to gather dry branches for a fire, while Mira tested her leg. Though the Hydra bite was healed, the day's tension had left her muscles stiff.

Soon, a small campfire crackled, the scent of burning pine drifting on the breeze. Cedric doled out the last of their dried rations, quietly resolving to forage or hunt in the days ahead. Elara took a seat on a broad rock, shield resting at her side, offering a prayer of thanks for their deliverance from the Cyclops's accidental boulder strike. Thalion scribbled notes in a battered journal, recording details of the Land of Giants, the monstrous thunderbirds, and the Cyclops's domain.

Mira stood on the edge of the terrace, gazing over the sweeping valleys below. From here, she could see the canyon that had nearly become their tomb. The sun hung low, bathing the mountains in red-orange hues. "So many obstacles," she murmured to herself. "But we keep going."

Elara joined her, resting a hand on Mira's shoulder. "We have to," the paladin said softly. "We've come this far. The fate of Stonehaven hinges on the relic and the Song of Severance. I won't let my kingdom fall to shadows."

Mira offered a small, tired smile. "Nor will I. Let's hope we find that amulet soon."

They turned back to the camp as dusk settled. Thalion closed his journal, rising to stir the fire. Cedric had already laid out bedrolls, while the horses grazed on sparse patches of grass near the pines. The wind hissed among the branches, a lullaby of sorts, as the group prepared for another night in precarious territory.

Night fell swiftly in the heights, stars winking into view above the jagged silhouettes of mountain peaks. A crescent moon emerged, casting silver light across the rocky slopes. Though exhaustion weighed on them, each companion took a turn standing watch—mindful that other creatures might dwell here, unseen.

During Mira's shift, she found herself gazing into the fire, recollections of the boulder's near impact replaying in her mind. If their illusions had been fractionally weaker, or if they had ridden a bit slower, the Cyclops's slip might have killed them all. She let out a shuddering sigh, feeling anew the fragility of their quest.

But she also felt gratitude—gratitude for her friends who fought by her side, for the strange luck that had saved them. She recalled Harrow's words about possible traces of void essence in her system, but tonight, she sensed only relief. If any darkness lurked within, it was overshadowed by the bond she shared with Elara, Thalion, and Cedric. She prayed that bond would be enough to carry them through the final challenges.

At dawn, they rose to clear skies. The faint chill of the high elevation bit at their cheeks, but also invigorated them. Over a sparse breakfast, they decided to push deeper into the mountains, forging a path that would hopefully reveal ancient ruins or a trail leading to the rumored hidden temple. The memory of the Cyclops lingered like a bruise on their minds, but they took solace in having slipped past without direct battle.

Before breaking camp, Cedric made a final check of their supplies. Food was dwindling, but there were enough streams and possible wild game along the way to keep them fed for a short while. They still had healing potions from Harrow, though not an unlimited supply. The relics in their possession—the Wyvern scale, Behemoth disc, and Pearl of Tides—remained stowed carefully, each humming with arcane resonance. Now they hoped to find the **Amulet of Divine Light**—the piece that was rumored to be located somewhere within the Labrynthian Mountains.

Elara adjusted her shield on her back, turning to the horizon. "We can't be far now," she said with quiet optimism. "The Labyrinthian Mountains are said to hold hidden labyrinths, old cathedrals carved into the rock. Perhaps we'll find a local guide or runes that point us in the right direction."

Thalion frowned thoughtfully, scanning distant spires of rock. "If memory serves, certain runic scripts might appear near cave mouths or carved pillars. Let's keep watch for any inscriptions. Failing that, we may rely on arcane detection spells to sense the relic's divine aura."

Mira nodded. "We proceed carefully, as always." She mounted her horse, patting its mane. Despite the calamities of thunderbirds and Cyclops, the creature remained surprisingly calm—evidence, perhaps, of the herbal potions and the trust built over weeks of traveling together.

Cedric took the lead once more, guiding them along a faint mountain trail that clung to the slopes. Pine trees dotted the path, their needles carpeting the ground in a soft hush. The wind carried the scent of resin and distant snow. As they rode, each found themselves glancing back at the canyon's direction, remembering the Cyclops perched with its lethal boulders. The terror of that near-crushing weighed on them like an unspoken vow never to rely on luck alone again.

But even near-misses can kindle new determination: they had outmaneuvered a foe many times their size through cunning, stealth, and cooperation. In the battles ahead—where illusions, valor, and faith would again be tested—the lesson would not be forgotten. If a single Cyclops could block an entire pass, what awaited them deeper into these mountains? No one knew, but the day's success reminded them that unity could triumph where raw force might fail.

Through perseverance, stealth, and a touch of fortune, the party slipped under the Cyclops's nose—almost literally—escaping certain doom when the giant inadvertently dislodged a massive boulder. The cliff-shaking impact served as a reminder of how precarious their quest was. One slip, one misread moment, and the heroes might have been crushed to dust against the canyon floor.

Yet they lived. They had navigated the Land of Giants, evading thunderbirds, outwitting a bull Gorgon, and surviving the Cyclops's domain. Standing now at the threshold of the Labyrinthian Mountains, they shared a sense of solemn triumph. Behind them lay a trail of monstrous foes and near-death scrapes. Before them lay uncharted peaks, cryptic ruins, and the rumored resting place of the next artifact.

As the group pressed higher into the winding paths, the sun rose overhead, bathing the mountains in shifting ribbons of light and shadow. With hearts resolute, they embraced the next phase of their journey—each step carrying them closer to the **Amulet Channeled by Divine Light**, and one step nearer to saving Stonehaven from the encroaching darkness of the Shadow Nexus.

21

THE LABRYNTHIAN MOUNTAINS

A biting wind whipped through the high mountain pass as Sir Cedric, Lady Elara, Thalion, and Mira crested the last switchback above the Cyclops's domain. Though they had narrowly evaded death beneath that colossal guardian's boulder, their relief soon turned to awe and trepidation: stretching northward rose the **Labyrinthian Mountains**, an unending sea of jagged peaks and hidden valleys. The range was so vast—and so complex—that even seasoned adventurers like them could only marvel at its immensity. Sheer cliffs, twisting passes, and pinnacles crowned in eternal snow gave the place an almost otherworldly grandeur.

Standing on a small outcrop, the companions took in the sight. Far above, wisps of cloud clung to a single massive peak, the summit lost to swirling gray mist. Sunlight grazed the upper slopes in shifting beams, highlighting ancient stone ridges and glacial shelves. Ever so faintly, they could see what appeared to be a trail winding up the mountainside, leading into the very clouds. A hush fell over them as they sensed an unspoken pull—some ancient aura that tugged at their hearts. After all, they had come here to find the next relic: the **Amulet of Divine Light**.

Thalion flipped open his field journal, riffling through notes. "According to the Sage Elder's tips from the Coastal

Temples," he murmured, "a golden dragon roams these heights, possibly near that cloud-shrouded summit. Or at least, that's the rumor."

Cedric rubbed the scar on his chin. "We've met plenty of monstrous foes, but a dragon... that's on another level. And if it's truly golden and gargantuan, we'd best be prepared. Dragons are legendary for guarding priceless treasures."

Elara adjusted the phoenix sigil on her shield, her eyes fixed on the looming peak. "We need that treasure. The sages believed the **Amulet of Divine Light** rests in the dragon's hoard, or is worn by the beast itself. Without it, banishing the Shadow Nexus remains impossible."

Mira brushed a few stray locks of hair from her face. "Just the thought of a golden dragon of unmatched size..." She sighed, half excited, half apprehensive. "Let's hope we find a way to retrieve the relic without getting scorched to ash."

The group exchanged determined nods. Then, with horses in tow, they ventured deeper into the Labyrinthian Mountains. The air grew thinner, crisp with an alpine chill. Pines gave way to hardy shrubs that clung to crags. Each step upward felt like entering a grand puzzle of switchbacks and hidden canyons, an endless labyrinth in stone. And somewhere in that maze, a giant golden dragon soared between clouds, standing between them and the next piece needed to oppose the Shadow Nexus.

Continuing onward, they followed a faint trail etched into the mountainside, occasionally reinforced with old stones or rotting planks from an era long past. The path wound precariously close to steep drops, where scree and gravel threatened to slip under the horses' hooves. Cedric dismounted at the worst sections, guiding his mare by the bridle, offering calm reassurance. The others followed suit. Twice, Thalion conjured illusions to mask treacherous ledges, preventing the horses from spooking at dizzying heights.

Midday found them at a narrow plateau dotted with stunted conifers. The wind carried the tang of distant storms. A fine drizzle misted the air, turning the trail slick. Looking up, they spied the far-off silhouette of the mountain's crown, half-buried in swirling clouds.

Elara paused to catch her breath and scanned the sky. "If a golden dragon is up there, we should see signs soon enough—scorched rock, abandoned bones, or at least unusual claw marks."

Mira pointed to a ragged tree trunk. Deep gouges raked the bark, as though from massive talons. "We might already be seeing them," she remarked, voice hushed. "Whatever did that was no ordinary bird of prey."

Cedric's gaze swept the slopes. "We must be close."

Just then, an echoing roar rolled from somewhere high above—an immense, bone-rattling sound that reverberated off the stone and made the horses whinny in fear. The travelers froze. Though they'd heard plenty of monstrous howls, screeches, and roars on their journey, this was something altogether different: deeper, more resonant, like thunder trapped in a beast's throat. There was only one likely source: **the golden dragon** they had come to find.

Thalion exchanged an uneasy look with Cedric. "We've come this far," he said softly. "No turning back now."

Gathering their courage, they continued up the path. The drizzle thickened to a cold drizzle, merging with thin mountain fog. Visibility dropped to a few dozen yards. Yet that roiling, thunderous roar sounded again, closer this time, guiding them forward as though the dragon itself was calling them out.

Late afternoon light bled through the cloud cover, painting the mountaintop in eerie half-gloom. Rounding a final bend, they emerged onto a broad, windswept ledge—a natural plateau from which the summit soared skyward. Jagged crags flanked the plateau, while swirls of low-lying cloud drifted at the edges like ghostly curtains.

Then, from that haze, it emerged: a colossal shape, gliding effortlessly on massive wings. Scales glinted **golden** in the dim light, each glimmer a reflection of unimaginable power. A ridged neck and powerful limbs ended in razor-sharp talons, each large enough to impale an armored knight. Spiraling horns arched back from a majestic head crowned by fin-like spines. There was something regal, almost sacred, in the creature's silhouette. Its flight exuded a leisurely confidence, as though it believed no foe could challenge it in these heights.

Mira's breath caught in her throat. "By the Light," she murmured. "It's... enormous."

Elara's hand tightened on her shield. "Bigger than the Hydra, bigger than any creature we've faced."

The golden dragon circled overhead, wings generating strong downdrafts that scattered loose gravel. Then it landed with a thunderous impact near the plateau's far side, talons gouging deep furrows in the stone. Its great head swung toward the party, that impossible single reptilian gaze pinning them. A growl, like distant thunder, rumbled from the dragon's throat. Wisps of smoke curled from its nostrils.

Cedric carefully dismounted and raised his free hand in a gesture of cautious respect. "Mighty dragon," he called, voice echoing across the plateau. "We come seeking an artifact of great importance—an amulet said to hold the Divine Light. We do not wish to desecrate your domain."

The dragon's eyes narrowed, a luminous gold flickering within. It lifted a clawed hand, revealing, clasped around one talon, a **shimmering chain** from which dangled an ornate pendant. Even at a distance, the travelers recognized its radiance: **The Amulet of Divine Light.**

A rumbling voice, low and resonant as shifting tectonic plates, reverberated from the dragon's maw. "You dare approach me... for **this**?" It lifted the chain slightly, showing it off. "A trifling mortal relic unworthy of my gold. Yet it shines with holy power. And you seek it, do you not?"

Elara stepped forward, shield lowered but gaze steady. "Yes, we seek it to save Stonehaven from an ancient evil. Grant us the amulet, and we'll leave your domain in peace."

A hiss parted the dragon's jaws. "I have little reason to entrust such power to you. Men have lied, stolen, slaughtered for far less. This realm is mine. Prove your worth—or be consumed by my flames."

Thalion raised a hand in supplication. "Mighty one, we have no desire for conflict. Please—"

But the dragon lashed its tail, sending a chunk of boulder tumbling off the ledge. Wings flared, posture shifting into lethal poise. **"Show me your convictions. Or die."**

There was no time to negotiate further. A swirl of golden scales and outstretched claws signaled the start of a fearsome confrontation.

The dragon lunged, inhaling sharply. The party recognized the telltale sign of a dragon's breath weapon. "Scatter!" Cedric shouted.

A column of searing white-gold flame erupted from the creature's maw. The scorching blast carved a molten path across the ledge, forcing the heroes to dive aside. Elara raised her shield, bracing behind it as the fiery surge battered her defenses, the edges of her cloak curling in the heat. Thalion dropped behind a broken slab of rock, illusions swirling around him to mask his form. Mira summoned a gale of frost-laced wind to counter the flames at her flank, while Cedric rolled behind a jagged outcrop, heart pounding.

The golden dragon roared, filling the plateau with deafening thunder. Sunbeams pierced the thin clouds overhead, glinting on the creature's majestic form as it rose on hind legs. Claws scrabbled at the stone, leaving gouges. Each movement exuded raw might. Then the dragon's head snapped toward Elara, the nearest target. "You, with the shield of dawn's crest," it rumbled. "I taste your faith. Let's see if it withstands my fury!"

Elara grit her teeth. With a silent prayer, she charged forward, shield raised high. The dragon's front claws lashed out, scraping her shield with a reverberating clang that rattled her arm to the bone. She stabbed upward with her sword, but the blade glanced off the dragon's golden scales, leaving only a faint scratch. Sparks danced, failing to penetrate. The dragon swiped again, nearly knocking Elara off her feet.

From behind, Cedric dashed in, runic sword glowing. He aimed for a joint between the massive wing and torso. His strike landed, drawing a shallow line of golden blood that sizzled on the blade. The dragon snarled in pain, spinning to face him. A tail whip forced Cedric to hurl himself backward, narrowly evading a fatal blow.

Thalion sprang from cover, staff crackling with arcane energy. "Mira, now!" he called. The pair unleashed a combined assault: illusions of swirling serpents coiling around the dragon's flanks, combined with a concentrated blast of ice-lances from Mira's staff. The serpents bit into the dragon's peripheral vision, while the ice-lances impacted the beast's shoulder, forming a thin crust of frost. The dragon roared, snapping at the illusions in confusion.

Elara seized that moment. She pressed in, channeling her divine aura into her sword for a powerful overhead slash aimed at a gap in the chest scales. A burst of radiant light flared. The dragon howled, stumbling back a step. Gold scale plates parted slightly, revealing a vulnerable seam. Elara's sword found purchase, drawing a hot spurt of blood. Yet the wound, while real, wasn't deep enough to cripple.

The dragon's eyes blazed. Smoke and steam poured from its jaws, and the creature unleashed another torrent of flame, forcing the heroes to retreat behind boulders or shield walls. The scorching air shimmered with radiant heat, and the plateau's surface cracked under the assault. Loose rock tumbled off the mountainside.

The fight raged across the plateau, each side testing the other's limits. Though the heroes inflicted small wounds, the golden dragon showed no signs of yielding. Its leaps and powerful wingbeats caused wind gusts that threatened to blow them off the ledge. Flames licked the crags, the smell of ozone and molten rock permeating the air. The clang of steel against gold scales, the hiss of spells, and the dragon's thunderous roars echoed among the peaks.

Cedric, battered but unbroken, circled around for a vantage on the dragon's backside. He waved frantically at Elara, who stood panting behind her shield. "We have to coordinate!" he shouted over the cacophony. "Keep it distracted so Thalion or Mira can strike a decisive blow!"

Elara nodded, bracing to engage again. She rushed the dragon's flank, forcing it to pivot. The dragon spun with grace belying its massive size, lashing out. Elara blocked the blow with her shield, wincing as the impact sent shockwaves through her arm. Her knees nearly buckled, but she stood firm.

Seizing the moment, Thalion conjured swirling illusions around the dragon's head—phantom copies of Elara danced in its peripheral vision. Distracted by the illusions, the beast slashed at empty air. Mira unleashed a volley of arcane force from behind a cracked boulder, striking the dragon's side. Another roar, another spurt of golden-hued blood. The dragon's anger soared, and with a tremendous beat of its wings, it launched itself into the air, flames trailing from its jaws.

"Brace!" Cedric shouted, eyes wide as the enormous creature hovered overhead. A shower of molten sparks rained down. Clutching the chain with the amulet, the dragon roared in defiance, spitting smaller bursts of flame.

"You are persistent... but you. Will. Burn!" The final word boomed like an oncoming storm.

Circling overhead, the dragon singled out Thalion, who was weaving illusions near the edge. With a shriek, it dove, jaws wide. Thalion gasped, trying to leap aside, illusions swirling too slowly. The golden dragon's talons closed in a lethal vise. But a moment before contact, Elara lunged, driving her sword into the dragon's flank. Distracted by the pain, it missed Thalion by inches. The mage tumbled away, heart pounding.

Elara's rescue earned her the dragon's wrath. The beast spun, tail smashing into her side. She flew backward, slamming into a rocky outcrop with a cry. Her shield clattered, and she collapsed, dazed. Blood trickled from her temple. The dragon inhaled deeply, flames dancing in its throat, prepared to unleash a final immolating blast on the downed paladin.

But Cedric was already running, sword at the ready, a frantic cry in his throat.

In a single leap, Cedric hurled himself between the dragon's open jaws and Elara's prone form. He raised his shield at an angle, bracing for the inferno. Fire spewed forth, slamming into the shield and rolling around it, scorching the stone behind Cedric's boots. The heat threatened to melt steel, yet the runic inscriptions on his shield glowed fiercely, holding the flame at bay for a heart-stopping moment.

Once the flame subsided, Cedric was half-blinded by the glare, but he thrust forward, jabbing his runic sword through the dragon's parted maw. The blade slid past thick fangs, scoring a deep gash along the creature's inner jaw.

The dragon bellowed in agony, recoiling, thick droplets of golden blood sizzling as they struck the plateau.

Elara coughed, forcing herself upright despite the throbbing in her ribs. She saw the dragon reeling, stunned by Cedric's daring move. "Now, Thalion—Mira!" she rasped, staggering to her feet.

Thalion unleashed a chain of arcane lightning, focusing it at the fresh wound along the dragon's jaw. Electricity crackled, dancing across the dragon's scales, causing the beast to convulse. Mira followed with an ice-lance barrage, aiming at the damaged spots in the dragon's flank and chest. The synergy battered the creature's defenses, forcing it to stagger back, wings flapping wildly.

At last, the dragon slumped onto all fours, breathing raggedly. Shudders racked its frame, smoke curling from new wounds. The chain with the **Amulet of Divine Light** dangled precariously from a rent in its front talon, the clasp nearly broken.

Gasping for air, Elara advanced. Her shield battered, her armor blackened, she clenched her sword. The dragon's single, furious eye locked onto her. A low, rumbling growl built in its throat, as though it might attempt one more defiant stand.

She raised her sword, voice shaking but firm. "We fight not for greed, but to save our realm from a darkness older than curses. **Yield**, or perish."

The dragon roared, half in rage, half in desperation. Its wings unfurled, but battered as it was, it could not fully lift off. A shimmering bubble of arcane energy from Thalion pinned it down, illusions weaving about its battered body. Cedric rushed in, shield raised, slashing at the talon that clutched the chain. With a final snarl, the dragon's grip slackened, and the chain fell free, the amulet clinking onto the stone.

Mira, seeing her chance, conjured a vortex of frost to freeze the creature's front limb in place. "Now, Elara!" she cried, voice echoing in the swirling mists. "End this!"

Elara advanced, sword blazing with her divine aura. The golden dragon glared in defiance. "If I fall this day... let it be known I succumbed only to a righteous cause." Its voice rumbled with a strange, ancient sorrow. Lashing its tail one final time, it mustered a last sweep of flame. But battered illusions and locked limbs betrayed the beast's weakening state. Elara thrust her blade into the vulnerable gap near the dragon's throat. A burst of radiant light flashed; the dragon roared in anguished fury. Then its colossal form slumped to the side, the thunderous impact shaking the mountain.

For a moment, the world hung still. The only sounds were the party's ragged breathing, the hiss of steam rising from the dragon's wounds, and the distant howl of wind across the cliffs.

In the hush that followed, Cedric bent over Elara, supporting her as her knees threatened to buckle. She clutched her ribs, pain etched on her face, but she looked up at him and managed a ghost of a smile. The two shared a silent moment of relief and gratitude. Mira stumbled forward, staff clattering on the stone, nearly weeping from exhaustion. Thalion pressed a trembling hand to his own wounded side, the arcs of illusions finally dissipating.

They stood around the dragon's massive body. Golden scales, even dulled by blood and soot, glowed like a hoard of treasure in themselves. The creature lay still, eyes closed.

One final rasping exhale escaped its maw, then silence. This being—so regal, so ancient—had challenged them in the fiercest battle yet. They had triumphed, but the cost could be seen in every gash and bruise on their bodies.

Slowly, as if in a trance, Elara approached the fallen talon where the amulet's chain had slipped free. The **Amulet of Divine Light**—a brilliant pendant shaped like a small sunburst, etched with intricate runes—glowed softly, illuminating the smoky air. She knelt beside it, her reflection shimmering in the polished gold of the dragon's scales. With reverent hands, she lifted the chain, feeling a pulse of warm energy resonate through her.

Thalion, eyes wide, whispered, "That's it. The final relic."

Mira exhaled in awe. "We truly have it? By the Light…"

Cedric, leaning on his sword, watched as Elara carefully clasped the amulet around her neck. The pendant rested against her dented breastplate, shining with gentle brilliance. A wave of radiant warmth coursed from the relic, washing over the group like a wave of dawn. Cuts and bruises eased slightly; the burning ache in their lungs from dragonfire soothed. It was as though the amulet recognized her devotion—her unwavering faith—and responded with a taste of its divine grace.

Her eyes glistened with gratitude. "We've found it," she whispered. "And together, we overcame the greatest foe yet."

Cedric let out a shaky chuckle, leaning down to give her a hug, mindful of her bruises. "And we're still alive to see it."

Thalion, tears of relief in his eyes, sank to one knee in the dragon's shadow, murmuring a quiet prayer. "With this, we might finally stand a chance against the Shadow Nexus."

Mira pressed a hand to her chest, feeling the last pulses of adrenaline fade. "By all the fates, we did it," she breathed.

The amulet's faint radiance seemed to dispel the gloom that had cloaked the plateau. Exhausted though they were, a surge of renewed determination filled the heroes. They had secured the final relic: **the Amulet of Divine Light**—essential for the Song of Severance that would purge the Shadow Nexus's ancient evil once and for all.

Cedric took a few moments to examine the amulet's intricate designs, each rune telling a story of solar blessings and dawn's purifying warmth. "This is truly a relic of the highest order," he said quietly, remembering the wonders they had collected so far: the Wyvern scale, the Behemoth disc, the Pearl of Tides. Each manifested a primal essence, but none quite radiated the raw hope this amulet possessed.

Elara placed a hand over the pendant, feeling the pulse of living light within. It awakened something in her, a deeper connection to the powers she served. She closed her eyes, breathing the crisp mountain air. "I sense a synergy with my faith. This relic... it was meant to be wielded by one who follows the Dawn's path." She reopened her eyes, meeting the group's gazes. "We must hurry back to the capital or wherever we can safely perform the Song of Severance. Time is short. The Shadow Nexus grows stronger."

Thalion rubbed his bruised ribs, wincing. "Yes. But first, we need to treat our wounds, recover our strength." He eyed the battered shape of the golden dragon's corpse. "What a tragedy. I wonder if it was corrupted by the Nexus or simply too proud to relinquish its treasures. Dragons... not all are inherently evil, but they do guard their hoards fiercely."

Mira nodded somberly, remembering how the golden dragon's final words hinted at a sorrow deeper than mere greed. "We gave it no choice. Or perhaps it gave *us* no choice." She sighed, guilt flickering. "Either way, the price was steep. But it was... necessary. Stonehaven depends on us."

Cedric turned to the edge of the plateau, gazing at the swirling clouds overhead. "Let's find a place to tend our injuries. We can't linger here—other beasts or storms might converge. We might even attempt a short rest in the dragon's lair, if it keeps a nest. Perhaps we'll find shelter from the cold winds."

Indeed, near the far side of the plateau, they discovered a wide cave opening carved into the mountainside. The ground near the entrance bore claw marks and scorch patterns, indicating the dragon had used this cavern as a lair. The place reeked faintly of sulfur and ozone, testifying to the creature's flaming breath. But inside, they found scattered remnants of rocky alcoves suitable for refuge— enough to set up a small camp if they dared.

Cautiously, they ventured in, finding the remains of a half-buried hoard. Twisted metal lumps, scorched chests, and the occasional glimmer of gold or jewels hinted that the golden dragon had once possessed far more wealth. Now, it lay mostly in disarray, fused by intense heat. Perhaps the creature had melted it intentionally or sealed certain spoils within the stone. The group searched but found no living occupant. The dragon had lived here alone.

They set up a modest camp in a relatively dry corner, out of direct wind. Thalion used illusions to mask their presence from any passing predators who might investigate the dragon's fate. Elara prepared healing salves and bandaged her side, wincing at each movement. Mira helped Cedric remove dents from his armor, carefully hammering out twisted sections. A hush fell in the lair, an unspoken mixture of sorrow for the fallen dragon and relief for their victory.

When they finished basic tending of wounds, Elara reclined against a slab of fused gold-and-stone, pressing the amulet to her chest. "If only we could have reasoned with it," she murmured. "But we had no choice."

Mira placed a comforting hand on Elara's shoulder. "You did everything you could. Dragons are proud creatures. In its eyes, we were invaders. We can honor its memory by using this relic for a truly righteous cause."

Cedric nodded. "We will. And soon." He paused, noticing how the amulet's glow cast gentle patterns on the walls. "With all the relics gathered, the final step is to unify them in the Song of Severance. But to enact it, we need the precise location of the Shadow Nexus—somewhere beyond these mountains, deep in the Frozen Lands where the **Village of Scholars** supposedly dwells."

Thalion tapped his staff lightly on the ground. "Yes, time is short. The Shadow Nexus grows each day, sending out monstrous abominations. We must rally. But for now, let's rest. Dawn will find us forging a path **down from these heights** and then onward into the Frozen Lands—assuming we can manage a route faster than the labyrinth we navigated on the way up."

A small, weary laugh passed among them. "We'll manage," Cedric said. "We always do."

The night in the dragon's lair passed quietly. No storms battered the mountains, no beasts intruded. The air was cold, but the **Amulet of Divine Light**, combined with meager campfires and illusions, helped them withstand the chill. Their horses, tied near the entrance, found enough dryness on a ledge to rest.

In the darkest hours before dawn, Elara awoke from a dream. She had seen flashes of bright white wings, a phoenix motif swirling around a cosmic tapestry, and a swirling blackness threatening to devour it all. The amulet glowed softly at her collarbone. She pressed a hand to it, feeling an echo of that vision. Something about the relic called to her, urging her to stand strong in the coming confrontation.

By morning, each companion rose with renewed purpose. Though battered and sore, the psychological weight of the quest felt lighter. The **final relic** hung around Elara's neck, a silent promise of hope. Cedric, Thalion, and Mira gathered the rest of their gear, salvaging a few gemstones from the melted remains of the dragon's hoard—plus a gilded scale or two that might prove useful as magical reagents.

Outside, the plateau lay draped in pale morning light, the wind crisp but not as harsh. The fallen dragon's colossal body remained where it had collapsed, a silent testament to their brutal clash. A swirl of crows or mountain scavengers circled at a respectful distance, uncertain how to approach a creature once so mighty.

Elara approached the carcass, bowing her head in a gesture of respect. "May your spirit find rest," she whispered, recalling the dragon's final roar of sorrow. Then she turned to rejoin her friends.

They mounted their horses, guiding them carefully around the plateau's edge to descend via a different path than the one they arrived on—hopefully one less treacherous than the route of the deadly Cyclops and the labyrinth of monstrous dangers. The descent would be no easy task, but the knowledge that they possessed the final relic spurred them onward. If they overcame a Hydra, Gorgon, thunderbirds, a Cyclops, and at last the golden dragon, surely they could navigate a safe exit.

Mira studied the **Amulet of Divine Light** as Elara rode beside her. "I can still feel its aura," she commented. "It's as if it's attuned to your faith—and the realm's greater cause. Once we combine it with the other relics, the Song of Severance might be unstoppable. The Shadow Nexus won't stand a chance."

Elara's eyes shone with conviction. "We'll do it. For Stonehaven. For all who have suffered under this darkness. This amulet is the final key."

Cedric, leading the way, glanced over his shoulder. "We must be careful not to underestimate the Nexus. Even with the relics, it'll be a tremendous battle. But yes—hope is on our side now. True hope."

Thalion nodded, staff resting across his saddle. "Once we leave these mountains, we'll skirt around Stonehaven's interior and head northeast into the Frozen Lands. According to the rumors, that's where the **Village of Scholars** is hidden. They might decipher the Nexus's exact location. Let's gather their knowledge before confronting the darkness."

So the party ventured down the winding trails, forging a path among the high ridges. They avoided the more perilous labyrinthine passages, relying on vantage points and illusions to mask themselves from lingering threats. The days of stealth, near-brushes with death, and cunning maneuvers had honed their instincts. No thunderbirds soared overhead; no Gorgons prowled these heights. Each day brought them closer to the lower valleys and, eventually, the outlying roads that curved around Stonehaven's farmland, turning northeastward toward the chill domain of legend.

Despite the physical toll—bruises, burns, and exhaustion—the group's spirits soared. At last, they had all the relics:

1. **Wyvern Scale** (Representing Fire)
2. **Behemoth Disc** (Representing Earth)
3. **Pearl of Tides** (Representing Water)
4. **Amulet of Divine Light** (Representing Air and the Celestial/Divine Aspect)

Elara felt the amulet's weight around her neck, physically and spiritually. It thrummed beneath her armor, resonating with her every breath. Cedric saw her contemplative calm and smiled. "Suits you," he remarked. "The relic, I mean. That glow matches the unwavering faith you've always carried."

She blushed slightly, but a resolute light shone in her eyes. "We stand on the brink of a new chapter for Stonehaven, Cedric," she said softly. "When we finally face the Shadow Nexus, we won't be helpless. We'll bring the might of these relics—and the combined resolve of everyone we've met on our journey."

Thalion's thoughtful gaze lingered on the path ahead. "We should be mindful that the Nexus won't remain idle. By the time we gather the scholars' insights, it may unleash horrors we can barely imagine. We must be ready."

Mira took in a steady breath. "All we can do is gather every ally, every resource. If the Arcadium library still has secrets, or if the Citadel's war mages can assist, we'll call on them. Together, we can triumph."

Their conversation continued as they navigated narrow switchbacks. Days of slow, careful travel passed. No monstrous foes confronted them, and the echoes of the dragon's roar were replaced by simpler forest sounds. Gradually, the air warmed, pines replaced by leafier woods, and the group found themselves near Stonehaven's outer farmland. Yet their true destination lay northeast, into the **Frozen Lands**: a realm rumored to hold ancient wisdom and the final clue to the Nexus's location.

One evening, they paused on a ridge, looking out over farmland in the west, mountainous peaks behind them, and the dark silhouette of looming icefields ahead. They made camp, a humble fire crackling in the twilight. Cedric stared into the flames. "We'll set off at dawn for the Frozen Lands," he announced quietly, glancing at each friend. "The path won't be easy, but if it leads us to the Village of Scholars, we gain the knowledge to seal the Nexus forever."

Mira nodded. "Our mission demands it."

Elara, the amulet softly illuminating her face, agreed: "And after all we've faced, a bit of winter's bite can't stop us."

Thalion merely smiled, leaning on his staff. "Let's rest, then. Tomorrow, we tread new ground—and gather the last piece of this puzzle."

22

INTO THE FROZEN LANDS

Icy gusts rippled across the high plateau, buffeting the four companions as they pressed **ever northeast**. Sir Cedric, Lady Elara, Thalion, and Mira had overcome countless trials—yet one final task remained: discovering the **Shadow Nexus**'s precise seat of power. Armed with the final relic, the **Amulet of Divine Light**, they rode headlong into the **Frozen Lands**, a place as unforgiving as it was mysterious.

The sun hung low over jagged peaks at their backs, casting elongated shadows across stark, frost-crusted tundra. The air carried a constant bite, an icy wind whistling through rocky passes, testing their resolve. Beneath their horses' hooves, the ground shifted from firm soil to a crust of compacted snow, cracking underfoot. In the far distance, glaciers rose like sapphire fortresses, reflecting the dim light in prismatic shards.

Elara pulled her fur-lined cloak tighter, the amulet's radiance warming her chest despite the penetrating cold. "We've come a long way, haven't we?" she murmured, gazing at the expanse of white ahead.

Mira, equally bundled, conjured a modest heat in her gloved palms. "The Frozen Lands... rumored to shelter the Village of Scholars who fled warmer realms long ago. If they can decode the final riddle of the Nexus's location, we might at last corner the evil that plagues Stonehaven."

Thalion, hood pulled low, nodded. "Yes. The apex of our quest lies here: the knowledge to find and destroy the Shadow Nexus once and for all."

Cedric exhaled, his breath fogging the air. "No time to lose. Every day we delay, the Nexus gains strength, twisting more creatures into nightmares. Once we glean the scholars' insight, we'll strike without hesitation."

So they pressed on, forging deeper into the snowy wilderness. Icy winds scoured their cheeks, swirling diamond-sharp flurries around them. Yet the unwavering bond among the heroes burned brighter than any hearth, dispelling doubts. They had braved monstrous labyrinths, undead hordes, and a golden dragon's fury; neither frost nor unknown terrors would halt them now.

By late afternoon, the travelers found themselves at the edge of a ravine where a half-frozen river glinted below. Long icicles hung from the rocky overhangs, and the sky turned steel-gray, threatening a snowstorm. Navigating these treacherous slopes forced them to slow their pace. At times, Thalion or Mira employed small illusions to confuse predators lurking in the white drifts, while Cedric guided the horses along relatively stable paths. Elara remained vigilant, scanning the horizon for any sign of monstrous threats.

They camped that night at the base of a cliff, taking advantage of a natural alcove that shielded them from the worst of the wind. Snow flurries drifted around the campfire, the orange glow dancing on the cave-like walls.

Thalion used a gentle warming spell on their bedrolls, preventing frostbite from creeping in.

Elara, stoking the flames with a half-burnt branch, let her gaze linger on the **Amulet of Divine Light** shining faintly at her collarbone. "This might be our best ally against the cold," she said softly. "I sense a kind of protective aura from it—like a warmth that staves off despair. Perhaps it's part of the amulet's divine nature."

Mira, seated on a flat rock, nodded in agreement. "I can feel it too. Not just the physical warmth, but... an emotional solace, a reminder that we're close to our ultimate goal."

Cedric, finishing a sparse meal of dried meat and hard bread, gave a half-smile. "We'll need every bit of solace if the rumors about the Frozen Lands prove true. Some say even frost trolls and ice wraiths roam here, drawn by ancient magics. We have to remain prepared."

Thalion, ever the scholar, flipped through pages of a worn notebook. "True. But our biggest advantage is unity. We overcame the golden dragon—together, we can weather this cold and whatever beasts lurk in these snows."

In the hush that followed, the wind howled around the alcove's edge, swirling powdery flakes into miniature whirlwinds. Despite the chill that numbed their toes, the group felt an undercurrent of excitement: they were close to gleaning the final puzzle piece—the precise location of the Shadow Nexus. Soon, they would unify the relics and bring the battle to the dark core that had haunted Stonehaven.

They took turns standing watch under the starlit sky, each shift accompanied by a hushed sense of both wonder and caution. The Northern Lights flickered across the heavens in faint ribbons of color, an eerie spectacle that lent the entire region an otherworldly feel. By dawn, fresh snow had drifted around their camp, burying footprints and smoothing the landscape into a pristine sheet of white.

The next leg of their journey led them deeper along a valley flanked by ice-laden cliffs. The horses plodded through shin-deep snow, their breaths puffing clouds into the air. Occasionally, the travelers spotted odd shapes in the distance—crooked pillars of ice, or perhaps the silhouettes of some creature peering from behind jagged ice spires. The howling wind masked smaller sounds, leaving them unsure whether illusions played on their eyes.

Midday brought a fresh swirl of snow, thick enough to hamper visibility. Thalion and Mira conferred over small illusions to highlight hidden ice fissures. Cedric scouted carefully with his runic sword, the blade's faint glow revealing cracks or hidden pitfalls. Elara kept her shield strapped across her back, focusing on guiding her mare. The amulet's presence provided some intangible fortitude, but forging ahead in a near-blizzard tested their will.

When the snow squall lifted briefly, the group found themselves at a wide plain of ice. Ahead, perhaps a mile off, stood a cluster of low huts or igloo-like structures— mysterious shapes half-buried in snowdrifts. Could this be the fabled **Village of Scholars**? The travelers quickened their pace, hearts beating in anticipation. They had expected something more fortress-like, but perhaps the real strongholds lay underground or hidden.

Yet as they drew near, a deep rumble shuddered the air, echoing across the plain. The horses stiffened, ears pinning back. Out of the swirling flakes stepped a hulking figure: a monstrous orc-like being, but thrice the size of any normal orc. Its skin was **pale gray**, pitted and scarred, and from its broad shoulders sprouted not one head, but **three**, each one crowned with curved black horns and teeth reminiscent of a monstrous lion. The center head let out a guttural snarl, while the left and right heads' eyes burned with a bestial rage.

The monstrous orc carried a massive spiked club, fashioned from iron shards bound to a heavy bone handle. Standing guard before the approach to the village, it stomped a three-toed foot, causing the ice beneath to crack. Clearly, this was no ordinary sentinel.

Cedric hissed a warning: "Three-headed orc. The rumors about orc mutations in the Frozen Lands are true. Looks like this one guards the entrance to the Village of Scholars."

Elara tensed, gently patting her horse's neck. "Any chance we can negotiate?"

Thalion grimaced. "We can try, but multi-headed orcs are said to be savage. Possibly corrupted by the same shadow that blights our kingdom."

Mira raised her staff, illusions flickering. "We'd better prepare for a fight."

No sooner had they drawn closer than the monstrous orc let out a trifold roar—three throats blending into a single, earsplitting challenge. It brandished the spiked club overhead, scattering chunks of ice with each swing. Then, with surprising speed, it barreled forward, aiming to crush the intruders.

Thalion reacted first, weaving illusions that conjured a swirling haze of snow to obscure the orc's vision. The left head snarled, swinging the club in a wide arc that parted the illusions. Cedric spurred his horse sideways, narrowly avoiding a crushing blow that gouged a deep trench in the ice. Shards flew in all directions.

Mira dismounted, staff blazing with arcane frost. She thrust her palms forward, releasing a wave of icy spikes that peppered the giant orc's chest. The creature roared in anger, two of its heads blinking furiously against the sudden cold. Yet the thick, pale skin seemed to shrug off minor wounds. The orc slammed the club down, cracking the ground again, sending Mira stumbling.

Cedric dismounted as well, runic sword drawn. He circled behind the creature, slashing at the orc's hamstring in a bid to hobble it. The blade bit into leathery flesh, drawing blackish blood. One of the orc heads bellowed in pain, spinning its body around with terrifying force. Cedric raised his shield just in time to block a backhand from the orc's free arm—still, the impact flung him back a dozen paces, crashing onto packed snow.

Elara, seeing Cedric momentarily pinned, darted in. The **Amulet of Divine Light** flashed, suffusing her sword with radiant energy. She aimed for the same wound Cedric had opened, hoping to deepen it. Her strike cut through the orc's tough hide, but the monstrous being retaliated, swiping downward with knifelike claws. Elara managed to block two swipes, but the third raked her side, scraping her armor and bruising flesh.

Thalion, trembling from the cold, summoned a crackling bolt of lightning. He channeled it through the illusions swirling around the orc's heads, attempting to disorient the creature. The orc's center head roared, thrashing its horns in confusion. The left head snapped at the illusions, its maw dripping saliva, while the right head swiveled around, trying to locate Thalion's position. The mage took cover behind a jagged ice outcrop.

Mira pressed her advantage. She conjured shards of frozen spear-like projectiles, launching them at the orc's torso. Each head snarled as the icy spikes embedded in the creature's thick hide. It tried to charge her, but the wounds to its leg slowed its pace. Spotting an opportunity, Elara lunged again, sword blazing with the amulet's power, slicing across the orc's side. The blow staggered the monstrous being, sending it to one knee.

The orc roared in agony, thrashing with its club. Cedric, having regained his feet, dashed in with runic sword raised. "Together—now!" he shouted. In unison, Thalion, Mira, and Elara unleashed concentrated strikes: illusions to blind the orc's heads, a barrage of frost-lances to its back, and a final slash of radiant steel across its chest. The creature swayed, collapsing onto one elbow, blood staining the snow black.

Breathing heavily, Cedric seized the moment, driving his sword into the orc's heart. A final, gurgling roar from all three heads melded into one tortured cry. Then the monstrous sentinel collapsed face-first, sending up a spray of powdered snow. A hush fell across the frozen expanse, broken only by the howling wind.

For a moment, the companions simply stood there, panting in the cold air, muscles shaking from the strain. The defeated orc's massive form sprawled across the ice, horns and pale hide painted in blackish gore. Elara clutched her side, where a claw swipe had dented her armor. Cedric wiped sweat from his brow, despite the sub-zero temperatures.

Mira stepped forward, staff alight. "It's... done?" she whispered.

Thalion nodded, leaning on his staff for support. "Yes. That was... intense." He peered at the orc's three heads, each slack-jawed in death. "Frightening how strong it was. But we had to pass."

They turned their gaze toward the small settlement beyond—the low huts or igloo-like structures now clearly visible at the far edge of the ice plain. Lanterns flickered in a few doorways, and faint silhouettes moved within. Evidently, the scuffle hadn't gone unnoticed. Slowly, as the travelers caught their breath, figures emerged from the huts, creeping cautiously onto the ice. Bundled in heavy furs, these watchers looked equal parts alarmed and relieved.

Cedric sheathed his sword, raising his hands in a gesture of peace. "We're here on a mission," he called across the distance. "We seek knowledge from your scholars. The orc attacked us... we had no choice."

A half-dozen robed or hooded individuals advanced, each bearing a staff or walking stick. Their faces, mostly hidden by fur hoods, showed signs of curiosity. One figure, taller than the rest, stepped forward. A thick scarf covered their lower face, but intense gray eyes locked onto the traveling party. With a slow, measured bow, the figure spoke:

"You have slain the **Three-Headed Orc** who barred our gates. We owe you a debt, travelers. Come, warm yourselves among us. We are the scholars you seek."

The group let out collective sighs of relief as they followed these robed figures to the settlement. Beyond a low palisade of sharpened stakes (heavily iced over), the huts revealed themselves to be half-buried in snow, connected by labyrinthine tunnels or semi-underground chambers. Despite the harsh climate, the interior boasted a snug warmth, thanks to cleverly designed heating from geothermal vents or cunningly channeled hot springs.

Their hosts ushered the heroes into a large communal hall. The space was lit by glowing crystals set into sconces along the walls, and the floor was layered with thick animal furs. Low tables ringed a central fire pit. Around them, men and women with wizened faces or scholarly eyes peered curiously at the newcomers. Stacks of scrolls and codices sat on shelves carved directly from the ice. Indeed, it was a place of study, deep in the frozen wilds.

The tall figure who'd greeted them lowered the scarf, revealing a woman of indeterminate age, silver hair braided with small beads of quartz. "I am Elder Sima," she said, voice resonant. "We do not often receive visitors, especially those who can dispatch a three-headed orc so efficiently. Please, sit. You must be weary."

Cedric gratefully complied, sinking onto a bench near the fire. Elara eased beside him, mindful of her bruised torso. Thalion and Mira joined them. The robed scholars brought cups of hot tea, spiced with local herbs. After days of freezing wind and rations, the warmth felt almost too good to believe.

Elder Sima gestured to a younger man who quietly wrapped the travelers in extra furs. Then she turned to the party. "We observe from a distance the changes in Stonehaven," she said, her gray eyes flicking to the **Amulet of Divine Light** glinting at Elara's chest. "Rumors swirl of a rising evil—some ancient nexus of shadow. And you come with relics said to unite powers against it."

Elara inclined her head. "That is so, Elder. We have traveled far, collecting relics from across the kingdom. But the Shadow Nexus moves. We must learn its exact location to strike."

Thalion pulled out a half-frozen parchment, offering it to Sima. "The High Seer's glimpses indicated a place older than curses, a seat of negative energies. Yet we have only partial coordinates. We hoped your archives might hold the missing piece."

Sima accepted the parchment delicately, scanning the cryptic symbols. "We are keepers of knowledge lost to the ages," she said, handing it to a bearded scholar at her side. "If it can be decoded, we shall find a way."

Mira sipped her tea, letting the fragrant steam thaw her face. "We heard you can decipher ancient tongues or runic wards," she explained. "We're short on time. The Shadow Nexus threatens to plunge Stonehaven into darkness."

Elder Sima offered a calm nod. "We are aware of the urgency. Rest assured, while you mend your wounds, we will consult the archives." Her gaze turned sharp. "However, you must know: deciphering such location spells, especially if they're partly shrouded by dark magic, could take time. Are you prepared to linger here a few days?"

Cedric glanced at Elara, who nodded. "We'll do whatever it takes. We can't face the Nexus blind. But rest assured, we do not have weeks to spare."

Sima acknowledged this with a thin smile. "Understood. We will begin at once." She motioned for the bearded scholar to hurry off. Then, glancing at the group's battered armor and bandages, she added, "Meanwhile, let our healers tend your wounds. The Frozen Lands are harsh, but we repay goodwill with hospitality. Consider yourselves our guests."

That evening, the heroes found themselves guided to a set of modest sleeping quarters carved into the ice. The walls were surprisingly insulated, with layers of dried moss pressed between ice blocks, and small braziers casting a gentle glow. Healers—equally adept with herbal salves and arcane touches—tended to Elara's claw marks and Cedric's bruised chest, mending torn ligaments and easing pain. Thalion, sore from multiple spells and illusions in the freezing cold, accepted a pungent ointment for stiff joints, while Mira—though less physically battered—underwent a mild check for any lingering venom residue from her hydra wound.

In these quiet hours, they felt a sense of serenity unusual for their quest. No immediate monsters lurked at the door, no thunderstorms threatened from overhead. Instead, the muffled hush of snow outside and the rustle of parchment from the scholars' corridors lulled them. A reprieve at last.

Cedric, lying on a straw-stuffed mattress, spoke softly to Elara, who sat reading by a small lamp. "We'll succeed," he murmured. "We've come too far to fail. The Shadow Nexus won't stand against all our relics—especially with your new amulet's divine power."

Elara nodded, fingers brushing the amulet's surface. "I feel more certain each passing day," she admitted, her voice resonating with quiet conviction. "Yet something in me dreads the confrontation. The Nexus... it's ancient beyond measure. We must be absolutely prepared."

Thalion, overhearing, turned from his corner seat. "Preparation is exactly why we're here," he said. "The Village of Scholars is our last chance to gather the knowledge needed for a direct strike."

Mira closed her eyes, remembering the monstrous orc's triple-headed roar. "The land itself is resisting the Nexus's corruption, but if we fail, Stonehaven's final strongholds will fall, even places like this village. We can't let that happen."

A hush fell as each reflected on the shared burdens. They had faced Hydra venom, Gorgon horns, thunderbird dives, Cyclops boulders, and the golden dragon's scorching flames. Now, in the last stretch, they needed a final boon of wisdom from these hidden scholars. Sleep eventually claimed them, warmed by the knowledge that, for once, they were safe.

The next day dawned with a hushed snowfall, softening the village's already muffled environment. Over a hearty breakfast of spiced porridge, Elder Sima summoned the four heroes to the main hall. Her expression was grave. Around them, other robed scholars busied themselves with ancient scrolls and worn codices.

"We have gleaned something from the partial coordinates you shared," Sima began. "This text references a 'cataclysmic convergence' hidden beyond Stonehaven's recorded maps. A place that once was sealed by wards older than our known kingdoms."

Thalion leaned forward, heart pounding. "Does that confirm it's the Shadow Nexus's seat of power?"

Sima nodded slowly. "Highly likely. The references match old records of a Shadow Rift we discovered in our archives. If these lines are correct, the location is near the

Ebon Veil—a forbidding territory far east of Stonehaven's normal frontiers. We suspect it's guarded by wards of negative energy. Even pinpointing its gateway might require a synergy of the relics you carry."

Mira exhaled. "So we do have a path. We can gather the relics, perform the Song of Severance... but only if we find the exact rift entrance."

Sima's eyes flicked to the amulet on Elara's chest. "Yes. The final lines indicate that the relic of divine light must act as a key. Combined with the other three relics, it can breach the negative wards. But the texts also mention that time is critical: if the Nexus finishes... something... perhaps an alignment or resurrection, it may unleash an unstoppable wave."

Cedric's grip tightened on his sword hilt. "Then we must hurry."

Elder Sima gave a thin smile. "Indeed. We will provide you with the necessary runic instructions, gleaned from our tomes, to ensure you can open the rift. But be warned— beyond that gateway, we cannot aid you. We are scholars, not warriors."

Elara placed a hand over her heart. "Your knowledge is more than enough. Stonehaven owes you."

Sima paused, glancing at her fellow scholars. "One more thing. We sense a stirring dark presence in these lands, as if the Nexus's corruptive influence tries to spread here, too. The monstrous orc you slew may have been a harbinger, twisted beyond normal orcish stature. You may face more abominations on your way out."

Thalion straightened. "We'll remain cautious. Thank you for the warning."

Later that day, Elara, Cedric, Mira, and Thalion each copied the runic instructions for the rift-breaching ritual into water-resistant parchments. The scholars meticulously double-checked each symbol, ensuring no stroke was out of place. Even the slightest error in the final incantation could doom the attempt.

Meanwhile, the village's healers completed their ministrations, leaving the group feeling stronger. The heroes' gear was repaired, new winter furs provided, and rations restocked with dried seal meat, fish, and a pungent cheese that, though strong-smelling, was high in calories—essential for the trek back out of the Frozen Lands.

That evening, the village held a subdued but heartfelt banquet in their communal hall. Stews of northern vegetables and smoked fish warmed the travelers. The scholars, mostly reclusive, offered modest toasts, acknowledging the group's valor against the orc sentinel. Candlelight flickered on icy walls, the hush of outside winds replaced by quiet conversation. Over cups of spiced wine, each companion felt a flicker of renewed optimism: they now possessed the location of the Shadow Nexus and a plan to breach it. The final confrontation drew ever closer.

Before dawn the next day, Elder Sima led them to the village gates. Snow swirled around the monstrous orc's corpse, which still lay half-buried at the outskirts, a grim testament to the land's dangers. Sima bowed respectfully. "Go with knowledge, and may fortune guide your quest. Stonehaven's fate may well hinge on your success."

Cedric, gripping the reins of his horse, nodded. "We won't fail."

Elara smiled gently, the amulet's faint glow illuminating her features. "Your knowledge has given us a fighting chance."

Mira and Thalion offered final thanks, and with that, the gates opened, revealing a pale sunrise over the icy plains. Together, the four rode forth, hearts brimming with determination. Their stay in the Village of Scholars had given them far more than healing—it had yielded the final piece of the puzzle. No longer were they searching blindly for the Nexus. Now they knew precisely where to strike.

Their route led back westward for a time, skirting the Frozen Lands' outer reaches before they could swing south toward Stonehaven's more familiar domains. Although the monstrous orc was defeated, new dangers seemed to lurk amid the snowdrifts. Once, a savage pack of frost wargs trailed them for hours, menacing from a distance, but a display of illusions from Thalion and a few well-placed arcane blasts from Mira warded the beasts away.

Near a glacial ravine, they found signs of an even greater threat: tracks that might have belonged to an ice giant or an enormous undead creature, though they never caught sight of it. The sense of being hunted lingered, prompting Cedric to keep a constant watch. The amulet's aura soothed their frayed nerves, but it couldn't banish the creeping unease that pervaded these frozen wastes.

One afternoon, as swirling snow battered them, they stumbled on a half-frozen waterfall feeding a crystal-clear pond. The reflection of the sky in the water was so vivid that Mira paused to admire it. A memory of the golden dragon's reflection on that high plateau flitted through her mind. So many battles behind them, yet they remained steadfast—

unbroken, if battered. She closed her eyes, offering a silent prayer that the final confrontation would see them all alive.

Elara approached, noticing her quiet reflection. "You alright?" she asked gently.

Mira exhaled a cloud of breath. "Yes. Just... reflecting on how close we are to the end. And how dangerous it will be to face the Nexus."

Elara nodded, placing a comforting hand on Mira's shoulder. "We'll face it together. That's our strength."

Their path eventually led them down from the highest reaches of ice into a region of tundra dotted with stunted pines. The weather improved slightly, shifting from constant blizzards to intermittent flurries. Some nights, the group even glimpsed faint starlight, a rarity in this land of swirling snow. The promise of less severe cold spurred them onward.

Yet on the final day before they would exit the Frozen Lands, danger found them one last time. As they navigated a narrow pass flanked by icy cliffs, a distant roar boomed— different from the orc's or the thunderbirds or any other beast they'd faced. It rattled the stones underfoot, and the horses reared in alarm.

Cedric jerked his mount to a halt, scanning the icy ridges overhead. A colossal shape emerged from the swirling snow—a hulking form that might have stood thirty feet tall if it rose to full height. Its hide was a patchwork of ice and dead flesh, a grotesque giant's frame twisted by necromantic energies. The skeletal face, half rotted, locked onto the group with a silent shriek. Some vile, undead giant, likely a sign of the Nexus's corruption creeping even here.

Elara grimaced, summoning a faint glow from her amulet. "More abominations," she muttered. "We have no time for this."

Thalion hissed. "We can't outrun it on this pass. Prepare to fight."

Mira tensed, illusions flickering at her fingertips. Cedric hefted his sword, heart pounding. Another grueling battle loomed. But then, the undead giant lurched awkwardly, as though the necromantic magic animating it were incomplete. Its limbs jerked in spasms, each step sending ice shards tumbling. With a pitiful, rattling moan, it abruptly collapsed on itself, rotted sinews snapping. The entire mass fell into a heap of icy bones, as if the leftover negative energy had dissipated.

The group stared in surprise. "That was... anticlimactic," Cedric muttered.

Thalion exhaled, relief mingled with unease. "A sign the Shadow Nexus's corruption attempts to reach this land but lacks a foothold? Or an experiment in controlling undead giants?"

Mira shivered, gazing at the remains. "Either way, we're seeing how close evil has come. We must hurry."

Thus, they bypassed the inert bones. By dusk, they crested a ridge where the whistling wind quieted, the sight of gentler forests in the distance. The boundary of the Frozen Lands was at hand. Each hero let out a silent thanks that they could leave this realm behind, carrying the crucial knowledge gleaned from the scholars.

Nightfall settled as they descended into lower altitudes. The deeper snow gave way to slush, then patches of brown earth. The temperatures, though still cold, no longer threatened immediate frostbite. When they finally set camp among scraggly pines in a region known as the Winterwood, it felt almost balmy compared to the frigid heights they had endured.

Gathered around a small fire, the group assessed their progress. Elara rechecked the runic instructions gleaned from the scholars, ensuring they were intact. Cedric spread out a rough map, while Thalion recounted possible outposts or hidden enclaves they might pass on the way. Mira, half lost in thought, considered how the final battle with the Nexus might unfold.

At last, Cedric put away the maps, and they let the conversation ease into a restful calm. The nights of constant threat in the Frozen Lands made this quiet moment precious. The Amulet of Divine Light cast soft reflections on Elara's armor, a gentle reminder of what they had come to do—and how close they were to the end of their quest.

Over the next few days, the group navigated rolling hills and pine forests, crossing half-frozen streams that crackled under hoof. A sense of urgency throbbed in their chests: the Shadow Nexus must be confronted soon, for each day might bring new horrors unleashed upon Stonehaven. Yet they also felt a guarded optimism. They now held all necessary relics. They had the Song of Severance's final incantations, plus the runic instructions from the scholars on how to breach the negative wards.

One dawn, as they paused to water the horses at a clear pond near the forest's edge, Elara took a moment to gaze at her reflection in the water's surface. The amulet around her neck glowed faintly, forming a halo of luminescence. She recalled the first time King Alaric had summoned them: how the kingdom's fields were touched by shadows, and dark rumors spread among the villages. Now, they had come so far—from four scattered heroes to a unified band that had braved the mightiest foes. The final test lay on the horizon.

Mira joined her, staff in hand, placing a gentle hand on Elara's shoulder.

"You look ready," she said softly. "I guess we both are, in our own ways."

Elara nodded, smiling. "Yes, though I fear what the Nexus might do. I fear the cost we'll pay." Mira sighed. "Costs there will be. But remember: Stonehaven stands behind us. The relics stand with us. And we have each other."

They embraced briefly before returning to the group, hearts bolstered by that unity. Cedric and Thalion, finishing their morning checks, gave silent nods reflecting the same sentiment: they faced the final step together.

By the end of another day's ride, they emerged onto a rugged trail that veered east—not back to Stonehaven's capital, but toward the very location the scholars had deciphered as the Shadow Nexus's seat of power. Warmer breezes whispered in the boughs overhead, carrying hints of an early spring. No longer did endless drifts of snow dominate the horizon. Instead, patches of green reemerged, a promise that life endured. Relief mingled with determination—relief at leaving the frigid realm, and resolve to carry out the final mission swiftly.

They made camp one last time before the final push, pitched in a quiet glen. The talk around the campfire turned to practical matters: uniting the relics for the Song of Severance, positioning themselves for the final ritual, and preparing for any ambush from the Nexus's monstrous agents.

Mira poked at the fire, sending up a flurry of sparks. "We should also consider whether the Nexus has cultists, undead, monstrous generals—some final blockade."

Cedric nodded. "We've faced countless horrors. If the Nexus sets a final trap, it could be worse than anything we've seen yet."

Elara rested a hand on her amulet, feeling its steady pulse. "Let them come. We have the power to withstand them now."

Thalion offered a small, confident smile. "And with the knowledge from the scholars, we won't be wandering blindly. The Nexus can't hide behind wards. We will find it— and break it."

Morning light brought renewed vigor. As they packed up, the final vestiges of the Frozen Lands faded behind them. The looming threat of endless ice gave way to rolling farmland in the distance. It was as though Stonehaven herself welcomed them back—stronger, braver, and ready to face the source of all darkness.

And so, with horses trotting on firmer ground, the four heroes rode onward. The memory of the three-headed orc that once barred the Village of Scholars lingered in their minds, evidence of how deep the corruption had run. Yet they had prevailed, gleaning the final secrets from the village's archives. Every step eastward now led them to the day they would stand against the Shadow Nexus itself, relics in hand, hearts united by the unwavering bond forged through trials.

In time, they would see the twisted horizon where the Nexus held sway. They would recall their victories, their trials, and all those who had aided them. The scholars' runic instructions would guide them to the exact rift that concealed the Shadow Nexus. The world seemed to hold its breath, waiting for these heroes to fulfill the promise they had carried so far.

Thus ended the Chapter: having conquered the Frozen Lands and secured the final knowledge, the heroes turned east—away from the safety of the Citadel—to face the Shadow Nexus directly. Worn yet confident, they pressed toward the final confrontation that would decide Stonehaven's fate, trusting that their unity and the relics' synergy would vanquish the ancient evil once and for all.

23

THE SHADOW NEXUS

A thin veil of morning mist drifted across barren plains as Sir Cedric, Lady Elara, Thalion, and Mira pressed onward, the faint silhouettes of crags and dead trees looming against a golden sunrise. Despite the crisp air and the steady clip of their horses' hooves on frost-limned earth, none could ignore the creeping unease that thickened around them like a gathering storm cloud.

Only days had passed since they left the Frozen Lands behind. Now, armed with the runic instructions gleaned from the Village of Scholars, they ventured straight into the lion's den: the Shadow Nexus. Far from Stonehaven's usual borders lay a corrupted wasteland, rumored to hold an ancient crystal amplifying dark magic. If not destroyed soon, it threatened to plunge the entire realm into perpetual night.

Within saddlebags slung across them, all four relics resonated with subtle arcs of light:

1. **The Wyvern Scale** (Representing Fire)
2. **The Behemoth Disc** (Representing Earth)
3. **The Pearl of Tides** (Representing Water)
4. **The Amulet of Divine Light** (Representing Air and the Celestial/Divine Aspect)

Lady Elara wore the last relic at her breastplate—the Amulet of Divine Light—its faint glow a quiet source of resolve. She glanced at it occasionally, feeling its pulse respond to her heartbeat as though encouraging her to stay resolute. Cedric rode at her side, runic sword sheathed but ready. Thalion and Mira followed behind, discussing final details of the cleansing ritual required to destroy the crystal's corruption.

They found a faint trail meandering between rocky outcroppings, the terrain soon giving way to a barren expanse of lifeless earth. Once vibrant fields lay wilted, pocked with blackened stumps of trees. It was as though a poisonous shadow had drained color from the land. The group exchanged uneasy glances, urging their mounts forward. The deeper they ventured, the more the environment bore marks of the Shadow Nexus's taint: twisted brambles, ash-laced soil, oppressive silence where birdsong should have been.

"It's like the land itself recoils," Mira observed grimly, staff resting across her saddle. "The corruption intensifies with every league."

Thalion nodded, scanning the horizon with tired eyes. "Soon, we'll be close enough to sense the Nexus's negative aura directly."

Cedric stiffened. "We'll destroy it by day's end," he vowed, quiet but certain. "Whatever form it's taken, we have the relics and the ritual. This ends today."

By midday, the skies had dimmed into a perpetual gloom, despite no thick clouds overhead. The sun's rays seemed weakened, as if the air itself drained warmth and light. A chill wind carried an eerie whisper. Ahead, the land sank into a shallow depression—a sprawling crater ringed with broken pillars of stone. Black tendrils of energy snaked skyward from its center, coiling like malignant smoke.

The horses grew skittish, snorting and pulling at the reins, sensing the malevolent energy that pooled in the hollow. Cedric dismounted first, placing a soothing hand on his mare's flank. "Easy, girl," he murmured. Elara, Thalion, and Mira followed suit, each feeling the weight of the dark presence intensify. The amulet at Elara's chest glowed more brightly now, as if reacting to a mortal foe.

Over the rim of the crater, they glimpsed a tall spire of twisted rock, ringed by black crystals that jutted like teeth. At the spire's base gleamed a single crystal formation, large as a grown man, pulsating with a violet radiance that made the air shimmer. The **Shadow Nexus** at last: a corrupted crystal, brimming with negative magic, set upon a natural pedestal of rock. The swirl of darkness around it seemed alive, rippling outward in waves.

Mira's throat went dry. "So... that's it."

Thalion took a moment to steady himself. "Yes. The crystals we've seen—shards here and there—were mere fragments. This is the Nexus's heart. It's far worse than I imagined."

Elara inhaled, her expression steeling. "The scholars were right. To cleanse it, we must enact the sacred ritual they outlined. The Song of Severance with the four relics." She placed a hand on the amulet, drawing strength from its calm pulse.

Cedric turned to the others. "We'll need a secure spot to set the relics. Then we channel magic to break the negative wards. Once the wards are down, we apply the final incantation to purge the crystal's corruption."

Thalion nodded solemnly. "We must remain undisturbed while we focus. Otherwise, the ritual might fail. The scholars warned monstrous creatures would swarm to defend the Nexus if threatened."

Mira's face set in determination. "Then let them come. We hold them off until the ritual's complete."

They descended the crater slope, careful not to slip on patches of black ooze that seeped from cracks in the earth. The air smelled acrid, like burned metal. Each step closer intensified the sense of dread, yet also ignited the relics' combined synergy. A faint luminescence from their satchels or scabbards created overlapping auras of color—fiery orange from the Wyvern scale, earthy green from the Behemoth disc, watery blue from the Pearl of Tides. Elara's **Amulet of Divine Light** shone brightest a radiant white, a beacon against the gloom and symbol of both air and divine light.

They reached a half-collapsed dais of stone near the spire's base—an ancient structure possibly built by whoever once attempted to seal the Nexus. The dais provided a flat enough surface to arrange the relics. Cedric and Elara cleared debris, while Thalion and Mira cast minor wards around the perimeter. The swirl of black energy above the crystal crackled ominously, as if sensing intruders. Faint moans, distant howls, and skittering echoes rose from the crater's edges.

"This place is vile," Cedric muttered, setting his jaw. "But we stand here to cleanse it."

Mira produced the scroll of incantations from the scholars. "Thalion, we have everything we need to begin. Let's place the relics in the diagram's formation."

Thalion indicated a roughly diamond shaped arrangement on the dais. One by one, they set the relics down at designated points:

1. **Wyvern Scale** (Fire) at the south corner.
2. **Behemoth Disc** (Earth) at the north corner.
3. **Pearl of Tides** (Water) at the west corner.
4. **Amulet of Divine Light** (Air) at the east corner.

Elara kneeling, still wearing it but aligning with the pattern.

A hush fell, broken only by the crackling hiss from the corrupted crystal. The relics glowed in resonance, arcs of multicolored light bridging them. The dais thrummed with an undercurrent of power. Thalion gestured for the group to stand at the points, each focusing on the relic near them. Mira took the Wyvern scale, Cedric the Behemoth disc, Thalion the Pearl of Tides. Elara knelt at the east corner, the amulet's glow intensifying.

"All right," Thalion breathed, staff raised. "Commence the Song of Severance, as the scholars instructed. We combine our energies to break the wards. Then, with the final incantation, we purge the Nexus from within."

The party closed their eyes, each intoning the memorized lines from the chant. Ancient words fell from their lips, weaving into a tapestry of harmonized magic. Colors from the relics flared, swirling overhead in a vortex. The ground quaked slightly. The black crystal across the spire responded with a low-pitched hum, as though fighting back.

Within moments, the land erupted in chaos. As the ritual's power blossomed, the **Shadow Nexus** reacted—calling forth a legion of monstrous defenders. Shapes emerged from the crater's edges: twisted beasts, undead abominations, and warped animals corrupted by dark energies. Grotesque forms half-lumbered, half-scrambled across the rocky ground, eyes glowing with malevolence.

A savage howl cut the air—a pack of large, wolflike creatures with skeletal patches tearing toward the dais. Winged monstrosities resembling harpies but with tattered bat-like membranes swooped overhead, shrieking. From behind jagged spires, lumps of animate flesh crawled, spitting black venom. The stink of rot and corruption thickened the air.

Cedric was the first to break from the chant. "They're coming—Elara, Thalion, keep focusing. Mira and I will hold them off!" he barked. Without waiting for protest, he gripped his runic sword, stepping from his position to intercept a charging beast. The ritual's partial momentum still flowed, the arcs of energy continuing through Elara and Thalion, though incomplete.

Mira, near the Wyvern scale, also lifted her staff, illusions dancing at her fingertips. She launched a barrage of frost-lances at the nearest wave of twisted hounds. The beasts yelped as ice skewered them, but more poured forth. With a flick of her wrist, Mira conjured illusions of fiery walls that corralled another pack, buying precious seconds before they discovered the illusions were intangible.

Elara, forced to remain at the east to sustain the amulet's resonance, clenched her fists around the chain. She closed her eyes, pushing deeper into the chant, bridging the relics' synergy. Her mind flickered with images of distant dawns, a promise of renewal. Thalion, sweat beading on his brow, maintained the incantation, occasionally extending illusions or mild wards to protect Elara from stray attacks.

The dais glowed with intensifying magic, but it needed more time to break the crystal's wards.

Cedric sliced through the first wave of beasts, runic sword flaring with holy power gleaned from the relic synergy. Each stroke cut down a monster in a burst of black ichor, though the creatures fought viciously, biting and scratching. One large abomination—a hulking mass of congealed flesh and bone—lurched forward, trying to crush him in a bear-like hug. Cedric jammed his sword upward, severing its spine. The creature collapsed in a heap.

Mira spotted vile harpy-bats swooping toward Elara, talons outstretched. She conjured a swirling vortex of wind and shards of ice, shredding two mid-dive. Their twisted screams rattled the dais. Another soared overhead, launching acidic spit that sizzled across the stones. Mira yelped, ducking behind a half-broken pillar. Sparks from the amulet's aura flickered around her, partially protecting her from the acid splash.

The battle raged in a frenzy of shrieks, snarls, and magical blasts, all under the looming presence of the corrupted crystal. The ground cracked, glowing fissures spewing noxious fumes. Yet the heroes held firm. They had faced monstrous hydras, cyclopes, a golden dragon—these twisted beasts, however numerous, wouldn't break them so easily.

As the group beat back wave after wave, the dais' arcane glow intensified. A swirl of radiant power coalesced in the east portion, anchored by the **Amulet of Divine Light**. The black crystal across the spire trembled, faint cracks forming on its surface. Dark lightning crackled from the crystal's apex, lashing out in arcs that battered the dais, nearly toppling Thalion once.

"We're close!" Thalion called, voice trembling with strain. "Another minute or two. Elara—push deeper into the incantation!"

Elara, face contorted with concentration, channeled every ounce of faith and magic she possessed. The amulet pulsed so brightly that it hurt to look at. Her lips moved in a continuous chant, sweat coursing down her temples. She felt the relic synergy building to a crescendo. With it, an unshakable intuition: the wards around the crystal demanded a final catalyst, something more than just raw magical energy. They hungered for a sacrifice—a trade of lifeforce or devotion to break the darkness.

A monstrous shape leaped onto the dais—some corrupted minotaur, wreathed in black flames. Cedric was too far to intervene; he was pinned by another beast. Elara flinched as the minotaur roared, lifting a jagged axe. But before the blow fell, Elara released a burst of radiant energy from the amulet, incinerating the creature in a flash of holy light. The effort cost her, nearly toppling her to the ground. She gasped, her vision blurring.

"Lady Elara!" Thalion cried, reaching a hand to steady her. But a fresh wave of monstrous hounds attacked, forcing him to defend their flank. Meanwhile, the swirling energies in the dais started to fluctuate, precariously close to unraveling if Elara's focus waned.

Chest heaving, Elara realized the only path to truly break the Nexus's wards might require her to channel the amulet's entire essence—likely at great personal cost. She rose shakily, voice raw. "Thalion, keep them off me just a moment longer."

The orc illusions, the swirling arc of frost-lances, Cedric's relentless swordplay—none could fully distract the wave of horrors converging on the dais. Elara steeled herself, clasping the amulet with both hands, and closed her eyes. She recalled every step of the vow she made when first she became a champion of the Light. If a sacrifice was needed, she would not flinch.

"In the name of Stonehaven..." she whispered, her voice resonating with the amulet's core. The relic's glow magnified, blazing into a pillar of brilliance that stabbed into the dark sky. "I give myself to break these chains of corruption!"

A roaring wind erupted, swirling around Elara. The dais' synergy soared. Thalion and Mira staggered at the force. Cedric, mid-swing, glimpsed Elara at the dais eastern most point, eyes shining with tears, body framed by a halo of pure luminescence. He realized with dread what she meant to do.

"Elara, no!" he shouted, voice hoarse.

She looked to him with a calm, tender expression—sorrowful but resolute. The pillar of light intensified, arcs of golden flame dancing across her armor. The relic synergy rushed into the amulet like a torrent, focusing into a single, blinding beam at the crystal. The monstrous hordes shrieked as the beam cut through them, forging a direct conduit to the Shadow Nexus. The black crystal cracked further, vile energies hissing in protest.

As Elara poured her soul into the final chant, pain lanced through her body. Her lifeforce ebbed, each breath a labored gasp. The cost was unimaginable, yet she pressed on. The wards around the crystal shattered one by one in brilliant bursts. The negative energies howled, swirling into a chaotic vortex that hammered the dais with shockwaves. In that moment, Elara cried out, a raw, anguished sound that tore at her companions' hearts. A final flash of light enveloped her, the amulet's glow erupting into an explosion of divine radiance.

In the aftermath of that explosion, a wave of light rolled across the crater, incinerating or dispersing swarms of lesser creatures. The larger abominations reeled, wounded or dazed. For a heartbeat, silence fell, broken only by crackles of black lightning and the hiss of dissolving monstrosities.

Cedric stumbled forward, blinking away tears from the afterimage. On the dais, Elara lay prone, her armor scorched and the amulet's chain still clutched in her hand. The rest of the relics lay strewn around her, each flickering with leftover resonance. Thalion and Mira rushed to her side, fear in their eyes. Cedric's heart pounded so loudly he could barely breathe. He knelt, gently turning Elara onto her back.

Her eyes fluttered, chest rising in shallow breaths. Pain etched across her face. "I—" She tried to speak, but no words came. The swirling brilliance around the amulet had dimmed, yet a faint glow lingered in her gaze.

Thalion pressed trembling fingers to her pulse. "She's alive," he choked, "but... she's so weak."

Mira, tears beading her lashes, squeezed Elara's hand. "You gave everything," she murmured. "We can't lose you now."

Elara's lips parted, voice a whisper. "Finish... the ritual," she breathed, eyes flickering to the corrupted crystal. Cracks marred its surface, thick purple smoke venting. The wards were gone, but the final banishing incantation remained undone. Unless they completed the Song of Severance's last lines, the crystal would remain a threat.

With renewed resolve, Cedric carefully laid Elara in Thalion's arms. He stepped to the dais center, retrieving the amulet from her slack hand. "Mira, Thalion—help me channel the relics!" he commanded, voice thick with emotion. "Elara has broken the wards. We can purge the Nexus now."

Nodding, Mira scooped up the Wyvern scale and the Pearl of Tides, Thalion grabbed the Behemoth disc. They formed a ring around Cedric as he held the **Amulet of Divine Light** overhead. The monstrous legions, though battered by Elara's blast, stirred anew, desperate to stop the final blow. Snarls and roars echoed as they converged from every angle.

But the heroes stood resolute. Cedric began the last lines of the Song of Severance, voice trembling but unbroken. "By the fires of creation... by the pulse of the earth... by the flow of waters... by the breath of winds... and by the dawn's pure light... we sever the bonds of darkness!"

Mira closed her eyes, channeling frost and illusions into the relic synergy. Thalion whispered incantations of disruption and banishment. The relics glowed, arcs of color weaving around them. Elara, too weak to stand, lifted her trembling hand, adding the faintest whisper of prayer. The runic instructions from the scholars flooded their minds, guiding the energies into a single, unstoppable surge.

The Shadow Nexus crystal howled, releasing a storm of black lightning that hammered the dais. Rocks splintered; the ground quaked. A final wave of monstrous beasts lunged forward—grotesque chimeras, undead knights, twisted drakes—throwing themselves into a desperate assault. Cedric roared, meeting them with a slash of runic steel infused by relic power. Mira cast illusions that caused the creatures to turn on each other in confusion. Thalion conjured elemental blasts, incinerating or freezing entire swathes. The synergy burned bright, each hero pushing to their limit.

In the midst of the chaos, a pillar of multicolored brilliance erupted from the dais, enveloping the black crystal. The relic energies converged upon it, dissolving the corruption in cascading waves of light. Cracks spread across the crystal's surface, now bursting with luminous fractals. The monstrous defenders screeched in agony as the source of their corruption faltered.

Cedric, voice hoarse, shouted the final incantation. Light lanced from the relic ring into the crystal's core, and with a thunderous detonation, the Shadow Nexus shattered. A vortex of negative energy spiraled upward, unraveling into a million flecks of black dust. The ground convulsed, then stilled, as the dark presence that once choked the land vanished.

For a breathless moment, everything was silent. An intense white radiance surged outward from the dais, sweeping across the crater, the plains beyond, and even the distant hills. The monstrous creatures convulsed, dissolving into motes of dust or retreating with shrieks back to the shadowed realms. The gloom that had stained the skies receded, letting pure sunlight break through. A new dawn seemed to bloom across Stonehaven, bright and untainted.

The dust of shattered crystal settled. The dais, scorched and partially collapsed, lay quiet. Cedric, trembling, lowered the amulet. Mira, panting, sank to her knees. Thalion, battered, stumbled to Elara's side. The land felt different—lighter, cleansed. A sense of unburdened air replaced the suffocating dark aura.

"Is... is it truly over?" Mira asked, disbelief in her voice.

Cedric nodded, tears clouding his vision. "Yes. The Nexus is gone. We did it."

They turned to Elara, who lay slumped where she had poured her strength into breaking the wards. Thalion cradled her head, checking her vital signs. Her breathing was shallow, her face deathly pale. The aura of the amulet, once bright, was now just a soft glimmer near her chest. The others rushed over, hearts pounding.

Thalion's eyes brimmed with tears. "Her lifeforce is... almost spent," he said thickly. "The amulet demanded too much. She gave everything for Stonehaven."

Mira clasped Elara's hand, fighting back sobs. "No, we can't lose you. Wake up, Elara, please."

A faint smile tugged at Elara's lips. Her eyes fluttered open, half-lidded. "We... succeeded," she breathed, voice a ragged whisper. "The land... is free..."

Cedric bowed his head, tears rolling. "You saved us. You saved everyone."

Elara's gaze lingered on each friend, love shining through her fatigue. "All of us... saved Stonehaven... together," she managed, each word a strain. "I—" She closed her eyes, a final exhale escaping her lips. The tension in her body eased.

For a long moment, the group sat frozen, the victory's euphoria crushed under a wave of grief. Cedric gently held Elara's lifeless form, tears dripping onto her battered armor. The light from the amulet flickered, a final pulse of warmth that washed over them. Then it dimmed, as though in mourning.

"She's gone," Thalion whispered, voice breaking.

Mira pressed a trembling hand over her mouth, stifling a sob. "Elara… Goddess of Dawn, guide her to peace."

A hush fell across the crater. Even the wind seemed to hold its breath in reverence of Lady Elara's sacrifice—a hero who gave her life so that all might live.

Time lost meaning as they grieved, the dais and shattered crystal a silent testament to the cost of victory. At last, Cedric lifted his gaze. The land around them glowed with a renewed vibrancy, fresh grass sprouting where corruption had reigned. Blue sky arched overhead, pure and unobscured. In the distance, birds called, returning to a realm freed from darkness.

Working gently, the companions prepared Elara's body, wrapping her in a cloak embroidered with the dawn sigil. The amulet lay quiet on her chest, yet Cedric felt an echo of her spirit within it. The relic would remain a symbol of her final stand.

They traveled west in solemn procession, carrying their fallen comrade across the same land once choked by gloom. Everywhere they went, they saw signs of renewal. Monsters that once haunted the roads had disintegrated or fled. Farms and villages they passed marveled at the sudden lift of the cursed pall. People emerged from hiding, celebrating the bright sunlight that no longer felt stifled by malevolent storm clouds.

Word spread like wildfire: the Shadow Nexus had been purged. Harvest fields that once withered bounced back with surprising vitality, animals lost to monstrous transformations returned to normal. The realm woke as if from a nightmare, breathing hope it had almost forgotten.

By the time Cedric, Thalion, and Mira reached Stonehaven's capital, throngs of joyous citizens lined the streets. King Alaric and High Seer Malachai greeted them at the palace gates, eyes brimming with gratitude. Yet their smiles faltered when they saw Elara's draped form. A hush fell among the crowd, realization dawning that victory had claimed a dear cost.

They laid Lady Elara to rest in the Royal Citadel's sacred garden, a place reserved for the greatest heroes of Stonehaven. Thousands gathered for a solemn ceremony. Candles glowed beneath a twilight sky, while priests of the Light chanted prayers of passage. King Alaric delivered a eulogy, voice trembling with reverence for the paladin who had embodied the dawn. The people wept openly, many having heard tales of her compassion and valor. Even nature seemed to mourn—a gentle rain of golden petals drifted from the blossoming trees overhead.

Mira, cloaked in black, leaned on Thalion for support, tears never far from her eyes. Cedric, standing at the front, gently laid the Amulet of Divine Light upon Elara's casket, letting it rest beside her in final tribute. He spoke only a few words: "She gave everything so that our world could live. May we honor her by living the light she fought for."

After the ceremony, as the sun rose over a kingdom free from darkness, King Alaric invited the remaining heroes into the War Chamber. There, before advisors and generals, they recounted the final confrontation. Cedric placed the shattered fragments of the Shadow Nexus crystal on the council table, proof of the ancient evil's demise. Thalion unrolled the relic tapestry, showing how each piece of the puzzle had aligned. A sense of closure lingered in the air.

High Seer Malachai, tears still glistening, concluded: "With the Nexus destroyed, Stonehaven shall rebuild. But we must never forget the cost—or the hero who paid it." His gaze turned to a painting being prepared: a memorial portrait of Elara in shining armor, the amulet glowing upon her chest.

In the weeks that followed, the three remaining relics— Wyvern Scale, Behemoth Disc, and Pearl of Tides—were enshrined in Stonehaven's grand temple, their power dormant now that the Shadow Nexus was gone. The Amulet of Divine Light, once the keystone of their victory, lay sealed with Elara in the Citadel's crypt. Some whispered that if the realm ever faced dire evil again, her spirit might answer through the amulet's glow.

Thalion returned to the Arcadium Library, ensuring the story of their quest and Elara's sacrifice was preserved in ancient tomes. Mira, after a period of mourning, resumed studying illusions and healing magic, traveling the kingdom to help rebuild villages scarred by monstrous raids. Cedric, quiet and solemn, spent time training new squires, imparting lessons of bravery, sacrifice, and unity. All bore the memory of Elara's final stand as a guiding star.

Across Stonehaven, roads once haunted by beasts lay peaceful under clear skies. Rivers ran free of taint, farmland produced bountiful harvests, and the common folk lived without fear of creeping shadows. The monarchy honored the heroes with ceremonial titles, but each refused lavish rewards. Their greatest reward was seeing the realm flourish, free from the darkness that once choked its future.

Even the Land of Giants and the Frozen Lands felt the Nexus's absence. Tales circulated of once-corrupted creatures reverting to normal. The scholars in the icy north wrote letters of marvel, describing how their environment no longer suffered creeping darkness. The minotaurs, once wary and beset by monstrous threats, found renewed peace in their labyrinthine domain.

On a calm spring morning, Cedric visited the sacred garden where Elara lay. Dappled sunlight filtered through blossoming cherry trees. He knelt by the polished memorial stone inscribed with her name, carefully setting a fresh lily at its base. A soft breeze stirred the petals, carrying distant birdsong. He closed his eyes, recalling her steady gaze in that final moment on the dais.

"You live on in all we do," he whispered, voice tender. "The light you ignited can never be snuffed out."

A gentle warmth seemed to brush his shoulder, as though some echo of her spirit lingered. With a faint smile, he stood, adjusting the runic sword at his side. The kingdom had dawned anew, and the threat of the Shadow Nexus had vanished into memory. Yet the lessons of unity, courage, and sacrifice would guide Stonehaven for generations to come.

As Cedric departed the garden, he spotted Mira and Thalion by the courtyard fountain, discussing an upcoming expedition to reclaim lost knowledge from the corners of the realm once overshadowed by the Nexus. They beckoned Cedric over with friendly waves. Together, they shared stories of the times they overcame monstrous odds, forging an unbreakable bond. The emptiness of losing Elara would always ache, but the love and respect for her sacrifice bound them closer still.

When the next festival of dawn was celebrated, an event dedicated to Elara's memory, throngs filled Stonehaven's capital. Lanterns glowed in swirling patterns of gold and white, symbolizing the banished darkness. Children in bright costumes reenacted the heroes' feats with wooden swords and painted relic props, culminating in a show of radiant lights as the "Shadow Nexus" puppet was triumphantly torn asunder.

King Alaric presided over the festival, tears shining in his eyes as he recounted how Elara and her companions traveled from Oakenshade to Brighthaven, from the Gravenshade Woods to the Labyrinthian Mountains, each chapter a tapestry of valor culminating in the final stand. The crowds cheered Cedric, Thalion, and Mira for their ongoing service, but always left a space for the absent figure who had once knelt with the Amulet of Divine Light.

At night's end, a new banner was raised atop the Citadel tower: a phoenix crest entwined with a morning star, symbolizing rebirth and hope. The entire city glowed under fireworks that arched across the sky, reflecting in the eyes of a liberated people. In that spectacle, the memory of Lady Elara soared—her spirit woven into Stonehaven's future.

Time would march on, bringing new challenges and wonders to Stonehaven. But no longer did the monstrous gloom of the Nexus threaten the kingdom's dawn. Farmers sowed crops without fear, pilgrims traveled roads that sparkled with reclaimed safety, scholars shared knowledge freely, and the lingering scars of undead or monstrous raids were gradually healed by communal effort.

Stories of the Shadow Nexus and its banishment became the stuff of legend, retold by minstrels who wove stirring ballads of four determined heroes. Some doubted the account of a Hydra or a golden dragon, labeling it hyperbole. Yet wise folk, who witnessed the transformations wrought by the Nexus, nodded in quiet affirmation. The heroism of Lady Elara, Sir Cedric, Thalion, and Mira had proven all too real.

And so, in a realm renewed by light, the heroes found their places. Thalion's knowledge shaped Stonehaven's magical renaissance, Mira's illusions and healing arts brought solace to once-suffering regions, and Cedric's leadership guided a new generation of knights who bore the paladin's memory as their moral compass. Each night, the stars shone bright and clear, free of the black storms that once choked the horizon.

Far from mortal eyes, the final resting place of the Amulet of Divine Light lay in quiet vigil with Lady Elara. Some believed that if ever the land faced a threat of equal magnitude, the amulet's glow would call a new champion to stand in her stead. Others believed her spirit lingered among the astral realms, watching over Stonehaven in a tapestry of dawn's gentle promise.

In the quiet hush before dawn one spring morning, Cedric stood on a balcony of the Royal Citadel, gazing at the eastern horizon. The first sliver of sun crested the hills, casting pink and orange streams across the sky. Warmth touched his features, a symbol of renewal. He closed his eyes, imagining Elara's voice echo in that gentle light.

A final sense of peace washed over him. The Shadow Nexus had threatened to blot out Stonehaven's future, but now, the kingdom stood radiant—testament to the sacrifices made by heroes unafraid to challenge ancient evil. Cedric inhaled, allowing the fresh air to fill his lungs, then turned away from the sunrise.

Down in the courtyard, Thalion and Mira waited with saddled horses, each preparing for a new journey across the realm to ensure that monstrous pockets of corruption had indeed been vanquished. Cedric smiled, descending the stairs to join them. No longer overshadowed by dread, Stonehaven's dawn glowed with unrestrained brilliance.

Thus ended the Chapter, not in sorrow, but in the promise of a tomorrow shaped by unity and courage. The Shadow Nexus was purged, its vile crystal shattered, and light reclaimed the lands. Though Lady Elara's sacrifice weighed heavily on every heart, her memory illuminated Stonehaven's path forward like an eternal sunrise. In that radiant dawn, the heroes' story became legend, reminding all that even when darkness looms, hope can shine, if only a few stand with unwavering hearts.

Their quest—long and perilous—found closure in the cleansing of the deepest evil. And Stonehaven, bathed in triumphant light, would stand free of shadow's chains for ages to come.

24

A KINGDOM REBORN

Soft breezes swept through Stonehaven's fields, carrying the sweet scent of budding flowers and fresh-tilled earth. Only weeks had passed since the Shadow Nexus was shattered, and already, the land showed signs of vibrant renewal. Farmlands greened under warm skies, travelers roamed without fear of monstrous ambush, and the capital's gleaming spires welcomed endless visitors who came to pay respects to the fallen hero, Lady Elara.

During the final days of winter, the heroes—Sir Cedric, Thalion, and Mira—had toiled tirelessly alongside villagers and royal forces to purge lingering corruption. Remnants of twisted creatures and faint pockets of shadow magic clung to remote corners of the realm. But with the Shadow Nexus gone, these remnants dissipated swiftly, losing the dark power that once sustained them.

Now, as spring burst into full bloom, Stonehaven stood on the brink of a golden age. Freed from creeping horrors, the realm's communities began to flourish. In dusty hamlets previously haunted by beasts, fresh paint covered boarded windows and children played without looking over their shoulders. Merchants traversed newly safe roads, hauling goods from city to city. Every corner of Stonehaven seemed lit by a gentle sunrise, a warmth more profound than mere sunlight—a warmth born of renewed faith and unity.

Yet for the three remaining heroes, it was a season of mingled joy and solemn reflection. They had saved Stonehaven, yes—but at the cost of Lady Elara's life. Memories of her sacrifice lingered in each sunrise, reminding them that the land's current peace was wrought by unwavering bravery and personal loss.

A month after the destruction of the Shadow Nexus, King Alaric summoned Cedric, Thalion, and Mira to the Royal Citadel once more. The War Chamber—where their quest had begun—looked different in the bright morning light. Gone were the anxious maps detailing monstrous sightings; in their place, fresh banners commemorated Stonehaven's liberation. Painted scenes of the Hydra, the Cyclops, and the Golden Dragon adorned tapestries on the walls, each monstrous foe receding under the heroes' might. At the chamber's center stood a newly constructed pedestal holding three relics in stasis: the Wyvern Scale, the Behemoth Disc, and Pearl of Tides. Around them hung a wreath of golden laurel, a symbol of honor.

Seated near the dais, King Alaric rose as the trio entered. A hush of respect settled over the assembled nobles, knights, and advisors. High Seer Malachai stood beside the king, his robes embroidered with sunrise motifs—no longer overshadowed by the fear of dark omens.

Alaric welcomed them with a soft smile. "My friends," he began, voice resonant in the high-ceilinged hall, "once we trembled at the approach of doom. Now, Stonehaven stands free from the Shadow Nexus. I cannot put into words our gratitude—or the sorrow we share at Lady Elara's passing."

Cedric inclined his head, a tightness in his chest at Elara's name. Thalion gripped his staff, eyes downcast, while

Mira pressed her lips together, remembering the final moment on the dais when Elara unleashed the relic's power.

"Your deeds belong to legend," Alaric continued, gesturing to the ornate pedestal. "These three relics—and the memory of Lady Elara's Amulet of Divine Light—shall be kept safe. Their unity saved us from an ancient evil." He scanned their faces. "But I would not keep you from the road should you choose to wander anew. Stonehaven is in your debt. Remain as honored knights, archmages, counselors—anything you desire."

A bittersweet smile tugged at Cedric's lips. "My liege, we shall each find our way. But first, we would visit Elara's resting place. There are final words we'd like to speak."

Alaric nodded, stepping down from the dais to clasp Cedric's forearm in a warrior's salute. "You have the run of the realm, noble knight. Wherever you go, Stonehaven stands with you."

That very evening, Cedric, Thalion, and Mira rode to the Citadel Gardens, where Lady Elara was entombed among statues of past heroes. The garden, once bleak under shadow, now flourished with blooming roses and twilight orchids. Illuminated by torches, the path glowed softly. Stone arches curved overhead, etched with the phoenix crest—a symbol of rebirth that Elara had once borne on her shield.

They found her marble memorial by a tranquil pond, water lilies drifting across the surface. A sculpture of Elara stood in prayerful repose, wearing the celestial armor that many recognized from her final stand. Though the Amulet of Divine Light had been laid to rest with her, the statue wore a replica, shining with faint starlight under the torches.

Thalion set down a bouquet of dawn-pink lilies at the base, eyes misting. Mira knelt, pressing a trembling hand to the cool marble, whispering words of gratitude. Cedric lingered behind, silent but overwhelmed by memories: Elara's radiant smile, her steadfast courage, her final sacrifice. The hush of the garden enveloped them, broken only by the rustle of branches in the evening breeze.

After a long moment, Cedric cleared his throat. "Elara... we've done all we can. The Nexus is no more, and your dawn shall never be forgotten." He paused, voice thick. "I—I wish I could hear you laugh again, or see your eyes light up at a new sunrise. But know that your spirit lives in our hearts."

Mira stood, tears glimmering. "We'll keep on, for your sake. And for all Stonehaven."

A gentle warmth brushed the night air, like an unseen caress—a whisper of presence that made their hearts stir. Thalion half-expected to see a glow from the statue, a sign that Elara heard them. Though the stone remained still, each friend felt the lingering echo of her essence in the hush. They departed quietly, resolute in carrying her legacy forward.

In the days that followed, the realm's reconstruction gained momentum. Fallow fields were tilled anew, roads repaired, and commerce thrived. Cedric, Thalion, and Mira stayed in the capital for a time, each contributing to the restoration. Cedric offered guidance to the Royal Knights, ensuring no corner of Stonehaven lacked protection. Thalion shared arcane insights with Malachai and the Citadel's mages, developing new wards in case vestiges of darkness stirred. Mira used her illusions and healing magic to uplift towns haunted by nightmares of the war.

One bright afternoon, a festival in Brighthaven—once besieged by vampires—marked the official reopening of its harbor. Lanterns and ribbons adorned streets filled with music. The heroes were guests of honor, greeted by Captain Farim and the grateful mayor. It felt surreal to see the once-frightened city so full of life. Children chased each other, playacting scenes of the heroes slaying monstrous foes. Tavern keepers toasted them with hearty cheers.

Mira, sipping sweet mead, caught Cedric's eye across the crowd. They shared a smile, remembering the night they had battled vampire thralls in Brighthaven's darkened alleyways. Now, the city's lamplights shone bright, free of the undead menace. High above, a pale moon glowed serenely, as though blessing the festivities.

In these moments, joy mingled with a lingering sorrow. Elara's absence hovered like a star that had vanished from the night sky—once bright, now gone, yet remembered in every story told. The sense of completion in defeating the Nexus was tempered by the knowledge of her sacrifice.

As spring matured into early summer, the roads dried, the rivers ran full, and trade routes bustled with caravans carrying exotic goods from the far corners of Stonehaven. Cedric, Thalion, and Mira found themselves restless, each drifting to new corners of the kingdom, ensuring no hidden pockets of darkness remained. Often they traveled together, forming smaller expeditions to the Land of Giants, or a quick foray into the Frozen Lands to confirm peace reigned there. At times, they split up, confident in each other's skill and that they could regroup if a fresh threat emerged.

Thalion, while exploring a remote region near the old Minotaur labyrinth, discovered traces of an ancient library rumored to hold knowledge about other realms. Mira, intrigued, accompanied him, illusions at the ready. Meanwhile, Cedric patrolled the kingdom's borders, forging alliances with small villages and ensuring local militias formed a first line of defense should a new evil ever arise.

Throughout these journeys, they carried Elara's memory as a guiding star. Her example of selfless devotion shaped every decision. The bond between the three heroes grew deeper, forged in sorrow yet radiant with purpose. They lived not just for themselves, but for the realm and for the ideal that heroes stand guard over peace.

A grand memorial for all those lost to the Shadow Nexus—knights, villagers, mages, and beasts corrupted beyond salvation—was organized in the capital's wide courtyard. Citizens from every province gathered, lighting thousands of small lanterns and setting them afloat in the central lake. Each lantern represented a soul claimed by darkness, including Elara's. The sight of shimmering lights drifting under a moonlit sky drew tears and hushed prayers. King Alaric's voice carried over the assembly, praising courage and unity as the true pillars of Stonehaven.

Cedric stood among the crowd, remembering each face lost—colleagues from the initial siege of Oakenshade, brave souls in Brighthaven, even the golden dragon that had fought so fiercely, and ultimately, Lady Elara. The echoes of their sacrifice rang in every glowing lantern. But the tears glimmering in the watchers' eyes were not just of grief— they carried gratitude for the dawn that followed every darkest night.

After the ceremony, Cedric stepped onto a balcony overlooking the lake. There, Thalion and Mira joined him.

None spoke for a long moment, content to watch the lantern lights fading into the distance. "Seems like an age has passed since we first met," Mira murmured. "And yet I still recall every detail—the call to Oakenshade, the whispering rumors of a Shadow Nexus."

Thalion gave a small, nostalgic smile. "We've lived an entire saga since then—like stepping into a legend. But all legends come with loss."

Cedric exhaled. "We do what we must. Stonehaven's future stands bright." He turned to them. "What of us, now? The kingdom is safe. There are no more shadows to chase."

Mira shrugged gently. "Perhaps we continue to watch over Stonehaven. Or we travel to rediscover places abandoned under the dark times—help them rebuild. Knowledge was lost. People fear the future might hold more evils. We can reassure them by being present, guiding them."

Thalion nodded. "Wherever the road leads, we walk it, in Elara's memory."

Cedric closed his eyes, nodding. "Agreed."

Weeks turned into months, and the capital settled into a peaceful routine. One sunny afternoon, Cedric, Thalion, and Mira rested in the Citadel's courtyard, preparing for a short journey to confirm that a remote fortress once besieged by undead was truly cleared. A messenger hawk swooped overhead, dropping a scroll into Cedric's hands.

He unfurled it carefully. The parchment bore an unfamiliar crest—two entwined dragons over a stylized mountain. The text read:

"To the Heroes of Stonehaven:

Word of your triumph against the Shadow Nexus travels far. We, the Dwarven King under the Emberstone

Range, request your audience. A matter of grave importance stirs in our depths—a darkness unknown. Please come if you can spare your blades and wisdom."

Cedric passed the note around. Mira's eyebrows rose. Thalion's eyes narrowed with concern. "Darkness unknown... So soon after the Nexus's fall?"

Cedric set his jaw. "Stonehaven stands free, yet the world is vast. If new darkness emerges in dwarven halls, we cannot ignore it. It might be unrelated, or it might be some remnant of the corrupt powers we faced."

Mira looked hesitant. "We only just ended a devastating threat. But if we're needed..."

Thalion gently rolled the scroll. "The dwarves rarely ask humans for help. If they've called us, it must be dire."

Cedric sighed, glancing at the empty place where Elara once stood in their circle. "We should go. For all we know, it may be nothing, but we can't let hidden shadows fester."

And so, with a final check of weapons and wards, they decided to heed the dwarves' call. The promise of peace was never guaranteed, and if evil stirred anew—somewhere beyond Stonehaven's borders—they would stand ready. For that was the vow they had all embraced, sealed by Elara's final act.

Before departing, they once again stepped into the Citadel Gardens to say quiet farewells to Lady Elara. Sunbeams cascaded over her stone memorial, haloing the carved phoenix crest. The three heroes laid a wreath of dawn-hued flowers, silent in their gratitude. The gentle wind whispered across the grass, almost as if giving a soft blessing.

Cedric stooped, brushing his hand against the marble. "Elara, we embark on another journey. The land you saved thrives. I only wish you could stand at our side."

Mira's voice wavered. "We carry your spirit in our hearts—forever."

Thalion bowed his head in prayer, staff clutched to his chest. "May the Light guide us, as it guided you."

An ephemeral warmth, faint yet comforting, suffused the garden air. Perhaps it was imagination, or perhaps Elara's presence lingered still. Whatever the truth, they left the garden with renewed conviction, spirits uplifted by the memory of her unwavering smile.

That evening, as they prepared to ride north to the dwarven realm, King Alaric and High Seer Malachai accompanied them to the city gates. A small crowd of well-wishers, knights, and townsfolk gathered to see the heroes off, reminiscent of the day they first rode out to fight unseen evils. Garlands hung from stone arches, and children offered shy salutes. The sun dipped low, setting the sky ablaze in oranges and reds, a fitting backdrop for a farewell.

Alaric clasped Cedric's forearm. "Your courage saved us all, and for that, we can never repay you. May the Light bless your next quest, though I pray it's a peaceful one."

Cedric managed a lopsided grin. "Perhaps it will be. But if it's not, we've learned how to stand firm."

Malachai smiled sadly. "Elara would be proud. You stand as the kingdom's beacons now, shining where darkness lurks."

Mira inclined her head respectfully. "She taught us that no light is too faint to pierce the shadows."

With that, they mounted their horses. The crowd parted, cheering softly as Cedric, Thalion, and Mira guided their mounts through the wide gate. The clatter of hooves on cobblestone echoed, mingling with the hush of approaching night. A wave of nostalgic pride swelled in them: once, they had left these streets uncertain, untested. Now, they departed as legends, forging ahead to yet another unknown horizon.

At the crest of a hill outside the city, the three paused, turning back for a final glimpse of Stonehaven's lit ramparts. Candles twinkled like starlight on the walls, a quiet testament to how love and unity overcame tyranny. Cedric closed his eyes, inhaling the crisp breeze. Then, in unspoken agreement, they spurred their horses onward, northward, into the deepening twilight.

As the last rays of sun gilded the heroes' silhouettes, a hush fell over the kingdom they left behind—Stonehaven, at peace under an unshadowed sky. Yet the world beyond her borders was vast, brimming with secrets and undiscovered perils. And while the Shadow Nexus lay shattered, dark corners of creation might yet spawn new threats, beckoning heroes to stand once more between doom and hope.

Riding side by side, Cedric, Thalion, and Mira carried not just steel and spells, but the memory of Elara's luminous sacrifice, a guiding flame that refused to be quenched. The dwarves' plea reminded them that evil could rise anywhere. Should it threaten innocence again, they would answer. For in the tapestry of fate, heroes walk an ever-winding path, each triumph forging the mettle for the next challenge.

Overhead, stars began to shimmer. The soft clop of hooves on the road mingled with a gentle night breeze. A distant call of an owl resonated among the trees, as if wishing them luck on the next leg of their unending vigilance. And far off, behind the horizon, lightning flickered—an omen, perhaps, or a mere passing storm?

The final chapter of their grand quest had closed with the Shadow Nexus purged and Stonehaven reborn. But in the wide world, the seeds of future legends waited to bloom. In the hush of night, one could almost hear destiny stirring. One day, their journey might continue—a new saga in the forging, a new horizon where the Light must stand against encroaching darkness.

For now, Stonehaven slept untroubled under starry skies, content in the warmth of a dawnless peace. And the heroes, though scarred by loss, pressed on, hearts brimming with the promise of tomorrow—a promise that, wherever evil rose, they would meet it with courage, faith, and unbreakable unity.

THE END....

542

ABOUT THE AUTHOR

Blair Edward Russell (B.E. Russell) was born in 1979 in Etobicoke, Ontario, just outside of Toronto. Summers were a blur of outdoor activities—roaming forests, wading through creeks in search of fish, and skateboarding around the neighborhood. After finishing high school, Blair pursued his education at York University in Toronto, graduating in 2007. Not long after, he embarked on a new adventure, relocating to Miami, Florida, with his wife, Ginna, to build their life together in the Sunshine State.

Blair's creativity doesn't stop at writing. He's also an avid oil painter, a domain name investor, and an accomplished internet entrepreneur. Most of all, he's a passionate angler, especially when it comes to fly fishing. He writes many types of novels—including Epic Fantasy Adventures, Light Horror, Mysterious Tales, and novels about the Outdoors—drawing heavily on his love of fishing to craft stories that hook readers and take them on thrilling, unforgettable journeys.

Today, Blair lives in South Florida with his wife Ginna. Whether he's crafting a new original tale, painting in his studio, or casting a line into tranquil waters, Blair finds inspiration in life's simple yet extraordinary moments.

ACKNOWLEDGEMENTS

I would like to thank the following people who have helped inspire me and supported me throughout my life in all the various projects and endeavors I have been through.

My wife Ginna, My father and mother Bob and Marie, My brother and sister Bobby and Stacey, all of my friends and extended family as well as you my passionate reader.

You are all the ones who inspire me to share my dreams and ideas with the world.

546

FURTHER READING

Please be sure to check out the other fine books from **B.E. Russell** including:

- *Trial by Fire*
- *Emberheart*
- *Stories from the Grave – BOOK ONE*

If you enjoyed reading this novel be sure to join my mailing list at www.BlairEdwardRussell.com. And check in on my website often to find information on my latest novels.